Conrad Allen is the author of the acclaimed series of mysteries featuring George Porter Dillman and Genevieve Masefield. *Murder on the Lusitania* is the first novel in that series. A playwright with a lifelong interest in history, he lives in England.

Also by Conrad Allen

Murder on the Lusitania
Murder on the Minnesota

(*see pages 304-307*)

Murder on the Mauretania

Conrad Allen

Duckworth Overlook

This edition 2013
First published in 2002 by
Duckworth Overlook
30 Calvin Street, London E1 6NW
T: 020 7490 7300
E: info@duckworth-publishers.co.uk
www.ducknet.co.uk
For bulk and special sales, please contact
sales@duckworth-publishers.co.uk
or write to us at the address above

© 2000 by Conrad Allen

First published in 2000 by
St. Martin's Press, New York

A catalogue record for this book is available
from the British Library

ISBN 978-0-7156-4570-3

Typeset by E-Type, Liverpool
Printed and bound in Great Britain by
CPI Group (UK) Ltd, Croydon, CR0 4YY

In loving memory of my grandfather,
Frederick Allen,
who first introduced me to the joys of sailing

An exceptionally smooth passage to
Queenstown, which we reached at 9:00
this morning, augurs well for the
prospects of what must prove a notable
voyage in the history of shipping....

—From Our Special Correspondent,
The Times, Monday, November 18, 1907.

ONE

Saturday, November 16, 1907

The largest ship in the world chose the worst day of the year on which to begin her maiden voyage. Omens were bad from the start. The boat train was an hour late leaving Euston Station, it was hopelessly crowded, and the journey was far too noisy and unpleasant to put anyone in the right mood for participation in an historic event. Trying to make up for lost time, the motorman increased speed at the expense of comfort, sending violent shudders and deafening rattles the whole length of the train. Polite irritation rose until it gave way to muted anger. Open resentment eventually broke out. No relief awaited them in Liverpool. When they finally steamed into the dockside station, they found the port shrouded in mist, drenched by rain, and sieved by a sharp wind. By the time the marine superintendent began to hurry the first-class passengers and their luggage on board, it was almost dark.

Gloom had also descended on many of those still trudging along the platform with their wives, husbands, children, relations, mistresses, lovers, friends, acquaintances, and assorted baggage in tow. Collars of overcoats were turned up, scarves tightened, gloves pulled on, and hats pulled down. People were tired, tense, cold, and depressed by the murky conditions. The station was a huge echo chamber of complaint. Some of the travellers looked less like eager passengers on a unique voyage than condemned prisoners about to be transported in chains to an unknown destination.

George Porter Dillman did not share the general pessimism. The tall, elegant, well-dressed American had learned to accept the shortcomings of rail travel and the vagaries of British weather. Nothing could dim his spirits. He was happy, relaxed, and urbane. While others moaned and criticized, Dillman had spent the train journey trying to cheer up his companions by listing all the virtues of the ocean liner on which they were about to sail and by telling them what a warm reception would await them in New York Harbour. His accent aroused mixed reactions among his exclusively English listeners in the second-class compartment, but all were impressed by his intricate knowledge of the *Mauretania* and grateful for the way in which he distracted them from the rigours of the hectic race northward. The polite stranger defeated time for them in the most easy and unforced manner. Dillman had made his first friends of the voyage.

When they alighted from the train, the most important of these friends fell in beside him. One hand enclosed in her mother's palm, eight-year-old Alexandra Jarvis, a cheerful, chubby little girl with an inquiring mind, positively skipped along the platform firing questions at Dillman.

'How do you know so much about ships?' she asked.

'Because they fascinate me,' he admitted.

'Why?'

'It's in my blood, I guess. I was born and brought up near the sea. My father builds yachts for a living. When I was your age, Alexandra, I probably spent more time afloat than on dry land.'

'Were you ever seasick?'

'Don't pester Mr. Dillman, dear,' scolded her mother gently.

'But I want to know.'

'Everybody is seasick at first,' he said.

'What does it feel like?' pressed the girl.

'Alexandra!' The rebuke was reinforced by a maternal tug on the hand. Vanessa Jarvis turned apologetically to Dillman. 'You'll have to excuse her. When she gets too excited, Alexandra sometimes forgets her manners.'

'No apology is needed, Mrs. Jarvis,' he assured her.

'There!' said Alexandra triumphantly. 'Will *I* be seasick, Mr. Dillman?'

'I think it's highly unlikely on a vessel of that size, Alexandra.'

'Good.'

'I bet you'll turn out to be a natural sailor.'

'That's what I think. It'll be Noel who's seasick all over the place.'

'No I won't!' countered her brother, walking close enough behind to jab her in the small of the back. 'Don't tell lies about me, Ally.'

'They're not lies.'

'Yes they are.'

'You've got a weak stomach.'

'Who has?' demanded Noel with righteous indignation.

'Stop bickering!' ordered their father. 'What will Mr. Dillman think?'

'He likes us,' said the girl confidently. 'Don't you, Mr. Dillman?'

Dillman replied with a grin and followed the crowd into the customs shed. He had already made his judgment about the Jarvis family. They were nice, friendly, civilized people who seemed, in his opinion, like typical members of the lower middle class. The father, Oliver Jarvis, a dapper man in his forties with a neat moustache, was, it transpired, manager of a branch bank in Camden, and he was taking his wife, a plump but still handsome matron, and their two children on their first trip abroad. Included in the party was his mother-in-law, Lily Pomeroy, a big, bosomy old woman with a fur-trimmed coat and a monstrous hat on which a whole flock of swallows had apparently elected to die. Dillman took time to break through the father's natural reserve and distant suspicion of a foreigner, but Mrs. Pomeroy was much more forthcoming, chatting amiably about the purpose of their visit to New York and yielding up details about her private life with a readiness that prompted an occasional wince from her daughter and put an expression of pained resignation on the face of her son-in-law.

Noel Jarvis was a silent, dark-eyed, sulking boy of thirteen bedeviled by shyness, a capacity for instant boredom, and a bad facial rash. His sister, Alexandra, had no such handicaps. She was alert, affable, and buoyant. When formalities had been completed in the customs shed, she glanced down at Dillman's small valise.

'Why have you got so little luggage?' she wondered.

'I sent most of it on ahead,' he explained.

'Shall we see you on the ship?'

'I hope so.'

'Are we going to break the record?'

'That's something I can't promise, Alexandra.'

'Didn't you tell us that the *Mauretania* was the fastest liner of them all?'

'Potentially, she is,' he said, 'but she may not be able to prove it on her maiden voyage. November isn't the ideal time to cross the Atlantic. Adverse weather conditions may slow us down, and there are all kinds of other hazards.'

'Such as?'

The question went unheard and unanswered because Alexandra's voice, though raised above the mild tumult around them, was drowned out by the clamour that greeted them as they came out onto Prince's Landing Stage. In spite of inclement weather, fifty thousand people had gathered to wave goodbye to the new liner, only a quarter of the number who had watched her sister ship, the *Lusitania*, set off on her maiden voyage a couple of months earlier, but enough to produce a continuous barrage of noise and to remind the newcomers that they were about to embark on a maritime adventure. Jaded passengers were suddenly exhilarated, shaking off their fatigue and striding forward with a spring in their step. History beckoned. The discomfort of the train journey was forgotten.

What really inspired them was the sight of the *Mauretania*, berthed at the landing stage, a massive vessel with lights ablaze from stem to stern, looming above them like a vast hotel floating on the water. While her dimensions had been well publicized, the statistics had not prepared anyone for the reality that rose up so majestically in the darkness, her size and shape defined by thousands of glowing lightbulbs as well as the four gigantic funnels picked out by the harbour illumination. Dillman had already been given a tour of the ship to familiarize him with her labyrinthine interior, but he was moved anew by her sheer magnificence.

Even in the rain-swept gloom, the *Mauretania* was an irrefutable statement of the supremacy of British ship-building. It would be a joy to work on her.

The long column of those from the boat train made its way through a sea of umbrellas and smiling faces, everyone now caught up in a mood of celebration that defied the elements. Police and port officials were on hand to control the crowd, but it was too disciplined and good-humoured to need much attention. Liverpool inhabitants knew better than anybody the significance of a maiden voyage. An amalgam of pride, curiosity, and excitement brought them to the docks. They had dispatched countless vessels down the River Mersey, but the *Mauretania* and her sister ship were special cases, two self-styled greyhounds of the Atlantic Ocean that would wrest the Blue Riband – the unofficial prize for the fastest crossing – from German hands and keep it where they believed it belonged, writing the name of their port into the record books once more. Like the *Lusitania* before her, the new vessel was another large feather in the already well-decorated cap of Liverpool.

When everyone was finally aboard, the ship would hold the population of a small town, with well over two thousand passengers – more than half of them in third class – and a crew of over nine hundred. Such a daunting number of people would only make Dillman's job more complex and difficult, but he dismissed such thoughts as he joined the queue at the gangway. He wanted to savour the communal delight. The Jarvis family was directly in front of him, and Alexandra kept turning around to send him a smile, her blue eyes dancing and her face shining with glee. Her brother, too, was overawed by the experience, and their effervescent grandmother, the chuckling Mrs. Pomeroy, nodded her head so vigorously in approval that the swallows on her hat almost migrated out of fear.

When their tickets had been inspected, they stepped

aboard and felt the ship under their feet for the first time. It was thrilling. A different omen then appeared. Before a steward could escort the Jarvis family to their cabin, a black cat suddenly materialized out of nowhere and curled up near the top of a companionway with an almost proprietary air. Alexandra clapped her hands in surprise, then turned to Dillman.

'Isn't that a sign of good luck?' she asked.

'Yes, Alexandra,' he confirmed.

'I knew this voyage was going to be wonderful.'

'It will be.'

'The girls at school will be so *jealous* of me!' she said with a giggle.

'Come along, dear,' urged her mother, still holding the girl's hand. 'Goodbye, Mr. Dillman. It was so nice to meet you.'

'Goodbye,' he said.

Dillman waved them off, but Alexandra had not finished the conversation yet. 'Oh, by the way, Mr. Dillman,' she called over her shoulder.

'Yes, Alexandra?'

'You can call me "Ally", if you like.'

'Thank you.'

It was an important concession in her world, and he was touched that she should bestow the favour on him after so brief an acquaintance. As he made his way to his cabin, he was superstitious enough to take some reassurance from the sight of the black cat. Had it dashed across their path, it might have been an evil portent, and he knew sailors who would not even put out to sea if they saw a black cat walking away from them. In this case, however, the animal's easy familiarity and purring contentment could only be construed as a sign of good fortune. It was an unexpected bonus.

Dillman also reflected on the pleasure of making new friends and suspected that he and Alexandra Jarvis – 'Ally' to selected intimates – would bump into each other quite often in the course of the voyage. It never occurred to him that a ship's mascot and an eight-year-old girl might help him solve a murder.

TWO

Genevieve Masefield was glad to be aboard at last. Unlike most of her fellow travellers on the boat train, she'd had a very enjoyable journey from London, sharing a first-class compartment with a congenial group of people who welcomed her into their circle without reservation. She had passed her first test with flying colours. Her confidence soared. In the lighthearted atmosphere, time had flown. There had been so much laughter and harmless fun that none of them had even noticed the jolting lurches of the train or the rhythmical clicking of its wheels. It was almost like being at a party. Long before they reached Liverpool, they were intoxicated with each other's company and further inebriated by the very idea of sailing on the *Mauretania*.

Notwithstanding all that, Genevieve was grateful to be alone again, if only to catch her breath. When she was conducted to her quarters, she was pleased to see that her luggage was already there, neatly stacked against a wall. The single-berth cabin in which she would spend the next five and a half days was luxurious to the point of excess. It was superbly appointed. Gilt-framed mirrors were artfully placed to give an impression of spaciousness and to reflect to their best advantage the intricate decorations on the panelled walls, the ornate lighting fixtures and the beautifully upholstered furniture. Beneath her feet was a delicately woven patterned carpet. All around her were expensive attempts to convince her that she was not in a ship at all, but in a luxury suite in some palatial hotel. The sense of newness was almost tangible.

Genevieve was thrilled. When she had sailed on the

maiden voyage of the *Lusitania*, she had been highly impressed by the quality of the first-class accommodation, but she was overwhelmed by what now confronted her. Enormous care and artistic talent had gone into the design of the interior of her sister ship. In the first-class cabins, comfort was paramount. It made Genevieve realize how truly fortunate she was. Her first voyage to America had theoretically also been her last because she had planned to settle on the other side of the Atlantic and make a fresh start there. Yet here she was, barely two months later, boarding another ocean liner in Liverpool for its maiden voyage and doing so in a far happier state of mind. So much had changed in the intervening weeks. She had a different outlook, increased zest, and a whole new purpose in life.

She removed her gloves, took off her hat, then slipped out of her coat and tossed it over the back of a chair. Genevieve felt at home. Appraising herself in a mirror, she gave a quiet smile of approval. Now in her mid-twenties, she had lost none of her youthful charms. Her face had a classical beauty that was enhanced by the silken sheen of her skin and her generous lips; her large blue eyes were surmounted by eyebrows that arched expressively; the high cheekbones and slight upturn of nose gave her a pleasing individuality. She brushed a strand of fair hair neatly back into place, then studied herself once more. Striking enough to turn men's heads, her face also suggested a wealth and social position that she did not, in fact, have but that enabled her to move easily in high society and gained her acceptance by the leisured class as one of its own. It would be a vital asset during the week that lay ahead.

A respectful tap on the door curtailed her scrutiny. Expecting it to be her cabin steward, she was surprised to open the door and find herself looking instead at two of her erstwhile companions from the train. Harvey Denning was a suave, smiling, dark-haired man of thirty with the kind of dazzling good looks that seemed faintly unreal. His smile broadened into a complimentary grin as he ran a polite eye over Genevieve's slender body. Susan Faulconbridge was a beaming, bright-eyed, vivacious young woman with dimples in her cheeks and auburn hair peeping out from beneath her hat. Both visitors were still wearing their overcoats and scarves.

'We've come to collect you,' announced Denning courteously.

'Collect me?' said Genevieve.

'Aren't you coming out on deck? We're about to set sail.'

'Oh, do join us,' urged Susan Faulconbridge effusively. 'We had such a lovely time together on the train that I wanted to share this experience as well. You're one of us now. Please say you'll come.'

'I will, I will,' agreed Genevieve.

'Good,' said Denning. 'After all, you're the expert.'

'Am I?'

'Yes, Genevieve. You hold the whip hand over us. You sailed on the *Lusitania*. We're the innocents here. You can teach us the ropes. The moment when we actually set sail must be so uplifting.'

'It is, Harvey.'

'That's the other thing,' said Susan happily. 'We're on first-name terms already. That so rarely happens, doesn't it, Harvey? Do you remember that dreadful couple, the Wilmshursts? It was months before I could bring myself to call that odious creature "Ellen". Then there was Mr. Ransome, whom we met at the Ecclestones' house party in the Lake District. We played bridge with him regularly after that, but it was over a year before he allowed us to use his first name.'

Denning grimaced. 'Obadiah! No wonder he kept it to himself.'

'Obadiah Ransome.'

'"He of the Unfortunate Teeth."' They laughed together at a private joke.

'I'll be out on deck shortly,' said Genevieve, 'but I'm not quite ready yet.'

'Do you want us to wait?' asked Susan.

'No, no. I'll find you.'

'There'll be a huge crowd out there.'

'I'll track you down somehow.'

'We'll be on the promenade deck.'

'Right.'

'Don't keep us waiting too long.'

'I won't, Susan, I promise you.'

'Happy with your accommodation?' asked Denning, glancing into the cabin over Genevieve's shoulder as if angling for an invitation to enter. 'Our cabins are splendid. Needless to say, Donald and Theodora have one of the regal suites. Only the very best for them, what? We'll be able to hold private parties there. Won't that be fun? All our cabins are on the promenade deck,' he added, pointing at the floor. 'Next one down. In fact, with luck, mine may be directly below yours, Genevieve. That would be convenient, wouldn't it? If you hear someone burrowing up through your carpet, you'll know who it is.'

'Behave yourself, Harvey,' said Susan with a giggle.

'You've changed your tune, Miss Faulconbridge,' he teased.

They shared another private joke and Genevieve felt momentarily excluded.

'I do beg your pardon,' said Denning, recovering quickly to make a gesture of appeasement to her. 'Frightful bad manners. We must let you go, Genevieve.'

'I'll be as quick as I can,' she replied.

'We'll be with Donald and Theodora,' said Susan. 'And with Ruth, of course.'

'Look for Theo's hat,' advised Denning. 'Even in a crowd, you can't miss that. It must be the largest chapeau on board, but then, that's Theodora. She and Donald must have the largest of everything. Including income, lucky devils! Search for the hat and you'll find all five of us sheltering underneath it.'

'I'll be there.'

After an exchange of farewells, the visitors walked away and Genevieve was able to withdraw into her cabin again. Of her new friends, Harvey Denning and Susan

Faulconbridge were by far the most amiable and talkative. Genevieve had still not worked out the precise nature of their relationship but felt that it would emerge in time. Donald and Theodora Belfrage were a pleasant young couple, still basking in the novelty of marriage. Ruth Constantine was both the outsider and the still centre of the quintet. They were an interesting group and Genevieve felt at ease in their company. She was glad to have been invited to join them on deck. It was only when she was putting on her coat again that a sudden thought struck her.

How had they known what cabin she was in?

Dismal weather did not deter either the passengers or the spectators. As the moment of departure drew close, the former moved to the decks or the windows and the latter surged forward along the landing stage. At 7.30 p.m., Captain John T. Pritchard gave the signal and the *Mauretania*'s siren rang out boldly. To cheering and applause, the lines were cast off and the tugs pulled the vessel clear of the land. The maiden voyage had begun. River craft of all sizes added their own salutation with whistles and hooters. When she passed the New Brighton pier, a fireworks display was set off in her honour, brightening the sky for fleeting seconds and drawing gasps of pleasure from all those watching. A new chapter in maritime history was being written. It was an invigorating experience.

Genevieve Masefield found it even more stimulating than the moment of the *Lusitania*'s departure, a fact she put down to her change of attitude and improved circumstances. Wedged in at the rail between Susan Faulconbridge and Ruth Constantine, she waved as long and energetically as either of them at the slowly disappearing well-wishers, wondering what it was that drove people who would never make a transatlantic voyage themselves to give such a wonderful send-off to those who did. For more reasons than one, she felt highly privileged.

Susan Faulconbridge was shaking visibly with excitement. 'Wasn't that marvellous?' she exclaimed.

'Yes,' said Genevieve.

'Oh, I'm so glad we decided to sail on her. Actually,' she confided, turning to face Genevieve, 'we wanted to go on the maiden voyage of the *Lusitania*, but Donald and Theodora were on their honeymoon in Italy in September, so that was ruled out.'

'Do you always take your holidays together, Susan?'

'Of course. We're friends.'

'That's right,' said Ruth Constantine, joining in the conversation. 'Holidays are a true test of friendship. If you can spend three weeks skiing in the Alps with people and still be civil to them afterward, then you've found kindred spirits.'

'Oh, yes,' agreed Susan. 'Do you remember the Glovers? What fools we were to go on a Mediterranean cruise with that gruesome pair! We found them out after only two days, and the holiday lasted a month. It was excruciating.'

'One learns from experience.'

'I hope so, Ruth.'

'Instincts are sharpened by time.'

Genevieve liked Ruth Constantine. It was not simply her poise and elegance that were so attractive. She had a deep, melodious voice that was informed by a clever brain and a keen sense of humour. Though she lacked the conventional beauty of Theodora Belfrage and Susan Faulconbridge, she had a composure that neither of them could match and a way of dealing with the two men in the party that compelled their respect. Genevieve hoped to get to know Ruth a lot better.

'Well, this is it!' declared Harvey Denning. 'Doctor Johnson time.'

'What on earth are you talking about?' asked Susan.

'The moment when we should take his warning to heart.'

'Warning?'

'Yes, Susan,' he continued, raising his voice so that the whole group could hear him. 'Do you know what Samuel Johnson said about the sea? "No man will be a sailor who has contrivance enough to get himself into jail, since being in a ship is being in jail, with the chance of getting drowned." Good point.'

'Harvey!' reproached Susan. 'That's a terrible thing to say!'

'Especially at a time like this, old chap,' noted Donald Belfrage, tightening an arm around his wife's shoulders. 'Don't want to spread gloom and despondency, do we? Occasion for celebration. Why try to upset the ladies?'

'He sent a shiver down my spine,' confessed Theodora Belfrage.

'And mine,' said Susan.

'Harvey never frightens me,' said Ruth calmly. 'It's just one more way of drawing attention to himself. Ignore him. Besides,' she observed dryly, 'there's something he forgot to mention about Samuel Johnson.'

Denning smiled tolerantly. 'What's that, Ruth?'

'He never sailed on a vessel the size of the *Mauretania*.'

'I have,' volunteered Genevieve, 'and it didn't feel at all like being in jail. It was liberating. The *Lusitania* was as solid as a rock beneath our feet.'

'I bow to your superior wisdom,' said Denning with mock humility.

'We're not really in danger, are we, darling?' asked Theodora, snuggling up to her husband. 'I thought that this was the safest ship afloat.'

'It is, Theo,' he said, ducking under the brim of her hat to plant a reassuring kiss on her cheek. 'Harvey is being Harvey, that's all. Look at those names we saw in the newspaper. The Princess de Poix, Prince Andre Poniazowski, Sir Clifton and Lady Robinson, and dozens of other famous people. Do you think they'd step aboard any ship that wasn't one-hundred-percent safe? Then there's Mr. Hunter, from the firm that actually built the *Mauretania*. He has complete faith in the vessel.'

'So do the sundry millionaires who are travelling with us,' conceded Denning. 'Believe it or not, Donald, there may be people on board with more money than you.'

Belfrage wrinked his nose. 'Ghastly Americans, most of them.'

'That's a contradiction in terms,' said Genevieve loyally. 'All the Americans I've encountered have been quite delightful.'

'Well, yes, there are always exceptions to the rule.'

'How many have you actually met, Donald?'

'Enough to know that they're a different species.'

'Different perhaps, but not inferior.'

'Let's not make an issue out of it,' he said dismissively. 'The truth is that I don't give a damn about Americans.'

'Then why are you so eager to visit their country?'

'Don't pester him, Genevieve,' complained Theodora, coming to her husband's defence. 'We're here because we've never been on a maiden voyage before. Isn't that justification enough? As for Americans, we must just live and let live.'

'You'll have to do more than that, Theodora,' cautioned Ruth.

'What do you mean?'

'A large number of first-class passengers will have hailed from the other side of the Atlantic. Indeed, I suspect there may be more of them than us. You'll be rubbing shoulders with Americans every day. Overcome your prejudices and make friends.'

'I don't have any prejudices,' squeaked the other. 'Do I, Donald?'

'None at all,' he flattered her.

'I just prefer to be with my own kind.'

'I rest my case,' said Ruth.

She caught Genevieve's eye and they traded an understanding look.

The lights of Liverpool had now dropped astern as the four monstrous screw propellers churned up the dark waters of the Mersey and sent the vessel onward with gathering speed. Half an hour after departure, a bugle sounded. Susan was startled.

'What's that?' she asked.

'The signal for dinner,' explained Harvey. 'We can adjourn to the dining saloon so that Donald and Theodora can patronize all those Americans.' He rode over their spluttered protests with a grin. 'As for the safety of the ship, you omitted the strongest argument of all, one that even Samuel Johnson would have to accept.'

'We're not back to him, are we?'

'No, Susan.'

'Then what's this strongest argument?'

'The *Mauretania* has the most valuable cargo ever to leave the British shore.'

'Is he trying to pay us a compliment?' asked Theodora suspiciously.

'No,' he returned gallantly. 'But then, anyone as gorgeous as you are will fly through life on a magic carpet of compliments. What you're all forgetting is the money famine in New York. This ship is carrying almost three million pounds in gold bullion to relieve the financial crisis across the water. Bankers are the most cautious people in the world,' he pointed out. 'Do you think they'd risk putting all that wealth aboard a ship if they were not absolutely certain that it would reach its destination? It's something to reflect upon while we dine this evening. We're not simply travelling with precious friends beside us,' he said, waving an arm to include them all, 'we're sailing with a veritable fortune. Britannia is ruling the waves with a gold-bullion smile.'

THREE

George Porter Dillman was called into action that very evening. After sharing a table with the Jarvis family in the second-class dining saloon, he hovered near the door for a few minutes, chatting to a steward while keeping one eye on a man in the far corner whose behaviour had aroused his suspicion.

'Splendid meal!' said Dillman with evident sincerity.

'Thank you, sir,' replied the steward.

'My compliments to the chef.'

'I'll pass them on.'

'What's on the menu for breakfast?'

'You're a man who likes his food, sir, I can see that.'

'One of the pleasures of travelling on the Cunard Line.'

'I'm glad you think so.'

While the steward listed the items on the breakfast menu for the following day, Dillman changed his position slightly so that he could get a better view of the dinner guest in the corner. The man had waited until everyone else had vacated his table, then shifted surreptitiously from his own seat to the next one so that his back faced into the saloon and obscured the movements of his hands. Dillman had no idea of what he was about to steal, but he saw the swift grab and knew that something had been snatched with professional ease. Draining his glass of whisky, the man rose to his feet, glanced around, then strode casually underneath the lofty dome in the centre of the room and toward the exit. Short, stubby, and smartly dressed, he looked more like a successful realtor than a thief. His bald head glistened under the light of the crystal chandeliers.

When he passed Dillman and the steward, he gave them a token smile of farewell before going out.

After waiting for a few moments, Dillman excused himself in order to follow the man. The second-class dining saloon was on the upper deck and opened off the grand staircase. It could accommodate two hundred and fifty people at its refectory-style tables, but only one of the diners interested Dillman at that juncture. Instead of joining the other second-class passengers in the lounge, the drawing room or the smoking room, the man headed for his cabin, sauntering along with a law-abiding gait, quite unaware of the fact that he was being trailed at a discreet distance. Dillman waited until the man reached his door before he moved in.

'Excuse me, sir,' he said, closing in briskly, 'but I believe you may inadvertently have taken something from the dining saloon that doesn't belong to you.'

The man stiffened. 'You're crazy!' he retorted.

'I watched you put it in your pocket, sir.'

'Then you need your eyes tested, mister.'

He glared at Dillman with controlled belligerence, as if deeply offended by the charge. His accent had Brooklyn overtones. Dillman remained deliberately polite.

'Would you have any objection to emptying your pockets, sir?'

'You bet I would!'

'Then we'll have to discuss the whole matter with the purser.'

'Whatever for?'

'He doesn't approve of theft.'

'And I don't approve of being accused of something I haven't done!' said the other, flaring up. 'Can't a man enjoy a meal without having someone spy on him? Who the hell are you, anyway?'

'I work for the Cunard Line, sir.'

'Well, I'm a passenger, buddy. That means I help to pay your wages, indirectly. It also means you're supposed to be nice to me. Got it?'

'In the circumstances, I'm being extremely nice,' said

Dillman, letting his voice and eyes harden slightly. 'The Cunard Line has certain idiosyncrasies, I'm afraid. One of them is that it doesn't condone the loss of its property. If you'd care to come with me to the purser, I'm sure that he'll explain the rules to you in full.'

'Listen here, wise guy!'

Squaring up to Dillman, he seemed to be on the point of striking him, but he quickly repented of his hasty action. Dillman did not flinch. Not only was the detective much younger and taller, he looked as if he knew how to handle himself in a fight. The man changed his tack at once, shrugging off his anger and extending apologetic palms.

'Look, there's been a misunderstanding here,' he soothed.

'Has there, sir?'

'Okay. I'll come clean. I'm no kleptomaniac. You did see me take something off the table,' he admitted, slipping a hand inside his coat, 'but it was only this.' The menu was waved under Dillman's nose. 'What's more, the steward told me I could have it as a souvenir, so I guess he's an accessory before the crime. Satisfied now?'

'Not exactly, sir.'

'You going to march me off to the purser because I take a lousy menu? Here,' he said, thrusting it at him. 'Have it back.'

'It's the other item I'm after,' persisted Dillman. 'The one that the steward didn't give you permission to steal. Let's do this properly, shall we? Perhaps you'd be kind enough to tell me your name, sir.'

'Mind your goddam business!'

'It won't be difficult to find it out. I know your cabin. All I have to do is check the passenger list. Now, why don't you start cooperating, Mr. –?'

Dillman's composure was slowly unnerving the man. He eventually capitulated. 'Hirsch,' he grunted sourly. 'Max Hirsch.'

'How do you do, Mr. Hirsch? My name is George Dillman.'

'I have another name for you.'

Three elderly passengers came along the corridor and walked past. Hirsch looked embarrassed. It was time to move the interrogation to a more private venue.

'Could I suggest that we step inside your cabin?' said Dillman.

'Why?' challenged the other with vestigial defiance.

'It's either here or in the purser's quarters. Your choice, Mr. Hirsch.'

Cursing under his breath, Hirsch unlocked the door of his cabin and led the way in. Dillman shut the door behind him and glanced around appreciatively.

'Almost identical to my own,' he commented. 'Second-class cabins on the Cunard Line are now as good as first-class accommodation on earlier vessels.'

'Yeah, I know.'

'You sound like a seasoned traveller, Mr. Hirsch.'

'Not really.'

'How many times have you crossed the Atlantic?'

'Enough,' said the other. 'And if this is the kind of treatment I get from Cunard, I sure won't be booking my passage on one of its liners again.'

'Unless we can sort out this matter amicably,' warned Dillman, 'you may not be allowed on board a Cunard ship again. Why not cut the shadow boxing? We both know that you took something off that table. I want to see what it is.'

Max Hirsch studied him with a mixture of exasperation and respect. Dillman was a handsome man with a hint of a dandy about him, but the broad shoulders and lithe movements indicated someone who kept himself in prime physical condition. There was a quiet intelligence about him, and his eyesight was evidently keen. Hirsch's only hope lay in trying to talk himself out of his predicament. Holding out both arms, he let them flap to the sides of his thighs.

'They put the right man on the job, Mr. Dillman,' he complimented.

'Thanks.'

'Trouble is, you picked the wrong culprit. That's to say,

I'm no light-fingered thief. I did what a lot of guys might've done in my position and acted on impulse.'

'And what did this impulse lead you to take, Mr. Hirsch?'

'These.'

Putting a hand in his trouser pocket, he extracted a silver saltcellar and a pepper pot. Dillman took them from him and wrapped them carefully in a handkerchief.

'You forgot the vinegar, Mr. Hirsch.'

'If I'd stashed that in my pocket, the stopper would've come out and I'd have ended up looking as if I'd pissed in my pants. That's it, Mr. Dillman. On the level.' He spread his arms. 'Frisk me if you don't believe me.'

'No need. I've got what I want. Apart from an explanation, that is.'

Max Hirsch let out a world-weary sigh and flopped into a chair. 'Where do I start?' he wondered, scratching his head. 'Do you want the full story, or will you settle for the shorter version?'

'The shorter one, please.'

'Then the truth is that I felt Cunard owed me a silver cruet. At the very least.'

'Why?'

'Because they managed to lose some of my baggage on the voyage from New York. God knows how. I mean, they load the stuff into the hold and they take it out again at the other end. How could it possibly go astray?'

'Pilfering is not unknown,' said Dillman impassively. 'Besides, I can't believe that you didn't insure the baggage against loss or breakage. The rates are very low.'

'Yeah. Everything was insured. But it takes an age for the dough to come through. In any case, some of the things they lost were irreplaceable. They had sentimental value. Rachel will be real upset.'

'Rachel?'

'My wife,' he said, heaving another sigh. 'She bought several of those things for me. I'm not looking forward to breaking the news to her, I can tell you. Rachel was to have made the trip with me, see, but she came down with an attack of shingles. I offered to cancel the whole vacation, of course, but she wouldn't hear of it. She's that kind of woman, wanted me to have the experience for both of us.' He grimaced. 'All the experience has amounted to so far is suffering a rough crossing on the *Saxonia*, losing some of my baggage, staying in a rotten hotel in London, missing my wife like hell, and getting hassled by you. Some vacation!'

'You said earlier that you acted on impulse.'

'Yeah, I did. And it wasn't only an impulse of revenge. Love came into it as well. Rachel begged me to bring her back a souvenir from the *Mauretania.*' Sadness came into his eyes. 'I couldn't help myself, Mr. Dillman. I promised her. My wife has a thing about silver, see.'

'So does the Cunard Line. It likes to keep its supply intact.'

'It's not going to miss a saltcellar and a pepper pot.'

'That doesn't give you the right to take them.'

'No, it doesn't,' confessed the other, 'and I'm ashamed of what I did. It was a dumb thing to do. I'll happily pay for them.' He produced a wallet and flipped it open. 'How much do you reckon they're worth, Mr. Dillman?'

'They're not for sale, sir,' said Dillman pointedly. 'Neither am I.'

'That wasn't a bribe I was offering you, I swear it. What kind of man do you take me for?' He put his wallet away. 'Look, let's be realistic here. I grabbed those things and I've told you why. Human nature being what it is, they won't be the only souvenirs that get snatched aboard this ship. So what do you say, Mr. Dillman?' he asked, adopting a jocular tone. 'It's hardly the crime of the century, is it? What are you going to do with me – lock me up in the brig?' He offered his wrists. 'Come on. Cuff me if you have to. I'll go quietly.'

Dillman needed a full minute to reach his decision. He shook his head. 'That won't be necessary, Mr. Hirsch.'

'So what happens? A diet of bread and water from now on?'

'No, sir,' said Dillman pleasantly. 'You can continue to

use the facilities that other second-class passengers enjoy. Now that you've explained it to me, I can see how it must have happened and I'm certain it was an isolated incident.'

'You can count on that.'

'Then I suggest we forget the whole thing.'

Hirsch brightened. 'You won't report this to the purser?'

'Not this time.'

'Thanks, Mr. Dillman. You're a pal.'

'No, sir,' said Dillman coolly. 'This has nothing to do with friendship. I'm hired to keep a lookout for genuine thieves, and I don't believe you fall into that category.'

'Hell, no!' exclaimed the other. 'If I were a pro, I wouldn't be trying to sneak off with a saltcellar and a pepper pot. Why settle for a pocketful of silver when there's almost three million in gold bullion aboard? *That's* what I'd be after, I tell you.'

'Fair comment, Mr. Hirsch.'

'Say, while you're here, can I offer you a drink?'

'No thanks.'

'Sure? I always keep a bottle handy.'

'Another time perhaps,' said Dillman, opening the door. 'I have to return these items to the dining saloon before anyone misses them. Good night, Mr. Hirsch. I'm glad we were able to sort this out.'

'So am I.'

'Confession is good for the soul.'

'Sweet dreams!'

Dillman stepped out into the corridor and pulled the door shut behind him. As he headed back to the dining saloon, he gave a wry smile. Max Hirsch was too plausible to be true. Dillman did not believe a word of his explanation and doubted if the man even had a wife, let alone one called Rachel, conveniently afflicted by shingles. When he first spotted Hirsch during the meal, Dillman saw him paying court to a middle-aged woman beside him in a blue-satin dress. Judging by the way she had lapped up his flattery, she had taken Max Hirsch at face value. It was a mistake that Dillman would never make.

Their paths would definitely cross again; Hirsch was no first-time offender who had learned his lesson. What gave him away was the fact that he'd recognized the detective for what he was without even asking to be shown credentials. He would soon be prowling after fresh spoils. Having caught him red-handed, Dillman had released him so the man would think he had gotten away with the crime. Hirsch would be emboldened to strike again. Dillman would be ready for him, eager to arrest the man for something more serious than the theft of a saltcellar and a pepper pot.

All he had to do was to bide his time.

— — —

Harvey Denning inhaled the smoke from his cigarette, then blew it slowly out again. 'Why have you never married?' he asked softly.

'I might ask you the same question,' replied Genevieve.

'There's an easy answer to that. I'm simply not the marrying kind.'

'What's that supposed to mean?'

'What it says. I enjoy the chase but have no wish to chain myself to the quarry for the rest of my life. I thrive on risk and novelty.'

'I gathered that.'

'Also,' he continued smoothly, 'I happen to think that connubial bliss is a myth. Show me a marriage that doesn't start to creak and groan very early on. A wedding ring may give you a momentary feeling of possession, but it's no guarantee of happiness.'

'Donald and Theodora seem happy enough.'

'A temporary illusion.'

'They're besotted with each other, Harvey.'

'Yes, I know. He's madly in love with her and she's infatuated with his money.'

'Don't be so cynical!'

Genevieve Masefield gave a laugh of reproof. The two of them were reclining in the first-class lounge, a sumptuous room on the boat deck. Designed in late eighteenth-century French style, the lounge was crowned by a large oval dome with bronze framing, set against a ceiling that was pristinely panelled in white. Sitting in chairs of polished beech with variegated brocade upholstery, they were the last survivors of a group that had slowly disintegrated as the evening wore on. The Belfrages had been the first to go, abandoning decorum when they reached the exit and clutching each other like drowning sailors clinging to their life rafts. Ruth Constantine had soon followed, pleading a headache. Susan Faulconbridge had stayed until her eyelids began to droop; then she, too, quit the field. Harvey Denning showed no sign of tiredness. Genevieve had agreed to have one last drink with him, less for the pleasure of enjoying his company than for the chance to probe the relationships within the little party.

'You haven't answered my question,' he prompted. 'Every mirror you've ever looked in must have told you what a beautiful creature you are, and no red-blooded male can fail to notice it. You must have had dozens of proposals.'

'One or two,' she conceded.

'Both rejected, it seems.'

'Not at all, Harvey. I was engaged to one gentleman for some months.'

'Ah!' he said with triumph. 'A broken engagement, eh? Do I detect a scandal? What happened? Did the fellow turn out to be a bounder? Or did you uncover some hideous secret about his family?'

She gave a shrug. 'I realized that I didn't love him enough.'

'Why not?'

'That's a private matter.'

'You can trust me,' he coaxed. 'I won't breathe a word of this to anyone else.'

'You won't get the opportunity.' Genevieve toyed with her glass. 'Did you say that Donald might be going into politics one day?'

'There's no "might" about it. All cut-and-dried. As soon as a seat becomes vacant, Donald Belfrage will have it.

Rather an alarming thought, isn't it?' he said, stubbing out his cigarette in the ashtray. 'Donald as a member of Parliament. I mean, he's the most generous soul alive, but he's hardly the stuff from which statesmen are made. The only two things that Donald has done well are to inherit wealth and to gain a rowing blue at Oxford. Did he tell you that he was president of a winning crew in the Boat Race?'

'Several times.'

'Donald's inordinately proud of that achievement. I can't think why. Mindless muscularity has never appealed to me but then, I was sent down from Balliol after only one term. It was a blessed release.'

'Do you have any political ambitions, Harvey?'

'Heavens, no! It would be the ruination of my career.'

'As what?'

He gave a brittle laugh. 'Haven't you worked that out yet?'

'Not completely.'

'How far have you got?'

'Not very far at all,' she lied tactfully. 'What I have noticed is how tightly knit the five of you are. You're genuine soul mates. You seem to have done so much together. Susan keeps reminding me of that. She's the archivist in the party, always taking out the scrapbook to jog your memories.'

'Genevieve Masefield will go into that scrapbook now.'

'Briefly.'

'We shall see.'

'A moment ago, you mentioned your career.'

'I was speaking metaphorically,' he said with a lazy smile. 'Most people would call it a life of sustained sponging, but more discerning eyes appreciate my true value. I'm not just a social butterfly, Genevieve, flitting here and there to brighten up the lives of my friends. I also act as their confidant, their adviser, their court jester, and – most important of all – their secret weapon at the card table.'

'Secret weapon?'

'Bridge. A game of infinite subtlety, which is why I took

such trouble to master its intricacies. That's why I'm in continual demand as a partner. Lady Ferriday made me stay for over three weeks this summer so we could trounce all and sundry. And I went straight from there to Sir Gerald Marmion's family seat. It's a gift,' he said with feigned modesty, 'and I exploit it to the full. There is the small matter of a couple of directorships I hold, but they don't deflect me from my main purpose in life.'

'Being a cardsharp?'

'That's unkind, Genevieve,' he protested. 'Bridge is an art form, not a mere game of cards. It's taken me all over England and the Continent in the company of the great and the good. How many people can claim that? And wherever I go, I earn my keep, I promise you. I have a system, you see.'

'Yes,' she said with a twinkle in her voice. 'I've noticed.'

He gave another laugh and rose slowly to his feet, holding out a courteous palm. Genevieve let him take her hand to help her up. He kissed her fingers lightly.

'Thank you, kind sir.'

'May I see you to your cabin?'

'That won't be necessary,' she said.

'An independent spirit, eh?'

'No, Harvey. It's just that I have someone else to see before I retire.'

'Oh? Anyone I know?'

'I don't think so.'

'Float a name past me.'

A shake of the head. 'Good night. I thoroughly enjoyed our chat.'

'The first of many, I hope,' he said, his hand gently resting on his heart.

'Possibly.' She was about to move away when she remembered something. 'One thing,' she said, turning back. 'You and Susan came to call on me earlier. How did you know which cabin was mine?'

'I told you,' he said with a grin. 'I have a system.'

FOUR

Maurice Buxton was a big, beefy man in his late thirties with curly brown hair and a well-groomed beard. Resplendent in his uniform, he conveyed an impression of trustworthiness and reliability. As purser on the *Mauretania*, he had enormous responsibilities, but he carried them lightly and discharged his many duties with cool efficiency, giving each worried passenger who came to him with a complaint or an inquiry a reassuring feeling that he was taking a personal interest in the matter. Buxton had a gift of creating instant goodwill. Dillman liked him from the start and was very grateful when, at the end of the day, the purser even found time to give him a private view of an exclusive part of the cargo.

'Well,' said Buxton, turning the last key in the lock and pulling the heavy door open, 'there it is, Mr. Dillman. You're looking at £2,750,000 in gold bullion.'

'All that I can see are strongboxes,' said Dillman.

'Ironbound and sealed. Every precaution has been taken.'

'Quite rightly, Mr. Buxton.'

'On the journey by special train from Euston, it was guarded like royalty by the railway police. When we got it aboard, the whole amount was checked and accounted for with meticulous care.' He grinned at his companion. 'Don't want to shortchange our American friends, do we?'

'The situation over there is desperate,' said Dillman, surveying the neatly stacked boxes. 'This couldn't come at a better time. Banks are collapsing right, left, and centre. Over two hundred state banks have failed already. When I was in New York a couple of weeks ago, there was an

article in one of the newspapers about the smart set having
to sell their jewels. The crisis is biting deep.'

'Let's hope that this little consignment helps to steady
things.'

'Where has it all come from?'

'Not from anyone on the Cunard Line,' said Buxton
with a chuckle. 'That's for sure. They pay us a fair wage, but
nothing in this league. No, I gather that six hundred thousand pounds of it was bought principally from South
African mining companies through the bullion brokers.
Needless to say,' he continued, hitting his stride and
revealing his love of statistics, 'they made a tidy profit,
charging seventy-eight shillings per ounce for it – that
includes brokerage, assay, and other costs. The metal was
refined during the week into gold bars.'

'What about the Bank of England?'

'Something like nine hundred and forty-seven thousand
pounds' worth was bought from them in bar gold, plus five
hundred and sixty-four thousand in American eagles. No
need to tell you what they are, Mr. Dillman.'

'I guess not.'

'The current value is around two pounds in sterling.'

'There must be hefty insurance for all this.'

'Prohibitive.'

'The insurance brokers stand to reap a rich harvest.'

'If all goes well and we get the gold to New York in one
lot.'

'No doubt about that, is there?'

'None at all, Mr. Dillman,' said the other confidently,
closing the door and using the different keys to lock it.
'You'd need dynamite to get into this security room. The
crown jewels would be safe in there. Then, of course, we
have our own special security device.'

'What's that?'

'The Atlantic Ocean. It's one vast insurance policy. Only
a fool would try to steal the gold when there's nowhere to
take it. In the unlikely event that we were robbed, we'd
simply have to search the ship in order to find the loot.'

'That's true.'

'Captain Pritchard is very proud of the fact that the *Mauretania* was chosen to transport the consignment. It gave us one claim to fame before we even set off. What you've just seen is the largest amount of gold bullion ever carried across the Atlantic. The *Lusitania* led the way before with two million pounds' worth. In one fell swoop, we've relieved her of that particular record.'

'What about the more important record you covet, Mr. Buxton?'

'The Blue Riband will come in time, have no fear. It's inevitable.'

They moved off down the corridor, then went up a companionway in single file. 'Are you managing to find your way around?' asked the purser.

'Just about. It's like being in a maze.'

'I know. I get lost myself occasionally.'

'Daresay I'll master the layout in time.'

'What do you think of second class?'

'Extremely comfortable. I've met lots of nice people there.'

'It's the bad boys that you have to look out for, Mr. Dillman. I expect that we have our share of those aboard as well. Pickpockets and confidence tricksters love to work these ships.'

'I know,' said Dillman as they reached the top of the steps and walked along another corridor. 'They get such easy pickings. People can be surprisingly off guard when they go on a voyage.'

'They surrender to the magic of oceanic travel.'

'Some of them, perhaps.'

'What do you mean?'

'It's all very well for passengers in first and second class, Mr. Buxton. They can relax and enjoy themselves in plush surroundings. And so they should, having paid handsomely for the privilege. But the largest group of people aboard are immigrants, travelling in steerage. Facilities are a little more spartan for them.'

'Yet a big advance on what they used to be,' argued the other. 'When I joined my first ship – not a Cunard vessel, by the way – steerage passengers were treated like cattle. No comforts, no trimmings, no privacy. They had to sleep in those awful open berths. I met some who actually stayed on deck throughout the entire voyage to escape the cramped conditions down below. Imagine that. Sleeping out under the sky.'

They paused when they reached a corner. Lips pursed, Dillman was somber. 'Ironic, isn't it?' he mused.

'What is?'

'The immigrants are leaving Britain because they can't make a decent living there. In their eyes, America is the land of opportunity. It's a cruel mirage,' he said ruefully. 'Hundreds of people in steerage are braving this voyage in the hope that they'll find the streets of New York paved with gold.'

'Instead of which, New York is having to import the gold from us.'

'Makes you think, doesn't it?'

The purser was businesslike. 'I'm not paid to cry into my handkerchief, Mr. Dillman,' he said briskly. 'My job is to see to the welfare of the passengers, whichever part of the ship they're travelling in. Once we get to New York, they're on their own. From a commercial point of view, westbound immigrants are a godsend to us in the cutthroat world of transatlantic travel. Traffic has peaked this year. Cunard made well over a million pounds taking them to the New World, and we're duly grateful. But they went of their own volition,' he emphasized. 'All that we can do is get them there. Don't ask us to improve their lives as well.'

The four-berth cabin was on the lower deck at the forward end of the ship. Not only could they hear the muffled roar of the engines, they could feel the vibrations as the ship powered its way across the Irish Sea. Glyn Bowen, a short, dark, thickset man in his twenties, lay on the top bunk with his eyes wide open. He gave an involuntary shiver.

'Mansell,' he whispered. 'You still awake?'

'How can I sleep with that bloody noise going on?' complained Mansell Price in the bunk below him. 'We might as well have had a berth in the boiler room.'

'At least it would have been warm there.'

'*Diu!* I can't stick this for five days, Glyn. It's worse than being down the pit. I didn't realize it was going to be so primitive in steerage. I mean, I didn't expect the Ritz Hotel, but this is terrible. Sharing a tiny cabin with complete strangers.'

'What if those strangers had been two gorgeous women?'

'That would've been different, mun,' said Price with a laugh. 'All four of us could've kept ourselves warm then. No such luck, though. We got shoved in here with those two drunken idiots from Huddersfield.'

'They're not too bad, Mansell.'

'Wait till you've spent a night with them.'

'Why?'

'Because you won't get a wink of sleep. I know their type. Selfish morons, the pair of them. No consideration for others. Talk, talk, talk. And if that old man plays his mouth organ in here again, I'll ram it down his bloody throat.'

'Hey, calm down,' said his friend.

'How can I stay calm when someone is playing "Auld Lang Syne" in my ear? Doesn't the old fool know any other tunes? It wouldn't be so bad if he could play a few Welsh songs on that mouth organ, but "Auld Lang Syne!" Makes me want to puke.'

Mansell Price was a tall, muscular young man with a rugged face animated by blazing brown eyes. Like his friend, he bore the legacy of years spent in the coal mines of South Wales. His forehead, body, and arms were flecked with the blue scars of a miner, but the deeper gashes were in his soul.

'It's got to work, mun,' he insisted.

'What has, Mansell?'

'This, of course. Going to America. Starting afresh. Trying to make something of ourselves. It's got to work, Glyn. We can't go back to the Rhondda with our tails between our legs. I'd rather die than do that.'

'Me, too.'

'I just wish we'd got off to a better start.'

'Could be worse.'

'What's worse than sharing a cabin with two drunks and a mouth organ?'

'Sharing one with even more people,' said Bowen reasonably. 'They've got six- and eight-berth cabins. Some are probably bigger than that. Hey, they might even have a fifteen-berth,' he added, brightening at the thought. 'Wouldn't it be great to share that with the rest of the boyos in the rugby team? We could shut out the noise of those propellers with a chorus of "Men of Harlech".'

'I'm going to shut them out right now,' decided Price, hauling himself out of his bunk. 'Come on, Glyn. Get dressed. We're out of here.'

'Where to?'

'Anywhere to escape this pandemonium. Up on deck, if need be.'

'It'll be freezing up there.'

'Then we'll explore the *Mauretania* and see if she's all she's cracked up to be. Yes,' he said, warming to the idea, 'we might even take a look at parts of the ship we're not allowed to go in. One thing about miners – we know how to find our way around in the dark. Hurry up, Glyn,' he ordered, slapping his friend on the shoulder. 'Let's have an adventure, shall we?'

Mansell Price reached for his trousers and clambered into them eagerly.

An extension of the grand staircase, the second-class lounge was on the boat deck aft. The room was panelled in teak and had gracious blue curtains and carpets. Its furniture was tasteful, its fittings eye-catching. Though it lacked the opulence of the first-class lounge, it offered Genevieve Masefield plenty to admire during her wait. Most of the passengers had retired, but there were still a few hardy spirits ensconced alone in chairs or deep in discussion with friends. George Porter Dillman glided in, sat down beside her, and apologized for the delay in his arrival.

'The purser wanted to show me the gold bullion he explained.

'Did he give you a free sample?'

'No, unfortunately. And I probably wouldn't have been able to carry it if he did. The bars are all sealed up in heavy boxes. Still, how are things with you, Genevieve?'

'Oh, I'm enjoying myself,' she said with a smile.

'I'm sorry that you have to come down the social scale into second class, but I thought this would be a good place to meet. Being seen here with me won't compromise your position among the wealthier passengers.'

'What about your position, George?'

'Right now it's just about perfect.'

He gave her a warm smile and let his affection show for a second. Genevieve replied with a twinkle of her eyes, then gave him an account of her experiences so far on the ship. Dillman listened intently, pleased with what he was hearing.

'You've made a good start,' he concluded. 'You're accepted by that party in a way that I could never be – especially not by this Donald Belfrage. He obviously hates Americans. What does he think is wrong with us?'

'You're not English.'

'Some people might find that appealing.'

'Stop fishing for compliments,' she said with mock reproach. 'Yes, I seem to have got off on the right foot, and Susan actually told me that I was one of them now. What worries me is that they may envelop me so much that I can't do my job properly.'

'Ration the amount of time you spend with them, Genevieve.'

'That's easier said than done. Susan Faulconbridge hardly left my side all evening, the Belfrages insist that I dine in their suite, and Harvey Denning looks as if he might suggest an even more intimate get-together.'

'What about this Ruth Constantine?'

'Ruth is the one that intrigues me,' she said, wrinkling her brow. 'The other four seem to be birds of the same feather – denizens of high society collecting a maiden voyage on the *Mauretania* in the same way they collect Ascot or Henley or any other event where it's important to be seen. Their life seems to be one long party, interrupted by an occasional game of bridge. That's not a criticism, by the way. Given the chance, I could probably take to it myself.'

'Could you?' he said doubtfully.

'For a short while, anyway.'

'Tell me more about Ruth.'

'There's not much to tell, George, except that she's the brightest and wittiest of them. She's also the only one who can put Harvey Denning in his place, and that takes some doing. He's incorrigible. He almost glories in the fact that he's a kind of parasite. As for Ruth,' she judged, 'she doesn't really belong with them, and yet they'd be lost without her. It's curious. I can't make it out.'

'Well, don't spend too much time trying to fathom Ruth Constantine,' he advised, 'or you'll be diverted from your real purpose on this voyage. Use your new friends as a useful camouflage but spread your net much wider.'

'I will. Just like you.'

'No, Genevieve. Don't copy me.'

'Why not?'

'You have to develop your own methods.'

'But you set such a good example, George,' she said with an approving smile. 'When I first met you on the *Lusitania*, I'd never have guessed that you were a detective working for Cunard. You blended in so easily.'

'When I first met you on that maiden voyage, I'd never have imagined that we'd be making a second one on the *Mauretania*, working alongside each other.'

'That was only thanks to you.'

'We made such a good team,' he reminded her. 'Without your help, I wouldn't have been able to solve that murder and bring the villains to justice. I had to recommend you. Apart from anything else,' he said with a grin, 'it was the only way I could be sure of seeing you again. Don't underestimate your skills, Genevieve. You're a natural sleuth. And you have one supreme advantage over me.'

'Do I?'

'You're a woman. You can go places where I could never venture.'

Genevieve stifled a yawn. 'The only place I want to go right now is to bed,' she murmured. 'It's been a long day, filled with heady excitement. Tomorrow, I promise, I'll be more alert.'

'So will I.'

Dillman helped her up and escorted her across to the grand staircase. A public situation dictated a certain restraint. Wanting to give her a farewell kiss, he instead settled for a brief handshake, then went off down the stairs toward his own cabin. Genevieve Masefield's assistance would be invaluable and her presence on the ship made the voyage even more attractive to him, but he knew he had to keep his mind on his job. Eyes that were trained on a beautiful first-class passenger might miss things they ought to have seen elsewhere. He was given proof of the fact within a matter of minutes.

The farther they went, the bolder they got and the more they marvelled. Mansell Price and Glyn Bowen picked their way furtively through the second-class areas of the ship and noted the marked increase in comfort and design. Creeping along dimly lit corridors, they gaped at thick carpets, exquisite panelling, an array of paintings, and all the other evidence of talent and investment. Bowen was less audacious than his friend, fearing they might be caught and conscious of the fact that though he wore his one suit, its quality and cut did not identify him as a second-class passenger. Price was untroubled by any feelings of social inferiority. Indeed, the nocturnal tour brought out the rebel in him. While his companion held back, Price even contrived a glimpse into some of the public rooms, bringing back whispered reports of unimaginable luxury.

Both men were fit and lithe; whenever they heard someone coming, they dodged around a corner or slipped into an alcove, each time eluding discovery. Their luck was bound to run out in the end.

'Can I help you?' asked Dillman politely.

He had silently come up behind them, allowing them no chance to hide. Bowen gave a yelp of surprise, but Price was mutinous. He put his hands on his hips.

'We got lost,' he declared.

'Where's your cabin?'

'Steerage,' volunteered Bowen, blurting it out before he could stop himself and earning a dig in the ribs from Price's elbow. 'It's true, Mansell.'

'What's it like down there?' asked Dillman pleasantly.

'Crowded.'

'Our cabin is like a rabbit hutch,' moaned Price. 'And it's so bare.'

'So you thought you'd see how the other half lives, did you?' said Dillman easily. 'And why not? I don't blame you. The only trouble is that the stewards patrol these corridors. If they catch you here, they'll give you a stern reprimand.'

Price was defiant. 'Just let them try!'

'Come on. I know a shortcut back to the third-class section. Let me show you the way.' They traded a glance as they hesitated. 'Well?' encouraged Dillman. 'You can't stay here all night.'

The two of them fell in beside him and they walked down the corridor.

'Are you an American?' asked Bowen tentatively.

A friendly smile. 'How did you guess?'

'We're from Wales.'

'That was pretty obvious as well,' said Dillman. 'Immigrants?'

'Yes.'

'Don't tell him our business, Glyn,' snapped Price, nudging his friend. 'It's nothing to do with him.'

'But he might be able to help us, Mansell. He comes from America. He might be able to warn us what to look out for.' He looked at Dillman. 'Could you?'

'If you like,' said the other obligingly. 'My name is George Dillman, by the way. I hail from Boston. However, I may not be the best person to praise my native country.

To be honest, I'm coming around to the view that I'd rather live in London. I'm an Anglophile.'

'You sound like a madman to me,' said Price. 'Who'd want to live in London?'

'We all have our weaknesses.'

Dillman led the two of them around a corner, then halted as he caught sight of a figure tripping nimbly up the steps of a companionway. The others also came to a halt. Torn between following the man and escorting the two Welsh miners back to steerage, Dillman opted for the latter. He would have time enough later to speculate on where Max Hirsch was going at that hour.

As they set off again, he looked across at them. 'Now then,' he said helpfully, 'what can I tell you about the States?'

'Will we get jobs there?' asked Bowen.

Price was more specific. ' Good jobs?' he stressed.

'Put it this way, my friend,' replied Dillman. 'People who work hard usually get on. And the pair of you look as if you're not afraid of hard work. But I must be honest. Don't bank on immediate success. You'll have to work your way up slowly.'

'We've proved we can do that, Mr. Dillman,' said Price jocularly, softening toward his new acquaintance. 'We've only been on the *Mauretania* one evening and we've already worked our way up from steerage to second class.' He let out a sudden laugh. 'Before we finish, we'll probably be wallowing in all that gold bullion we're supposed to be carrying.'

FIVE

Alexandra Jarvis was the family alarm clock. Waking early out of sheer excitement, she made sure that her parents and her brother did not sleep blissfully on but roused them from their beds with tales of her vivid dreams about typhoons, killer whales, and the pirate ship that attacked the *Mauretania* in the night. Only her grandmother, the formidable Lily Pomeroy, slumbering peacefully in a separate cabin, was spared the persistent ringing of a child's voice in her ear. It meant that four members of the Jarvis family were among the first passengers to have their breakfast that morning.

Alexandra was in her usual interrogatory mood. 'Isn't this wonderful?' she asked, chewing on a piece of toast.

'Don't speak with your mouth full, dear,' chided her mother.

'Why not?'

'Because it's not polite.'

'Who decides what's polite and what's not polite?' wondered the girl.

'We do,' said her father firmly.

'But Christobel Wilkinson always talks with her mouth full at school and her father is a bishop.' She washed down the remnants of the toast with a drink of orange juice. 'Is it different for girls whose fathers work in the church?'

'No,' asserted Oliver Jarvis.

'Then why does Christobel do it, Daddy?'

'Sheer ignorance. She doesn't know any better.'

'But she's ever such a polite girl most of the time. When she says her prayers, Christobel talks to God as if he's our headmistress. She's so respectful.'

'Let's drop the subject, shall we?'

'Why?'

'Because we don't want to hear about Christobel Wilkinson.'

'Don't you like her, Daddy?'

'I don't want to share my breakfast with her, that's all.'

'Do you think the bishop talks with his mouth full?'

'That's immaterial.'

'No it isn't. Children are supposed to copy their parents, aren't they?'

'Yes,' agreed Vanessa Jarvis, smiling. 'So why don't you watch us and simply follow suit? In a public situation, good manners are vital.'

'Are they?'

'We're on display. People are looking at us.'

'But there's hardly anyone else in here,' said Alexandra, glancing around. 'Who's going to see what we do?' She munched on more toast but swallowed it before speaking again. 'Mr. Dillman has good manners, doesn't he, Mummy?'

'Yes, dear. He does.'

'Why was Daddy so funny with him?'

'I was nothing of the kind,' said her father testily.

'Yes you were.'

'Alexandra – '

'You were so suspicious at first. What was wrong with him?'

'He was a stranger,' explained Oliver Jarvis. 'There are rules.'

'What sort of rules?'

'You'll learn them in time, Alexandra,' said her mother.

'I hope so!' sighed Jarvis.

'But Mr. Dillman was such a lovely man,' recalled the girl. 'He was even nice to Noel, and that takes a lot of doing.'

'What do you mean?' demanded her brother, bridling.

'Well, you just sat there and glared at him.'

'No I didn't, Ally!'

'Noel is more reserved than you are, dear,' said Vanessa Jarvis. 'He takes a little longer to make new friends.'

'Only because of those spots on his face.'

'Ally!' snarled the boy.

'It's true. You look as if you've got measles, yet Mr. Dillman pretended that he didn't even notice them. That's how polite he is.'

'Shut up, will you!'

'That's enough!' said their mother sharply. 'I won't have language like that at the table. Do you understand?'

'She started it,' grumbled the boy.

'Your sister has a name, Noel. Please have the grace to use it.' She switched her gaze to Alexandra. 'As for you, young lady, I think you owe an apology to your brother. What you said was very hurtful. Don't you ever let me hear you say it again.'

'But he *does* have spots,' she contended. Three angry faces surrounded her and she became repentant. 'I'm sorry, Noel,' she said, twisting her napkin between her fingers. 'It was only meant as a joke.'

'A very cruel joke,' added her mother.

'I won't do it again, I promise.'

'Make sure you keep that promise,' said her father, wagging an admonitory finger. 'Or you'll be sent to the cabin to spend the rest of the voyage there.'

'Oh, no,' she protested. 'I'd miss all the fun if that happened. Please don't do that to me, Daddy. It's not fair. I'll be friends with Noel from now on. He can't help being shy. I love him, really.'

There was a long pause. Oliver Jarvis gritted his teeth as the first signs of indigestion made themselves known. His wife looked across at their daughter with a mixture of affection and exasperation, while her son, only partly mollified, spread marmalade on his toast, his head kept well down. Alexandra had the sense to say nothing. Pushing her plate away, she folded her arms and sat there with a patient smile. It was Vanessa Jarvis who eventually broke the silence.

'Well, now,' she said, taking a sip of tea, 'what are we all going to do today?'

'Try to wake Granny up,' suggested Alexandra.

Her mother tensed, her father sighed inwardly, and her brother sniggered.

'That wasn't a very kind thing to say,' scolded Vanessa Jarvis.

'I'm sorry. Can I be excused, please?'

'No, dear,' said her mother.

'Perhaps it's not such a bad idea,' decided Oliver Jarvis, overruling his wife. 'At least we could eat the rest of the meal in peace.' The warning finger came back into play. 'Wait outside for us, Alexandra, do you hear? Don't wander off.'

'I won't, Daddy.'

'And don't talk to any strangers.'

The girl nodded, set her napkin aside, then got down from her chair. Wanting to run to the exit, she instead opted for a dignified walk, knowing that her parents would be watching her all the way. When she reached the grand staircase, she was out of sight and celebrated her freedom by dashing up the first flight of carpeted steps. A familiar figure was waiting for her at the top. It was the black cat she had seen when embarking in Liverpool. Resting in an alcove, it was grooming itself absentmindedly while keeping the staircase under surveillance. Alexandra smiled and went down on one knee.

'Hello,' she said, beckoning the animal over. 'What's your name?'

The cat stopped grooming and studied her intently, then rose up lazily on its paws. After further appraisal of the young passenger, it put a long, quivering tail in the air and padded across to her to seal the introduction. Alexandra was delighted, stroking the fur gently and drawing a contented purr from the animal. She was so absorbed in what she was doing that she did not see the man descending the stairs toward them. The uniformed officer came to a halt and gave her a smile of congratulation.

'Well done!' he said. 'Bobo must really like you.'

'Is that his name?' she asked.

'Yes. Bobo is the ship's mascot. I'm the only person on board he allows near him as a rule. You're honoured, young lady.'

*

It was an exceptionally smooth crossing. At that time of year, the Irish Sea could be very choppy, but it was as calm as a millpond while the *Mauretania* steamed across it. When land was first sighted, several passengers were already at the rail, and hundreds more joined them as the southwestern coast of Ireland slowly appeared on the horizon. In Queenstown itself, a large crowd had been gathering since dawn to welcome the new ship and to give her a send-off worthy of her eminence. It was 9:00 a.m. on Sunday when the vessel finally pulled into her berth to receive her dock-side ovation and submit herself to the waiting cameras. The *Mauretania* did not linger. Additional passengers were swiftly embarked along with bags of mail, and the post office ashore was deluged with a record number of cables and letters. Activity among the crew and the port officials was at its peak. Nothing was allowed to delay departure.

A large press corps was making the historic voyage, and the correspondents' first wireless messages to their respective newspapers and magazines were uniformly positive. Having luxuriated in the ship's interior, sampled its excellent cuisine and enjoyed a good night's sleep, reporters of various nationalities were profoundly impressed, none more so than Hester Littlejohn, a correspondent from a ladies' journal that was sold in all the major cities on the eastern seaboard of America. A short, fair-haired, roly-poly woman in her late thirties, she gazed down from the boat deck at the seething crowd.

'They're certainly pleased to see us,' she said with a grin.

'It's a big day for them,' explained Dillman. 'They're letting us know it. We had exactly the same welcome on the *Lusitania*'s maiden voyage.'

Hester's interest was sparked. 'You sailed on the *Lusitania*?' she asked, turning to peer at him over the top of her glasses. 'That must have been a terrific experience. I begged my editor to let me make the trip, but it just wasn't possible. She said that I could sail on the *Mauretania* instead. What was it like?' she pressed. 'How do the two ships compare? Which do you prefer?'

'There are no short answers to those questions.'

'Then we must get together sometime so you can fill in the details. Some of the British reporters aboard were on the *Lusitania* as well, but they're too busy blowing their own trumpets to be taken seriously. Besides,' she insisted, 'I want to hear it from a passenger's point of view – an American passenger at that – and not from someone who's drinking his way through his newspaper's expense account.' She removed a glove to extend her hand. 'I'm Hester Littlejohn. Ladies' Weekly Journal.'

'George Dillman,' he replied, shaking her pudgy hand.

'From up near Boston, by the sound of it.'

'You've got a good ear, Miss Littlejohn.'

'Mrs. Littlejohn,' she corrected, pulling the glove back on. 'Unfortunately, my husband hates sailing or he'd be with me. Hal's idea of a vacation is to go hunting with the other men from the office. That suits me fine. I like to do my hunting on assignment. Hal aims his rifle at deer. I prefer to get a good story in my sights.'

'Then you're in the right place.'

'Looks to me as if I might have stumbled on the right person as well.'

Hester gave him a toothy smile of approval. Dillman's job on the ship allowed him free access to all sections of it, and he had come up to the boat deck partly to get a good view of Queenstown, and partly in the hope of catching a glimpse of Genevieve Masefield. The meeting with Hester Littlejohn was providential. He sensed that she might be a useful contact, not merely an agreeable companion with whom he could pass an occasional hour, but a vigilant woman who was trained to look into the nooks and crannies in search of copy. Hester might see things that neither he nor Genevieve were in a position to notice.

'So tell me, Mr. Dillman,' she resumed, 'is the *Mauretania* really the biggest ship in the world? That's what all the Brits are claiming.'

'With some justification.'

'I thought its dimensions were identical to those of the *Lusitania*.'

'Theoretically, they were,' he explained. 'Both were supposed to be seven hundred and eighty-five feet in overall length, but the *Mauretania*'s rounded stern adds an extra five feet, giving her a slight advantage. The width of each ship is the same – eighty-seven and a half feet. Look, I hope this isn't too technical for you.'

'No, no. Go on. I'm fascinated.'

'This is definitely the larger ship,' he continued. 'Its gross tonnage is just under the thirty-two-thousand mark, almost five hundred tons more than that of the *Lusitania*.'

'So we're that much heavier as well, are we, Mr. Dillman?'

'No, Mrs. Littlejohn.'

'But you just said that we were.'

'Gross tons is a measure of the ship's cubic capacity, not its weight.'

'Well, I never!' she said with a chortle. 'You live and learn. None of this would have the slightest interest for my readers, I'm afraid, but I love it. You certainly know boats. Anybody would think you'd designed the vessel yourself.'

'I come from a family that builds yachts, so I have a professional interest.'

'Then you're a real find, Mr. Dillman. I have a habit of bumping into people like you and it's one I don't intend to break. We need to sit down in a corner and have a proper conversation. If you don't mind, that is.'

'I'll look forward to it.'

'Good. Are you travelling alone?'

'More or less.'

'I suppose that I am as well,' she said with another grin. 'More or less. What took you to England? Vacation or business?'

'A little of both, Mrs. Littlejohn.'

'Did you go there to sell some of your yachts?'

'Not exactly,' he answered, 'but it was my maritime interest that got me there and put me on this remarkable vessel.'

'You, me, and all that gold bullion we're carrying.'

'We're the richest ship that ever sailed. Tell that to your readers.'

'I will, Mr. Dillman. Oh,' she said as she heard the siren, 'we're about to cast off.'

A concerted cheer went up from the spectators at the dockside. Every vessel in the harbour added its salutation. Wrapped up in their coats, scarves and hats, the passengers gave a valedictory wave and felt another surge of pleasure. It was precisely 11:00 a.m., and they would soon be passing Daunts Rock Lighthouse, the point from which the Atlantic crossing would be measured. All over the ship, people checked their watches and made a note of the time. The race for the Blue Riband had begun. The maiden voyage was fully under way.

Mansell Price and Glyn Bowen witnessed it all from the main deck, waving their caps at the receding crowd and forgetting, in the general euphoria, the shortcomings of third-class travel. As soon as the ship left Queenstown Harbour behind, however, they had to face up to the reality of four more nights in steerage.

'We took on a lot of new passengers,' observed Bowen.

'Yes,' said Price. 'And it looked to me as if most of them are here for the same reason as us. Especially those poor chaps carrying bundles on their shoulders or all their worldly possessions in a battered old case. They had third class written all over them. It's going to be more cramped down here than ever.'

'We keep on the move, Mansell, that's all.'

'How can we, mun?'

'There's lots of places to go. Out on deck, in the dining saloon or the lounge. And what about the smoking room? It's quite comfortable in there.'

'Only trouble is that we can't smoke.'

'We would if we had enough money to buy tobacco. Maybe we could cadge a couple of smokes off someone. Yes,' he said, considering the notion. 'We should have asked that Yank we met last night. Friendly sort of bloke. I bet he'd have given us a smoke or two. What did he say his name was?'

'Can't remember.'

'Hilton? Was that it?'

'No, it was Dilly or something like that.'

Bowen snapped his fingers. 'Dillman,' he recalled. 'That was it. George Dillman.'

'Where did he come from, that's what I want to know,' muttered Price.

'Who cares? He was no problem.'

'Yes he was. Spoiled our fun. I was enjoying our little prowl.'

'We're not supposed to go into second class, Mansell.'

'Nobody stopped us – until that Dillman bloke came along, that is.' A grin slowly spread over his face. 'If we'd left in an hour or two, I reckon we could have got into first class and had the run of the place.'

'That'd be asking for trouble.'

'We're entitled to a bit of fun. Tonight, maybe.'

'No, Mansell!'

'What's the problem? You scared?'

'Of course not.'

'Go on my own, if I have to.'

'Why go at all?'

'Because it gets me away from the cabin and out of earshot of that bloody mouth organ. Honestly, I'd like to toss the thing over the side of the ship, then throw the old man after it.'

'Fair play, mun. He was quiet as a mouse last night. So was his mate.'

'Only because the pair of them were dead drunk.'

'Lucky devils! Wish I could afford to go on the beer!'

Price rallied. 'Wait till we get to New York,' he asserted. 'You can have all the beer you like there.'

'If we can find ourselves a job,' said Bowen ominously. 'Mr. Dillman was very honest about our prospects. It won't be easy. According to him, there's a crisis in the American banks. That's why we're taking all that gold to them.'

'Yes, I been thinking about that.'

'About what?'

'The fact that we're sitting on a king's ransom. What about that, Glyn?' he said, eyes glistening. 'Somewhere in this ship there's almost three million pounds in gold bullion stashed away. I've just got to take a peep at that before we land.'

'Whatever for, mun?'

'Curiosity.'

'But you've got no idea where it's kept, Mansell.'

'Then I'll find out.'

'No,' said Bowen, deeply troubled. 'Wandering around second class in the night is one thing, but I'm not going anywhere near that gold. It's probably guarded. They'd nab us for sure.'

'Not if we're careful.'

'It's too dangerous.'

'I just want to see it, that's all.' He gave a chuckle. 'And touch it maybe.'

'Mansell!'

'Must be thousands of gold bars aboard. They wouldn't miss one.'

'You're mad!'

'Am I?' said Price, his mouth close to his friend's ear. 'Where's your ambition? Where's your guts? For once in your life, have the courage to dream.'

'It'd be a nightmare!'

'Would it?'

'Yes, Mansell.'

'Use your imagination,' urged the other. 'Just think of how much beer and smokes we could buy with a single bar of gold.' He smacked the rail hard with the flat of his hand. 'That would show the boyos back home!'

Mindful of Dillman's advice, Genevieve Masefield made a conscious effort to widen her social circle a little. Though she'd had to eat breakfast in the company of the gushing Susan Faulconbridge and the droll Harvey Denning, she managed to elude them for the rest of the morning. While her friends were watching the coast of Ireland gradually fade away, Genevieve adjourned to the first-class lounge, choosing a seat in the corner in order to read the book she had borrowed from the ship's library. As she expected, it was not long before she had company.

'That must be a mighty fine story you've got there,' commented a man's voice. 'Since you opened that book, you haven't lifted your head once.'

'I didn't realize that I was being watched,' she said, looking up.

'Oh, I think you did. My guess is that you've spent a whole lifetime being watched. If I had your looks, I'd not only expect it, I'd demand it.' She acknowledged the polite compliment with a brief smile. 'Do I get to know the title?'

'*Moby Dick.*'

'My, you're a brave young lady, reading a story like that on a voyage. Some people might say you were tempting fate. However,' he said, backing away slightly, 'it's your choice, so I won't keep you from it. My apologies for intruding.'

'Not at all,' she said, responding to his warm smile and courteous manner. 'I was only whiling the time away.'

'Then you need almost any author other than Melville. If all you want is mild diversion, find someone lighter and more inconsequential. *Moby Dick* is the kind of book that grabs you by the throat. It calls for real concentration.'

'I found that out.'

'Then why choose it?'

'I wanted an American writer.'

'You should have picked Mark Twain or Washington Irving.'

'I toyed with Henry James at first,' she admitted, putting the book down on the table. 'They have several of his books in the library.'

'Let them stay there,' he counseled. 'James is far too dull for you. He's less of an American than a fake Englishman. Believe me, I've met the guy. He's not the author to give you a true flavour of our country.'

'Then who would you recommend?'

'It would be presumptuous of me to say,' he replied seriously. 'I only stopped by to say hello. I'm not offering to take charge of your literary education.'

'But I'd value your advice.' She indicated the chair. 'Would you care to join me?'

There was a momentary hesitation before he spoke. 'I'd love to,' he said, lowering himself into the seat beside her and offering his hand. 'The name is Delaney, by the way. Orvill Delaney.'

'How do you do, Mr. Delaney?' She shook his hand. 'I'm Genevieve Masefield. And this,' she added, pointing to the book, 'is the Great White Whale.'

'Hardly suitable reading for a charming young lady.'

'Perhaps that's why I picked it.'

Genevieve had no qualms about inviting him to sit down. Orvill Delaney was a pleasant, relaxed, sophisticated man of fifty with long, wavy hair streaked with grey and a luxuriant moustache. Thin, wiry, and of medium height, he was impeccably dressed and exuded a mixture of culture and wealth. There was something completely unthreatening about him, and if nothing else, the presence of an American would at least keep Donald Belfrage away from her. Unlike the potential member of Parliament, her new acquaintance had a cosmopolitan air about him and a tolerant smile. He had the look of someone who had long outgrown his prejudices.

'Did you really meet Henry James?' she asked.

'Of course.'

'Where?'

'The first time was in London. I heard him give a lecture there. Well, most of it, anyway,' he confessed. 'I dozed off toward the end. The next time I came across him was down in Rye. I guess you know where that is.'

'Sussex.'

'Beautiful little place. I was strolling along the sidewalk one morning and there he was in front of me, crossing the street. Henry James. In the flesh, so to speak. You don't expect great writers to do anything as mundane as crossing a street. Not that I rate him as a great writer, mark you, but you take my point.'

'So who would you advise me to read?'

'My own favorite is O. Henry. Best short-story writer in creation.'

'That's a bold claim, Mr. Delaney.'

'Read him. Judge for yourself.'

'I will.' She studied him for a moment. 'What were you doing in Rye?'

'You might well ask,' he said evasively.

'In other words, you're not going to tell me.'

'Let me put it this way. The reason I went to hear Henry James lecture is that he and I are in what you might call associated walks of life.'

'Are you a publisher or a bookseller?'

'Both, Miss Masefield,' he explained, noting the absence of a wedding ring on her left hand. 'Indirectly, that is. I'm in the lumber business. At least I was. I sold to paper mills all over the country. Who knows?' he joked, nodding at the book. 'That may even have started life as one of my trees in Wisconsin.'

'A sobering thought. What took you to England?'

'The prospect of sailing back on the *Mauretania*. It was too good to miss. I had an enyoyable vacation as well, of course, doing all the things I like to do. Visit with friends, go to the theatre, buy lots of books. Oh, yes,' he said as an afterthought, 'I bought something else in England. A new automobile.'

'Why?'

'Because I wanted to take it back home with me.'

She was amazed. 'It's on board?'

'Tucked away down in the hold.'

'Don't they make enough cars in America for you to choose from?'

'I took a fancy to this one,' he said easily, 'so I reached out and took it. That's not quite as mercenary as it sounds, Miss Masefield.'

'I suppose I should be grateful that a British car tempted you.'

'There's a lot more than automobiles to tempt me in your country. That's why I plan to visit again in due course. Often.'

'Does that mean you're retired?'

He shook his head. 'People like me never retire. When I got out of lumber, I bought a controlling stake in a copper mine. When that palled on me, I moved into the construction business. And so it's gone on,' he said with a self-effacing smile. 'When I see what I like, I usually have it, though there are always sound commercial motives involved. Not with that automobile, however. That was different.'

'In what way?'

'Promise you won't hightail it out of here if I tell you?'

'Why should I?'

He leaned slightly forward. 'Because the horrible truth is that I responded to a sudden and uncontrollable urge. You'll be relieved to know that it's quite uncharacteristic of me,' he stressed, drawing a whisper of a smile from her. 'But let's talk about you,' he went on, stroking his moustache reflectively. 'I'm just a businessman looking to make an honest dollar. What about you, Miss Masefield?'

'I'm curious to visit America, that's all.'

'Oh, I think there's more to it than that.'

'Is there?'

'Yes,' he said, eyeing her shrewdly. 'When I saw you in the dining saloon yesterday evening, you seemed to be part of a merry little group, carousing happily with your friends. Yet here you are now, all alone, with no one for company but that weird old one-legged Captain Ahab.'

'So?'

'In a short space of time, I've been privileged to see two completely different Miss Genevieve Masefields. That's why you interest me so much.'

'There's only one of me, Mr. Delaney.'

'Not from where I sit. You're split right down the middle.'

'Into what?'

'The reveller and the reader.'

'I do like to curl up with a book,' she admitted.

'You also like to drink champagne and have fun. One woman, two aspects. The party-goer and the recluse. My question is this,' he said casually. 'Which is the real you?'

It was her turn to be evasive. She gave a noncommittal shrug.

'I wish I knew,' she replied.

SIX

The Sunday luncheon menu was particularly enticing, and George Porter Dillman was looking forward to working his way through it in the company of the Jarvis family. Having seen nothing of them that morning, he wanted to catch up on their news and gauge their first impressions of life afloat. However, duty intervened. When he arrived at the second-class dining saloon, the steward was waiting for him with a message.

'The purser's compliments, sir, and could you please join him in his cabin?'

'Now?' said Dillman.

'As a matter of urgency.'

Luncheon was postponed. Dillman asked the steward to convey his apologies to the Jarvis family and to express the hope that he might join them later. Long strides took him off in the direction of the purser's quarters. Maurice Buxton was waiting for him, smoking a pipe and filling the room with a pleasant aroma of tobacco.

'Sorry to haul you away from the feeding trough, Mr. Dillman,' he said.

'What's the problem?'

'There are five in all, I'm afraid.'

'Oh?'

'A spate of theft seems to have broken out.'

'Where?'

'Largely in second class,' said Buxton, 'though one of the first-class passengers also reported something missing.'

'What was taken?'

'Various things. A purse in one case, and a silver snuffbox. The most expensive item was the gold watch stolen from a lady in first class.' He rolled his eyes. 'Angry is too mild a word to describe Mrs. Dalkeith. She was pulsing with fury. Came charging in here like a she-elephant on the rampage.' The purser gave a wry smile. 'Anyone would think that *I* was the thief.'

'When exactly was the watch stolen?' asked Dillman.

'That's the problem. Mrs. Dalkeith was not quite sure. The old dear is nearly eighty and her memory is not all that reliable. She remembers taking the watch off in the ladies' room yesterday evening when she washed her hands, but she's fairly certain that she put it on again. When she woke up this morning, however, it wasn't lying on the dressing table, as it should have been.'

'Does she recall putting it there?'

'Yes and no.'

'So she may simply have mislaid it?'

'Not according to her. Mrs. Dalkeith is certain that she's the victim of a heinous crime. She wants the culprit caught immediately. If she had her way, he'd be strung and given a hundred lashes.' He gave a dry laugh. 'Her memory may be failing, but there's nothing wrong with her lungs. Mrs. Dalkeith could bellow for Scotland.'

'Give me the details, Mr. Buxton.'

The purser drew on his pipe and reached for the ledger in which he'd recorded all the thefts that had been reported. Taking pad and pencil from his inside pocket, Dillman listened to Buxton's litany and jotted down the information in a neat hand, looking for connecting links between the crimes as he did so. When he folded his pad, he had already reached an interim conclusion.

'The thefts in second class may well be related,' he said thoughtfully, 'but my guess is that the gold watch was taken by someone else entirely.'

'That'll please Mrs. Dalkeith.'

Dillman smiled. 'Tell her that even thieves observe class distinctions.'

'The only thing I'd dare tell her is that we've recovered her watch. Anything less than that would set her off again.' Buxton closed his ledger and took the pipe from his mouth. 'If I were you, Mr. Dillman, I'd put my earplugs in before I spoke to her.'

'I have a much better idea.'

'What's that?'

'I'll ask Genevieve Masefield to handle that part of the inquiry,' he decided, putting the pencil and pad away. 'A woman's touch is obviously needed here. Genevieve will be able to tease out details from the victim that may prove crucial. She knows how to deal with the Mrs. Dalkeiths of this world.'

'So do I – but I didn't have my elephant gun handy.'

'Was she really that difficult?'

'No,' replied the other with a ripe chuckle. 'I just felt a bit trampled on, that's all. Still, that's part and parcel of the job. A purser has to take the brickbats along with the plaudits, and there've been a fair number of the latter, I'm pleased to say. But we can't have thieves loose on the ship,' he added, brow furrowing. 'Bad for business and bad for passenger morale. We have to nip this in the bud before it gets out of hand.'

'We will, Mr. Buxton.'

'Where will you start?'

'In the dining saloon.'

Buxton frowned again. 'Are you *that* hungry, Mr. Dillman?'

'No,' said the detective, 'and I may have to forgo luncheon altogether in the interests of law enforcement. Four second-class passengers have had something stolen since we set sail from Liverpool. I'd like to know exactly where they were sitting for dinner yesterday evening. Especially the gentleman who had the silver snuffbox taken.'

'That was Mr. Rosenwald,' recalled Buxton, putting his pipe back into position. 'A charming man. The complete opposite to Mrs. Dalkeith. He more or less apologized for having to report the theft. Some of your countrymen can be a little demanding at times, but Stanley Rosenwald was politeness itself. You'll get every cooperation from him.'

'Good. He'll be my first port of call.'

'Keep me informed of developments.'

'Of course, Mr. Buxton.'

Dillman let himself out of the cabin and walked along the passageway. His mind was racing. Four people had been robbed under his nose and that was a blow to his pride. He was determined to root out any criminal activity early on. Instincts honed by his years with the Pinkerton Detective Agency, he knew the importance of solving a crime as soon as possible after it was committed, while the trail was still warm and the details still fresh in the minds of the victims. Since three of the four thefts had taken place overnight, his thoughts immediately turned to the two Welshmen he had found loitering in the second-class section. When he had shown them the way back to their cabin, Dillman had found out as much as he could about them, suspecting that they had ventured into that part of the vessel only out of a mixture of curiosity and bravado.

That opinion might have to be revised. Both men were extremely short of money and facing an uncertain future in America. Though the nervous Glyn Bowen did not look like a thief, there might well be enough desperation and social resentment in Mansell Price to provoke him into random theft. He was a creature of impulse. Dillman made a mental note to speak to them again in due course. He still doubted that they were the culprits; there was a distinct amateurism about them, and they had made no effort to get away when he cornered them. But they had to be investigated. Even if they were innocent, they might, in the course of their nocturnal exploration of the second-class facilities, have spotted someone on the prowl.

That brought the name of Max Hirsch into play, and it leapfrogged immediately over those of the miners to the top of the list of suspects. Hirsch's predilection for silver had already been demonstrated, and he had been seen flitting up a companionway the previous night. Dillman wondered if Stanley Rosenwald's silver snuffbox was hidden away in Hirsch's cabin, along with the rest of his spoils. One thing was clear: Two immigrants from the

Welsh valleys would hardly have any use for a snuffbox; it was hardly standard issue in the coal-mining industry. Bowen and Price would probably never have seen such an item before, let alone possessed one. Dillman came slowly around to the view that Rosenwald's property had followed the same route as the silver saltcellar and the pepper pot. It was time to reacquaint himself with Hirsch.

When he returned to the dining saloon, Dillman had a discreet word with the chief steward about the seating arrangements on the previous evening. Swift inquiries were made among the staff. The waiter who had served Stanley Rosenwald and his wife remembered the man very well because the American had left such a generous tip. He indicated the table at which the couple had been sitting. Dillman was satisfied. The table was adjacent to the one from which Max Hirsch had removed the cruet set. If, as was likely, Rosenwald had taken a pinch of snuff at some stage, the thief could not fail to have noticed the silver box.

Dillman checked the position of the three other victims whose names had been given him by the purser, but none had been seated anywhere near Hirsch. That did not matter. The proximity of the silver snuffbox was enough to lend extra weight to Dillman's suspicions.

Hirsch had to be questioned again, but a second interrogation, Dillman realized, might have to be delayed. When the detective caught sight of him, he saw that the man was at one of the tables in an alcove, holding forth to his companions with such authority that they all gaped at him in admiration. One of the people at the table was exhibiting more than admiration. Seated beside Hirsch, touching his arm affectionately as he made them all burst into laughter, was the woman whom Dillman had seen him paying his attentions to on the previous evening. Short, stout, and wearing a wide-brimmed hat, she was holding middle age at bay with mixed success, but friendship with Max Hirsch had apparently taken years off her manner. Teeth bared in an adoring smile, she was gazing at him with an almost girlish intensity.

It was not the ideal moment for Dillman to speak to his

prime suspect. In any case, he did not get the opportunity. Another priority suddenly beckoned as Alexandra Jarvis came trotting across the room to beam up at him.

'There you are, Mr. Dillman,' she said. 'Where've you been?'

'Hello, Ally,' he said fondly.

'Come and join us. We've been waiting for you.'

Before he could stop her, the girl grabbed him by the hand to lead him off.

Because her maiden voyage was in November, when a rough crossing was feared, the *Mauretania* was not full to capacity. Nevertheless, she was carrying a record number of passengers for that time of year, and there was certainly no visible sign of a shortage of numbers in first class. Almost every table was taken in the dining saloon for Sunday luncheon. It was one of the most spectacular rooms in the vessel. Set on two levels on the upper and shelter decks, the saloon was designed in the style of Francois I, each panel of light oak with a different carving, with the richer and more elaborate work in the lower half of the panels. The splendid glass dome, a thing of wonder in itself, gave the upper half of the saloon an additional sense of light and space. Between the two rooms was an open space, defined by the carved balustrade that encircled the upper area with decorative solidity.

Genevieve Masefield was glad there was no room for them in the upper section, where tables could accommodate from two to six guests. Instead of being an exclusive unit, she and her friends had to share with four complete strangers a table for ten in the lower section. What pleased her even more was that she collected a courteous nod of acknowledgement from Orvill Delaney as she took her seat. The gesture did not go unnoticed by Ruth Constantine.

'Someone you know, Genevieve?' she asked.

'Yes,' said the other. 'Mr. Delaney.'

'An American, by any chance?'

'From Wisconsin. He gave me some advice about what to read.'

'Is he an author or something?'

'No, Ruth. I think he's what you would describe as a man of means.'

'He looks prosperous enough,' said Donald Belfrage with condescension. 'I'll grant him that. But where does his wealth come from, that's what I want to know.'

'The slave trade probably,' suggested Harvey Denning mischievously.

'That wouldn't surprise me at all.'

'He's not like us, darling,' said Theodora Belfrage. 'We have Old Money.'

'What does it matter where it comes from,' said Ruth crisply, 'as long as you have it? Besides, I don't think that you can occupy the moral high ground with an entirely clear conscience, Donald. I seem to recall that one of your illustrious ancestors owned a fleet of ships that was engaged in the slave trade.'

'That was almost a century ago!' protested Belfrage.

'Quite,' she said. 'Old Money.'

'The slave trade has long been abolished, Ruth.'

'Except inside marriage.'

'That's an appalling thing to say,' squeaked Theodora.

'Ruth was only joking,' soothed her husband.

'If only I were!' sighed Ruth.

'I think that Mr. Delaney looks more like a captain of industry,' decided Susan Faulconbridge, stealing a glance at him over her shoulder. 'Something deliciously vulgar. An oil magnate perhaps.'

'I'd say he owns a steelworks,' said Theodora. 'Or something equally beastly.'

'Beastly, but essential,' Denning argued.

'Congratulations, Harvey,' teased Ruth. 'Your first sensible comment today.'

'And your first pleasant remark to me, my darling,' he countered. 'But you're all way off the mark. My guess is that Genevieve's new friend is a newspaper tycoon.' He smiled at her. 'Am I right?'

'Not exactly,' she replied.

'Then what is he? A politician? He looks wily enough.'

'Politicians are not wily,' said Theodora with a protective hand on her husband's arm. 'Donald is going into Parliament one day. Nobody would call him wily.'

'Certainly not!' murmured Ruth.

'Donald is a man of real integrity.'

'Let's put the dazzling career of Donald Augustus Belfrage, M.P., aside for a moment,' Denning interrupted. 'I want to hear about the mysterious Mr. Delaney. Tell us the truth, Genevieve. What is he?'

'A timber merchant,' she explained. 'At least he was.'

Susan was horrified. 'A lumberjack!' she exclaimed.

'Far from it, Susan. He inherited thousands of acres of forest.'

'And made his living by chopping down trees.'

'Mr. Delaney didn't need to swing an axe. He could employ others to do that for him. His real interest is in literature,' she continued. 'He's a very cultured man.'

'Yes,' said Denning with light sarcasm. 'I can just see him, trapped in some remote lumber camp, reeking of stale perspiration after a day of sawing up logs and reading Bret Harte by the light of the fire.'

'O. Henry is his favourite, actually.'

'Who?' asked Theodora.

'An American writer,' explained Genevieve.

'Well, I've never heard of him,' said the other as if that were the sole criterion of literary excellence. 'Have you, Donald?'

'Of course not,' replied her husband. 'Why are we talking about Americans anyway?' He brought a fist down on the table. 'We're British through and through and we should be proud of the fact!'

'You should work that sentence into your political speeches,' said Denning waspishly. 'It has such a ring of originality.'

'Why are you being so cruel to Donald?' asked Theodora, flapping a hand at Harvey. 'You and Ruth are doing it all the time.'

'Only because we love him,' said Denning with a conciliatory smile.

'They're jealous of him, Theo,' confided Susan, 'that's all. Everyone is. I mean, he's got everything. A beautiful home, a happy marriage, a glittering career ahead. That's my definition of perfection. What more does he need?'

'A brain?' muttered Ruth under her breath.

Donald Belfrage was saved from any further sniping by the arrival of the guests who were obliged to share their table. The waiter escorted them to their seats, and the four newcomers exchanged a flurry of nods with the incumbent diners. The two couples who settled down at the other end of the table were middle-aged, patently English, and endearingly old-fashioned. Indeed, one of the husbands, a tall man with muttonchop whiskers and a rubicund complexion, wore the attire and manner of a mid-Victorian *pater familias*. Their presence imposed a restraint and formality on the proceedings. Harvey Denning acted as an interlocutor between the two parties, but it was Genevieve who profited most. Sitting alongside the Victorian gentleman, she engaged him and his wife in conversation and was amazed to learn how progressive some of their ideas were. They had sent their son to be educated at Harvard, and since he had married and settled down in Albany, New York, they were now planning to visit him with their friends for an extended vacation.

A general discussion began on the relative merits of English and American universities, and Donald Belfrage rid himself cheerfully of his worst prejudices before telling the newcomers about his moment of triumph in the Boat Race. Pleased to widen her circle of acquaintants, Genevieve nevertheless kept one eye on the rest of the saloon, looking for the telltale signs that Dillman had warned about. She saw nothing untoward, however, though she knew that by the law of averages, at least someone in such a large gathering would have criminal inclinations. Harvey Denning was utterly charming toward the quartet at their table, and Ruth Constantine showed a more compassionate side to her nature, expressing genuine sympathy when one of the newcomers talked about her recent bout of illness.

Though he was sitting some distance away, Orvill Delaney was never far from Genevieve's thoughts, and whenever she glanced in his direction, his friendly gaze always met hers. She was sorry when he and his companions finished their meal and left the saloon. Unknown to Genevieve, her own departure was imminent. She had just eaten her dessert when a waiter brought a note for her. As soon as she read it, she rose to her feet and excused herself from the table.

Susan Faulconbridge tried to identify the mystery correspondent. 'It's from that lumberjack,' she said in a hoarse whisper. 'That Mr. Delaney.'

'I'm terribly sorry to put you to all this trouble, Mr. Dillman,' he said meekly. 'I'm sure you have more important things to do.'

'Nothing is more important than recovering stolen property, sir.'

'If indeed it *was* stolen.'

'Is there any doubt about that?' asked Dillman.

'Only a very slight one.'

The purser's description of Stanley Rosenwald was quite accurate. The man was mild-mannered, with a bearing of excessive politeness. Of average height and with a sallow complexion, Rosenwald had a substantial paunch that was largely disguised by a resourceful tailor. His wife Miriam was equally unassuming, a quiet little mouse of a woman in an expensive but totally anonymous grey dress. Both were verging on old age, but Dillman suspected that they might have reached it, in some ways, several years earlier. The interview took place in the Rosenwald cabin. They were sitting, while the detective remained on his feet.

'A slight doubt, you say?' probed Dillman.

'Yes,' said the other. 'I can be rather careless at times, can't I, Miriam?'

'Not really, Stanley,' she said loyally.

'What about that invitation card I mislaid?'

'That was quite different.'

'The fact is, Mr. Dillman,' he said, looking up at their visitor, 'there is an outside possibility that I may simply have put the snuffbox down somewhere and forgotten to pick it up. Unlikely, I grant you, but not impossible.'

'Where do you normally keep it, Mr. Rosenwald?' asked Dillman.

'In my waistcoat pocket,' he explained, opening his coat, revealing the paunch. He jabbed a finger into the appropriate pocket. 'Right here. I always carry it with me.'

'And you had it during dinner yesterday evening?'

'No question about that, Mr. Dillman.'

'Did you take it out in the course of the meal?'

'Oh, yes,' said Rosenwald firmly. 'That's one thing I'm never careless about. I always have one of my pills after I've eaten.'

'Your pills, sir?'

'That's what I keep in the box. I don't take snuff, Mr. Dillman. I think it's a disgusting habit. An occasional cigar is the height of my indulgence. No, the snuffbox was a present from my dear wife.'

'Stanley needed a box for his pills,' she explained. 'I saw it in an antiques shop.'

Rosenwald smiled benignly. 'Miriam spoils me.'

'You deserve the best,' she murmured.

Dillman was satisfied that the silver snuffbox had been visible during the meal and might conceivably have been noticed by a vigilant diner at an adjacent table. He jotted down details of Stanley Rosenwald's movements since the man had been aboard and was also given a loving description of the stolen item.

'If you need some more pills, sir,' he suggested, 'you should get a prescription from Dr. Hordern. The dispensary is well stocked and the pharmacist should be able to provide you with what you need.'

'That won't be necessary, Mr. Dillman,' said the other. 'I always carry an emergency supply with me. In the circumstances, it's just as well.' He put a hand on his wife's arm. 'But we would appreciate the return of that snuffbox.'

'I'll do my best to track down the thief.'

'My problem was that it took me such a long time to accept that it might actually have been stolen. I prefer to think well of my fellowman,' admitted Rosenwald with a sad smile. 'I suppose that I'm a little too ready to trust people.'

'The vast majority of passengers are entirely trustworthy,' Dillman assured him, 'but we may have the odd villain in our midst as well. Finding him is my job. Meanwhile, I'd be grateful if you didn't tell anyone about this.'

'Oh, we wouldn't dare do that, Mr. Dillman.'

'It's too embarrassing,' added his wife.

'Keep it to yourselves,' advised the detective, closing his pad. 'There's no point in spreading unnecessary alarm among the other passengers. And I hope you won't let this incident spoil your enjoyment of the voyage.'

'We won't,' said Rosenwald. 'It's a privilege to sail on the *Mauretania*.'

'Unfortunately, someone has abused that privilege. I'll do everything in my power to hunt him down,' promised Dillman. 'Carry on as if nothing has happened. Have you made many new friends since you've been aboard?'

'A few, Mr. Dillman. But then it's difficult not to make friends in such a cordial atmosphere. And, of course, we'd already met some of our fellow passengers on the boat train. That helped to break the ice, didn't it, Miriam?'

'Yes,' she agreed. 'The Sinclairs are a delightful young couple. We had the feeling that they're on their honeymoon. It was the way they kept looking at each other. Oh, and Mrs. Cameron is a lovely woman.'

'To be frank,' resumed her husband, 'we're rather shy in public, so we were very grateful to share a compartment with someone who took control of the introductions. He was so adept at bringing people out. It was remarkable. We set out as a group of complete strangers, but – thanks to him – we arrived in Liverpool as firm friends.'

'We owe it all to Mr. Hirsch,' said Miriam Rosenwald.

Dillman blinked. 'You shared a compartment with a Mr. Hirsch?'

'Yes,' she confirmed. 'Max Hirsch. Such pleasant company.'

Genevieve Masefield was pleased to be given a specific assignment at last. Hers had been a mere watching spell until now, and she'd felt a trifle guilty to be enjoying all the delights of first-class travel without having to pay for them. She now had an opportunity to earn her keep in another way. Dillman's note had sent her hurrying to his cabin, where he had given her the details of the thefts, then issued his instructions. When he went off to make contact with the owner of a silver snuffbox, Genevieve returned to the first-class dining saloon, established from the chief steward that Mrs. Dalkeith was not there, so repaired to the latter's cabin. A thin, anxious, breathy young woman in a maid's uniform invited her in, then vanished swiftly into the adjoining room so that Genevieve could speak alone with Mrs. Cynthia Dalkeith.

Having had her luncheon served in the privacy of the cabin, the old lady was fairly quiescent, reclining in a chair and looking remarkably well preserved for her years. She was fleshy without being fat, poised without being arrogant. Genevieve took note of the delicately embroidered long blue skirt and the zoave jacket in a navy hue, trimmed with gilt braid applied in a serpentine fashion. Beneath the jacket was a white silk blouse. At her neck, like a bejeweled Adam's apple, was a large black-and-gold brooch that bobbed up and down as she spoke. Her mottled fingers were encrusted with diamond rings. There was a thick gold bangle on her left wrist. Evidently, Mrs. Dalkeith liked to display her wealth. Dillman had warned his colleague about the old lady's sharp tongue and fierce temper, so Genevieve trod carefully, introducing herself with a respectful smile and explaining her role on the vessel.

Mrs. Dalkeith was caught between astonishment and disbelief.

'You're far too young to be a detective,' she said, peering at her visitor and speaking with a light Edinburgh accent. 'And far, far too beautiful.'

'Nevertheless, that is what I am, Mrs. Dalkeith.'

'And you're going to find my gold watch for me?'

'I hope so.'

'How?'

'With a combination of inquiry and persistence.'

'But what will you do when you catch the thief?' asked the other with concern. 'You could hardly overpower the wretch and drag him off to the captain. Suppose the man turns violent? You could be hurt, Miss Masefield.'

'In the event of violence, I have someone to help me.'

'I'm relieved to hear that.'

She waved Genevieve to a chair, then summoned the maid to pour them each a cup of tea. The latter was summarily dismissed with a flick of the hand before Mrs. Dalkeith resumed the conversation. She stirred her tea with methodical care.

'I must have that watch back,' she declared.

'Rest assured that we'll do all we can to recover it,' said Genevieve, opening her purse to take out a pencil and a small notebook. 'Now, if you would, please, I'd like you to tell me exactly when you discovered that the watch was missing.'

'I've given all the details to the purser.'

'I'd like to check them, Mrs. Dalkeith, to be absolutely sure. There may be a few things that you forgot to tell Mr. Buxton.'

'That's true,' conceded the old lady. 'I was quite upset when I reported the theft. Rightly so, Miss Masefield. I mean, one doesn't expect to be robbed in broad daylight on the Cunard Line.'

'Are you certain that the theft occurred during the day?'

'Well, no. I'm not, to be quite candid.'

'Let's go back to yesterday evening,' said Genevieve patiently. 'Describe your movements from the time you stepped aboard. Presumably, you were wearing the watch when you embarked.'

'Of course.'

'What happened then?'

Cynthia Dalkeith needed a long sip of tea before she

could begin. The river-delta of lines on her face acquired new tributaries as she summoned up her concentration, going over the events of the previous evening as if picking her way barefoot over a pathway strewn with sharp stones. Valuable new details emerged and went straight into her notebook. When the recital ended, Genevieve allowed herself a drink of tea from her own cup. Mrs. Dalkeith adjusted the brooch at her throat.

'Was that helpful, Miss Masefield?' she asked.

'Extremely helpful.'

'It's so much nicer talking to you than to Mr. Buxton. It wasn't only the robbery that annoyed me, it was that foul smell of pipe tobacco in his cabin. It set me on edge. Mind you,' she added with a shrill laugh, 'the purser was very fortunate.'

'Fortunate?'

'Having to deal with me rather than with my husband. Alistair really does have a vicious tongue. Compared to him, I'm a model of restraint.' She laughed again. 'Alistair always says that I'm a West Highland terrier, while he's a man-eating tiger. All I did to Mr. Buxton was to nip at his ankles. My husband would have torn him to shreds.'

'He's not on the voyage, I take it?' said Genevieve.

'No, he's already in New York. We have family there. If I was going to travel all that way again, I wanted to do it on the maiden voyage of the *Mauretania*.' Her voice darkened. 'Though I didn't expect to be robbed in the process.'

'You have my sympathy, Mrs. Dalkeith.'

'I need a lot more than that to smooth my ruffled feathers.'

'Understandably.' Genevieve glanced down at her notes. 'When you visited the ladies' room yesterday, you took off your watch to wash your hands. Did you also remove your rings, Mrs. Dalkeith?'

'Of course. I always do. Don't you?'

'The rings and the watch were set down beside you. Is that correct?'

'Yes.'

'Was anybody else in there with you at the time?'

'Three or four people.'

'Did any of them stand next to you?'

'A French lady in a rather appalling green dress that was most unbecoming. I know that the French have a reputation for setting fashion,' she said tartly, 'but it's very undeserved in my opinion. This lady was a case in point. She was too old and far too overweight to appear in public in such an unsuitable evening dress.'

'Do you happen to know the lady's name?' wondered Genevieve.

'I'm afraid not, but I could easily identify her.' Her jaw tightened vengefully. 'You don't think that *she* might have taken my watch?'

'Not at all, Mrs. Dalkeith. I'm just wondering if she might have noticed when you put it back on again. Along with your rings. But you say that there were other people in the room with you,' said Genevieve. 'Might any of them have seen you taking the watch off and putting it back on?'

'Only that American lady.'

'American lady?'

'Yes, Miss Masefield. She spent a lot of time in front of the mirror, brushing her hair and applying a little rouge to her cheeks. Heaven knows why. I would have thought that she was the last person who needed to worry about her appearance.'

'Why is that, Mrs. Dalkeith?'

Scrutinizing her visitor, the old lady spoke with a slightly wistful air. 'Because she was almost as beautiful as you are.'

SEVEN

Mansell Price and Glyn Bowen were thoroughly chastened. Having spoken to some of the other immigrants on board, they came to see their own situation in a new light. Compared to the predicaments that others were facing, they had every reason for optimism. Both were young, healthy, and accustomed to hard physical work. They had a variety of labouring skills to offer. More to the point, they lacked the family commitments that hindered so many of their fellow passengers in steerage. One unemployed Irish navvy who embarked in Queenstown had a wife, three children, and a disabled sister in tow. They had barely managed to scrape together the money for the voyage. Another family, from Cumbria, five in number, had been evicted from their tied cottage by a vindictive farmer, who ensured that the labourer got no more work in the county by spreading cruel lies about him. Despair was driving the man and his young family to travel three thousand miles across the ocean in search of a new life.

Other tales were even more harrowing. Some people scarcely owned more than the clothes in which they were standing. Most had no idea of what they would do once they reached New York, or indeed if they would even be allowed into America. Among the immigrants, there was a stench of poverty and a quiet sense of panic. The incongruity was startling. On the most elite liner in existence, the bulk of the passengers were beleaguered human beings making a last bid for survival. The two Welshmen had seen widespread deprivation in the Welsh valleys but nothing on the scale that surrounded them now. Glyn Bowen was shocked.

'Did you notice his wife?' he asked. 'That bloke from Wigan, I mean.'

'Aye, mun,' said Price.

'She was all skin and bone. I thought she was forty, not twenty-one.'

'It was that kid that worried me, Glyn. Too weak even to cry. He just clung to his mother. You wonder if they'll even make it to New York alive.'

'Maybe we're not so badly off after all, Mansell.'

'Matter of opinion.'

'Against some of this lot, we're rich.'

'Well, I don't feel rich,' said Price rancorously. 'I'm sorry for these other poor blokes, but we have to look out for ourselves, Glyn. Fact is, we're going to land in New York with empty pockets and slim prospects. Where do we go from there?'

'We'll find something.'

'Will we?'

They were standing on the main deck, wrapped up against a searching wind in flimsy overcoats, woolen scarves, and flat caps. Sobered by his contact with the other passengers, Bowen was trying to remain positive and make the most of the voyage, but Price was a malcontent. He pointed an accusing finger upward.

'That's where the rich people are,' he sneered. 'Up there in first class, drinking their champagne and eating their five-course meals. Well, you saw what second class was like, Glyn. Luxury, compared to what we have to put up with down here. First class is even better than that. Cost us more than a year's wages to have a berth there.'

'Some people have all the luck.'

'Why them and not us?'

'They were born to it, Mansell,' Bowen replied with a fatalistic shrug. 'All we were born to was a life down the pit. Just like our fathers.'

'Your father maybe,' retorted the other vehemently. 'He's still swinging a pick at the coal face right now. Not my dad. When the roof collapsed on him, he was trapped for days before they dug him out. And what did the bastards do?'

'Took him home to your mam on a stretcher.'

'With nothing but a blanket thrown over him,' recalled Price, eyes smoldering. 'Mam fainted when she saw him. Someone came 'round next day and gave her a five-pound note like they was doing us a favour. Thirty years down that hellhole and all he's worth is five quid!' He spat over the bulwark. 'That isn't going to happen to me, I tell you. I'm not going to be buried alive under tons of coal because some clever fool of a manager, who works above ground, doesn't know how many pit props are needed to shore up a tunnel. Mam won't ever have me brought home on a stretcher.'

'But she'll miss you, Mansell.'

'Can't be helped. I had to go.'

'So did I.'

'It's a dog's life.'

'Got to be better in America.'

Price nodded. 'Let's get out of this bloody wind,' he said irritably.

They headed for the lounge, a cavernous space with a functional air about it, lined with wood panelling and built to accommodate the large number of steerage passengers in revolving chairs that were fixed to the floor. As they entered, one of the stewards was coming toward them, a jaunty little Irishman with a tray under his arm. Price's manner changed at once. He grinned at the steward and adopted a familiar tone.

'Hang on a minute, boyo,' he said. 'Want to ask you something.'

'Yes, sir?' said the steward.

'Is it true we got a fortune in gold aboard?'

'You know it is, Mansell,' said Glyn.

'I want to hear it from someone in authority,' returned the other, silencing him with a glare. He grinned at the steward again. 'Is it?'

'Yes,' replied the Irishman, 'but you're not hearing that

from someone in autority, sir. Steward in third class is about as low as you can get on board. The ship's mascot has more autority than I do. As for the gold, there's heaps of the stuff here. Enough to keep every man jack of us in clover for the rest of our lives.'

'And where's it kept?' asked Price.

'In the security room.'

'Under armed guard?'

'Who knows? I'll never get near it, that's for certain.'

'Did you see it come aboard?'

'Now that I did,' confessed the steward. 'A small army of railway police brought it to the dockside. The boxes were unloaded one by one.'

'Boxes? What kind of boxes?'

'Drop it, Mansell,' said Bowen uneasily.

'How big were they?'

'Oh – so big,' explained the steward, tucking the tray between his legs and holding his arms apart to indicate dimensions. 'And heavy as lead. You could see that from the way they lifted them.' He grabbed the tray again. 'Anyway, I have to be off.'

'One last question,' said Price.

'No, Mansell,' urged his friend.

'Keep out of this, Glyn.'

'But this is ridiculous, mun.'

'Shut your gob, will you!' He turned to the steward. 'Don't mind him.'

'What's this last question, sir?'

Price tried to sound casual. 'Where is this security room?' he asked.

Max Hirsch was singularly elusive. George Porter Dillman made three circuits of the second-class section and two visits to the man's cabin before he finally ran him to ground. Wearing a fur-collared overcoat and a black homburg, Hirsch was about to go out on deck. Dillman touched his arm to restrain him.

'Excuse me, Mr. Hirsch,' he said politely. 'Might I have a word?'

'As long as it's a quick one,' replied Hirsch, looking over his shoulder. 'I've arranged to go for a stroll on deck with a friend.'

'Talking of friends, sir, I believe that you know a Mr. and Mrs. Rosenwald.'

'Stanley and Miriam? Yes, they were in my compartment on the boat train. Nice people. Very civilized. I've never met a couple who were so shy. Not a common failing among Americans, is it? I got on very well with both of them.'

'So they say.'

'Has anything happened to them?' asked the other with mild concern.

'Mr. Rosenwald had something stolen, I'm afraid.'

Hirsch clicked his tongue. 'I'm sorry to hear that. What was it?'

'A few other things went astray in the night as well.'

'That's a rather poor advertisement for Cunard security,' mocked Hirsch.

Dillman did not rise to the bait. 'After we spoke last night,' he said evenly, 'did you have reason to leave your cabin at all?'

'What's that to you?'

'I'd like to know, please.'

'That's your problem.'

'Do I need to spell it out for you, Mr. Hirsch?'

'Ah!' exclaimed the other as if it had just dawned on him. 'I get it now. You think I'm the culprit. It all fits. You believe that as soon as you left me, I sneaked off to the Rosenwald cabin and stole whatever it is that was taken.' He smirked. 'By the way, what was it? Money? Jewellery? State secrets of some kind?'

'A silver snuffbox.'

'Oh, I remember that. Stanley was so proud of it.'

'He showed it to you?'

'Of course. On the train. After I'd shown him my silver cigarette case.'

'So you know where Mr. Rosenwald kept it.'

'In his waistcoat pocket. There were pills in that box, not

snuff. I teased him about it, actually,' said Hirsch with a chuckle. 'I asked him if he kept his snuff in a pillbox.'

'Let's go back to last night,' said Dillman.

Hirsch checked his watch. 'Must we?' he sighed.

'Yes, sir. Did you leave your cabin?'

'I may have.'

'Can't you remember?'

'I just don't see that it's relevant, Mr. Dillman.'

'Then let me be a little more explicit,' said the other, stepping in closer. 'Three cabins were entered last night by a thief. Valuable items were stolen. You had already been apprehended earlier on, helping yourself to a silver salt-cellar and a pepper pot from the dining saloon.'

'I explained that,' said Hirsch in anguished tones. 'They were a gift for my wife.'

'Husbands tend to buy gifts, sir – not steal them.'

'I was impulsive.'

'Thieves often use that excuse.'

'Rachel has a thing about silver. I told you that.'

'Yes, sir. You did. So why did you leave your cabin last night?'

'What makes you think I did, Mr. Dillman?'

'Because I saw you, sir.'

He looked deep into Hirsch's eyes and saw a momentary flicker. The suspect recovered his composure with great speed. Putting a hand in his pocket, he took out a key and offered it to Dillman.

'Go on,' he encouraged. 'Take it. Search my cabin. Find all this loot I'm supposed to have taken. Stanley Rosenwald's silver snuffbox is hidden inside one of my black shoes, by the way. Why not start with that?'

'There's no need for sarcasm, sir.'

'Then get off my back, Mr. Dillman,' he said, pocketing the key once more. 'Yes, I did leave my cabin last night, but only because I wanted some fresh air. I went out on deck for a stroll. If you really saw me, you'd have noticed I was wearing this coat.' He undid the buttons and held it wide open. 'And in case you think I've got the booty sewn into the lining, give this the once-over while you're at it.'

'There's no point, Mr. Hirsch. We both know that.'

'Yes, my friend. We also know that it's perfectly legitimate for any passenger to move about the ship of his own free will whenever he or she chooses. I was simply exercising that right. If you have evidence to the contrary,' he taunted, buttoning his coat again, 'show it to me right now or stop pestering me.'

Dillman hesitated. Before he could speak, another voice rang out behind him.

'Where've you been, Max? I've been waiting for ages.'

'I'm sorry, Agnes,' said Hirsch, a picture of contrition. 'I was on my way when I was intercepted by Mr. Dillman here.' He beamed at the detective. 'Have you met Mrs. Cameron?' he asked, then turned back to her. 'Agnes, this is Mr. Dillman.'

'Oh, how do you do?' she said.

'Pleased to meet you, Mrs. Cameron,' he replied with a reflex smile.

Her hand emerged from the muff to shake his. Though she was immersed in a fur coat and hat, Dillman recognized her as the woman he had seen with Hirsch in the dining saloon. Clearly, their relationship had started in a compartment on the boat train. Agnes Cameron was a pleasant, pale-skinned Englishwoman with a mole on her left cheek that served as a kind of beauty spot. She gazed fondly at Max Hirsch. He offered his arm and she slipped a hand through it before tucking it back into her muff. On land he might be a loving husband but at sea, he allowed himself certain bachelor freedoms.

'You'll have to excuse us,' he said with a broad grin. 'Mrs. Cameron and I have a lot to discuss. Goodbye.'

'Goodbye,' said Dillman, giving them a token wave of farewell and wondering why a woman like Agnes Cameron had been ensnared by Hirsch's seedy charm.

The two made an odd couple, but Dillman never made it his business to pass judgment on any nascent romances between passengers. There were far more unlikely pairings aboard, and others would develop over the next few days as the seductive power of oceanic travel worked on people's emotions. He was annoyed with himself. After his brief confrontation with Hirsch, he was no nearer to deciding whether or not the man was involved in the spate of thefts. All that he had done was to alert him that he was under suspicion. Hirsch had, however, saved him the trouble of searching the cabin. Had any stolen property been hidden there, he would never have offered the key to Dillman with such blatant confidence. Firm evidence was needed, but before the detective could go in search of it, someone swooped down on him like a hungry seagull spotting a morsel of food.

'Mr. Dillman!' she said with a cackle of triumph. 'We can stop playing hide-and-seek at last. I want that long talk with you right now. Where shall we go?'

Hester Littlejohn would not be denied.

Oliver Jarvis made a considered decision. Convinced that his children would be safe if they stayed together, he allowed them a degree of freedom that afternoon. It meant that he and his wife could spend some quiet time together in the lounge, unencumbered by his mother-in-law, who retired to her cabin to sleep off a gargantuan luncheon, or by Noel and Alexandra. The children, meanwhile, roamed the decks, stared at the sea, argued about the speed at which the vessel was going, talked about what they would do when they reached New York, and engaged in the ceaseless banter of childhood. It was only when they stepped in out of the wind that Alexandra realized something. She stared up at the clock on the wall.

'Is that the time?' she asked.

'Yes, Ally.'

'I've got to go!'

'Where?' asked Noel.

'Wait here for me!'

'You can't just run off.'

'I won't be long.'

'Daddy said we had to stay together,' he reminded her.

But the parental decree had already been forgotten. Alexandra went rushing off along a passageway, then turned a corner. Her brother set off in pursuit, wondering what could possibly have made her bolt like that. When he reached the corner, he turned into another long passageway, but it was quite deserted. Where had his sister gone? There were so many options. Companionways led up and down. At the far end of the passageway was a T junction that gave her further possibilities. Was it conceivable that Alexandra had gone into one of the cabins? Noel was puzzled and anxious. He knew that he would get a stinging reprimand from his parents if he returned to the lounge alone. They would blame him for Alexandra's disappearance. He began a hasty search.

The girl, meanwhile, was on the deck above, scampering toward a half-open door at the far end of a passageway. She was almost out of breath when she reached it. When she tapped on the door, it was opened immediately by one of the officers.

'Hello, Alexandra,' he said. 'I had a feeling that you might turn up.'

'You told me that Bobo was always fed at set times.'

'Oh, yes. He never misses his grub. You could set your watch by him.'

'Can I come in?' she asked.

'Of course.'

The officer stood back so that Alexandra could step into the cabin. On the floor in a corner was a plate with a few remnants of scraps that had just been eaten by the cat. With an urgent tongue, Bobo was now lapping up milk from a bowl. Alexandra waited until he had finished before she bent down to touch him. Licking his lips with satisfaction, he turned to look at the girl; then, with no warning, he hopped up onto her knee. Alexandra cradled him and stroked his fur with a gentle hand. The purring was like the revving of an engine.

'Hello, Bobo,' she said. 'Did you enjoy your meal?'

'He's never let anyone pick him up before,' observed the officer. 'Not even me.'

Alexandra giggled. 'Bobo is my friend. Aren't you, Bobo?'

By way of reply, the black cat rubbed his head softly against her arm.

Her patience was finally rewarded. Genevieve Masefield had no difficulty in identifying her. The woman had a natural beauty that was subtly enhanced by a sparing use of cosmetics and a stylish silk dress in a shade of green that matched her eyes. Though she seemed to be in her early twenties, there was a poise and maturity about her that hinted at more years than were at first apparent. Her smile, frugally used, seemed to light up her whole face. Genevieve watched her talking to a distinguished-looking man with a dark beard. Their conversation was long and intense. When it finally came to a close, the man rose to his feet, kissed her hand with great courtesy, then left the room. Genevieve got up from her own seat and glided across to the woman.

'Excuse me,' she said affably. 'I wonder if I might have a word with you?'

'Of course,' replied the other. 'Please sit down.'

'Thank you.' Genevieve lowered herself into the chair beside her. 'My name is Genevieve Masefield, by the way.'

'Katherine Wymark,' said the other, appraising her. 'To be honest, I was rather hoping for the opportunity to meet you, Miss Masefield. You aroused the envy of every woman in the dining saloon. Myself included.'

'I can't believe that.'

'Oh, come on. You must surely have grown used to being the centre of attention by now. The women were envious because the men couldn't take their eyes off you. There's nothing to touch that classical English beauty,' she said with a confiding smile. 'It has such purity. An all-American girl like me just can't compete with that.'

'I wouldn't have thought that you had any shortage of male attention,' remarked Genevieve pleasantly. 'There are probably dozens of jealous women here who'd be only too glad to scratch your eyes out as well.'

'Not really, Miss Masefield. I'm spoken for, you're not.' She held out her left hand to show off the gold wedding ring, partnered by an engagement ring that featured a large sapphire in a circle of diamonds. 'It's amazing what a difference that makes. But,' she said, folding her hands in her lap, 'I'm sure you didn't come here to talk about that. What can I do for you?'

'Actually, I've come on behalf of a friend,' said Genevieve. 'Mrs. Dalkeith.'

'I don't believe I know the lady.'

'Your paths did cross yesterday evening. In the ladies' room.'

Katherine Wymark gave a laugh. 'My! This conversation is taking a strange turn,' she said, raising an eyebrow. 'Who is this friend of yours?'

'Mrs. Dalkeith is an elderly Scots lady. Grey-haired and dignified.'

'Oh, yes. I think I remember her. We exchanged a word or two.'

'Did you happen to notice that she removed her rings and her watch?'

'Why do you ask?'

'Because the watch has gone astray,' said Genevieve, 'and Mrs. Dalkeith wonders if she simply forgot to put it back on again after she'd washed her hands. She is rather prone to do something like that. But she's dreadfully upset about the disappearance of the watch, so I offered to try to track it down.' She looked into the green eyes. 'Do you recall seeing her leave the room without a gold watch?'

'No, Miss Masefield,' said the other firmly. 'If I had, I'd have picked it straight up and gone after her. The truth is that I hardly looked at her. It's not the kind of thing you do in those circumstances.'

'I appreciate that.'

'Though I do seem to recall someone else in there at the time. A French lady.'

'Madam Coutance. I've already spoken to her.'

'You *have* been diligent.'

'I promised to help Mrs. Dalkeith,' said Genevieve. 'She's very distressed.'

'Was this Madame Coutance able to help you?'

'I'm afraid not.'

'And nothing was found in the ladies' room when it was cleaned?'

'No, Mrs. Wymark. That was the first thing I checked.'

'Then the mystery thickens.' Katherine gave a wry smile. 'I stepped in there only to brush my hair. I didn't realize that I'd get involved in a search for a gold watch. Incidentally,' she wondered, 'how did you know that I was even in the room? I didn't give my name to your friend.'

'Mrs. Dalkeith gave me a clear description of you.'

'Yet she can't remember if she put her watch back on or not. What a curious thing memory is! Well, Miss Masefield, I'm sorry I can't help you.' Her eyes twinkled. 'And I won't embarrass you by asking what this "clear description" of me was. Besides, I'm not sure I want to know how I'm viewed by an absentminded elderly Scots lady.'

'Very favourably.'

'I'll settle for that and ask no more. So where will you go from here?'

Genevieve gave a shrug. 'I'm not sure, to be honest.'

'Dozens of women must have been in and out of that room after we left. If the watch was there, any one of them might have picked it up. You could be in for a long search, Miss Masefield.'

'I know.'

'Good luck!'

'Thank you for talking with me, anyway.'

'My pleasure.'

Disappointed that she had made no progress in the search, Genevieve was nevertheless pleased to have met Katherine Wymark. She was an interesting woman, with an easy drawl in her voice and a relaxed manner. There was none of the reserve and formality that might have been encountered in an Englishwoman of the same age. Katherine had a sophistication that made friends like Theodora Belfrage and Susan Faulconbridge seem almost naive. Even the worldly Ruth Constantine would have looked inexperienced beside her. There was a composure about Katherine Wymark that was formidable. Only one thing was troublesome: The woman was far too intelligent to believe that Genevieve was acting on behalf of an elderly lady out of the kindness of her heart. Genevieve's disguise had been penetrated.

Out of the corner of her eye, she saw a man approaching them and turned to face him. Orvill Delaney bore down on them with a magazine in his hand.

'Pardon this intrusion, ladies,' he said, distributing a smile evenly between the two of them. 'I just wanted to give you this, Miss Masefield,' he explained, handing the magazine to her. 'It has a story by O. Henry in it. I think you'll appreciate it.'

'Thank you, Mr. Delaney.'

'And while I'm here, Mrs. Wymark,' he said, turning to face her, 'could I ask you a favour, please? Remind your husband about that game of chess he promised me.'

'I will, Mr. Delaney.'

'No better way to end the day than with a game of chess.' He looked back at Genevieve. 'And with a story by O. Henry, of course.'

'So, on balance, Mr. Dillman,' she concluded, 'you'd prefer the *Lusitania*.'

'I didn't say that, Mrs. Littlejohn.'

'But that's what it amounts to. From what you've told me, it was obviously a memorable and exciting maiden voyage.'

'Yes,' agreed Dillman, 'it certainly didn't lack for excitement. And it gave me some very precious memories,' he confessed, thinking of Genevieve Masefield and the firstlings of their romance. 'But that doesn't mean I'd rate the *Lusitania* as the finer vessel. It's far too early to judge. Ask me when we reach New York.'

'What about the interior decoration of the two ships?'

'I'd have to say that the *Mauretania* has the edge there. I hold the highest esteem for what Mr. Peto has done. He was known for his work on country houses before he got this commission, and he's incorporated a lot of ideas from stately homes into the design. The panelling throughout is a revelation, and those lavish plaster ceilings are works of art. Everywhere you look,' he said with admiration, 'there's an arresting design feature.'

'I know,' said Hester Littlejohn. 'I've used up half a dozen pencils just trying to list them. Harold Peto will certainly get a mention in my magazine. He's left the stamp of his genius on this ship.'

'Even though that stamp can be a little too firm at times.'

'What do you mean, Mr. Dillman?'

'Well, he does tend to gild the lily,' argued Dillman. 'In the first-class smoking room, for instance, the Italian Renaissance style is a trifle forced, I think. And I do have my doubts about those encrusted mullions.'

They were seated in the second-class lounge, sharing a pot of tea and their impressions of the vessel. Hester Littlejohn had a pad on her lab, but she was committing far more to memory than to the page. She was also making no secret of the fact that she enjoyed Dillman's company, grinning at regular intervals and even touching his arm when he made a polite joke. Dillman gave a highly edited version of the maiden voyage of the *Lusitania*, concealing the fact that it was essentially a work assignment for him. There had been little time to relish the event.

Hester Littlejohn was as irrepressible as ever, wearing a travelling dress of a reddish hue that softened the contours of her body, and a brown cloth-and-felt hat shaded with plumes. Her eyes sparkled over the top of her glasses.

'Tell me about the things I can't see, Mr. Dillman,' she invited.

'I'm not sure that I understand you,' he said.

'Well, I looked at all the public rooms when I was given a tour of the ship this morning with the rest of the scribblers. We were even given a glimpse of the bridge and allowed two minutes with Captain Pritchard. But it's difficult to get the proper measure of a vessel when you're being shunted around in a group.'

'What else would you like to know?'

'What happens out of sight. In the boiler rooms, for example.'

'I don't think your readers would be interested in that.'

'I am, Mr. Dillman.'

'Then you'll need some basic knowledge of engineering to understand how the steam turbines work. They're geared to quadruple screw propellers that are capable of generating a speed of approximately twenty-five knots under good conditions.'

'Such as we have now.'

'Exactly,' he confirmed. 'The *Mauretania* has twenty-five boilers, a hundred and ninety-two furnaces, and a storage capacity for six thousand tons of coal. That may sound like a lot, but then we use up a thousand tons of coal a day. Think of how much shovelling is involved in that, Mrs. Littlejohn,' he said solemnly. 'While you and I are sitting here, those boilers are being fed by the real heroes aboard this ship. Out of sight.'

'Now we're getting somewhere. How much are they paid?'

'Who?'

'The men who sweat away in the boiler room.'

'The different grades have different wages. The chief engineer and his officers will obviously be at the top of the tree.'

'I'm talking about the men who do the hard work. How many of them are there?'

'Oh,' he said, scratching his head, 'I couldn't give you an exact figure. My guess is that we have around two hundred firemen and over half that number of trimmers. Those are the men who bring the coal from the bunkers to the boilers. Then there are around thirty greasers, I'd say. All told, I reckon there won't be far short of four hundred men in the engineering department.'

'Yet I haven't seen a single one of them.'

'Do you ever see motormen when you ride the train, Mrs. Littlejohn?'

'No, that's true.'

'It's a world apart down there in the boiler room. Stokers earn their wages.'

'But do they get their just deserts?' she pressed. 'Or are

they cruelly exploited by the Cunard Line?' She saw his look of surprise. 'I think you have the wrong idea about the *Ladies' Weekly Journal*, Mr. Dillman. We don't only give our readers nice recipes and offer them guidance with regard to fashion and etiquette. The magazine does have a conscience as well. Are you familiar with the name of Ida Tarbell?'

'Of course,' he replied. 'She published a series of articles in *McClure's*, exposing the coercion and double-dealing in the oil business. Mr. Rockefeller was hopping mad with the woman they called Miss Tarbarrel. I happen to think she performed a great public service. Standard Oil had a monopoly, and that can so easily lead to corruption.'

'I knew we'd talk the same language!' she said, patting his knee. 'My magazine can't match *McClure's* or *Munsey's*, or even the *Ladies' Home Journal*, but my editor does like to court controversy from time to time. That's why I've been sniffing around, you see. I've talked to stewards, cooks, bakers, mail sorters, barbers, even the two typists aboard. Most are too loyal to Cunard, but one of the stewardesses told me what she was paid. It's pitiful. Without tips, her income would be derisory.'

'Cunard pays as well as anyone else afloat.'

'That's no excuse, Mr. Dillman. They should give their lowliest employees a decent wage. That's why I want to find out about the stokers and those other men. What did you say they're called?'

'Trimmers. Though I'd warn you against a direct approach.'

'Why?'

'The language is a little raw down there, Mrs. Littlejohn. I'm afraid you'd get rather more than a flea in your ear. Stick to the stewardesses,' advised Dillman. 'That's more of a human-interest story for your readers. There are only ten stewardesses aboard the ship and two matrons, a tiny percentage of the entire crew. Why not examine the women's role in a male environment? I'd have thought that was worth investigation.'

'I'm ahead of you there,' she said, flipping back through

the pages of her notebook. 'I've got lots of material along those lines. But I'd like something more sensational as well. You know,' she said, grinning happily. 'A strike by underpaid laundry stewards. A mutiny among the stokers. Or even,' she added, patting his knee again, 'a daring gold-bullion robbery. That would give me the hottest story of all!'

A man's shadow fell across the door of the security room. A hand reached out to touch the locks in sequence, caressing the last one with affectionate fingers. Every detail of the door was noted with care. It was tested by a shoulder that applied slow but firm pressure. The visitor was content with his findings, and the shadow swiftly flitted away.

EIGHT

Dinner that evening was a much more formal affair in the first-class dining saloon. On the day of departure, there had been no dress code and diners had worn a variety of apparel, from the ostentatious to the dowdy, from the elegant to the downright casual.

Sunday brought an entirely different mood. Evening dress was the norm, and passengers seized the opportunity to put on their finery. While the gentlemen paraded in white ties and tails, the ladies took their most striking gowns from their wardrobes and added a stunning array of diamond brooches, pearl necklaces, ruby rings, gold bracelets, and glittering tiaras with which to set them off. Silk and satin swished the floor as people glided into the room to the strains of the orchestra. Seated at the helm of his own table, the captain was in his best uniform, radiating goodwill. Waiters, too, were at their smartest, taking up their posts with starched and gleaming readiness. The first night on the Atlantic Ocean promised to be a festive occasion in every sense.

Because they were dining in the saloon that evening, Genevieve Masefield agreed to join the five friends she had made on the boat train. Had the invitation been to the regal suite occupied by Donald and Theodora Belfrage, she would have been less willing to accept, and she was not quite sure of how she would react when the couple did decide to host a dinner party in their cabin.

Genevieve had looked forward to Sunday evening. Apart from the fact that she could keep the saloon under surveillance while appearing to be only one more guest at a table, she had the opportunity to raid her own wardrobe, choosing, after some deliberation, her black-velvet evening gown trimmed with pink and red rosettes. Her hair was swept up at the back and held in position by a comb of black jet edged with silver. Around her neck she wore a silver pendant that gleamed against the soft whiteness of her half exposed shoulders. Admiring herself in the mirror, Genevieve felt for a moment that she was a genuine first-class passenger, but the illusion soon faded when a sharp tap on the door brought her back to reality.

Harvey Denning had come to call for her. She opened the door to be greeted by his smiling face. He gave a courteous bow. There was no sign of Susan Faulconbridge.

'Ah!' he said with an expression of dismay. 'I've come too late.'

'For what?' she asked.

'To lend assistance to a lady, of course. I rather hoped that there'd be a necklace to fasten or a dress to be hooked at the back. Is there nothing left for me to do?'

'I'm afraid not, Harvey.'

'That's not what a gentleman likes to hear.'

'It's what this one has to be told,' she said, running an approving eye over him. 'You look as if you were born to wear tails, by the way. A study in elegance.'

'Then I'm a fitting escort for a beautiful lady in a dress that borders on the ethereal,' he complimented, 'even if it induces thoughts that are a little more terrestrial. Are you sure there are no final touches I can help you with?' he asked, lowering his voice to a confidential whisper. 'I'm known for my deft fingers.'

'It must be all that practice you get at dealing cards.'

'There's more to life than a game of bridge, Genevieve.'

'I had the impression that life *is* a game of bridge to you,' she said pleasantly. 'You seem so attuned to winning each round. Well, I am ready, as it happens. If you wait a second, I'll be right with you.'

'Aren't you going to invite me in?'

'We don't want to keep the others waiting, do we?'

'Oh, dear!' he said with mock horror. 'We mustn't do that.'

While not blind to his defects, Genevieve liked Harvey

Denning. He took no offence when she kept him at arm's length or prodded him with an occasional quip. Even the more caustic assaults by Ruth Constantine only bounced off him harmlessly. Denning was a model of imperturbability, sailing across high society with the same relentless smoothness as the *Mauretania* was cleaving her way across the ocean. After taking a last look at herself in the mirror, Genevieve collected her purse, then let herself out of the cabin. When her escort offered his arm, she took it and they headed for the saloon.

'Incidentally,' he confided, 'we've all signed a pact.'

'A pact?'

'Not to bait Donald quite so much. Underneath all that pomposity and patriotism, he's a decent fellow and generous to a fault. Susan, Ruth, and I decided to give him an evening off. I hope you'll support us.'

'Of course,' she said. 'I feel sorry for him. Donald is such a sitting target.'

'There's so much of him to aim at. I mean, if I were part of the Oxford eight in the Boat Race, there's nobody whose broad back and strong arms I'd rather have in front of me. Donald Belfrage is a wizard of an oarsman. When it comes to witty conversation, however, his shortcomings are all too visible.'

'Does he really mean to enter politics?'

'There are lesser men warming the benches at Westminster, I assure you.'

'But Donald would be exposing himself to certain ridicule.'

'That's in the nature of politics, Genevieve,' he said. 'Even someone as worthy and dignified as Gladstone was ridiculed – by Queen Victoria on occasion. Not that Donald is exactly out of the Gladstonian mould. Different party, for a start.'

'I'm glad that you're sparing him tonight,' said Genevieve. 'It upsets Theodora very much when you and Ruth snipe at him. It's so unfair to her.'

'She knows how to get her own back,' he said with feeling.

Before she could ask him what he meant, they found themselves joining the queue that was descending the staircase to the dining saloon. Bright lights illumined a scene of shimmering privilege and the air was charged with the accumulated scents of delicate perfumes. Evening gowns of every cut and colour moved ahead of them in a graceful line. Genevieve noticed the exquisite hairstyles, the sequinned purses, the costly jewellery, the random fans, and all the other feminine accessories that had been carefully packed for the voyage. Even the most shapeless bodies and the plainest faces were given a decided lustre by a well-chosen evening dress and a diamond necklace, especially when thrown into prominence by the black-and-white standardized attire of the gentlemen. It was the sort of occasion for which the dining saloon had been expressly designed.

When they entered the room itself, Harvey Denning gave her a gentle nudge. 'Don't look now, Genevieve,' he warned, 'but there's your lumberjack.'

'Where?'

'Swinging his axe at that side of beef.'

'Don't be so unkind. Mr. Delaney is a cultured man.'

When she caught sight of him, Genevieve saw that Orvill Delaney was talking to a short, compact young man with thinning hair that was slicked straight back over his skull. Delaney looked sleek and prosperous. Sensing that he was being watched, he glanced up to give Genevieve a welcoming smile. Someone else at the same table then commanded her attention. Denning supplied another nudge.

'That's Katherine Wymark,' he said.

'You *know* her?'

'I know of her, Genevieve. But then, I make it my business to find out about any woman as gorgeous as that. One never knows when one might need a new bridge partner. I've had to rule the divine Mrs. Wymark out, alas, because there is a Mr. Wymark to be taken into account.' He breathed in heavily through his nose. 'At a guess, I'd say that the fellow was a rather possessive type.'

Genevieve made a swift assessment of the husband. He was not at all what she had expected. Twenty years older than his wife, Wymark was a rather ugly man with a short body whose shoulders seemed too wide for his coat. Silver hair lent him an air of distinction that was vitiated by the grim set of his jaw and the piggy eyes. Katherine Wymark was the unrivalled cynosure in a magnificent turquoise-silk evening gown perfectly tailored to display her shapely body. A diamond necklace glinted in the light from the chandeliers. She was in her element, even outshining the Princess de Poix, who sat beside the captain in regal splendour. Katherine smiled serenely at all around her, but her left arm was securely anchored by her husband's strong hand.

'He must have money,' decided Denning cynically.

'Do you know his name?' asked Genevieve.

'Walter. Walter Wymark.'

'His wife seems very attached to him.'

'By invisible chains.'

They were sharing a table for six in the lower half of the saloon. The last to arrive, they settled down with the others and joined in the general exchange of compliments about appearance and dress. Susan Faulconbridge had chosen a rather daring evening gown of white satin, revealing chubby arms and sufficient of her full breasts to collect curious glances from passing diners. Ruth Constantine, by contrast, had made little concession to fashion or allure. Her plain black dress, with its high neck and puffed sleeves, was serviceable rather than attractive. Whereas Susan wore a string of pearls, Ruth spurned jewellery of any kind, yet the very severity of her appearance gave her an almost dramatic quality.

It was Theodora Belfrage who had taken the greatest pains. Her hair was neatly braided, curled up atop her head and held in place by a series of pins concealed beneath a diamond tiara. The silk evening gown, of a blushing-pink hue that suited her perfectly, had a tight waist to emphasize her slim frame, and a full skirt. Theodora seemed to have put on the entire contents of her jewellery box for the evening. Admiring her porcelain beauty, Genevieve could see what had drawn Donald Belfrage to her. By the same token, she could understand his appeal for her more easily. White tie and tails flattered his muscularity and gave him an almost stately air. This was his world.

Champagne was ordered and a general survey of the menu took place, all six of them making, then revoking, decisions as alternative dishes tempted their palates. Though contributing to the genial badinage, Genevieve kept glancing around the saloon to watch developments at other tables. Orvill Delaney was still chatting to the young man beside him, and Katherine Wymark was exchanging pleasantries with a tall figure who had paused on his way to the other side of the saloon. Genevieve recognized him as the bearded man who had been in the lounge earlier with the American woman. Walter Wymark was no possessive husband now. Grinning up at the newcomer, he treated the man with a mixture of respect and affection, cheerfully waving him off when the latter withdrew to his own place, then leaning over to place a fond kiss on his wife's cheek.

As interesting as she found this marital exchange, Genevieve dismissed it from her mind when her gaze drifted across to the captain's table. As well as the Princess de Poix, Sir Clifton and Lady Robinson, and Prince Andre Poniazowski, the guests included an Oxford professor and his wife, a wealthy American industrialist, and a French diplomat, but it was none of these who startled Genevieve. It was the presence of Mrs. Dalkeith in the party, holding her own with assurance and wearing a gown of black taffeta that matched the black ribbon in her hair. What made Genevieve sit up was the sight of something on the old lady's left wrist. As Mrs. Dalkeith extended an arm to reach for the menu, the object was unmistakable. It was a gold watch.

Dressed for dinner, George Porter Dillman sat at the small table in his cabin and poured over a list of second-class passengers. Four of them had been the victims of a robbery since they had been aboard. Apart from the money taken from two cabins, everything else that was stolen was made of silver. Even the purse that went missing had silver sequins on it, and according to its owner, Mrs. Dobrowski, it contained a small, silver-backed mirror.

The name of Max Hirsch automatically suggested itself, but there were mitigating factors. When the detective had glimpsed the man on the previous night, Hirsch had been ascending a companionway to the deck above, yet none of the four victims had cabins on that level. Had the thefts already taken place when the putative thief was sighted, or did they occur later, in the dead of night? Everything turned on the assumption that Hirsch was responsible for the crimes. Dillman decided that he should keep a more open mind. The two Welshmen who had strayed out of steerage still had to be interviewed, though he was fairly certain that they could be discounted. A passion for collecting silver seemed improbable in two former coal miners.

Dillman was about to put the list away when another name slipped into the equation. Hirsch claimed that he had merely been going up on deck to take a stroll in the night air, but why had he used a narrow companionway when he could have climbed the grand staircase? Why, in fact, had he gone to the upper deck at all when he could more easily have stepped out onto the main deck, the same level on which his cabin was located? The answer sent Dillman's index finger tracing its way down the alphabetical list until it reached the name of Agnes Cameron. Not only was her cabin on the upper deck, it was, he now learned, situated conveniently near the top of the companionway that Hirsch had tripped up with such alacrity. Again, the man had been wearing a thick overcoat at the time, hardly the preferred costume of a thief who was scouring the interior of the vessel. Could it be that Max Hirsch was simply on his way to an hour under the stars with the impressionable Mrs. Cameron? Dillman was confused.

After popping the list into a drawer, he left the cabin and went along to the second-class dining saloon. Dress was less formal there than in first class, but that had not prevented the ladies from looking their very best or stopped some of the men from reaching for their white ties and tails. As he stepped into the room, Dillman was aware of a distinct sense of occasion. The room was filled with contented passengers, determined to savour every moment of their first evening on the waters of the Atlantic. Menus were being consulted, dishes ordered, toasts given, glasses clinked, anecdotes circulated, and new friendships formed.

A place had been kept for Dillman at a long table that the Jarvis family was sharing with six other people. Making apologies for his delay, the detective took a seat between Alexandra and her grandmother. The girl was wearing a floral dress that had been ironed for the occasion; her brother, Noel, was in a grey-flannel suit, and her parents had settled for a nondescript smartness. Lily Pomeroy provided the colour and vivacity. Wearing a voluminous purple skirt of dotted muslin net, she also had on a white-silk blouse with a profusion of buttons down the front of it, peeping out from beneath a jacket of mustard-hued brightness. The string of false pearls around her neck was so tight that it was partially obscured by her double chin and fleshy jowls. Whenever she moved, her jacket gave off a pungent whiff of mothballs.

'We're in for a real treat tonight, Mr. Dillman,' she said.

'Are we, Mrs. Pomeroy?' he replied.

'Wait until you see the menu. It's mouth-watering.'

'Granny loves her food,' explained Alexandra.

'One of the few pleasures left to me at my age,' she said with a cackle, pinching the girl's cheek affectionately. 'That and being with my grandchildren. Aren't they lovely creatures, Mr. Dillman?'

'Yes, Mrs. Pomeroy,' he agreed.

'I'm blessed with my family.'

She let out another throaty laugh. Vanessa Jarvis gave a warm smile, Noel contrived a nod of gratitude and Alexandra giggled, but Oliver Jarvis could manage nothing more than a look of suppressed exasperation as he took a sidelong glance at his mother-in-law's extraordinary outfit.

Accepting that he had a cross to bear in life, the bank manager would have preferred it to be wearing more muted colours.

'I saw Bobo again today,' said Alexandra.

'Bobo?' echoed Dillman.

'The black cat. I told you about him over lunch.'

'Yes, you did.'

'Mr. Reynolds – he's the officer who looks after Bobo – said that I could watch him being fed. Bobo, that is,' she added with a laugh. 'Not Mr. Reynolds.'

'You obviously like cats, Ally.'

'I've always wanted one myself, but Daddy won't hear of it. He says they do too much damage to the furniture with their claws. Anyway, I went to Mr. Reynolds' cabin to watch Bobo finishing his meal and do you know what he said to me?'

'Who?' he teased. 'Bobo or Mr. Reynolds?'

'Mr. Reynolds, silly!' she replied with another laugh. 'He told me that I had an affinity with cats. Yes, that's the right word. Affinity. Do you know why?'

'Tell me, Ally.'

'Bobo let me pick him up. He's never let anyone do that before. Mr. Reynolds told me something else as well,' she continued. 'Do you remember saying that a black cat was a symbol of good luck when we stepped aboard and saw Bobo?'

'Yes.'

'According to Mr. Reynolds, sailors have a lot of...oh!' She sighed, bringing her hands up to her cheeks. 'I've forgotten the word.'

'Superstitions?' he prompted.

'Yes, that was it, Mr. Dillman. Superstitions. Mr. Reynolds told me that there were some sailors' wives who kept a black cat when their husbands went off on a long voyage. In a sailing ship, that is.'

'There are still plenty of those putting to sea, Ally,' he remarked. 'Not everyone can afford to travel on an ocean liner by means of steam turbines. Though even here, as we've found out, a black cat stills comes in useful.'

'Bobo is a lot more than useful.'

'I'm sure.'

'He's my friend. I'm going to feed him myself tomorrow.'

'Think about feeding yourself now, Alexandra,' said her mother kindly. 'And give Mr. Dillman a chance to read the menu.'

'I'm having the soup,' announced Lily Pomeroy. 'Then the duck. Vanessa?'

'I may as well have the same,' said the other.

'What about you, Oliver?' pressed the old woman.

'I still haven't decided,' he answered, burying his head in the menu.

'You can tell that my son-in-law is a banker, can't you?' she said, leaning across to Dillman and giving off a further whiff of mothballs. 'Oliver is so cautious. He has to study everything carefully before he reaches a decision. With me, it's quite different. I know at once what I want to eat.'

'As much as possible!' said Alexandra.

Noel sniggered, Oliver Jarvis frowned, and his wife administered a swift rebuke, but Lily Pomeroy was neither hurt nor offended. Throwing her head back, she let out a merry laugh, then turned to pinch both her granddaughter's cheeks simultaneously. Dillman chose that moment to examine the menu, marvelling at its richness and variety. Second-class passengers were being offered fare of the highest quality. A waiter came up to the table. While the members of the Jarvis family took turns placing their orders, the detective sneaked a look around the saloon. Familiar faces were seen on all sides. Stanley and Miriam Rosenwald were at a nearby table, and Mrs. Dobrowski, another victim of robbery, was seated in a corner. Dillman also noticed the other two people whose property had been stolen and whom he had earlier interviewed. Both appeared to be enjoying themselves at their respective tables, putting their losses out of mind to share in the communal pleasure.

It took Dillman a little time to pick out Agnes Cameron. Attired in a black-velvet gown trimmed with black lace, she had clearly made a supreme effort to look her best, wearing a diamond necklace and matching earrings in a slightly tentative way, as if the jewellery was very rarely put on view. Mrs. Cameron was sharing a table with the most animated group of people in the room. While her companions were bubbling with excitement, however, she was completely subdued. Detached from the proceedings and feeling increasingly self-conscious, Agnes Cameron kept looking at the empty chair beside her with a wistfulness that soon shaded into pain.

Someone had let her down. Dillman could guess who the man was.

The atmosphere, facilities, and food in the third-class dining saloon were of a very different order from those in the saloons above. The area was more akin to a factory canteen than to a restaurant. Seated in serried ranks at the refectory tables, passengers had a much more restricted menu and far less attentive service. The level of noise was much higher, and it contained a far greater proportion of childlike pandemonium than elsewhere. While those in other sections of the vessel were dining in style, these passengers merely ate. That did not necessarily diminish their pleasure. Some people were wolfing their food with an enthusiasm that showed it was the best meal they had consumed in ages. Others were behaving as if they were at a party. In spite of the large number crammed into the saloon, there was a prevailing spirit of camaraderie. The immigrants, in particular, were bonding together as they broke bread.

Glyn Bowen struck up a conversation with a couple of redundant steelworkers from Yorkshire, enduring the discomforts of steerage in the hope of finding employment on the other side of the Atlantic. While the three men compared their individual tales of hardship, Mansell Price stayed on the fringe of the conversation. The meal was almost over when a hitherto suppressed fact tumbled out.

'Why did you leave the pit?' one of the steelworkers asked Price.

'He had to,' said Bowen. 'Mansell punched the foreman.'

'I'll punch *you* in a minute!' warned Price. 'It's none of their business.'

'Sorry, Mansell.'

'What did you say that for, Glyn?'

'It just slipped out.'

'You need a padlock on that bloody gob,' said Price, getting up. 'Come on. Let's get out of here. This noise is driving me mad.'

It was left to Bowen to bid farewell to the two Yorkshiremen. He followed his friend out of the saloon and as soon as they were alone, was given a severe shaking by Price. The bigger man did not mince his words.

'You do that again, Glyn, and I'll kick seven barrels of shit out of you.'

'I didn't mean to say it.'

'You never do.'

'Well, it's the truth, Mansell. You knocked Dai Watkins out stone-cold. That's why you got the sack and I decided to quit with you.'

'I didn't *get* the sack,' corrected the other sharply. 'I went in search of it. Nobody was keeping me down that pit after what happened to Dad. So when Dai Watkins tried to push me around, I let him have it between the eyes. It was my way of resigning. Got it?'

'Yes, yes,' agreed the other. 'Anything you say.'

'Use your head for once, will you? If we get an interview for a job, one of the first things they'll ask is why we left the pit. How much chance have *I* got if you blurt out that I slugged the foreman? They wouldn't touch me.'

'Never thought of it that way.'

'Try, Glyn. Bloody well try!' He took his friend by the arm and led him off down a passageway.

'Where are we going, Mansell?' Bowen asked.

'You'll see.'

They followed a tortuous route through the bowels of the ship, pausing at corners to make sure they were not seen, then descending a companionway with lumbering stealth. Eventually they reached a large metal door that was heavily reinforced.

'There it is,' said Price expansively. 'The security room.'

'How did you find it?'

'By following the directions that Irish steward gave us.'

Bowen stared at the door. 'Is that where the gold bullion is kept?'

'Only yards from where we're standing. Exciting, isn't it?'

'Yes, Mansell.'

'It'll be even more exciting when we actually see it.'

'But that's impossible!'

'Is it?' said the other. 'Look at the door, mun.'

'It's far too solid, and it's got all those locks.'

'Locks can be broken, Glyn. Only a question of applying pressure at the right points. Call yourself a miner?' he sneered contemptuously. 'We've dug our way through seams of coal a hundred times thicker than that door.'

'Only because we had a pick and shovel.'

'Exactly. Get the right tools and we can do anything.'

'We can't dig our way in there,' said Bowen fearfully. 'Think of the noise it would make. They'd be down on us like a ton of bricks.'

'Then we make sure we do it quietly,' resolved Price, running a meditative hand over his chin as he studied the door. 'A ship of this size is bound to have what we need. Hammers and chisels and so on. What about those boxes of food we saw being loaded? They must have crowbars to open them. All we have to do is to borrow the tools, muffle them with rags, and get to work.'

Bowen was alarmed. 'You're serious about this, aren't you?'

'Dead serious.'

'Even though we're bound to be caught?'

'There you go again. Always fearing the worst.'

'It's lunacy!' wailed Bowen. 'It's not the same as taking a swing at Dai Watkins. All you got for that was the sack. This is a serious crime, Mansell. We could go to jail.

Besides,' he said, indicating the door, 'there's no way you could get through there.'

'Let me be the judge of that.'

'And even if you did, what would happen then?'

'We'd make off with a couple of bars of gold bullion, Glyn.'

'Until the ship was searched and we were caught red-handed.' Bowen waved dismissively. 'I want no part of this, Mansell. What's the point of going to all that trouble when we'd never get off the boat with one ounce of gold?'

'We won't even try,' explained Price slyly. 'Why not hear me out before you decide? I got it all planned, see? With the right tools and a torch to help us, I reckon I can get through that door in an hour or so. You act as lookout. Even you can manage that, Glyn. Now,' he continued, licking his lips, 'once we get inside, we open the first box and steal as many of the bars as we can carry.'

'And where do we take them?' asked Bowen in disbelief. 'Back to our cabin?'

'No, you fool. Straight to the purser.'

'The purser!' exclaimed the other.

'Of course.'

'But that's stupid.'

'Is it?'

'Yes, Mansell.'

'Listen, boyo. I thought this right through. We just have to put on an act.'

'What do you mean?'

'We tell the purser that we caught these two blokes making off with the gold, so we tackled them. They got away, but we managed to stop them from taking any of the loot. We won't be criminals, Glyn,' he stressed, 'we'll be heroes. They're bound to give us a big reward. Might even move us up to first class for the rest of the voyage. Whatever happens, we're far better off than we are now. And all for an hour with a jimmy or a crowbar. Well?' he said with a wild grin. 'Interested?'

'It could just work,' agreed the other uncertainly.

'Only if you let me do the talking.'

'Why?'

'I don't want you telling the purser that I knocked out Dai Watkins, do I?'

Dillman's meal was interrupted for the second time by a note from Maurice Buxton, but at least he had eaten the main course on this occasion. Excusing himself from the table, he strolled toward the door, gathering a smirk from Max Hirsch as he did so. He also got a nod of recognition from Agnes Cameron, mollified now that her beau was at her side and displaying her jewellery with a new confidence. Dillman had no time to speculate on why Hirsch had arrived so late for dinner. The purser had summoned him, and it would not be to pass on any good news.

Maurice Buxton was smoking his pipe again when the detective was admitted to his cabin. Scratching at his beard, the purser indicated the ledger on his desk.

'The phantom strikes again!' he moaned.

'How many times?'

'Twice. He got away with a fair amount of cash, a silver jewellery box, and two silver bracelets. Why people don't let me lock away their valuables in our safe, I don't know!' he sighed. 'They will leave things lying around in their cabins.'

'That's asking for trouble.'

'I know, Mr. Dillman. Yet strangely enough, most passengers get away with it. I've been on voyages when the only thing that got lost was someone's virginity. Then you have something like this to deal with. There's no rhyme or reason to it, is there?'

'Give me the details,' said Dillman, taking out pencil and pad.

The purser was succinct. Both thefts had occurred during the day from unoccupied second-class cabins. No sign of forced entry was found. The thief appeared to have come and gone at will, without leaving any clue behind as to his identity. Looking through his notes, Dillman was almost certain that the same man was responsible for all the crimes in second class, but he had to admit that his inquiries had so far failed to lead to an arrest. He made no mention of his confrontation with Max Hirsch.

'He must be halted in his tracks, Mr. Dillman!' declared Buxton.

'I know.'

'We don't want him running amok.'

'I'll interview these latest victims immediately.'

'Let them finish their dinner first. It might help to calm them down.' He pulled on his pipe and relaxed slightly. 'Anything else to report?'

'Only that you've got a rabble-rouser aboard, Mr. Buxton.'

'Who is he?'

'It's a woman called Hester Littlejohn,' said Dillman with a smile. 'A lively lady, I must say. She's a journalist with an American magazine, but she's not content with trumpeting the virtues of the *Mauretania*. She wants to uncover the ship's vices as well.'

'I didn't know we had any.'

'Mrs. Littlejohn thinks that Cunard may be underpaying its employees.'

'Oh, well, I'd go along with that. We could all do with more cash,' he said with a chuckle. 'But seriously, is this lady anything more than a nuisance?'

'She might be if she gets wind of this outbreak of theft,' admitted Dillman. 'That's one more reason to clear everything up. We don't want to read an article by Hester Littlejohn about the Cunard Crime Wave. I suggested that she concentrate on the women employed on the ship and take up their cause.'

'That'll keep her out of mischief.'

'I'm not so sure. Mrs. Littlejohn is very tenacious.'

'A troublemaker?'

'A well-intentioned woman in search of a scoop.'

'Saints preserve us!'

They chatted amiably for a few more minutes, then Dillman turned to leave.

'Hold on,' said Buxton. 'I've saved the one bright spot until the end.'

'Bright spot?'

'Yes, you'd better pass this on to Miss Masefield because I haven't had the opportunity to tell her. Cross one name off the list. The most important one in some ways. Mrs. Dalkeith has got her watch back. I daresay she's wearing it in the first-class dining saloon right now.'

'That's a relief. Where did she find it?'

'She didn't, Mr. Dillman. It was pushed under my door in a brown envelope.'

'When?'

'Sometime this afternoon.'

'Was there no note of explanation with the watch?'

'Not a syllable,' said Buxton, picking up a brown envelope from the table. 'As you can see, there's nothing on this either. Our benefactor wishes to remain anonymous.'

'If he really is a benefactor.'

'Who else would return an expensive gold watch?'

'Someone who prefers silver.'

NINE

What are we going to do when we get to New York, darling?' asked Theodora Belfrage.

'What we always do,' said her husband smugly. 'Be ourselves.'

'Do you think America is ready for Donald Belfrage?' teased Harvey Denning.

'Now, now,' warned Ruth Constantine. 'Remember what we agreed to, Harvey.'

'I sit corrected,' he said, putting both hands over his mouth.

'What's going on?' asked Theodora.

'Nothing,' said Susan Faulconbridge.

'Are you making fun of Donald again?'

'On the contrary, Theodora.'

'Because I won't have it, do you hear? My husband is a wonderful man.'

'And so say all of us!' agreed Denning, lifting his glass. 'To Donald!'

Genevieve Masefield, Ruth, and Susan joined him in the toast. Donald basked in their admiration, but his wife suspected a plot. She fixed her eyes on Genevieve.

'That wasn't a joke, was it?' she asked.

'Of course not, Theodora,' replied Genevieve softly. 'Donald is a very special person. Particularly when he's dressed like that. Haven't you noticed how much attention he's been getting from the other ladies in here? You're not only married to one of the most handsome men on board, he's also among the most desirable.'

'Listen to that, everybody!' said a delighted Belfrage.

'It's true, darling,' purred Theodora. 'You are desirable.'

'And handsome. Genevieve said so.'

'If compliments are flying around freely,' said Denning, 'are there any for me?'

'Yes,' replied Ruth. 'You're to be congratulated on getting through an entire meal without a sneer, a snipe, or a cruel innuendo. We may house-train you yet, Harvey.'

'Oh, I hope not. It would ruin my reputation.'

'You don't have one,' said Susan with a grin.

He shot her a look of mock reproach, then the two of them shared a laugh.

The meal was drawing to a close, and Genevieve was wondering how she could escape the little group before she was lulled into a sense of belonging and surrendered to the pleasure of their company. Repartee had flown with its usual speed, but the verbal persecution of Donald Belfrage had been notably absent. It had given him an opportunity to reveal sides of his character that had hitherto been obscured from her. Belfrage not only turned out to have a gift for political anecdote, he also showed that he was capable of self-mockery. Another aspect of him was more unexpected. Although his wife was at his side throughout, he kept staring at Genevieve as if seeing her properly for the first time, and at one point, she felt a foot touch her own quite deliberately under the table. Suspecting at first that it belonged to Harvey Denning, she began to wonder if the man's shoe that stroked her own was, in fact, worn by Donald Belfrage.

In any event, Genevieve did not have to manufacture any excuses. When they finished their coffee, the group broke up of its own accord. Theodora pleaded tiredness and took her reluctant husband off to their suite, while Denning and Susan went off to partner each other in a game of bridge against some acquaintances they had made. Genevieve was quietly delighted. Left alone with Ruth Constantine, she felt that she had the best of both worlds: an interesting companion with whom to talk, and greater freedom to keep up her reconnaissance of the other passengers. They adjourned to the first-class lounge and found a corner where they could settle into polished-

beech chairs in the shade of a potted palm. Ruth was char-
acteristically direct.

'Well,' she said. 'What do you make of us?'

'Do I have to deliver a report?' asked Genevieve with a
smile.

'Early impressions.'

'I think you're all very nice people.'

'Honest impressions,' stipulated Ruth. 'Don't pull any
punches. The men first.'

'Isn't that ungallant?'

'Stop sounding like Donald.'

'As you wish,' said Genevieve. 'Let's start with him. I
have to confess that when I met you all on the boat train, I
thought that Donald was something of an oaf. A very
friendly oaf, mark you, but one of those people who blun-
ders well-meaningly through a conversation without
noticing that he's bumping into people. Also, he can be a
prig. In fact, he's the only man I've met who can be both an
oaf and a prig at the same time.'

'Donald is both of those things, but he's a lot more
besides.'

'So I'm discovering. I'm told that he's very generous.'

'He's positively philanthropic, Genevieve. Did you
know that he booked the passages for all five of us? Yes,'
she said, seeing the other's astonishment. 'We each wanted
to pay our own way, but Donald wouldn't hear of it. He
likes to share his good fortune. In that way, he's very
unselfish.'

'Why do you all gang up on him?'

'Because he thrives on it.'

'Theodora doesn't seem to think so.'

'She has a lot to learn. Not least, how to make a husband
want to take *you* back to your cabin instead of having to
inveigle him there with that nonsense about a headache.
You must have seen how unwilling he was to go.'

'Yes,' said Genevieve, remembering the foot that
touched hers under the table. 'Do you think that he'll be
faithful to Theodora?'

'In the short term.'

'And then?'

'He's a man,' said Ruth bluntly. 'Part of the reason he wants to go into politics is so that he can buy a townhouse in London and spend nights away from his wife. I don't expect for a moment that he'll be entirely celibate during his time at Westminster.' She raised a cautionary eyebrow. 'Brace yourself for an invitation to visit a certain Tory member of Parliament.'

'I hardly know him, Ruth.'

'That makes no difference. Let's move on to Harvey.'

'He's already given me his speech about being a parasite.'

'Then he's being unfair to himself,' said Ruth. 'He has many good qualities, one of them being loyalty to his friends. But he also has his weaknesses, as you've probably discovered already. I heard my first tap on the door within hours of meeting him.'

'He does it with such charm.'

'Oh, yes. Lots of women fall for that charm. Susan, among them, I'm afraid. But he was wasting his time outside my bedroom. As appealing as he can be, I want more from a man than the feeling that I'm being fitted in between two games of bridge. That's his real passion. What of Susan?'

'She's in love with Harvey, isn't she?'

'Is she?'

'They seem to have this secret code between them.'

'That comes from sharing a bed with a man, but it doesn't mean you're madly in love with him. Susan's is a rather tragic case,' said Ruth. 'She got involved with Harvey in order to stay close to Donald. Ridiculous as it may seem to us, that amiable oaf with a degree from Oxford is the love of her life. Susan Faulconbridge would give anything to be where Theodora is, but she isn't beautiful enough or silly enough for Donald. So she just stays in his orbit. Like the rest of us.'

'What's your interest in him?'

'You tell me, Genevieve.'

'Let me have more time to work on it,' said the other

warily. 'You're more inscrutable than the rest. As for Susan and Theodora, however, you've summed them up perfectly. I can't add anything to your description of Theodora as beautiful but silly. And though I didn't know there was some history between Donald and Susan, it doesn't surprise me.'

'That brings us around to Genevieve Masefield.'

'Me?'

'Yes,' said Ruth, watching her carefully. 'Where do you fit in?'

'I'm just a willing travelling companion who's grateful for the way you've all taken me into your circle. It's been an absolute joy to me.'

'That answer might satisfy the others, but it doesn't persuade me. I've seen you looking around when you've been with us. It's almost as if we're a kind of stockade in which you can take refuge.' She leaned in closer. 'Who are you hiding from, Genevieve?'

'Nobody.'

'Then what's his name?'

'Whose name?'

'The man who's making you behave the way you do,' argued Ruth shrewdly. 'Any other single woman with your assets would make the most of them. Look at you, Genevieve. You could have almost any man aboard this ship eating out of your hand. In your position, I certainly would,' she said harshly. 'I'd make them *suffer*. Yet you don't seem to be interested in using any of the power you have. Why not?' she pressed. 'Why do you use our little party as a form of protection? It can only be because you're already committed to someone else. What's the fellow's name?'

'Orvill Delaney,' announced a voice.

They looked up to see him bearing down on them with another man. Genevieve recognized the person who had sat beside Delaney over dinner. The American beamed.

'Do forgive the interruption,' he said with an apologetic smile, 'but I couldn't resist a cue like that. I'm Orvill Delaney, by the way,' he said to Ruth. 'Miss Masefield and I are already acquainted.'

'Genevieve speaks very well of you, Mr. Delaney,' said Ruth, weighing him up. 'I'm Ruth Constantine and I'm pleased to meet you.'

'Likewise, Miss Constantine. Oh, and this is a colleague of mine,' he continued, easing the other man forward. 'Patrick Skelton. A fellow countryman of yours.'

'How do you do?' said Skelton with a polite bow. 'Are you enjoying the voyage?'

'Very much,' replied Genevieve.

'So are we. It's a unique experience.'

'Well,' said Delaney, adjusting his bow tie, 'we won't intrude any longer. I could see that you were deep in an important conversation.'

'Not at all, Mr. Delaney,' said Ruth, taking charge of the situation. 'You and Mr. Skelton are most welcome to join us, if you wish.'

'That sounds like an invitation too good to resist. What do you think, Patrick?'

'I agree,' said Skelton. 'Thank you, ladies. It's an honour.'

Ruth smiled. 'That remains to be seen, Mr. Skelton,' she said.

George Porter Dillman wasted no time in talking to the latest victims of the ubiquitous thief. They were still smarting at the outrage. The silver jewellery box had been taken from a cabin belonging to an American doctor and his wife, a robust couple who were threatening to sue the Cunard Line if their property was not recovered. The other victim was a nervous Englishwoman, a widow in her fifties, who was less upset by the theft of her jewellery than by the fact that someone had gained entry to her cabin so easily. Dillman managed to placate all three of them. One significant fact emerged. During luncheon that day, the doctor and his wife had been at the same table as Max Hirsch. It could just be another coincidence, but Dillman somehow doubted it.

He decided to speak to the two Welshmen. Dillman had caught them wandering about in a part of the vessel that was out-of-bounds to steerage passengers, but he did not believe that they would venture into second class during the day, when there were far more stewards cruising about to enforce the rules. Since both of the recent thefts had occurred during the afternoon, the two former miners could be absolved of any blame. Notwithstanding that, Dillman was anxious to interview the pair of them. The detective's immaculate appearance would make him an incongruous figure in steerage, but he did not worry about that. Solving crimes took precedence over sartorial considerations.

When he finally traced them, Mansell Price and Glyn Bowen were in the smoking room. They had each cadged a cigarette off a garrulous old man from Birkenhead, who was telling them his life story in a meandering voice. Surprised to see Dillman, the Welshmen warmed to him slightly when he bought each a drink and detached them from the maudlin reminiscences of the old man. Price sipped his beer and eyed the newcomer.

'Not exactly dressed for steerage, are you?' he observed.

'There's a more relaxed atmosphere down here,' said Dillman. 'I like it.'

'You wouldn't like it if you had to share a pokey cabin with a couple of strangers and listen to one of them playing the mouth organ.'

'Mouth organ?'

'He never stops.'

'It gets on Mansell's nerves,' explained Bowen. 'But what brought you here, Mr. Dillman? Nobody would be in steerage unless he had to.'

'I wanted to have a chat with you,' said Dillman. 'About last night.'

'Last night?' echoed Price, going on the defensive.

'We got lost, that's all,' said Bowen. 'It's the truth.'

'I'm sure it is,' said Dillman. 'It's very easy to lose your way in a ship as big as this. But you might just be able to help. It's a bit of a long shot, I know, but I wondered if you saw anybody behaving strangely when you were in second class.' They traded a glance with each other. 'Let me explain,' he went on. 'I have a friend who was playing cards in the smoking room until it was quite late. When he got back to his cabin, he found that someone had broken in and stolen something.'

'It wasn't us!' denied Price aggressively.

'I'm not saying it was.'

'We never went near any cabins. Did we, Glyn?'

'No, Mansell,' chimed the other.

'You'd better watch who you're accusing, mister.'

'It's not an accusation,' said Dillman calmly. 'I'm certain that neither of you is involved in any way. All I'm hoping is that you might be able to provide us with a clue.'

'What sort of clue?' asked Price.

'Any sort would be valuable. Now, did you see anyone last night?'

'Loads of people. We kept dodging them.'

'Were any of them behaving suspiciously?'

'We didn't hang around to find out.'

'How long had you been in second class before I bumped into you?'

'Not long,' lied Price, taking a swig of his beer. 'And we didn't see anyone suspicious. Did we, Glyn?'

'No, Mansell.' Bowen pondered. 'Except for that little bloke.'

'Who?'

'You remember. We met him two or three times.'

'When was this?' asked Dillman.

'Just before you turned up,' said Bowen. 'Well, no, a bit earlier, probably.'

'So you did spend some time roaming around?'

'No,' said Price, sticking to his story. 'Five minutes at most.'

'Tell me about this man,' coaxed Dillman. 'What was he like?'

'Short,' said Bowen, indicating the man's height with his hand. 'And stocky.'

'Ugly little chap,' added Price. 'Had a bald head.'

'So he wasn't wearing a hat?' asked Dillman.

'No.'

'What about an overcoat?'

'He just had this suit on.'

'Did you see him on the main deck?'

'Yes,' volunteered Bowen. 'And on the two decks above that.'

'The upper deck and the shelter deck?' He smiled. 'You obviously got around.'

'Only because we was trying to find our way back, Mr. Dillman.'

'Of course. So you saw this man – what? Three times?'

'Yes.'

'Close enough to get a good look at him?'

'He passed within a couple of feet of us,' said Price. 'We ducked into an alcove and he walked by with this little case in his hand.'

'A briefcase?' The other nodded. 'What was suspicious about him?'

'It was the way he kept pausing at different cabins, tapping their doors.'

'He had this list in his hand,' recalled Bowen. 'Kept checking it.'

'This is all extremely helpful,' said Dillman. 'I had a feeling that you might just have seen something. Do you think you'd recognize this man again?'

'Yes,' said Bowen.

'No!' boomed Price, countermanding him at once. 'We wouldn't, Mr. Dillman. Glyn and me don't want to get involved, see? We told you all we know.'

'Is there anything else you can remember about him?'

'We only got these glimpses of the man.'

'Short, stocky, bald-headed. Wearing a suit.'

'An expensive suit,' said Bowen. 'You could see that. And there was one other thing.'

'Go on,' said Dillman.

'Well, we never heard him speak, mind, but I got the feeling that he wasn't British. It was the way he looked and strutted along. Like he owned the ship. No offence, Mr. Dillman,' he said cautiously, 'but I think he was an American.'

*

'Have you had time to read that story I gave you, Miss Masefield?' asked Orvill Delaney.

'Yes,' said Genevieve. 'It was very clever and wonderfully amusing.'

'O. Henry is more entertaining than *Moby Dick*. Besides, you don't look like a Melville devotee. I'd say that you were more attuned to British authors. When I first saw you,' he admitted, 'I put you down as a Jane Austen reader.'

'Is that good or bad?'

'I leave you to judge that.'

'What about me, Mr. Delaney?' asked Ruth Constantine. 'Since you can classify us so readily at a glance, who's my favourite author?'

'I don't think you have one.'

'Why not?'

'You don't read books, Miss Constantine. You read people instead.'

'That's very perceptive of you.' She gave him a smile of approval, then switched her gaze to the other man. 'What about you, Mr. Skelton? Are you a literary man?'

'I'm afraid not,' he said diffidently.

'Patrick is an accountant,' explained Delaney. 'All that he reads are balance sheets. Though some of those can have a swirling drama to them, can't they?'

'Yes, Mr. Delaney.'

'Figures can be just as expressive as words.'

Genevieve was pleased to be able to talk to Orvill Delaney and she could see that he was making a good impression on Ruth, but she was finding his colleague far too stiff and reticent. A personable young man with a deep voice, Skelton never actually initiated conversation. He confined himself to polite nods of agreement and the briefest of neutral comments. Genevieve could not decide whether he was shy or merely uninterested in their chatter. Ruth tried to draw him out with a few acid comments about the British male, but Skelton did not respond. He left most of the talking to Orvill Delaney.

'I once met O. Henry,' said the latter airily. 'At least, I met the man who used that name as his pseudonym. It wasn't what you might call a marriage of true minds. We were in a bar in Manhattan at the time and he was rather more enthusiastic about drinking his whisky than in listening to my fulsome praise. But,' he continued, 'I still think he writes like an angel, albeit a tarnished one.'

'The best kind,' remarked Ruth.

'Do you have a liking for tarnished angels, Miss Constantine?'

'That depends on how far they've fallen from grace, Mr. Delaney.'

'What about you, Patrick?' he asked. 'Where do you stand on angels?'

'I'm not sure that I believe in them,' replied the other quietly.

'When you have two of them sitting right in front of you?' scolded Delaney.

'Present company excepted, of course,' added Skelton, dividing an awkward smile between the two ladies. 'Well, it's been a pleasure to meet you both,' he said, rising to his feet, 'but you must excuse me. I have some work to do before I retire.'

'Work?' said Ruth. 'At a time like this?'

'I'm afraid so. I'll see you tomorrow, Mr. Delaney.'

After an exchange of farewells, Skelton marched swiftly out of the room.

'You'll have to excuse Patrick,' said Delaney, looking after him. 'Accountants are not the most sociable people at the best of times. Also, it's his first voyage and he's heard too many horror stories about Atlantic crossings at this time of year. Patrick still has a sneaking fear that we're all going to finish up at the bottom of the sea.' He looked at Genevieve. 'He has none of that indomitable Captain Ahab spirit.'

'You're obviously a veteran sailor,' she said.

'Well, I have been lucky enough to visit your country a number of times.'

'Have you never encountered bad weather while en route?'

'Of course, Miss Masefield. But always we came through it without any problem.'

'How do you rate the *Mauretania*?' asked Ruth.

'She has to be my first choice.'

'Why is that?'

'Lots of reasons, Miss Constantine. Two of them are seated opposite me.'

Ruth tried to probe more deeply into his background, but it was soon Delaney's turn to leave. On the other side of the lounge, Katherine Wymark and her husband got up from their seats and walked arm in arm toward the door. Before they went out, Walter Wymark waved a hand in the direction of Delaney.

'Ah!' said the latter. 'I'm sorry, ladies, but that's my signal to go. I promised to play chess with someone and I always keep my promises.' He stood up and looked down at Ruth. 'Do you play chess, Miss Constantine?'

'I thought that we'd just been having a game,' she answered.

Delaney laughed, then bowed. 'Good night, ladies! Sleep well.'

'Good night.'

Genevieve added her own farewell, then waited until he was out of earshot. 'What did you think of him, Ruth?' she asked.

'Exactly the same as you. He's witty, sophisticated, and very wealthy.'

'He obviously liked you.'

'Oh, let's not fool ourselves, Genevieve. You were the person he really came to see, though I wish he hadn't brought that dry stick of an accountant with him. Orvill Delaney is entranced with you.'

'Don't be absurd!'

'I was using a polite word for it,' said Ruth. 'Put it this way – if there's a tap on your door tonight, it won't be Harvey Denning, I assure you. It will be Mr. Delaney.' She looked after him. 'And he won't be carrying a chess set.'

*

Dillman had to admire the man's effrontery. When he got back to the second-class lounge, the detective saw him at once. Seated in a chair beside Agnes Cameron was the stubby figure of Max Hirsch, gesticulating with both hands as he talked to Stanley and Miriam Rosenwald holding them enthralled with his tale and treating them as good friends, when in fact he had, Dillman believed, stolen property from them. Hirsch was a consummate performer. He might have been their stockbroker, advising them about an investment, or a lawyer, reassuring them about some litigation in which they were involved. Judging by the expressions on their faces, the Rosenwalds were very happy with what they heard, and Mrs. Cameron was plainly entranced. Her gaze never left Hirsch's mobile face and her hand fluttered to his arm more than once.

Eventually the Rosenwalds made their excuse and began to leave. Dillman saw Mrs. Cameron lean across to squeeze Hirsch's hand. When he whispered something in her ear, she gave a laugh and administered a harmless slap on the wrist. Standing near the exit, Dillman offered the Rosenwalds a token smile as they approached.

'Any news, Mr. Dillman?' asked Stanley Rosenwald.

'Not yet, sir.'

'I'd so like to get that snuffbox back.'

'It was an antique,' his wife insisted. 'An expensive one at that.'

'That's why it was taken, I'm afraid, Mrs. Rosenwald. Thieves don't usually bother with trinkets. They tend to know the value of things.'

'Can we hold out any hope?' asked Rosenwald.

'Yes,' said Dillman with more confidence than he actually felt. 'There's every hope, sir. It's simply a case of amassing enough evidence to make an arrest.'

'Do you have any idea of who the thief is?'

'I think so.'

'We didn't realize that criminals operated on these ships,' said Rosenwald with rueful innocence, 'but our friend Mr. Hirsch was just telling us about a pickpocket whom they caught on the *Campania*. He made a comfortable living out of it, apparently.'

'Until they arrested him,' said his wife.

'We always catch them in the end, Mrs. Rosenwald.'

He sent them off to their cabin with at least a degree of optimism, then looked across at Max Hirsch again. The man replied with an impudent grin. Dillman strolled across and exchanged polite greetings with him and Agnes Cameron.

'Did you enjoy the meal, Mr. Dillman?' Agnes asked.

'Very much,' he said.

'Then why did you charge off in the middle of it?' demanded Hirsch. 'A call of nature?'

'Not exactly, Mr. Hirsch.'

'Agnes and I had a wonderful time, didn't we, honey?'

'Yes, Max. Heavenly.'

'This is the best voyage I've ever had, bar none.'

'Better than your trip on the *Campania*?' asked Dillman meaningfully. 'I understand that you were talking about that to Mr. and Mrs. Rosenwald. You warned them to be wary of pickpockets.'

Hirsch's grin returned. 'That's right, I did. You can never be too careful when you're in the middle of so many strangers. Some people have no respect for other people's property.'

'You surprise me,' said Dillman with faint sarcasm.

'I feel completely safe,' affirmed Mrs. Cameron. 'Especially now that I have you to protect me, Max. He has such wonderful knowledge of the ways of the world, Mr. Dillman,' she went on. 'He's so cosmopolitan. You'd never think it of a man with his background.'

'And what sort of background would that be, Mrs. Cameron?' asked Dillman.

'He had his own business in Brooklyn.'

'His own business?'

'Yes,' she explained. 'A very successful one at that.'

'Oh?'

'Max was a silversmith.'

Hirsch gave his broadest grin yet. He was revelling in his invincibility.

*

Emboldened by the unexpected pint of beer, Glyn Bowen decided to speak his mind. 'I think we should call it off, Mansell,' he declared.

'What?'

'This wild idea of yours about that gold.'

'It's not wild,' insisted Price. 'I was talking to one of the lads who helps out in the galley. It's his job to open up the boxes that he fetches from the storeroom down below. Know what he uses? A crowbar.'

'So what?'

'We borrow it, that's what.'

They were in a corner of the third-class smoking room, taking turns to pull on the remains of a discarded cigarette that had been retrieved from the floor. Bowen was rapidly losing faith in the plan that his friend had worked out.

'Too many things can go wrong,' he said.

'Not if we choose our moment.'

'Suppose someone catches us?'

'How can they if you're acting as lookout?'

'We were both on the lookout last night, mun, but that Mr. Dillman still managed to steal up on us. He worries me, Mansell.'

'Why?'

'I don't know. There's something funny about him.'

'Yes,' said Price with a sneer. 'He's a Yank.'

'There's something else. I mean, why should he be so friendly to us?'

'Haven't you worked that out yet? Honestly, Glyn, you must be blind.'

'What do you mean?'

'You forgotten Sergeant Roberts already, mun?'

'Of course not.'

'Don't you remember what he used to do?'

'Yes,' said Bowen with bitterness. 'Give us hell during the week. Treat us like the scum of the earth. But on Saturdays, it was different. Off would come his uniform and on would go that old suit of his. There he'd be, propping up the bar in the pub, pretending to be one of us. It wasn't Sergeant Roberts then.'

'No,' recalled Price. 'He wanted us to call him "Denzil" in there. Not a chance. Whatever he wore, he was still a lousy copper. On or off duty.'

Bowen was perplexed. 'What are you trying to say, Mansell?'

'I think we got another Sergeant Roberts aboard.'

'Mr. Dillman?' said the other in surprise.

'I didn't believe that rubbish about a friend having had something stolen,' said Price, pulling on the cigarette stub for the last time, then dropping it to the floor. He ground it beneath a foot. 'He's a copper of some sort. On the sniff.'

'All the more reason to drop your idea.'

'Never!'

'But he's on to us, Mansell. He must sense something.'

'How can he, mun? All he wanted to know from us was whether or not we saw anyone on the prowl last night in second class. That's Dillman's beat. He won't bother us down by the security room. Besides,' he said, hitching his belt, 'he likes us. What we told him was a great help. You could see that. He trusts us.'

'Does he?' asked the other, unconvinced.

'Yes. If we turn up at the purser's cabin with that gold, Dillman will be able to vouch for us. They'd have to give us a reward then.'

'I still have doubts, Mansell,' admitted the other.

'Then keep them to yourself. When the time is ripe, we go ahead with my plan. I'm not having you backing out on me, Glyn. Understand?' He squeezed the other's arm until his friend yelped. 'Understand?'

'Yes,' said Bowen, rubbing his arm. 'I understand.'

The boat deck was swept by a stiff breeze, but it was not enough to frighten away the elderly couple who were taking a walk before they retired to bed, the two ladies who were exercising their dogs, or the young couple who were embracing impulsively behind one of the large ventilation cowls. Nor was it enough to make Genevieve

Masefield wish that Dillman had suggested somewhere else for a meeting at the end of the day. Warmly wrapped in a coat, scarf, and hat, she found him waiting for her beside one of the lifeboats. He, too, was wearing a thick overcoat, and a hat that all but concealed his face.

'Step behind here,' he suggested. 'It's out of the wind.'

'I could do with some fresh air after being inside for so long,' she said, following his advice, 'but I hadn't expected it to be quite so raw.'

'This is relatively mild weather, Genevieve.'

'Then I'd hate to see it when it takes a turn for the worse.' He slipped an arm around her and she snuggled up to him. 'Thank you, George. That's better.'

'How did you get on this evening?' he asked.

'It was very enjoyable.'

'Meet anyone interesting?'

Genevieve nodded. She gave him a brief account of events in first class, omitting most of the badinage at the table and concentrating on her time spent in the lounge afterward.

'You sound as if you like this Orvill Delaney,' he noted.

'I do, George.'

'Does that mean I have reason to be jealous?' he teased.

'Oh, I don't think so,' she said, kissing him on the cheek. 'The awful truth is that Mr. Delaney preferred a game of chess with Walter Wymark to spending more time with me. That's not very flattering to a lady.'

'Tell me more about Wymark's wife.'

'Katherine? She's a remarkable woman.'

'In what way?'

It was only when she described her earlier conversation with Katherine Wymark that Genevieve remembered why she had spoken to the woman. Her memory was jogged.

'Oh!' she said with self-reproach. 'I forgot to mention Mrs. Dalkeith.'

'I was wondering when you'd get around to her.'

'She was dining at the captain's table, George, and guess what?'

'Mrs. Dalkeith was wearing her gold watch.'

Genevieve was hurt. 'You knew?'

'The purser told me.'

'Well, I wish that he'd tipped me off as well. It took me completely by surprise.'

'I'm sorry about that, Genevieve,' he said. 'I only learned about it myself when I was hauled away from the dinner table. According to Mr. Buxton, the watch was pushed under his door without explanation in a brown envelope.'

'Somebody must have found it,' she concluded. 'Though I don't see why they wish to remain anonymous. Mrs. Dalkeith would have been thrilled to get that watch back. She'd have wanted to thank the person who stumbled on it.'

'I'm not at all sure that that's what happened.'

'How else could it have turned up?'

'That's for you to find out,' he said. 'The case is far from closed.'

'What about your cases, George?'

'They're like the animals that left Noah's ark,' he sighed. 'They went forth and multiplied. We're up to six at the present time, but my guess is that he'll double that before too long.'

He told her about the progress of his inquiry and of how he was convinced that Max Hirsch was responsible for the crimes. Dillman also explained why he lacked enough evidence to make an arrest. Genevieve was interested in the mention of Agnes Cameron.

'Doesn't she realize what a crook he is?'

'No, she thinks he's a wonderful man.'

'Is he that attractive?'

'Not to my eye, but Mrs. Cameron seems to think so.'

'Somebody ought to warn the poor woman,' said Genevieve, 'or she's going to have the most enormous shock.'

'I know,' said Dillman sadly, 'but what we can do? Our job is to prevent and solve crimes, Genevieve. We can't intrude into a romance, and that's what it is to Mrs. Cameron. She'd never forgive us.' He pulled her close.

'How would you like it if someone told you to have nothing whatsoever to do with George Dillman because he's the most appalling character?'

'But I already know that,' she said. 'That's why I'm here.'

He kissed her on the lips and she responded. It made up for some of the time they had spent apart, working in different sections of the ships and pretending to be travelling independently. Genevieve shivered in the cold.

'Could we meet somewhere a little warmer the next time?' she asked.

'Of course. You'd better get back inside.'

'What about you?'

'Oh, I'm going on patrol tonight. Just in case Max Hirsch is up to his little tricks again.' He gave a hollow laugh. 'There is one consolation, I suppose.'

'What's that?'

'He's only interested in silver. Thank heavens it's not gold.'

The sheet of paper was inserted two thirds of the way into the narrow slit beneath the door of the security room. A match ignited the paper, then an eye was swiftly applied to one of the keyholes. The blaze lasted no more than a few seconds, but its glare lit up the stacked boxes with vivid clarity. The visitor was satisfied. After removing all trace of the burned paper outside the door, he padded off silently to his cabin.

TEN

The message received by the Cunard Company headquarters in Liverpool was sanguine:

MAURETANIA 207 MILES WEST OF FASTNET AT 10 P.M. SUNDAY STOP ALL WELL STOP

Monday morning found the ship maintaining good speed as her turbine engines settled into their routine and powered the huge vessel along. By noon, she was 571 miles out of Queenstown, a distance that encouraged many people to believe that the coveted Blue Riband might actually be within her grasp at the first attempt. All hope of that was soon shattered beyond recall. That afternoon, the *Mauretania* ran head-on into a November gale, with winds of over fifty miles an hour buffeting the ship remorselessly and whipping up the waves into steep mountains.

Even a ship as large and well built as the latest Cunard liner was at the mercy of the tempest. Experienced mariners had endured worse conditions before, but most of the passengers were new to such violent pitching and rolling. They either locked themselves for safety in their cabins or found seating in the public rooms, gripping the arms of their chairs with desperate fingers and trying to make light of their ordeal with laboured humour. A few stoics sat over the vestiges of their meals in the dining saloons. No passenger was courageous or foolhardy enough to go out onto the decks.

George Porter Dillman was more accustomed than most to hostile weather. While engaged in the long-distance trials of the yachts built by the family firm, he had often been given proof of the sea's capricious moods and drenched by saltwater for hours on end, as if someone were playing a hose on him. At least he would not have to lash himself to a mast this time to save himself from being washed overboard. After a morning spent pursuing his inquiries, he took time off to worry about Genevieve Masefield, who had never encountered conditions like this before. When she was not in her cabin, he went to the first-class lounge in search of her and hovered near the door. The faces that gazed over at him were white and apprehensive. Even the stewards had a pinched look about them, moodily shifting their feet to accommodate the unpredictable movements of the vessel and trying not to show their anxiety to the passengers.

He saw Genevieve on the far side of the saloon, sitting beside a woman of such striking appearance that she had to be the Katherine Wymark about whom he had heard so much. Dillman was relieved to observe that Genevieve showed no signs of distress or queasiness. He was about to slip away when she caught sight of him and raised a hand in greeting. Dillman hesitated. It might be his only opportunity to meet Katherine Wymark, and Genevieve obviously wanted to speak to him. A fleeting encounter with her in a public room would not give anything away. Letting curiosity get the better of him, he walked across the saloon.

Genevieve introduced him to her friend with studied politeness and Dillman had a closer look at Katherine Wymark. He decided that she was every bit as remarkable as he had been led to believe. Though it was difficult to retain poise when the ship was tilting to and fro, Katherine managed it better than most. She was wearing a pale-blue dress with long, vertical box pleats down the skirt. A series of small blue buttons was arranged in diamond patterns across the chest, half hidden by a light brown jacket, meticulously tailored to add style and warmth. His appraisal of her was brief, but Katherine took a much more detailed inventory of Dillman, admiring what she saw and turning to Genevieve with a smile.

'Mr. Dillman is a friend of yours?' she asked. 'Where've you been hiding him?'

'I'm more of an acquaintance, really,' he explained. 'Miss Masefield and I bumped into each other on another voyage.'

'Lucky for her!'

'How are you coping with this bad weather, Mrs. Wymark?'

'Badly.'

'You seem very calm under the circumstances.'

'An optical illusion.'

'What about you, Miss Masefield?' he asked.

'I decided that we just have to grin and bear it,' she said.

'I'm not sure that I can rise to a grin,' warned Katherine. 'I'm just gritting my teeth and bearing it. But you seem to take it all in your stride, Mr. Dillman,' she went on. 'You walked across the room just now as if this turbulence was quite normal. Are you a seasoned mariner?'

He nodded. 'I spent some years helping design and sail yachts.'

'No wonder you look so hideously at ease. It's unfair. Most of us in here are still trying to hold on to our luncheon.'

'The friends with whom I'm travelling took to their cabins,' said Genevieve, feeding the information to Dillman. 'They daren't even look out of their portholes. I felt I'd rather be in a larger space, where the pitching was less obvious. So I came into the lounge. I thought I'd be sitting here all alone, until Mrs. Wymark came to my rescue.'

'We came to each other's rescue,' said the other. 'I didn't want to stay in the cabin and listen to my husband being ill in the bathroom, so I came here in search of company. Look,' she said, indicating the chair, 'why not join us for a few minutes?'

'I can't stay,' said Dillman. 'I only came over to say hello to Miss Masefield.'

'And to me, I hope.'

'Well, yes, of course.'

'Good.'

'But I'm sorry to hear your husband is unwell.'

'It's not only the bad weather, Mr. Dillman. Walter had a very late night.'

'How did his game of chess go?' asked Genevieve.

'Chess?'

'I thought he was playing against Mr. Delaney.'

'Yes, he was,' said Katherine, pursing her lips. 'That was the trouble. The game dragged on. I was fast asleep by the time my husband got back to the cabin. I'll complain to Mr. Delaney about that.' She smiled at Dillman. 'Have you met Orvill Delaney yet?'

'No, Mrs. Wymark,' he said.

'He's a gentleman who makes himself known.'

'In the nicest possible way,' said Genevieve. 'I've had some very pleasant talks with him. He has a keen interest in literature.'

'And business.'

'And people.'

'And chess,' noted Dillman. 'Mr. Delaney is obviously a man of many parts.'

'I'd go along with that,' agreed Katherine.

'Did you know that he bought a car in England?' asked Genevieve.

'No, but it's just the kind of crazy thing he'd do.'

'It's in the hold, apparently.'

'Well, I hope it's well secured,' said Dillman as the vessel tilted once more. 'This kind of weather can play havoc with any cargo that's not properly stowed away.'

'It's playing havoc with me,' admitted Katherine. 'I know that.'

'Nobody would guess it, Mrs. Wymark.'

She acknowledged his compliment with a warm smile. Dillman took a moment to study her more carefully. Katherine Wymark was a beautiful woman, but she was a little too aware of her beauty for his liking. Composed and sophisticated though she was, he detected a faintly calculating air about her. Looking into the handsome face, he could understand why he preferred Genevieve Masefield, but he schooled himself to give no indication of his true feelings for her.

'Ah!' said Katherine, looking across the saloon. 'One of the walking wounded!'

A short, thickset, broad-shouldered man was waddling toward them, his face darkened by a scowl. Walter Wymark was not enjoying this phase of the voyage. When he was introduced to Dillman and Genevieve, he barely gave them a glance. His manner was almost curt. Katherine sensed that he needed her and made her excuses. Holding his arm, she led her husband out of the saloon.

'What an odd couple,' remarked Dillman.

'Yet she was talking so fondly of him before you came in.'

'He's not exactly the most courteous passenger aboard, is he?'

'No, George, he isn't. What did you make of his wife?'

Shrugging, Dillman tried to suppress a grin. 'I only know which one of them *I'd* rather play chess with,' he said.

When conditions suddenly worsened, the Jarvis family took to their cabin. Alexandra was crestfallen at the thought that she might miss the opportunity to feed the ship's mascot, and she sought for a way to escape. Her grandmother proved an unwitting ally. Alarmed by the shifting position of the vessel, she was afraid to suffer its undulations alone and asked for company to sustain her through the ordeal. Alexandra volunteered at once. Standing beside the old woman, she fought off her own feelings of nausea by thinking about her friendship with the black cat. Lily Pomeroy was reassured by her presence, lying on her bunk and stroking the girl's hair, wishing that she still had the fearlessness of childhood. The ship began to settle into a more definite rhythm, rocking to and fro like a giant cradle. Protected from its howl and brutality, Mrs. Pomeroy heard the wind as a kind of distant lullaby that slowly sang her to sleep.

Alexandra watched carefully as her grandmother's

eyelids flickered, then closed. Only when she was certain that the old woman was asleep did she steal out of the cabin. Racing along deserted passageways, she reached the officer's quarters just as Reynolds was about to feed Bobo. He looked at her in astonishment.

'I didn't expect to see you, Alexandra,' he said.

'I couldn't let Bobo down, Mr. Reynolds,' she replied, panting from her exertions.

'In that case, you'd better take over, hadn't you?'

'Thank you,' she said excitedly, taking the plate of meat from him. 'Here you are, Bobo. You've been waiting for this, haven't you?'

She set the plate down on the floor and stroked the cat's back affectionately. Bobo, however, had no interest in the food. After giving it a cursory glance, he turned away in disdain. The girl looked over at Reynolds with dismay.

'Perhaps he wants a drink of milk first,' he suggested.

'Let me give it to him, please.'

Reaching for the bottle of milk, she poured some into the cat's bowl, but he did not even look at it. Bobo was unsettled, pacing the cabin restlessly and emitting a high-pitched cry when the ship lurched with increased violence.

'He's afraid,' said Alexandra. 'Maybe he just wants a cuddle.'

But the animal was in no mood for anyone's attentions. As she bent down to pick him up, Bobo gave a hiss of protest and darted between her legs. Before either of them could stop him, he dived swiftly through the gap in the door and scurried off down the passageway. Alexandra was shaking with disappointment.

'What's wrong with him, Mr. Reynolds?' she bleated.

'Bobo will soon come back,' he said, forcing a chuckle. 'Where else can he go?'

It was as if they were trapped on a gigantic roller coaster. The bow of the *Mauretania* was rising and dipping with increased speed and suddenness. Waves pounded her from all sides and washed her decks relentlessly. Wind tested her defences with renewed ferocity. The noise was earsplitting.

Down in the purser's cabin, Dillman could feel that the storm was intensifying.

'The *Mauretania*'s having a rough baptism,' he said, looking through the porthole at the heaving sea. 'It was always in the cards with a November crossing.'

'Yes,' agreed Maurice Buxton, plucking at his beard. 'The Atlantic is the most treacherous ocean in the world and it's letting us know it once again.'

'She seems to be holding up well.'

'So far, Mr. Dillman. But she was built for speed rather than for stability and comfort. I'm afraid our passengers are finding that out right now. I'm bracing myself for a bumper supply of complaints from them.'

'You can't control the weather, Mr. Buxton.'

'That makes no difference. If there's a complaint of any nature, it somehow lands on my desk. I've been blamed for rain, fog, ice, delays, engine noise, navigational errors, tardy service in the dining saloon, and unacceptable toilet paper. On my last ship, I was castigated by one lady because she found a spider in her bathroom and thought I had put it there on purpose.' He gave a sigh. 'Who'd be a purser?'

'You would, Mr. Buxton. You love it.'

'Most of the time perhaps. Not at the moment.'

'Does that mean our thief has been at work again?'

'I'm afraid so, Mr. Dillman.'

'How many victims this time?'

'Three,' said the purser. 'All from second class, and the thefts all occurred within a specific time frame. In each case, people went off to dinner last night and returned to their cabins to discover they'd been robbed.'

'I think I can narrow the time down even more,' said Dillman, recalling the late arrival of Max Hirsch in the dining saloon. 'My guess is that all three crimes occurred shortly before eight o'clock.'

'How do you know that?'

'Because that's when my prime suspect was going about his business.'

'Who *is* the man?'

Before Dillman could reply, the ship was lifted by

another mountainous wave, her bow reaching over sixty feet before she was dropped down again without warning. The force of the impact was so great that the spare anchor was dislodged on the foredeck, sliding against the fore-castle with an awesome thud. Dillman looked up with concern.

'That sounds serious,' he said.

Max Hirsch heard the noise as well, but it was so distant and muffled that he paid no heed to it. Far more important matters commanded his attention. As he had learned from experience, bad weather was good for his business; there was little movement around a vessel during a storm. Passengers tried to stay in one place, members of the crew were all on duty, and stewards were less likely to patrol passageways that seemed to have a life of their own. Hirsch could walk with relative impunity throughout the ship, searching for empty cabins to enter with a skill born of a long apprenticeship. One of the master keys he had collected over the years almost invariably did the trick. Speed was his defining characteristic. Once inside a cabin, he sensed immediately where money and valuables were kept. He was out again in less than a minute.

Having pillaged only the second-class passengers so far, Hirsch decided to go farther afield and explore the rest of the ship. It would exasperate Dillman even more. Hirsch was proud of the way he had outwitted the detective. It took cunning and bravado. Though Dillman was on his trail, he always managed to keep one step ahead of him. The burden of proof lay with the detective, and Hirsch vowed that the man would be given no evidence on which to make an arrest. Dillman was chasing shadows. Clutching his briefcase, Hirsch congratulated himself on his profes-sional expertise and went along another passageway with an arrogant strut.

When he turned the corner at the far end, however, his manner changed at once. The sight that confronted him made him come to a dead halt. He pointed a finger.

'What the hell are you doing?' he demanded.

Something hard and metallic struck him on the back of his head. Blood spurted across the bald pate as he staggered to the ground. A second blow was even more vicious, knocking him unconscious and forcing him to drop his briefcase.

'Don't let that blood get on the carpet,' ordered a voice. 'Use a handkerchief.'

'Right,' said another voice.

'Then get rid of him.'

'Where?'

'Where do you think? And be quick about it. I need help here.'

— — —

It was a case of all hands on deck. Detached from its mooring, the spare anchor was slithering all over the foredeck, dragging its chain behind it like a monstrous serpent. Wind and waves intensified their assault. The damage was extensive. Several windows on the promenade deck were shattered. The teak rails on the monkey island, high above the waterline on the top of the bridge, were twisted out of shape by vengeful waves. Ventilator cowls were dented, a tarpaulin was ripped off a lifeboat, and rivulets of cold, green seawater poured in to soak carpets and lap at interior walls. Securing the anchor was the main priority, but its vast size and weight made that a formidable task. It dwarfed the men who were trying to control it, and threatened to crush them each time it slid across the deck.

The captain took swift measures. Turning the *Mauretania*'s stern to the wind, he reduced her speed drastically to three knots, leaving himself barely enough power to steer by. The possibility of a record crossing had been sacrificed, but his crew was at least able to grapple more effectively with the crisis. Dillman was in among them. Knowing that every pair of hands was useful, he donned some borrowed oilskins and quickly joined the others on deck, throwing himself wholeheartedly into the struggle and responding to the orders that were shouted above the banshee screech of the wind. Hawsers were used to lasso the anchor in an attempt to bring it under control, but it was impossible to hold on to them when several tons of solid iron were skidding around wildly in circles.

Dillman was exhilarated. It was not just a sense of duty that had prompted him to lend his assistance; it was also the ambiguous pleasure of battling against the elements, of surviving the hazards that only a storm at sea can bring. Dillman was out of practice. It took him a little time to adjust himself to the conditions and to display the instant reflexes that were required in the situation. Part of a team, he was determined not to let it down. When another hawser was looped around the anchor, he and the other men pulled with all their might. It was hard, dangerous, exacting work in appalling weather, but Dillman was thriving on it. Like everyone else on deck, he was completely absorbed in his task.

None of them heard the splash of a man's body as it hit the water.

— — —

'Well, at least we're moving in the right direction now,' said Donald Belfrage. 'When we turned around, I thought we were going back to Ireland.'

'Why did the captain do that?' asked Theodora, prodding a potato.

'To get out of the headwind,' explained Harvey Denning. 'I spoke to one of the crew about it. Apparently the spare anchor came adrift and rolled around on the deck, smashing anything within reach. Captain Pritchard slowed us down so the crew could secure the anchor again. It took them over two hours.'

'I hope they've made a better job of it this time,' said Belfrage.

'I think they deserve our admiration,' said Ruth Constantine. 'Would you have gone up on deck in such foul weather, Donald?'

'Of course. If I was paid to.'

'No amount of money would have got me up there,' said Susan Faulconbridge. 'I saw the waves through my port-hole. They were colossal.'

'They've calmed down a bit now, thank heavens,' sighed Belfrage. 'That means we can start to eat properly once again.' He raised a glass. 'Welcome to the regal suite, everyone. Theo and I are delighted to be your hosts.'

'I think that we should be toasting the crew,' argued Ruth.

'Hear, hear!' supported Genevieve Masefield. 'They were Trojans.'

'Trojans didn't have turbine-driven oceanic liners,' observed Denning tartly.

'Don't be so fatuous, Harvey,' said Ruth.

'I'm just striking a blow for historical accuracy.'

'Then you're being absurdly pedantic as well as fatuous.'

'Who exactly *were* the Trojans?' asked Theodora innocently.

They were dining in the Belfrages' suite that evening, a sumptuous collection of rooms with a degree of luxury to rival any hotel. Having accepted their friendship and hospitality so far, Genevieve found it difficult to refuse the invitation, and she was, in any case, curious to see the inside of a regal suite. Now that the wind had lost some of its venom, the ship was back on a more even keel, steaming at her optimum speed on her intended course. A degree of normality had returned to the *Mauretania* and to the table presided over by Donald Belfrage. He was the common target once more.

'A Trojan was a person from Troy,' explained Denning. 'They were big, strong, industrious people – just like Donald, really. You ought to know what a Trojan is, Theodora. You married one.'

'No I didn't,' she said. 'I married the perfect Englishman.'

'Technically, he was born in Scotland,' argued Ruth. 'What does that make you, Donald? An Anglo-Scots Trojan?'

'Yes,' added Denning, seizing his cue. 'Donald ought to have his portrait painted wearing a kilt, waving a Union Jack, and sitting astride a wooden horse. Just think what that would make you, Theodora.'

'What do you mean?'

'Helen of Troy!'

'Is this the face that launched a thousand Cunard liners?' intoned Ruth.

Susan giggled, Denning rolled his eyes, and Ruth took a sip of her wine. Genevieve took no part in the amiable baiting. Seated opposite Belfrage, she was concerned about the glances he kept flicking in her direction. They signalled far more than affection. For a man who had not long returned from his honeymoon, he was behaving with a worrying lack of decorum.

'How is your tame American?' he asked her.

'Who?' said Genevieve.

'That timber merchant.'

'Mr. Delaney is not a timber merchant.'

'Then what is he?'

'A man of the world.'

'Didn't you say that the lumberjack gave you a magazine?' Susan asked.

Genevieve smiled. 'Yes, Susan, but he's not a lumberjack.'

'What was in the magazine?'

'A short story that Mr. Delaney wanted me to read.'

'Beware of Americans bearing gifts,' said Denning.

'I'd never trust any foreigner,' insisted Belfrage, slicing his way through a steak. 'You never know where they've been. As for Americans, I feel as if I'd have to put newspapers down on the floor before I invited them into my house.'

'That's unkind,' protested Genevieve.

'No,' said Ruth. 'It's typical of Donald's attitude. He still thinks that the Welsh should be kept in cages and fed twice a week, and he's even more critical of the Irish.'

'Barbarians!' said Belfrage.

'See what I mean, Genevieve?'

'Well, I won't have him sneering at Mr. Delaney. I thought him delightful.'

'So did I. Delightful in a peculiar sort of way,' said Ruth. 'He has depths to him.'

'That's a rare compliment, coming from you,' said Denning with surprise. 'As a rule, you don't have a good word to say for any man.'

'Only because most of them don't deserve it.'

'What was the story he wanted you to read, Genevieve?' asked Susan.

'It was by that American writer I mentioned before – O. Henry. I did read it, and liked it immensely.'

'The only author I have time for is Rudyard Kipling,' said Belfrage.

'Oh, yes, darling,' said Theodora. 'I've heard of him.'

'The supreme accolade,' mocked Denning. 'Being heard of by Theodora.'

'Splendid fellow, Kipling,' said Belfrage. 'Has the right attitudes.'

'That's one vote you can count on, then,' said Denning sarcastically. 'If old Rudyard happens to be in your constituency, that is. But that's enough literary table talk.' He tapped his fork against his glass to call for silence. 'Listen, everybody. We're going to have a round of predictions. This voyage still has over four days to run, remember, and a lot can happen in that time. What each of you has to do is to choose someone else and predict what's going to befall that person before we reach New York. Be serious, all of you. Who's going to start?'

'I will,' said Ruth levelly. 'My choice is you, Harvey.'

'Fire away.'

'I predict that by the end of the voyage, you will have rapped on the cabin door of every woman in first class in search of new conquests.'

'Not every one!' he protested over the laughter. 'Only the pretty ones. Right, it's my turn now. I'm picking Donald and Theodora.'

'You can't have them both at once,' said Susan.

'Why not?'

'It spoils it, Harvey.'

'Who's making the rules here? They must be together. You'll see why.'

'Is he going to poke fun at us again, Donald?' asked Theodora.

'He'd better not. Go on, Harvey,' he said warningly. 'What about us?'

'I predict that one night this week, all things being equal, given ideal conditions and a following wind, the son and heir will be conceived within these four walls.'

'Gosh!' exclaimed Theodora, blushing a deep crimson.

'That's a bit personal, isn't it?' chided Belfrage. 'We haven't even discussed that, have we, Theo? On the other hand,' he added as the notion slowly grew in appeal, 'it's not something I'd find altogether unwelcome. We have a dynasty to consider.'

'Susan's turn,' said Denning.

'Oh, I'll pick Ruth,' she said without hesitation. 'My prediction is that she'll actually find a man on board this ship who'll make her fall head over heels in love with him and regret all those years she's spent attacking the entire male sex.'

'That's not a prediction,' retorted Ruth. 'It's a dire threat.'

'The simple truth is that you're afraid of men.'

'No, Susan. I'm afraid of tying myself to one of them for life, that's all. Men are like that spare anchor that got loose this afternoon. They drag you where they want to go.'

'But Donald and I always want to go to the same place,' said Theodora.

Denning smirked. 'What did I tell you? Conception is imminent.'

'That's not what I meant, Harvey, and you know it.'

'Your turn now, Ruth.'

'Then I'll get my own back on Susan,' said the other.

'What's going to happen to me in the next four days?' challenged Susan.

'Nothing,' said Ruth with a shrug. 'Absolutely nothing.'

'That's a silly thing to say!'

'Is it? Wait and see.'

There was an awkward pause. Genevieve tried to heal the rift with her contribution. 'My turn,' she offered. 'I don't know any of you well enough to make an accurate prediction, so my forecast is for all five of you. No matter how many arguments and misunderstandings you have between now and the time we arrive in New York, I predict that you'll still be the best of friends and that you'll go on to have a wonderful time in America. I raise my glass to all five of you.'

There was warm approval of her prediction and they all clinked her glass with their own. Susan was beaming again, Denning was pleased, and Ruth refrained from any cutting remark. Theodora was touched by the prediction. She nudged her husband.

'You do it for both of us, darling,' she suggested. 'There's only Genevieve left.'

'I hardly need to be told that,' said Belfrage.

'So what does the future hold for Genevieve?' prompted Denning.

'Romance with the lumberjack?' suggested Susan.

'Dinner at the captain's table would be my guess.'

'Nobody is asking either of you,' said Belfrage, staring hard at Genevieve, his glass in his hand. 'I'll tell you what my prediction for her is. Genevieve has been a delight to have at our table and she deserves a just reward. That is why,' he continued, a smile forming around his lips, 'I can confidently predict that sometime in the next four days, something very, very special is going to happen to her.'

There was general agreement and everyone made flattering comments about her. Genevieve was touched by the affection she had generated, but her pleasure was marred by a highly disagreeable fact. At the very moment when he was making his prediction about her, Donald Belfrage, an adoring wife at his side and his closest friends around him, was trying to stroke Genevieve's leg under the table with his foot.

— — —

Glyn Bowen felt well enough to sit up on his bunk, but he had no inclination to lower himself to the floor. The turbu-

lence that afternoon had given him a severe bout of
seasickness and confined him to the little cabin in third
class. Mansell Price was spared any discomfort. He had
gone off to the dining saloon with relish, leaving his friend
to suffer alone. Gradually the pain and the queasiness
began to relent. Bowen even had the strength to turn his
mind to matters other than his health.

Price's scheme to break into the security room alarmed
him. It seemed to belong to the realms of fantasy, yet he
could not convince his friend of that. Price was single-
minded. Once set on a course of action, he persevered until
the very end. Regardless of his dissent, Bowen would be
dragged along behind him, as he always had been in the
past. He could see no way out of the dilemma. He began to
wish he had never left the Rhondda. It was Price who had
been sacked for violent behaviour, not him. Nostalgia for
the coal mine surged up inside him.

A banging sound on the door brought him out of his
reverie. He lowered himself gingerly to the floor and
groped his way across the room. The banging was
repeated.

'Open up, Glyn!' ordered a voice.

'I'm coming, Mansell.'

'Quick, mun!'

When he opened the door, Bowen saw the reason for
the haste. Cradled in his friend's arms was something
concealed in a piece of sacking. Price kicked the door shut
behind him, then placed his cargo on the lower bunk.
Laughing quietly to himself, he unwrapped the sacking to
reveal his haul. Bowen stared down in dismay at two crowbars, a bolster chisel, and a lump hammer.

'Where did you get that lot, Mansell?' he asked.

'Never you mind.'

'You're going ahead with this, aren't you?'

'Oh, yes,' said Price with a grim chuckle. 'We both are.'

Dinner with the Jarvis family was a more muted affair on
Monday evening. Dillman was grateful that the table also
contained a young married couple from Birmingham, as

well as two American businessmen returning to New York from a conference. Alexandra Jarvis was unusually subdued, fretting over the disappearance of the black cat, yet unable to raise the subject in front of her parents because it would be a confession of guilt. Oliver and Vanessa Jarvis had taken a jaundiced view of their daughter's friendship with the ship's mascot ever since their son had described the way in which Alexandra had abandoned him in favour of the animal. The girl was terrified to own up to the fact that she had not only sneaked off from her sleeping grandmother, but that she had disobeyed her father's express command to stay away from Bobo altogether.

Oliver Jarvis was the most animated member of the family, coming out of his shell for once to discuss with the two businessmen the difference in banking practices between their country and his. Unable to join the conversation, his wife merely supported him with a series of smiles and nods. Noel Jarvis was the ghost at the feast, a pale, dark-eyed creature, still not rid of the trailing effects of seasickness and rejecting with a groan everything put in front of him. Lily Pomeroy, having recovered her voracious appetite, was not in a talkative mood and directed her energies to clearing her plate and making odd, embarrassing interjections. It was Dillman who provided what unity the table had, drawing everyone into a review of the afternoon's mishaps on deck.

Alexandra was preoccupied with another kind of mishap. 'Have you seen Bobo today, Mr. Dillman?' she asked.

'I don't think so,' he said. 'Why?'

'Oh, I just wondered. I hope he wasn't frightened by the storm.'

'Were you, Ally?'

'No. I'm never frightened by bad weather. Noel is scared of lightning,' she said with contempt, 'but I'm not. Noel is scared of lots of things.'

Her brother came out of his silence to glare at her and poke out his tongue.

'So where were you this afternoon?' asked Dillman.

'Looking after Granny in her cabin.'

'She was as good as gold,' said Mrs. Pomeroy, wiping her lips with her napkin. 'My granddaughter watched over me like a guardian angel, Mr. Dillman.'

'That's because she loves you so much,' said Vanessa.

'I know. It's a great consolation.'

'Where do you think he is now, Mr. Dillman?' said the girl. 'Bobo, I mean.'

'Don't keep on about that cat, dear,' cautioned her mother.

'I'd like to know, Mummy.'

'Then the most probable answer is that he's fast asleep somewhere,' said Dillman. 'Cats spend a large part of the day curled up asleep, Ally. Especially when there's such dreadful weather. Bobo would have far more sense than to go out on deck in that storm.'

'Would it be a sign of bad luck if he disappeared?'

'Disappeared?'

'Yes,' she said artlessly. 'Got lost or something.'

'I don't think a ship's mascot is likely to get lost. He has far too many friends aboard for that. And you needn't have the slightest fear that any harm has come to him.'

'Why not?'

'Because he's a cat,' said Dillman. 'Cats have nine lives.'

'That's true,' added Mrs. Pomeroy. 'My husband ran over a cat with his wheelbarrow once. A ginger one with a frayed ear. He thought he'd killed the poor animal, but it suddenly jumped up off the grass and scratched him on the arm.' Her laugh set the double chin wobbling. 'He'd have killed it for sure if he could have caught it.'

'Bobo wouldn't scratch anybody,' said Alexandra.

Vanessa frowned at her. 'Forget about him, dear.'

'He'll be fine,' said Dillman. 'I'll keep an eye open for him.'

The girl brightened. 'Thank you!'

As he gazed around the second-class dining saloon, however, Dillman was not in search of the cat. He was more interested in watching the behaviour of the various people with whom he had come into contact before.

Stanley and Miriam Rosenwald were dining with a family of eight, Mrs. Dobrowski was sharing a table with friends, and the others who'd been robbed in the course of the voyage were also seen about the room. Hester Littlejohn had made an appearance, but it was less to consume a meal than to give the chief steward a verbal questionnaire. From the hunted look on the man's face, the detective concluded that she was asking him about rates of pay. A pad was taken out of her purse so that any new detail could be inserted. While almost everyone else was content to enjoy the meal, Mrs. Littlejohn had the earnest look of a missionary in search of a tribe to convert to Christianity.

It was Agnes Cameron who worried him most. She was in a position she had occupied once before, sitting at a table and manufacturing small talk with her companions while waiting for the empty chair beside her to be taken. Dillman's first thought was that Max Hirsch was using people's absence from their cabins as an opportunity to steal their property, and he had to resist the urge to go in search of the man. When half an hour rolled past, Mrs. Cameron's hopeful expression slowly turned to bitter disappointment. After an hour, she looked utterly betrayed.

By the time the dessert arrived, she could stand it no more. Dabbing at tears with a handkerchief, she got up abruptly and hurried out of the room. Dillman's compassion surged; he did not dismiss her merely as a gullible woman who had been taken in by a deceitful man. She deserved as much sympathy as Hirsch's other victims because, as Dillman now realized, he had taken far more from her than from any of them. They had only lost property. She had surrendered her love and her trust.

Max Hirsch was leaving more damage in his wake than the tempest had.

ELEVEN

Though he had two able deputies to assist him, Maurice Buxton took the bulk of the work on his own shoulders, applying himself to the welfare of the passengers with a blend of tact and professional charm. Nobody seeing him at the entrance to the second-class lounge would have guessed that the first full day at sea had been fraught with such severe difficulties. He beamed reassuringly at all around him and fielded dozens of anxious inquiries without losing either his bonhomie or his equanimity. With his sturdy frame in its smart uniform, his friendliness and air of supreme competence, the purser was a comforting presence.

The lounge was quite full after dinner that evening, but Buxton eventually picked out the person he had come to see. Realizing that he was wanted, George Porter Dillman soon detached himself from the friends to whom he was talking and left the lounge. A minute later, the purser casually followed him. He and Dillman met in the lift and ascended alone together.

'Aren't you ever off duty, Mr. Buxton?' asked the detective.

'A purser is on tap for twenty-four hours,' said the other, 'but you had your own experience of that with the Pinkerton Agency, didn't you? What was your motto?'

' "We Never Sleep." '

'I've forgotten what sleep is, Mr. Dillman.'

'More trouble?'

'Yes,' said the purser, 'though you may think it's really Genevieve Masefield's territory. Two thefts in first class, carried out this afternoon while the tempest was raging and you and the rest of the crew were doing heroics on the fore-deck. Here are the names of the passengers involved,' he went on, slipping a piece of paper into Dillman's hand. 'They were irate. You might prefer to let Miss Masefield soothe them. She obviously did that very well with Mrs. Dalkeith.'

'What was taken?'

'A silver-and-ivory eyeglass case from one cabin.'

'And the other?'

'You won't believe this, Mr. Dillman.'

'Astonish me.'

'A complete set of cutlery.'

'Cutlery?'

'Yes,' explained the other. 'Solid silver. Bought from an antiques shop on Bond Street at great expense. Unfortunately, when the people opened the box to gloat over their purchase, it was empty. Sixty-four pieces of silver cutlery had vanished into thin air.'

'No,' sighed Dillman. 'I think I know where they may have gone. The same place as the other stolen items. He's starting to spread his wings.'

'Who is?'

'My little silversmith. After concentrating on second class, he's now moving up in the world to richer pickings. I bet the eyeglass case was valuable as well.'

'It was. Mr. Tavistock was more upset by the loss of that than of the four hundred dollars that also disappeared.' The lift stopped and they got out. 'When I asked him why he was so reckless as to leave that much money in his cabin, he said that he trusted the Cunard Line.'

'The Cunard Line is entirely trustworthy,' said Dillman. 'It's human nature that you have to guard against.' He glanced at the piece of paper. 'I'll get on to this at once, Mr. Buxton. Unless there's anything else on the docket.'

'Yes and no.'

'What do you mean?'

'Well,' said the other, stroking his beard, 'I'm not sure if this is a crime or a case of absentmindedness. A couple of crowbars have disappeared.'

'Crowbars?'

'They use them to open boxes of food brought up from the storage area.'

'Where were they taken from?'

'The third-class galley, Mr. Dillman. Except that we're not certain they *were* taken. The lad who normally uses them is not the brightest star in the firmament. My guess is that he may have forgotten where he put them.'

'I wonder.'

'We can rule out your prime suspect, anyway.'

'Can we?'

'The crowbars were solid iron,' said Buxton, 'not silver.' Two passengers walked past and the purser smiled at them, waiting until they were out of earshot. 'We'd better not be seen talking shop together, Mr. Dillman. To all intents and purposes, you're just one more passenger on the *Mauretania*.'

'Then I'd like to report another disappearance, Mr. Buxton.'

'Are you serious?'

'Ally was deeply upset about it, I could see that.'

'Who's Ally?'

'Alexandra Jarvis,' said Dillman. 'A little girl I met on the boat train. It seems that she struck up a friendship with the ship's mascot, and now he's vanished. When I had dinner with Ally and her family this evening, she kept sending up silent distress signals to me. Bobo has disappeared.'

'Leave it to Mr. Reynolds. He looks after the cat.'

'Mr. Reynolds can't find Bobo either, apparently.'

'Well, don't come to me,' said the purser with a grin. 'I've got more than enough on my plate as it is. Let's catch this thief first, Mr. Dillman. He's our top priority. Don't worry about Bobo. He'll be back. Cats have a way of looking after themselves.'

— — —

The lavish meal offered in the first-class dining saloon that evening had included Tortue Verte, Crème Chatrillon,

Supreme de Sole, Sirloin and Ribs of Beef, served with a selection of vegetables as well as Boiled, Mashed, and Chateau Potatoes, and a range of desserts to suit all palates, the whole banquet served up on exquisite crockery embossed with the Cunard emblem. What the guests saw was a magnificent repast, set out before them with quiet efficiency by an army of stewards, who removed the plates between each course at precisely the right moment. The sense of organization was all-pervasive. What the passengers did not see was the controlled hysteria in the kitchens, making it all possible. While the French chef had devised the menu, it was his industrious *sous*-chefs who were charged with the job of reproducing hundreds of meals to his exact specification, submitting them for inspection before they were allowed into the dining saloon. High standards of cuisine were an essential element of the voyage.

As each set of plates, bowls, and cutlery was returned to the kitchen, it was handed over to the real galley slaves: the lowliest stewards, with the task of washing everything in readiness for the next meal. Before they could plunge the crockery into the water, they had to clean off any remaining food, invariably marvelling at the amounts that were sometimes left on a plate and making trenchant comments about the prodigality of the rich. Some of them popped an occasional leftover tidbit in their mouths, but most of the food was scraped off into the waiting bins.

It was between these bins that a black cat lurked in readiness. Bobo knew where to come. The first-class kitchens supplied the richest fare on the ship. It was almost as if he sensed that there was fish on the menu. When another piece of sole was pushed into a bin, Bobo came out of his hiding place, leaped nimbly onto the rim of the receptacle and retrieved the fish before anyone could see him.

Darting out of the kitchen, he found a quiet corner where he could dine in style.

It took took time for Genevieve Masefield to extricate herself from the private dinner party, and even more time to shake off the respective offers from Donald Belfrage and Harvey Denning to escort her to her cabin. In any event, she and Ruth Constantine left the regal suite together. The latter was complimentary.

'You're becoming quite adept at it,' she observed.

'At what?'

'Dodging the outstretched hands of Donald and Harvey.'

'I didn't want an embarrassing scene outside my cabin door,' said Genevieve briskly. 'Donald might have settled for a kiss on the cheek, but Harvey seemed to have rather higher ambitions.'

'He always does.'

'It was a lovely party, though. The five of you are such entertaining company. I thoroughly enjoyed it. You were in such good form, Ruth.'

'No,' said the other cynically. 'I wasn't nearly malicious enough.'

Genevieve smiled as they came to a halt outside Ruth's cabin. She now had a much clearer idea of how the other fitted into the scheme of things. Theodora Belfrage and Susan Faulconbridge were agreeable members of the leisured class, but their roles were largely decorative. Ruth was an altogether more positive character. She was the catalyst in the group, controlling the balance of power between Belfrage and Denning, while bringing out the hidden traits in the other women. She might affect a world-weary disdain at times, but Ruth Constantine needed her friends as much as they needed her.

'Good night, Ruth,' said Genevieve.

'You still haven't answered my question. What's his name?'

'How do you know that he even exists?'

'Intuition.'

'Then you'll have to rely on it to provide you with a name as well,' said Genevieve, teasing her. 'And when you find it, perhaps you'd be good enough to tell me who he is, because I'd like to know myself.'

Ruth laughed, gave a farewell wave, then let herself into

her cabin. Genevieve walked on down the passageway to the stairs, but instead of going up a flight to her own deck, she descended the steps and made her way to the second-class cabins. A glance at her watch showed her how late it was, but she knew that Dillman would be waiting for her. When he let her into his cabin, he made no complaint, giving her a kiss of welcome and offering her a chair. Genevieve settled down.

'This is a warmer place for a rendezvous than the deck,' she observed.

'But not quite so romantic.'

'That depends on the weather. It was foul earlier on.'

'I know,' said Dillman. 'I was out in it. Conditions are still pretty unpleasant out there, but we seem to have come through the worst of it. According to Mr. Reynolds, we're making good time.'

'Mr. Reynolds?'

'One of the officers. He looks after the ship's mascot, that black cat you may have seen loping around. I met Mr. Reynolds when I was on my way back here. He tells me that the captain still expects us to cover over four hundred and sixty miles today,' he said, checking his watch, 'which is due to end very shortly. Given the fact that we had to slow down this afternoon, that's an achievement.'

'Has the Blue Riband been ruled out?'

'More or less. Anyway, that's not our problem. We have enough of our own.'

'Do we, George? What's happened?'

'Tell me about your evening first.'

Genevieve recounted the details of her dinner party in the regal suite, glossing over any mention of the subterranean foot that had tried to stroke her leg during the meal. Dillman was amused to hear of Ruth Constantine's suspicion about her.

'So she knows that I do exist, does she?' he said.

'But you don't, George,' replied Genevieve. 'Not on this voyage, unfortunately. We're nothing more than employees of the Cunard Line, travelling independently.'

'Ships that pass in the night.'

Genevieve laughed. 'What about your evening?' she asked.

'More perplexing, I'm afraid.'

'In what way?'

When Dillman told her about the latest developments, Genevieve was alarmed. 'Two victims in first class?'

'Yes,' he said, handing over the piece of paper given him by Maurice Buxton. 'Here are the names. Something tells me we won't have the same happy outcome as we did in the case of Mrs. Dalkeith. Apart from anything else, you can't slip a complete set of cutlery under the purser's door in a brown envelope.'

'Why on earth keep something so valuable in a cabin?'

'That's the question I put to the Goldblatts.'

'You've spoken to them already?'

'I felt it was important for one of us to make contact with them as soon as possible in order to get all the details and to offer some reassurance. I also had a word with Mr. Tavistock,' he explained. 'The old man whose eyeglass case was stolen.'

'I would have thought he carried it with him wherever he went.'

'I'll come to that in a moment, Genevieve. Let's go back to the Goldblatts first. They're a middle-aged couple from New Jersey. Their daughter is getting married in the New Year and they felt that a set of solid silver cutlery would make an ideal wedding present. When they saw it in the shop, they fell in love with it and couldn't bear to be parted with it on the voyage. Mr. Goldblatt told me that they liked to take it out so they could just look at it. Thank goodness they did.'

'Why?'

'The theft might not have been discovered otherwise. Only the cutlery was taken, not the box it came in. The Goldblatts were devastated when they found out.'

'What about this other victim?' asked Genevieve, looking at the name on the piece of paper. 'Mr. Clifford Tavistock.'

'He was enraged,' recalled Dillman. 'Mr. Tavistock was

born in England but he now lives in retirement in Washington, D.C. Collecting old eyeglass cases is his hobby. He has some that date back over a hundred years.'

'Did people wear glasses then?'

'Yes, Genevieve. From what Mr. Tavistock was telling me, I'd say they took more care of them in those days. They certainly spent more on cases to keep them in. The one that was stolen was made of silver and ivory. It cost vastly more than the glasses it was designed to hold.' He spoke through clenched teeth. 'As our discriminating thief knew only too well.'

'Is it this Max Hirsch you've told me about?'

'Who else? There's a definite pattern here.'

'It won't be easy to conceal sixty-four pieces of cutlery.'

'No,' he agreed. 'That's why I went straight to his cabin when Mr. Buxton told me the news. Hirsch wasn't there, and he didn't show up in the dining saloon this evening either. I think he was out on the prowl again.'

'Breaking into people's cabins while they were eating their food.'

'Exactly. My guess is that he's still at work right now, Genevieve. When I've taken you back to your cabin, I'm going to search for the elusive Mr. Hirsch.'

'At this time of night?'

' "We Never Sleep." '

'It certainly looks as if *he* doesn't.' She put the slip of paper in her purse. 'What about these latest victims? Should I speak with them?'

'Yes, please. They could do with some soft words and reassurance. Tell them that we're making every effort to recover their property. Mr. Tavistock was in a terrible state. You'd have thought he'd lost a wife, not an eyeglass case. Calm him down.'

'I'll do my best, George.'

'In the meantime, I'll go out on patrol.' He took her hand to help her up. 'I can think of more enjoyable ways to spend a night, but duty comes first, alas.' He gave her a warm hug. 'I feel revived already.'

'You don't have to escort me back to my cabin, you know.'

'Try stopping me.'

She brushed his lips with a kiss. Dillman opened the door and they stepped out into a deserted passageway. They walked side by side toward the grand staircase.

'Nobody about,' she remarked. 'Everyone must have gone to bed.'

'Not everyone,' he said quietly. 'Some people work a night shift, I'm afraid.'

As they went ever deeper into the bowels of the ship, Glyn Bowen was puzzled. 'Where are we going, Mansell?' he asked, trailing behind his friend.

'Shut up and follow me,' grunted the other.

'But where are you taking that stuff?'

'To a safe hiding place.'

Price stopped and whirled around to face him. In his hands were the stolen implements, covered in the piece of sacking. He extended his arms toward Bowen.

'We can't leave this lot in the cabin,' he said.

'Why not?'

'Because someone might find them, you idiot.'

'Not if you stuff them under your mattress.'

'No? And what happens when the steward comes to make the bed?'

'I never thought of that, Mansell,' admitted the other.

'You wouldn't.' He set off again, Bowen at his heels. 'Why take chances? All we need is a hiding place before we get the lie of the land around that security room. Then tomorrow – we dig for gold.'

Bowen gave a shudder. He had profound misgivings about the plan but knew he was powerless to dissuade his friend from going ahead with it. Trying to overcome his sense of foreboding, he went down the companionway that led between the orlop deck and the lower orlop. Mansell Price seemed to know where he was going. Bowen tagged along, conscious that they were now well below the water-line and suffering from the first hints of a claustrophobia that he'd never experienced when down a coal mine. They reached a large metal door and Price came to a halt.

'Nobody will find the tools down here,' he asserted, putting them on the floor.

'Where are we?'

'The cargo hold.'

'But that'll be locked, won't it?'

'I thought of that, Glyn.'

Taking a penknife from his pocket, Price selected a blade, then inserted it in the lock. He had to twist it experimentally for a couple of minutes before he heard the telltale click. Easing the door open, he peered inside. The hold was at the forward end of the vessel, filled with the passengers' luggage and items of freight for delivery to New York. As their eyes grew accustomed to the gloom, they picked out a shape that was looming above everything around it.

'Hey,' said Bowen, his curiosity rising. 'What's that?'

'Looks like a car,' said Price.

'I didn't expect to find one of those down here.'

'Forget that. The only thing we're interested in is that gold. Though I daresay we'd have easier pickings if we rifled our way through some of this luggage. Problem is that we'd have nowhere to stash it.' He snapped his fingers. 'Pass me that stuff.'

'Where are you going to put it?'

'In here somewhere.'

Price stepped into the dark cavern and worked his way around a large wooden box, proceeding with care. He found a gap between the box and a crate that stood behind it and inserted a leg to see how much room there was.

'Give it to me, Glyn,' he hissed.

'I'm coming,' said the other, gathering up the tools and moving into the cargo hold. 'It's so creepy. I wouldn't fancy being stuck down here on my own.'

'Look where you're going,' scolded Price as his friend bumped into him. He took the tools from Bowen and placed them in the gap between the box and the crate. 'There,' he said, straightening up. 'Perfect place to hide them. We can pick them up tomorrow night when we actually do the job.'

'If you say so, Mansell.'

'I do say so,' affirmed the other. 'Don't try to back out on me now.'

'I won't.'

Bowen gave a sudden yelp of surprise and bumped into Price once more.

'What the hell's going on?' complained the latter.

'Sorry,' said the other, bending his knees slightly to grope around with his hand. 'I thought I felt something brush against my ankles.'

'A rat probably. You ought to be used to them after all those years down the pit. I've had dozens of them running over my boots in the dark.'

'This was bigger than a rat, Mansell, believe me.'

'Whatever it was, it can stay down here. Come on. Let's get out.'

Bowen was eager to comply. Price followed him out, grasped the door and pulled it hard. There was a satisfying click. Pleased with his choice of a hiding place, he went off in the direction of the security room with his reluctant accomplice in tow.

When they reached her cabin, Genevieve Masefield wanted to invite him in, but she abided by the terms of their agreement. Dillman had made the suggestion and she saw its value; while they were working in the ship, they had to set their personal relationship aside. There would be ample time for togetherness when they reached New York. Meanwhile, she contented herself with a brief kiss.

'It seems so unfair to you, George,' she said.

'What does?'

'I have this wonderful cabin in first class while you're down in second.'

'It could be worse,' he said with a grin. 'I might be in steerage, sharing a cabin with five other people. Think of that. Besides, you deserve the best, Genevieve.'

'You're a perfect gentleman.'

'My one big failing.' He kissed a finger, then tapped the end of her nose with it. 'But seriously, it's much better this way. We widen our opportunities. You cover first class while I cover second. And you blend in more easily up here. Let's face it,' he pointed out, 'I'd never have been accepted into the Belfrage circle in the way you were. Donald Belfrage despises Americans.'

'Some of us are more discerning.'

'I'm glad to hear it. Pleasant dreams.'

'Don't stay up too late.'

He raised a palm, then went off toward the grand staircase. Genevieve watched him go and heaved a sigh of disappointment. When she first met Dillman, on the maiden voyage of the *Lusitania*, she had completely misjudged him and had never suspected for a moment that he was a detective in the employ of the Cunard Line. Adversity had drawn them together and allowed her to see the man concealed behind the professional mask. In the months since then, she had learned a great deal about George Porter Dillman, all of it to his credit, and in the process, she had been taught a lot about herself. She was still musing on that fact when she let herself into the cabin and switched on the light.

Something stared up at her from the floor. It was a white envelope that had been pushed under her door. Genevieve picked it up. Nothing was written on the envelope itself, and the note inside was perfunctory. Three words were written in a looping hand: 'Where *were* you?'

The message was unsigned, and that only served to make it rather unsettling. Genevieve wondered who sent it and why it had such an aggrieved tone. She had made no arrangement to meet anyone in her cabin. It troubled her that someone had come here in expectation of seeing her alone. Had the note been written by Harvey Denning? He seemed the most likely correspondent. Or had Donald Belfrage somehow slipped away from his wife to visit her cabin while she was in second class talking to Dillman? Only one other possibility came to mind. Perhaps the message was referring to the fact that she did not appear in the dining saloon that evening. Unaware of her invitation to join the Belfrages in their regal suite, had someone missed her enough at the table to register a protest by means of an anonymous note?

That brought the name of Orvill Delaney to mind....

Dillman's perambulations were not without incident. He patrolled the ship for well over an hour, during which time he directed three hopelessly lost passengers back to their cabins, rescued a drunken man from spending the entire night asleep in an alcove, and acted as the peacemaker between a furious wife and the repentant husband whom she had locked out of their cabin. What the detective did not see was anything that gave the slightest grounds for suspicion. There were no trespassing Welshmen pretending to have gone astray, and no bald-headed thief with a brief-case in his hand. Dillman decided to call it a day and retire to bed.

On Tuesday morning, while the *Mauretania* was still feeling the effects of the storm, Dillman was being reminded of his part in the securing of the spare anchor. The muscles in his arms and shoulders ached and there were sharp twinges in his back. In spite of the discomfort, he was up at the crack of dawn to pursue his inquiries. Having located the steward who was responsible for Max Hirsch's cabin, he took the man along with him and pounded on the door. There was no answer.

'Maybe he's still asleep,' said the steward.

'Knock harder.'

The steward, a beefy little man with a red face, used his fist to beat on the door, but the noise produced no response. At a signal from Dillman, he used his key to open the door and step deferentially into the cabin.

'Good morning, Mr. Hirsch,' he said. 'I'm sorry to intrude, but there's a gentleman who's anxious to see you.' He looked over at the bed. 'He's not here, Mr. Dillman.'

'Are you sure?' said the other, coming into the cabin.

'Look, sir. The bed hasn't been slept in.'

'Did you turn it down last night?'

'Yes, sir. Usual time.'

'Was the cabin empty then?'

'Completely.'

'Thank you,' said Dillman, gazing around. 'I'll take over here now. You have other things to get on with, I'm sure.'

'Oh, yes. Lots of them, sir. Excuse me.'

Letting himself out, the steward closed the door after him. Dillman began a systematic search. He went carefully through every drawer and cupboard, paying particular attention to every item of clothing in the wardrobe. No hidden booty came to light. He even burrowed underneath the mattress in case something was secreted there, but it was all to no avail. Everything was as it should be. A tidy man, Max Hirsch kept all his things neatly arranged. Unless they were put back where they should be, he would be aware that the cabin had been searched. Dillman made sure that each item was returned to its rightful place. He did not wish to alert the thief.

After one last look around the cabin, he let himself out and walked down the passageway. His departure was timely. Seconds after he left, someone walked up to the cabin and tapped politely on the door. Dillman heard the noise and turned around. A rather pathetic sight greeted him. Tired and anxious, Agnes Cameron was trying to make contact with her newfound friend. Dark pouches under her eyes showed that she'd had little sleep during the night. Her hunched shoulders and tense body indicated the state of distress she was in. Dillman's sympathy for her welled up. Deserted by Hirsch at the dinner table, Mrs. Cameron had come in search of explanation and solace. He could see her fighting to hold in tears. When she knocked again on the door, Dillman walked back toward her.

'I'm afraid that Mr. Hirsch is not there,' he said softly.

'What?' she replied, turning to face him. 'Oh, it's you, Mr. Dillman.'

'Good morning, Mrs. Cameron. I wanted to speak with him myself, but he didn't respond when I knocked on the door of the cabin.'

'But he *must* be here. Where else can he be?'

'I've no idea, I'm afraid.'

'He promised me faithfully that we'd dine together yesterday,' she said, taking a handkerchief from her sleeve to dab at a solitary tear. 'But he never turned up.'

'Did he leave no message for you?'

'None at all, Mr. Dillman.'

'When did you last see him?'

'Over luncheon yesterday,' she explained. 'We had such a lovely time together. Then the weather took a turn for the worse and Max – that's Mr. Hirsch – very kindly escorted me back to my cabin. We arranged to meet last evening in the dining saloon.'

'Did he give you any hint as to where he was going after he left you in the afternoon?'

'Back here, he said. To his cabin. He was feeling a little unwell and wanted to have a lie-down. That's the sort of man he is, Mr. Dillman,' she said proudly. 'Even though he was queasy when the ship started to roll, he insisted on taking me back to my own cabin first. Mr. Hirsch was so considerate. He'd *never* let me down.'

'I'm sure he wouldn't, Mrs. Cameron.'

'This must be reported to the purser,' she announced. 'He's disappeared.'

'So it would seem.'

'When I left the dining saloon yesterday evening, I came straight here, but there was no sign of him. I looked high and low. That's why I got up so early this morning,' she said, fatigue in her voice. 'I was hoping against hope that I'd find him safely back in his cabin. He *must* be somewhere on the vessel.'

'Then he'll soon be found. But there's no need for you to distress yourself any further, Mrs. Cameron,' said Dillman, seeing another tear form. 'Let me report this to the purser. I'm sure that Mr. Buxton will organize a search at once.'

'And when they find Mr. Hirsch...'

'I'll make sure that you're the first to know.'

Agnes Cameron could contain her feelings no longer.

Bursting into tears, she brought both hands up to her face. Dillman put a consoling arm around her.

'Let's get you back to your cabin, shall we?' he said.

With a busy morning ahead of her, Genevieve Masefield decided to make an early start. Breakfast at this time of day, she reasoned, would also free her from the attentions of her mystery correspondent since he probably was not even awake yet. When she reached the dining saloon, however, she was surprised to see how many other early risers were already there, examining the menu or munching their food. Choosing a table in an alcove, Genevieve ordered her own breakfast, then looked around. There was no sign of Donald Belfrage, and she had the feeling that Harvey Denning was a man who preferred to languish in bed of a morning. That ruled out two suspects. But the third was actually in the room. Sipping his orange juice, Orvill Delaney was listening to something his companion was saying, then nodding in agreement. Neither he nor Patrick Skelton, beside him, paid any attention to Genevieve. She was grateful for that and shifted her seat to keep her back to them.

Her presence did not go unnoticed for long. A graceful figure materialized. 'Good morning!' said Katherine Wymark cheerfully.

'Good morning,' replied Genevieve. 'Would you care to join me?'

'As long as your friends don't mind. They seem very territorial.'

'They were also very tired when I left them last night. My guess is that they're all still snoring peacefully in bed. Besides,' she went on, 'I'm not their exclusive property.'

'I'm glad to hear it.'

Katherine lowered herself into a seat and reached for the menu. Even at this time of the morning, she looked her best: sleek, well-groomed, and immaculately dressed. Genevieve estimated that she must have spent far longer in front of a mirror than she herself had been prepared to do. A waiter took Katherine's order, freeing her to concentrate on her companion.

'What has you up so bright and early?' she asked.

'I like to make full use of the day,' said Genevieve. 'Somehow, I just can't lie in bed of a morning for hours on end.'

'My husband can. Walter rarely gets up before ten.'

'Isn't that rather unfair to you?'

'Not at all,' said Katherine airily. 'I just begin the day quietly on my own. Being apart from time to time is an important part of marriage. *Our* marriage, in any case. You have to give each other space in which to grow and blossom.' She gave a smile. 'But I'm quite certain that you've already found that out.'

'I've never been married, Mrs. Wymark.'

'A wedding ring is not always necessary. You understand men.'

'Do I?'

'Oh, I think so, Miss Masefield.'

There was a pause. 'Do you play chess yourself?' asked Genevieve.

'Chess? No, it's far too complicated for me.'

'But your husband seems to enjoy it.'

'Walter will play anything when there's a chance of winning money at it.'

Genevieve was shocked. 'There's cash involved?'

'Of course,' said the other. 'Orvill Delaney is something of a gambler as well. He and my husband talk the same language. Instead of playing cards in the smoking room, they prefer to have a quiet game of chess. No law against that, is there?'

'None at all, Mrs. Wymark.'

'Good.' A thought nudged her. 'Oh, I meant to ask you about that friend of yours.'

'What friend?'

'You may well ask, Miss Masefield. You've made so many in such a short time, and I'm pleased to be among them. But the lady I have in mind is the one who managed to lose her watch.'

'Ah, yes. Mrs. Dalkeith.'

'That was the name. Did she ever find the watch?'

'Fortunately, she did.'

'I'm pleased to hear that.'

'Mrs. Dalkeith had simply mislaid it,' said Genevieve, making no reference to the way in which the watch had been returned. 'She was thrilled to have it back.'

'Then it was in vain, was it?'

'What was?'

'Your detective work,' said Katherine with the tiniest hint of mockery.

'The watch is back where it should be, Mrs. Wymark. That's all that concerns me.'

'Quite so.'

There was another pause as their breakfast arrived. The two waiters unloaded it onto the table, then quietly withdrew. Katherine reached for her grapefruit juice.

'What does the day hold for you?' she asked, taking a first taste.

'Oh, I have a number of people to see and things to pack in.'

'I'm in the same position myself. I just hope that the weather is a little less menacing today. It takes the edge off one's enjoyment.'

At that moment, a middle-aged man strolled up to their table and stopped to give a polite bow. Tall, stiff, and rather formal, he had a faintly old-fashioned air about him.

'Oh, good morning, Mr. Fenby,' said Katherine smoothly. She indicated her friend. 'Have you met Genevieve Masefield?'

'I've not had that pleasure.' He gave another bow. 'Edgar Fenby.'

'How do you do, Mr. Fenby?' said Genevieve, recognizing him as the bearded man whom she had seen talking with Katherine Wymark on an earlier occasion. 'Are you enjoying the voyage?'

'Very much. One meets such interesting people.'

After a third bow, he went off to join friends at a table on the other side of the saloon. Genevieve found his manner a little strained, but Katherine looked after him with an indulgent smile.

'We met Edgar in London,' she explained. 'He's so irre-
deemably English, isn't he? Walter likes him, and that's not
always the case with his business associates.'

'Business associates?'

'He and Edgar have done a few deals in the past.'

'I see.'

'My husband buys and sells, Miss Masefield. He uses a
more polite word for it, but that's what it comes down to,
and it's certainly lucrative enough. Also,' she said, taking
another sip of her grapefruit juice, 'it does bring characters
like Edgar Fenby into our social circle. I think he's rather
sweet in a subdued kind of way.'

'Yes,' said Genevieve without conviction.

'Do I hear a note of disapproval?'

'No, Mrs. Wymark. I've only just met him. I haven't
formed a judgment one way or the other. Mr. Fenby seems
like an extremely nice man, but you know him much better
than I do. He is, as you say, a typical Englishman.'

'I find that refreshing.'

They addressed themselves to their breakfast and
confined themselves to more neutral topics of conversation. Genevieve was not relishing her company as much as
she had in the past, and she could not understand why. For
her part, Katherine Wymark was as relaxed and urbane as
ever. They were eating their toast before the American
woman dropped a casual remark.

'What do you think of your new admirer?' she asked.

'Admirer?'

'You must've spotted him, Miss Masefield. He hasn't
taken his eyes off you for the last ten minutes. I ought to
be jealous, I suppose,' she teased, 'because at first I thought
he was looking at me, but you're the one who has caught
his eye.'

'Am I?'

'No question of that. Look to your left. Orvill Delaney's
table.'

Genevieve tensed. She had deliberately taken up a position with her back to Delaney so that she would not have
to meet his glances. The thought that he might have sent

the anonymous note worried her, and she wanted to be spared any meaningful looks he might send her way. When she glanced around now, she saw that Delaney had already left the room. Four people were still at the table he had vacated, but only one was gazing in her direction. He was the last person whose interest she expected to arouse. Staring at her with a quiet intensity was the young Englishman whom she had met briefly on the previous day. Patrick Skelton was not as reserved and preoccupied as he had been on that occasion. His gaze was polite, but unrelenting. Genevieve thought about the note that had been pushed under her door, and her stomach lurched.

The search began at once. As soon as Dillman reported the disappearance of Max Hirsch, the purser summoned four men and put them under the direction of the American. They were thorough. Beginning on the boat deck, they worked their way slowly down through the whole vessel, looking, questioning, searching every corner, using an array of master keys to let themselves into unoccupied cabins, even scouring the boiler rooms in an attempt to find the missing man.

Dillman had a growing sense of unease. A man as cunning and experienced as Max Hirsch was unlikely to have gone astray. Nor would he have taken up with another woman when he and Agnes Cameron had become so close. As they worked their way through steerage, then shifted their search to the lower decks, Dillman's fears began to harden. Something had happened to the thief with the penchant for silver. Three patient hours failed to turn up the slightest clue as to his whereabouts. When he returned to the purser's office, Dillman was pessimistic.

'No sign of him, Mr. Buxton,' he announced.

'The man must be on the ship somewhere.'

'Well, we couldn't find him and we left no stone unturned, I promise you.'

'What on earth could have happened to the fellow?'

'I'm wondering if he may have chanced his arm once too often.'

'What do you mean?' asked Buxton.

'Hirsch has been very lucky so far,' explained Dillman. 'He was my prime suspect for all those thefts, but I just didn't have any firm evidence. He made sure of that. At one point he almost laughed in my face. I think he may have become overconfident and chosen the wrong victim.'

'Someone caught him and gave him a good hiding?'

'It could be even worse than that, Mr. Buxton.'

'Worse?'

'Yes,' said Dillman solemnly. 'There's only one conclusion that we can reach. For reasons unknown, Max Hirsch is no longer on board the *Mauretania*.'

'There has to be a hierarchy aboard ship, Mrs. Littlejohn.'

'You're a seafaring man yourself. You're bound to defend it.'

'I don't really have time to defend anything just now,' he said, trying to get away.

'But I haven't told you about the worst theft, Mr. Dillman.'

'The worst one?'

'Yes,' she said. 'I caught wind of it by accident, and I'm on my way to the purser now to see if the rumour is true or not.'

'What rumour?'

'Someone in first class had a complete set of solid silver cutlery stolen.'

'Indeed?'

'I'm wondering if the crimes might be related.'

'Related? I'm not sure that I follow, Mrs. Littlejohn.'

'Then you'd never make a detective,' she teased, giving him a playful nudge. 'Think of what was taken. Crowbars, a trolley, and presumably a large box in which the cutlery was kept. What if the crowbar was used to get into the cabin and the trolley to wheel away the stolen property? It might have been concealed in some way. I mean, a man with a box of cutlery under his arm would be rather conspicuous. But someone wheeling a trolley that was loaded with other items would pass unnoticed.' She touched his arm. 'Do you see what I'm getting at, Mr. Dillman?'

'You think a member of the crew is involved?'

'He must be. Who else would know where to find those things? Besides, if you or I or any other passenger were seen with a trolley, we'd arouse immediate suspicion. But it would look quite normal for a steward to be delivering a load of boxes somewhere.'

'That's true,' he conceded.

'I'm going to mention my theory to the purser,' she said smugly. 'Yes, and I want to ask him about that black cat as well. Wherever I go, I keep seeing it.'

'That's Bobo.'

'Who?'

'The ship's mascot. Bobo has the run of the ship.'

'That's certainly true. He's ubiquitous.'

'Just like you, Mrs. Littlejohn,' he said with a smile.

Before she could detain him any longer, he made an excuse and withdrew.

Dillman was irritated by the conversation with the journalist. Much as he liked the woman herself, he was annoyed that she had heard about the theft of the tools from the third-class kitchens, and perplexed that she knew about the disappearance of a trolley when that crime had not even been reported to the purser.

What really peeved him was the fact that she had somehow become aware of the theft of the silverware from the Goldblatts' cabin, though her assumption that it was taken in its box showed that she had no knowledge of the details. Maurice Buxton, he knew, would not provide those details to her or to anyone else. Like Dillman, the purser had impressed upon the Goldblatts the need to keep the news about their loss from the other passengers because it would cause unnecessary fears and might, in practical terms, hamper the investigation carried out by the detectives. If rumours of the theft had reached Hester Littlejohn's ears, they might also have spread farther afield, and that was a source of worry.

There was one consolation to be drawn from the chat. Bobo had been sighted. In her ceaseless movement about the ship, the inquisitive Mrs. Littlejohn had seen the black cat a number of times. Dillman would speak to Alexandra Jarvis on the subject, grateful that there was at least one person aboard to whom he could give good news.

— — —

It was her third visit to a distraught passenger that morning. After spending an hour with Ralph Goldblatt, trying to offer sympathy and comfort, Genevieve Masefield had gone on to Clifford Tavistock's cabin to repeat the process. The Englishman was still mortified at the loss of his eyeglass case, baffled that someone should take an item that only a collector like himself would truly appreciate. It took even longer for Genevieve to placate him, and she was forced to listen to an instructive, if meandering, lecture on his hobby while she did so. Dillman caught up with her outside the first-class lounge. After passing on the tidings about Max Hirsch's strange and inexplicable disappearance, he gave her another assignment.

It proved to be the most difficult of the three. Agnes Cameron was in torment. 'What can have happened to him, Miss Masefield?' she wailed.

'We'll soon find out, Mrs. Cameron.'

'But I reported him missing *hours* ago. The purser promised me faithfully that he'd instigate a search at once. Hasn't he done that?'

'I believe that it's still under way,' said Genevieve.

'After all this time?'

'Mr. Hirsch is proving rather elusive.'

They were in Mrs. Cameron's cabin, and it looked as if the woman would not be stirring from it for some time. It was almost as though she were in mourning. Eyes red-rimmed from continuous weeping, she sat on the edge of her chair with her body contorted, her hands clasped tightly, and her face lacerated with anxiety. Genevieve was patient. Whatever she and Dillman might suspect about the man, Mrs. Cameron obviously loved him and that fact had to be respected. It would be cruel to even hint that she had given her affection to a man who was a compulsive thief. Pencil poised, Genevieve sat with her notebook on her knee.

'Let's go through it all from the start,' she suggested. 'You say that you first met Mr. Hirsch on the boat train from Euston?'

'That's right. I shared a compartment with him. He was extraordinary,' Mrs. Cameron replied, a nostalgic smile breaking through the cloud of despair. 'He made us all laugh. I tend to be rather shy on such occasions, and the Rosenwalds – an American couple who were also in the compartment – were even more diffident. But that didn't trouble Max. I think he saw us as a challenge. In no time at all, he had us chatting away as if we'd been friends for years. That's quite a gift, Miss Masefield.'

'It must be.'

'And it was all done so effortlessly.'

'What happened then?' asked Genevieve. 'When you reached Liverpool.'

'He took me under his wing,' said the other. 'He insisted on carrying my bag and escorting me through the customs hall. It was wonderful to be looked after again.' A defensive note came into her voice. 'I don't want you to get the wrong idea about him,' she insisted. 'Max wasn't taking advantage in any way. Nobody could have been more courteous. I know that I was the only person in the compartment travelling on my own, but that wasn't why he took such an interest in me. It was mutual. I suppose you might call it an attraction of opposites. We had this affinity. Has that ever happened to you?'

'Only once, Mrs. Cameron.'

'It was a little breathtaking, to be honest.'

'I'm sure.'

'Things like that just don't happen to women of my age.'

'They did in your case.'

'Yes. It was magical.'

Genevieve made a few notes and gave her a brief opportunity to bask in her memories. Agnes Cameron had a reflective glow. Her spirits were temporarily lifted.

'What I really need,' said Genevieve softly, 'is a precise record of the time that you and Mr. Hirsch spent with each other. Obviously, you embarked together.'

'Yes, Miss Masefield. And we stood side by side at the rail to wave at the crowd. What a moving occasion that was! I've never been on a maiden voyage before and had no idea that there would be so much excitement.'

'It was rather overwhelming, wasn't it?'

'Completely. But to return to your question, Max and I shared the same table that evening in the second-class dining saloon, and we got even closer. He asked me if I'd care for a short stroll on deck later on.'

'Later on?'

'He said that he had a few things to do first.'

'Did you agree to go with him?'

'Of course.' The defensive note intruded again. 'Please don't misunderstand. I'm not given to casual relationships with complete strangers. In fact, if anyone had told me that I'd be walking around a deck that evening with a man I met on a boat train, I'd have thought they were mad. It's so out of character for me, Miss Masefield, and yet it seemed so perfectly natural at the time.'

'When did you next see Mr. Hirsch?' asked Genevieve.

'Over breakfast on Sunday. We also met for a mid-morning cup of coffee.'

'What about luncheon?'

'We were at the same table as the Rosenwalds. And for dinner.'

'You and Mr. Hirsch hardly ever seem to have been apart.'

'Oh, we were,' corrected the other. 'Max had work to do. He went off from time to time. Also, he told me that he didn't want to monopolize me in case it prevented me from making other friends. But he was the only one that I cared about,' she said with feeling. 'As far as I was concerned, he could monopolize me all he wanted. It was like a dream, Miss Masefield. I just never thought it could happen again.'

'It?'

'Meeting someone who aroused such strong feelings in me.' She raised a hand to brush back a strand of hair. 'When my husband died, I hardly dared to look at another man. It seemed vaguely improper. I'd been very happily married for fifteen years, you see, and wanted to stay true to my husband's memory. It turned me into something of a recluse, but I didn't worry about that. I almost enjoyed it. Does that sound peculiar?'

'Not at all, Mrs. Cameron.'

'We had no children, alas, so I was left completely alone. What kept preying on my mind was the fact that we'd never managed to fulfil an ambition that my husband had nursed for years. He always wanted us to visit America.'

She gave a rueful smile. 'It wasn't so much an ambition as an obsession. After brooding on it for months, I thought I'd make the trip on his behalf, so to speak.' She winced slightly. 'Nobody warned me about the kind of weather we might run into on an Atlantic crossing in November. Yesterday was really frightening.'

'You saw Mr. Hirsch at breakfast, I believe?'

'Yes. Then we met again for luncheon.'

'And after that?'

'He brought me back here before going off to lie down in his own cabin.'

'Could you give me an exact time, please.'

'It must have been around two-thirty in the afternoon,' recalled the other. 'Just as the storm was building up. And that was the last time I saw him.'

'Did you arrange to dine together?'

'We did, Miss Masefield. And I made him promise to be there on time. He was rather late for one of our other meals and I chided him a little about that.' She used a handkerchief to blow her nose. 'You can imagine how I felt when I sat there in the dining saloon for well over an hour. It was humiliating.'

'So what did you do?'

Agnes Cameron told her about the sudden flight from the table and the fruitless search for her admirer. Genevieve had already heard Dillman's account of his meeting with the woman that morning, but it was interesting to be given the other's version. She was deeply sorry for Mrs. Cameron. All the evidence was pointing to the fact that Max Hirsch might no longer be on board, but she did not wish to distress her companion any further by suggesting that. The latter had obviously suffered enough already. She looked to Genevieve for a crumb of comfort.

'Where can he be?' she asked softly.

'We'll soon have the answer, I'm sure.'

'I couldn't bear it if anything nasty had happened to Max.'

'Then let's hope it hasn't, Mrs. Cameron.'

'You don't think...' The woman's voice trailed away.

Then she made an effort to ask a question that clearly caused her pain. 'You don't think he may have found someone else, do you?'

'There's no chance of that,' said Genevieve, quick to reassure her. 'You and Mr. Hirsch obviously had a deep and trusting relationship, even though you've known each other for such a short time. From what you tell me, he was a very loyal man.'

'He was, Miss Masefield. He doted on me.'

'Then rule out any fears on that score.' Genevieve looked down at her notes. 'You and Mr. Hirsch were in each other's company so much that he wouldn't have had time to meet anyone else. Besides,' she said, glancing up, 'why would he look elsewhere when he had the friendship of someone like you?'

'It's kind of you to say so.'

'You and he were effectively a couple.'

'We were, Miss Masefield. That's exactly what Max called us. A couple.'

'And is this a complete list of the times you spent together?' asked Genevieve, tapping her notebook with the pencil. 'You haven't left anything out, have you?'

'No,' replied the other quickly. 'I haven't.'

But they both knew she was lying.

Still continuing his search, Dillman elected to forgo luncheon, but he did make a point of stopping into the first-class kitchens. He found the steward who was responsible for bringing up supplies from the storage areas and the refrigeration units. Dillman took the man aside and explained his position on the vessel.

'I understand you had a trolley stolen?' he began.

'Yes, sir.'

'Why didn't you report the theft to the purser?'

'Because I wasn't completely sure it was stolen,' said the steward. 'I thought someone might just have borrowed it. That sort of thing often happens.'

'When did the trolley go missing?'

'Yesterday evening.'

'Did you go in search of it?'

'Of course, sir. But there was no sign of it until this morning.'

'What do you mean?'

'It turned up again.'

'Where?'

'In the place where I normally keep it,' explained the steward. 'The little room at the back. So I was right. It wasn't stolen at all. I knew it would turn up eventually.'

'Who could have taken it?'

'Somebody from one of the other galleys, probably. Or even some joker from around here. Working in a kitchen all day can get a bit boring. There're a couple of stewards who're always trying to liven things up by playing tricks on the rest of us. One of them may have hidden the trolley on purpose.'

'That's one explanation, I suppose.'

'The most likely, sir,' said the other. 'I mean, it has to be a member of the crew. What use would any of the passengers have for a trolley like that?'

Dillman smiled inwardly as he remembered Hester Littlejohn's theory about the theft of the cutlery. Even the industrious Max Hirsch, pillaging on a regular basis, could not have stolen enough property to justify the use of a trolley. The steward's suggestion was the most convincing, and it gave Dillman a degree of comfort; one allegedly stolen item could be crossed off his list. Like Mrs. Dalkeith's watch, the trolley seemed to have come back of its own accord.

After thanking the steward, he made his way to the second-class lounge, hoping for a brief word with Alexandra Jarvis. Seated beside her grandmother, the girl was reading a book. She looked up with a grin as her friend bore down on her.

'Hello, Mr. Dillman,' she said.

'Hello, Ally,' he replied. 'Nice to see you again, Mrs. Pomeroy.'

'Thank you,' said the old woman. 'We didn't notice you in the dining saloon.'

'No, I wasn't hungry.'

Alexandra spoke up eagerly. 'Is there any sign of Bobo yet, Mr. Dillman?'

'Yes, Ally,' he told her. 'That's why I came over to see you.'

'Where is he?'

'I can't say for sure, but he's definitely about. I spoke to someone earlier who'd seen him lots of times in the past twenty-four hours.'

'Has he been back to Mr. Reynolds' cabin for his food?'

'I'm not sure.'

'I'd be ever so grateful if you could find out for me. Daddy won't let me go anywhere near Bobo, and I think that's cruel. Isn't it, Granny?' she asked, stroking the old woman's arm. 'You'd let me feed the cat, wouldn't you?'

'Yes,' agreed the other, 'as long as you didn't take food off my plate.'

She let out a cackle. Dillman was fond of Lily Pomeroy. She took an almost childlike glee in flouting convention and in expressing herself freely. Her gaudy attire was an act of senile rebellion in itself. Alexandra was much happier in the company of her grandmother than she was under the more repressive regime of her parents.

'I wonder where Bobo is now,' she said wistfully.

'Safe and sound, Ally.'

'Thank you so much for telling me that, Mr. Dillman.'

'I hope it's put your mind at rest,' he said. 'I never had the slightest worry about him myself. Cats have a knack of making the most of things. On a cold day like this, Bobo has probably sneaked off to the warmest place on the ship.'

'Where's that?'

'The boiler rooms. I'll bet he's curled up in front of a furnace right now.'

Bobo liked his new domain. The cargo hold was quiet, spacious, and filled with interesting objects to sniff and explore. He spent hours simply pacing out his new territory, scrutinizing boxes, rubbing against wooden crates, picking his way through neatly stacked piles of luggage, and jumping up on the multifarious items that were stowed away in the bottom of the ship. There was even a new car on which he could leave the dusty signature of his paws. When his inventory was complete, he found some sacking and settled down to spend the night on his comfortable bed, untroubled by the weather and undisturbed by any passengers. It was the happiest time he had spent so far on the ship.

Tuesday morning compelled him to revise his judgment slightly. While he still enjoyed the privacy that he had found, he noticed one alarming deficiency in the hold. It had no food supply. A careful tour around the perimeter of his empire showed him that it also lacked an exit. Bobo had no opportunity to slip back to the cabin for one of his regular meals or to forage in the kitchens for scraps. Since it was a problem he could not immediately solve, he decided to bide his time. Finding his way back to the door through which he had entered on the previous night, he hopped onto a box nearby and curled up into a ball. He was soon drifting off into a deep and restorative slumber.

'That's what it was,' said Glyn Bowen after long deliberation. 'It must have been a cat.'

'What are you going on about?' grumbled Mansell Price.

'That thing I felt brushing against my leg in the cargo hold last night. It was a cat.'

'Or a large rat.'

'No, Mansell,' said the other. 'Rats dart over your feet. They don't rub against you like this animal did. I'm certain it was a cat of some sort.'

'That must've been a disappointment for you.'

'Why?'

'Wouldn't you rather have a woman rubbing up against you in the dark?' asked Price with a lecherous grin.

'Fat chance of that!'

The two men were in the third-class smoking room, seated in two of the revolving chairs. Price was trying to manufacture a cigarette out of a series of discarded butts that he had collected from the floor. Bowen was preoccupied with the second visit he would have to make to the cargo hold. He screwed up his courage to voice his protest.

'I still have my doubts about tonight,' he said. 'I think we should call it off.'

'Too late, mun.'

'Why?'

'Because I've set everything up. I didn't go to all the trouble of borrowing those tools just to leave them in the cargo hold for a night. We've come too far to turn back now, Glyn. Don't you see that?'

'Yes, Mansell.'

'Then what are you moaning about?'

'I got this feeling in my stomach.'

'Excitement,' diagnosed the other. 'It's the same feeling you get before a rugby match. You're all worked up and raring to go.'

'But I'm not. It scares me stiff.'

'Rubbish!'

'It does, Mansell.'

Price finished rolling his cigarette, then got up to ask for a light from an old man with a clay pipe in his mouth. Returning to his seat, the Welshman inhaled deeply while staring at his friend. His eyelids narrowed to a thin slit.

'This is a two-man job, Glyn,' he warned. 'I need you.'

'Too risky.'

'Is it? Been very easy so far. We got the tools, found a hiding place for them, and staked out the security room. Stewards only patrol it once an hour. We had to hang around even longer for one of them to turn up.'

'We may not be so lucky tonight.'

'Of course we will.'

Bowen writhed in discomfort. 'Think what'll happen if we're caught,' he urged.

'I'd rather think about what'll happen if we don't take our chances,' retorted Price. 'We'll go on as we are, cadging drinks, scrounging smokes, and arriving in New York with barely enough money to last us for a week. Is that what you want?'

'You know it isn't.'

'Then do something about it. Stick to my plan.'

'It worries me.'

'This time tomorrow, you'll be thanking me,' said the other confidently. 'We'll have pocketed a tidy reward by then. You'll see.'

'If only I could believe that, Mansell.'

'You've got to believe it,' snarled Price vehemently. 'Lose your nerve and the whole thing falls to pieces. You can't go soft on me now. You're as much part of it as I am. You helped to hide those tools and you helped to keep watch on that security room. That makes you an accomplice, Glyn, like it or not.'

'I don't like it,' confessed Bowen. A hand grabbed his wrist and squeezed hard. 'But I'll go through with it,' he said reluctantly. 'I suppose I have to now.'

'Yes,' said his friend, relaxing his hold. 'You do.'

Genevieve Masefield had a late luncheon in the company of her friends. The table for eight also included the couple with whom Susan Faulconbridge and Harvey Denning had played bridge. Donald Belfrage was at his most expansive, talking about his plans to improve the estate that he had inherited and promising that he would hold regular shooting parties there.

'Good,' said Ruth Constantine. 'There are lots of people I'd like to shoot.'

'I hope I'm not on your list,' said Denning.

'No, Harvey. I don't think your head would look very nice mounted on a wall.'

'It prefers to be mounted on my shoulders.'

'What about you, Genevieve?' said Belfrage solicitously. 'You'll join us at some of our weekends, won't you?'

'If I'm invited,' she replied.

'You will be,' said Susan firmly. 'I shan't go without you, I know that. You're part of our circle now. You've been initiated.'

'Not completely,' said Denning under his breath.

Belfrage's glance seemed to convey a similar message.

Genevieve responded with a bland smile. The anonymous note was still causing her concern, and she was never allowed to forget that she might be eating a meal in the company of its sender. Belfrage was more attentive to his wife today, as if trying to atone for some earlier neglect, but he still managed to let Genevieve know that he harboured certain feelings for her. She had been careful to choose a seat that put her well out of reach of even his long legs. Denning was directly opposite her but attempted no clandestine manoeuvres beneath the table with his foot. His technique consisted of suave compliments, gentle innuendos, and the raising of a loquacious eyebrow. Neither man confirmed or denied by his manner the authorship of the note.

Genevieve was relieved to see that one of her other suspects, Patrick Skelton, was not even in the dining saloon, but she could not decide if his absence ruled him out or if he was merely lurking in readiness to ambush her elsewhere. Orvill Delaney was at a table nearby, chatting happily with a group of people as if they were lifelong friends instead of acquaintances he had made on the voyage. Genevieve was interested to see that Edgar Fenby was in the party, pushing each topic of conversation around as if passing the salt with excessive care. Walter Wymark, his business associate, was at a table in an alcove with his wife. In an almost exclusively male party, Katherine Wymark was in no way abashed, and Genevieve admired the way in which she was palpably holding her own. Her husband seemed more animated and gregarious than hitherto.

'Where've you been *all* morning, Genevieve?' asked Susan.

'Here and there,' she replied.

'I looked for you all over the place.'

'I had someone to visit, Susan.'

'Donald and I had breakfast in bed,' announced Theodora.

'Is that what they call it these days?' said Denning archly. 'There was a time when "connubial bliss" was the accepted phrase. I always regretted that I never experienced it myself.'

'Not with a wife of your own, anyway,' observed Ruth.

Brittle laughter greeted the comment. Denning did not mind that it was at his expense. He blew a kiss across the table at Ruth and got a cool stare in return. The laughter was just dying away when Orvill Delaney came over to the table.

'I didn't think that the menu was all that funny,' he said amiably. 'How do you do, Miss Masefield? Oh, and I believe that we've met as well, Miss Constantine.'

'We have indeed, Mr. Delaney.'

Ruth took charge of the introductions, and the newcomer could soon put names to all the faces. He made a few neutral comments about the weather, then started to move off. Genevieve put up a hand to catch his attention.

'I must let you have that magazine back, Mr. Delaney,' she said.

'Please keep it, Miss Masefield.'

'Are you sure?'

'I'm always looking for converts to the joys of O. Henry.'

'Well, you've certainly found one in me.'

He gave her a gracious bow, then strode out of the room. Genevieve was puzzled. His manner toward her had undergone a subtle change. He was still very courteous, but there was a wariness that had not been there before. She wondered if he might be having second thoughts about an anonymous note he had dashed off. Her companions were uniformly impressed by Orvill Delaney.

'He was almost human,' said Belfrage grudgingly.

'Unlike you,' murmured Ruth.

'Do you suppose he plays bridge?' asked Denning.

'Mr. Delaney prefers chess, actually,' said Genevieve.

'You're obviously on intimate terms with him.'

'I hardly know the man.'

'Accepting presents from him. Taking his advice about what to read. Knowing his habits and preferences.' He gave her a shrewd look. 'You've obviously been improving Anglo-American relations, Genevieve.'

'I'm glad that somebody has,' said Ruth sharply. 'If it was left to Donald, we'd be sailing to America in order to declare war on the country.'

'Colonials must be kept in their place.'

'They're not in the Empire any longer, Donald.'

'More's the pity!'

On that slightly sour note, the meal came to an end. As they got up from the table, Genevieve refused the invitation to join them in the lounge, saying she had an appointment. Denning clutched his hands against his heart in a gesture of despair, but Donald Belfrage was even more expressive. Touching her lightly on the elbow, he gave Genevieve a kiss on the cheek and whispered something in her ear that she did not quite catch. She responded to the communal farewell and made for the grand staircase, more confused than ever about the authorship of her nocturnal missive. Three men had spoken to her in the dining saloon, and each one of them was a potential correspondent.

As she descended the stairs, a fourth name resurfaced. Standing at the bottom of the first flight, Patrick Skelton looked up at her with the same intensity he had shown before. It was almost as if he were waiting for her. Genevieve was determined not to stop.

'Hello, Mr. Skelton,' she said.

'Good day to you, Miss Masefield,' he replied civilly.

Skelton stepped aside so that she could move past him. Genevieve went on down the next flight without daring to look behind her, feeling his gaze follow her all the way.

Alone in his cabin, George Porter Dillman unrolled the map on his table and held its curling edges in place with a tooth mug, a bunch of keys, and two bars of soap. A detailed plan of the *Mauretania* lay before him, showing him all that he needed to see of her interior. To Dillman's practiced eye, the ship was a true marvel, but he did not allow himself to savour the finer points of naval architecture. What he was looking for were places where Max Hirsch could conceivably be hiding, held against his will, or – the possibility had to be considered – lying dead from natural or foul means. There were nine decks in all, seven above the load line. Each offered an array of potential refuges. The orlop deck was given over exclusively to machinery, with the exception of the forward holds, where insulated space was provided for the storage of food and perishable cargo. The lower orlop deck could also be discounted.

Passenger and crew accommodations accounted for large areas of the vessel. The missing man could be in any one of several hundred cabins. The more Dillman studied the plan, the more difficult the problem became. It would take days for him to search every last corner of the vessel, and instinct was telling him that his efforts would be futile. By the time Genevieve arrived, he was starting to accept the inevitable conclusion.

'Sorry to keep you waiting,' she said, accepting his kiss of welcome as he admitted her to the cabin. 'It was tricky getting away from the luncheon table.'

'At least you sat down at one, Genevieve. I missed out on food altogether.'

'An upset tummy, or a devotion to duty?'

'I simply want to find Max Hirsch.'

'I can endorse that wish, George. So can Mrs. Cameron.' She saw the map. 'That's a novel use for a couple of bars of soap.'

'I had to improvise.'

'So did I,' sighed Genevieve. 'All the way through the meal.'

'How did you get on with Mrs. Cameron?'

'She was on the verge of collapse, poor thing. I did all I could to be supportive, but she's starting to fear the worst. It's now over twenty-four hours since she last saw him.'

'Did she have no idea of where he might be?'

'None at all. She was very grateful for the way you consoled her earlier, but rather ashamed that she'd broken down in front of you like that.'

'I didn't mind, Genevieve.'

'I don't think she realized just how much she cared for Max Hirsch.'

'How *did* he do it?' asked Dillman sceptically. 'Hypnosis?'

Genevieve sat down and took out her notebook to refresh her memory before giving him a concise account of her interview with Agnes Cameron. Dillman heard nothing he did not expect. He ran a meditative hand through his hair.

'As I see it,' he decided, 'there are three possibilities. Suicide can be excluded because Hirsch just wasn't the type. Besides, he had far too much to live for. That leaves us with the possibility that he's on board somewhere, alive or dead. The second option is that he went up on the deck during that storm yesterday and was washed overboard.'

'Only a maniac would have gone out in that tempest.'

'You're looking at one,' said Dillman with a smile. 'We now come to the third and most serious possibility. Max Hirsch is no longer on the vessel because somebody deliberately helped him off it.'

'Why would anyone do that, George?'

'Ask the Goldblatts. Ask Clifford Tavistock. Ask any of the people he robbed.' He raised a finger. 'Apart from the Rosenwalds, that is. If Hirsch went into the water, they'd be more likely to raise the alarm and man a lifeboat. Stanley and Miriam Rosenwald don't have a vengeful bone in their bodies.'

'What about his other victims? Would they hate him enough to kill him?'

'To *want* to kill him perhaps,' said Dillman, 'but I can't see any of them actually going through with it. Besides, they don't even know that Max Hirsch is the man who stole their property. They simply couldn't strike out at him.'

'So who did?'

'We don't know that anyone did, Genevieve,' he cautioned. 'All we can do is to make educated guesses, based on our knowledge of Max Hirsch and his movements.'

'Most of those seem to have been in the direction of Mrs. Cameron.'

Dillman nodded and walked across to the porthole. He gazed out at the sea, which was still turbulent but causing none of the havoc of the previous day. After again sifting through all the unanswered questions in his mind, he turned to face Genevieve.

'Where's that briefcase?' he asked.

'Briefcase?'

'According to those two Welshmen who saw him on the prowl, Hirsch was carrying a briefcase. He'd needed something to put his loot in, and a briefcase would attract less notice than a large bundle marked "Swag".' Where is it?' he asked, moving across to her. 'Yesterday afternoon it must have contained a silver-and-ivory eyeglass case and sixty-four pieces of solid silver cutlery. Nobody would throw that kind of haul overboard, surely?'

'It must still be on the ship, George.'

'And so must all the other stuff he stole. There was no sign of it in his cabin, nor of that briefcase. I was very thorough in my search. In fact,' he recalled, 'when I first began to put pressure on Hirsch, he offered me the key to his cabin. That meant he had nothing incriminating stowed away in it.'

'So where did he hide his loot?'

'With an accomplice. Except that he gave every indication of being a lone wolf.'

'Wait a moment,' said Genevieve, getting to her feet. 'Perhaps he did have an accomplice. An unwitting one maybe, but she might have provided a hiding place for him.'

'She?'

'Mrs. Cameron. I sensed that she was holding something back from me. Now I know what it was, George. Ridiculous as this may sound, I believe that Hirsch spent Sunday night in her cabin.'

'They *slept* together?' he exclaimed in astonishment.

'That's their business. I'm not their moral guardian. What I can say is that their relationship had reached a very critical point. Mrs. Cameron more or less admitted it.'

'But they only met on the boat train.'

'Passion can bubble very quickly at times,' she said with

a twinkle in her eye. 'It has to be the explanation, don't you see? Hirsch wooed her in order to have somewhere safe to hide whatever he stole. He spent the night with her on Sunday.'

'Are you certain about that?'

'Yes, George, and I'm certain about something else as well.'

'What's that?'

'Hirsch took a lot more into that cabin than a pair of pyjamas.'

THIRTEEN

Alexandra Jarvis was young enough to look disarmingly innocent, but old enough to have mastered the arts of manipulation. When she wanted something enough, there were usually ways to secure it. After displaying ten minutes of sincere but calculated affection for her grandmother, she nestled into the old woman's shoulder.

'Can I go for a walk, please, Granny?' she asked.

'No, Ally. You're to stay in here with me.'

'But I've finished my book and there's nothing else to read.'

'You heard what your parents said.'

'All they told me to do was to look after you,' said the girl artlessly.

Lily Pomeroy grinned. 'I thought it was the other way around,' she remarked, 'but I suppose that it's a bit of both, really. Anyway, you're staying put, young lady.'

'Not if *you* come for a walk with me.'

'What?'

'You must be as bored as I am with looking at the same walls. Let's go for a stroll. That's where Mummy and Daddy have gone.'

'Then you should have tagged along with them.'

'But I'd much rather be with you, Granny,' said Alexandra, leaning over to give her a kiss. 'You're kind to me. And I didn't want to have another row with Noel.'

Mrs. Pomeroy sighed and hauled herself out of her seat. 'I suppose it won't do me any harm to stretch my legs, though we're not going out on deck. It's far too cold. Hold my hand,' she ordered, grasping the girl's palm. 'I don't want you running off.'

'I wouldn't dream of it, Granny.'

'Yes you would.' They headed for the door. 'Where shall we go?'

'It doesn't matter. We'll just walk and be together.'

But she knew exactly where she wanted to take her grandmother. For her part, Lily Pomeroy had the feeling that the casual stroll had a fixed destination. She did not mind. Though she had been manoeuvred into the situation, she was prepared to indulge Alexandra. She remembered the warnings that Oliver Jarvis had given his daughter, but for the moment, her son-in-law's strictures could be quietly forgotten.

Delighted to have her own way, Alexandra led her grandmother toward the officers' quarters at a gentle pace. When she saw the door of Reynolds' cabin ajar, her hopes were raised and she broke clear of the old woman to run forward. She tapped on the door, then opened it, expecting to see Bobo munching his way through his afternoon meal. But there was no sign of the black cat. The scraps of meat in his feeding bowl were untouched. She looked up in despair at the officer.

'Where *is* he, Mr. Reynolds?' she whimpered.

'I don't know, Alexandra,' he admitted. 'Bobo will turn up soon, I'm sure.'

His smile was confident, but she saw the lingering doubt in his eyes.

Agnes Cameron was both surprised and alarmed when the two of them called on her. It was only when Dillman introduced himself properly and explained that he was leading the search for her erstwhile friend that she agreed to let them both into the cabin.

'Is there any news, Mr. Dillman?' she asked.

'I'm afraid not, Mrs. Cameron,' he said, 'but the search continues.'

'Why on earth can't you find him?'

'The *Mauretania* is the largest ship in the world. It takes time to work our way through it. After I reported Mr. Hirsch's disappearance this morning, I led a team of men

on an immediate sweep of the vessel. We looked everywhere but saw no trace of him.'

'Something has happened to him,' she said, sinking into
a chair.

'Don't jump to conclusions, Mrs. Cameron,' advised
Genevieve softly.

'Max has had an accident of some sort.'

'We don't know that.'

'I do, Miss Masefield,' said the other wearily. 'I sensed it
as soon as I woke up this morning. Max just wouldn't let
me down this way. He's far too considerate.' She turned to
Dillman. 'Tell me the truth, Mr. Dillman. Please. Don't hide
it from me.'

'Very well,' he said, lowering his voice. 'Until we learn
otherwise, Max Hirsch is missing, presumed dead.'

Agnes Cameron gasped. Genevieve touched her shoulder
in a gesture of sympathy then sat beside her. Dillman
remained on his feet. The older woman was in a delicate
condition. Her hands tightly bunched, she was trembling with
apprehension. Dillman knew that he would have to proceed
with great care. Not wishing to cause her more pain, he
foresaw that some distress was inevitable. Tact and discretion
might help to alleviate it. Genevieve's presence was another
valuable factor. They had rehearsed their approach.

'Mr. Dillman would like to ask you a few questions, Mrs.
Cameron.'

'But I've told you all I can,' protested Mrs. Cameron.

'You were extremely helpful,' said Genevieve, 'and
we're very grateful. But there are one or two things that I
didn't touch on.'

'What sort of things?'

'I'll let Mr. Dillman explain.'

'Mrs. Cameron,' he said gently, 'I'm sorry that we have
to intrude into your private life, but we need to build up a
clear picture of Mr. Hirsch.'

'But you knew him yourself, Mr. Dillman,' said Mrs.
Cameron. 'That's how we first met. You were talking to
Max on Sunday night.' She sounded faintly betrayed. 'Of
course I didn't know then that you were a detective.'

'I need to ask you about Mr. Hirsch's briefcase.'

'His briefcase?'

'Were you aware that he had one?'

'Well, yes. He came in here with it, as it happens.'

'How many times? Once? Twice?'

'I don't think that's any business of yours, Mr. Dillman,' she said, bridling.

'It's important for us to know,' explained Genevieve, leaning over to her. 'We believe that the briefcase may give us some important clues.'

'I don't see how, Miss Masefield.'

'You admit that he did bring it in here?' asked Dillman, taking over again.

'Yes,' conceded Mrs. Cameron.

'And is it in here now, by any chance?'

'No,' she denied hotly. 'It's not, Mr. Dillman. And I fail to see that Max's briefcase has anything to do with his disappearance. The most likely place you'll find it is where it should be – in his cabin.'

'I've already searched that, Mrs. Cameron. The briefcase is not there.'

'Oh. I see.'

'So Mr. Hirsch must have had it with him when he disappeared. However,' he went on, 'since he did bring it into your cabin, there's a possibility that he might have left some of its contents here.'

Mrs. Cameron jumped to her feet. 'He left nothing here!' she insisted.

'Are you quite certain?'

'Yes, Mr. Dillman.'

'Mr. Hirsch didn't ask you to hide anything for him?'

'Why should he?'

'I was hoping that you might tell me that.'

'Max never asked me to keep anything in here,' she answered firmly. 'I'm bound to say that I find some of your questions very impertinent. You've no right to come in here and badger me like this. If this goes on, I shall complain to the purser.' She sat down again. 'You should be out there right now searching for Max, not bothering me with irrelevant questions about his briefcase.'

'Unfortunately,' he said, 'they're not irrelevant.'

There was no easy way to secure her cooperation. It was time to let Genevieve take over once more. Moving a step back, Dillman gave her a nod and watched Mrs. Cameron closely. Her anger was natural and her denials genuine. If she had been Hirsch's accomplice, she obviously knew nothing about it.

'Mrs. Cameron,' began Genevieve, 'there are certain things that you don't know about Mr. Hirsch. He may have been everything that you describe, and I can understand your affection for him. By the same token,' she said, slipping in a soothing compliment, 'I can see why he was drawn to you. Mr. Hirsch was a fortunate man.'

'What is it that I'm not supposed to know about him?'

'It may come as something of a shock.'

'I won't listen to any slander about Max!' cautioned the other.

'It's not slander, Mrs. Cameron. Do you recall what you told me about Saturday evening? Over dinner, Mr. Hirsch invited you to take a stroll on deck.'

'What's wrong with that?'

'Nothing. Except that he postponed the walk until later on.'

'Max said that he had some business to attend to. I went back to my cabin to wrap up warmly and he stayed in the dining saloon.'

'The business he had to attend to was witnessed by Mr. Dillman.'

'Yes,' he confirmed. 'I saw him steal some items from the table.'

'Never!' protested Mrs. Cameron.

'I have sharp eyes. There was no doubt about it.'

'Max isn't a thief! He's the most honest man I've ever met.'

'He didn't show much of that honesty when I challenged him,' said Dillman. 'After the usual bluster that I get on these occasions, he admitted the theft and told me he'd acted on impulse. What he'd taken were a silver saltcellar and a pepper pot. He claimed that he wanted them as souvenirs for his wife.'

'But he doesn't have a wife.'

'Who knows? At the time, I gave him the benefit of the doubt. It was a grave mistake,' said Dillman, sighing heavily with regret. 'I let him go with a stern warning. If I'd had the sense to arrest him and report the theft, none of the other robberies would have occurred, because I'd bet my bottom dollar that he's behind them.'

Mrs. Cameron could not take it all in. The disappearance of a dear friend was a hard enough blow to bear. To hear that the man she revered was actually a thief was unendurable. She could only cope by disbelieving the charge. Swaying to and fro, she beat her fists on her knees.

'No, no, no!' she exclaimed. 'It's not true! It can't be true!'

'He was caught,' whispered Genevieve. 'Mr. Hirsch admitted the theft.'

'But he had no reason to steal. He was comfortably off.'

'On the proceeds of other robberies.'

'Max was a good man, Miss Masefield.'

'He was a thief, Mrs. Cameron,' she said, 'and we believe that he might have disappeared as a result of his criminal activities. That's why we need your help.' She held the other woman's hands to stop the drumming fists. 'You loved him, didn't you?' she went on. 'In his own way, I'm sure that Mr. Hirsch loved you.'

'He did,' murmured Mrs. Cameron. 'He said so.'

Genevieve left a long pause. 'When I spoke to you earlier,' she said at length, 'there was something you held back from me. I don't want to pry, but I have to ask you a very personal question. I think you can guess what it is, Mrs. Cameron, can't you?'

The other woman nodded, then glanced up with embarrassment at Dillman.

'During the time that Mr. Hirsch stayed here on Sunday night – or on any of the other occasions when he was here, for that matter – was he alone for any length of time?'

'I had to visit the bathroom, if that's what you mean.'

'What about Monday morning?'

'Really, Miss Masefield!' said the other, flushing visibly.

'I assume that Mr. Hirsch returned to his cabin?'

'Quite early in fact. He didn't want to compromise me in any way.'

'Nor do we, Mrs. Cameron,' said Genevieve. 'I can promise you that none of this will be heard outside these four walls. You've told us what we needed to know.'

Genevieve looked over at Dillman, convinced that their theory had substance to it. Mrs. Cameron was still trying to come to terms with what she had heard, shifting between disbelief and despondency, refusing to accept the charges they were making against her friend, yet sensing in her heart that the accusations might have some foundation. Her febrile mind replayed some of the conversations she'd had with Max Hirsch. Touching moments now came to seem like cruel charades. She turned to Dillman.

'Did he really tell you that he had a wife?' she asked.

'He said her name was Rachel,' he replied, 'but there's no reason to think that she ever existed. Mr. Hirsch may well have invented her on the spot.'

'Then again...'

'Forget about that,' said Genevieve, patting her wrist. 'There's no point in torturing yourself about whether or not he was married. The only way to learn the full truth about Mr. Hirsch is to find him. That brings us back to his briefcase.' She took a deep breath. 'Mrs. Cameron, we're going to ask you a very big favour.'

'Well?'

'We need your permission to search the cabin.'

'Whatever for?' retorted the other, colouring again.

'Evidence.'

'But there's nothing here. I can't let you go through my things, Miss Masefield. That would be a terrible invasion of my privacy.'

'Would you agree to conduct a search yourself?'

'There's no point.'

'I'm afraid there is, Mrs. Cameron,' said Dillman, applying gentle pressure. 'We're making a polite request at the moment. If the purser is summoned, he'll point out to you that we can insist on searching this cabin. We'd rather spare you any coercion.'

'Please,' coaxed Genevieve. 'It won't take long.'

'It would be a complete waste of time.'

'In that case, we'll apologize and leave you alone.'

'You won't find a thing, I tell you,' said Mrs. Cameron, getting up suddenly to pull open every drawer in the cabin. 'See for yourself, Miss Masefield. Go on. And look in here while you're at it,' she continued, flinging open the doors of the wardrobe. 'I have no idea of what you're after, but I'm certain it couldn't possibly be here.'

Genevieve carried out a quick but fruitless search of the drawers before moving to the wardrobe. She pushed all the garments aside so she could peer into every corner. Nothing was hidden away. Moving from indignation to open anger, Mrs. Cameron stood over her with her arms folded.

'Now are you satisfied?' she demanded.

'What's in that box?' asked Dillman, indicating the upper shelf in the wardrobe.

'A new hat I bought in London.'

'Have you worn it on board?'

'No, Mr. Dillman. Max preferred me in one of my other hats.'

'So he would know that the new one would stay in its box?'

'May I?' said Genevieve, taking down the box. She put the lid aside. 'What a pretty hat, Mrs. Cameron!' she added, lifting it out to admire it. 'Where did you buy it?'

'On Oxford Street.'

Genevieve held the hatbox in front of her so she could look down into it. 'Did you buy all these other items on Oxford Street as well?'

Mrs. Cameron blanched. 'They're not mine!' she gasped.

Moving in swiftly, Dillman extracted the silver snuffbox. 'No, Mrs. Cameron,' he confirmed. 'This belongs to Stanley Rosenwald.'

*

Maurice Buxton completed his tour with a smile of satisfaction. The last of the property stolen from second class had now been restored to its grateful owner. The purser was content. Crimes had been solved and the good name of the Cunard Line had been vindicated. He felt a weight being lifted from his back. Two major problems still existed, however, and they brought the chevrons back to his brow. Though Max Hirsch's haul had been found, the whereabouts of the thief himself were unknown. Also missing, and presumably hidden in the man's briefcase, were the eyeglass case and the cutlery taken from first-class passengers. Ralph Goldblatt and Clifford Tavistock would continue to bang on the purser's door to demand action. When Buxton reached that door, he found another unwelcome visitor loitering outside it.

Hester Littlejohn was consulting the notes in her pad. She looked up. 'Ah, here he is!' she said, beaming at him. 'Your assistant told me that you'd be back at your post very soon.'

'What can I do for you, Mrs. Littlejohn?'

'Confirm those rumours, for a start.'

'All I can say is what I told you earlier. Don't listen to idle speculation.'

'But a trolley was stolen from the first-class kitchens.'

'If you care to go back there now, I think you'll find that it's been returned. It was probably only taken by way of a practical joke.'

'What about those tools from third class?'

'Mrs. Littlejohn – '

'And that box of silverware that went astray. Was that a practical joke as well?'

'If anything goes missing,' he said with controlled politeness, 'the normal procedure is that the incident is reported to me before being handed over to the trained detectives we have on board. They are very efficient, Mrs. Littlejohn, as I have good reason to know, but they can do their job more effectively if they're not tripping over inquisitive passengers.'

'But I'm not an inquisitive passenger,' she said. 'I'm a nosy journalist.'

'That's even worse.'

'So you don't deny that those tools were stolen? And that cutlery.'

'Some people eat with crowbars. Others prefer knives and forks.'

Hester Littlejohn burst out laughing. 'I like your sense of humour, Mr. Buxton,' she said. 'I may even quote you. One last question, if I may.'

'Only if you promise to give me some breathing space afterward.'

'It's a deal.'

'Right. Ask your question, Mrs. Littlejohn.'

'Who or what are they after?'

'I don't understand.'

'Oh, come on, Mr. Buxton. You understand everything that goes on aboard the *Mauretania*. Nobody clears his throat without you having a report of it. So tell me. What is the search looking for? And don't try to fob me off. I've seen a team of men working their way along various decks today. Why?' she pressed. 'I'm no sailor, but I've got a nasty feeling that they weren't looking for leaks.'

'And I have a nasty feeling that *you* are.'

'What are they trying to find?'

'Something that I've been missing ever since we met, Mrs. Littlejohn,' he said with a friendly grin. 'Something that's very precious to me.'

'And what's that?' she asked.

'My peace of mind.'

He went into his office and closed the door firmly behind him.

'You were right, Genevieve,' he said with a congratulatory smile. 'Wonderful intuition.'

'I was getting rather worried when we seemed to have drawn a blank.'

'So was I.'

'But I was convinced the loot was in there somewhere.'

'Tucked away in a hatbox.'

'Unknown to Mrs. Cameron.'

'Who but Hirsch would have thought of a place like that?' said Dillman. 'When you opened that box, I wouldn't have been at all surprised if he'd popped out of it like a white rabbit.' He became serious. 'Except that he's given us another trick from his extensive repertoire.'

' "The Vanishing Act." '

After handing over the recovered property to the purser, they had adjourned to Dillman's cabin to review the situation. Delighted to have made some progress, they were both saddened that they'd had to do so at the expense of Agnes Cameron. She had been horrified at the discovery in her wardrobe, and heartbroken to learn that her romance with Max Hirsch had a mercenary side to it. Genevieve wanted to stay to comfort her, but the older woman insisted on being left alone. A woman of delicate sensibilities, she was hurt by the way her private life had been exposed. All that Mrs. Cameron wanted now was to withdraw from sight in order to lick her wounds.

'I hope she has the courage to venture out for dinner,' said Dillman.

'I doubt it, George. In her position, I'd barricade myself in.'

'We'd better keep an eye on her. Have food sent to her cabin, if necessary. We don't want Mrs. Cameron to die of starvation. She must feel rotten.'

'And so guilty. To realize that she'd been party to a series of thefts.'

'Only indirectly.'

'It still cut her to the quick. You could see that.'

'Max Hirsch has a lot to answer for, Genevieve – '

'We'll never find him. He's gone for good.'

'Yes,' he agreed. 'But I don't imagine that Hirsch dived off the boat deck just to prove that he could swim. Someone else was involved. We have to find out who it was.'

'How?'

'It means going back over Hirsch's tracks, talking to all the people he met since he came aboard. The ones he befriended and, more important, the ones he may have upset.'

'They'll all be in second class, won't they?'

'For the most part,' he said, rubbing his chin thoughtfully. 'That's my territory. But he may not be unknown in first class. My guess is that Hirsch sailed to and fro on a regular basis, taking advantage of gullible ladies like Mrs. Cameron and helping himself to anything that would fit into that briefcase of his. He could probably afford to travel in style but shifted between first and second class as a safety measure. Who knows?' He went on. 'Perhaps one of his former victims recognized him when he was embarking and decided to get revenge. The man we're after may be sleeping soundly in a first-class cabin tonight.'

I wish they all did that, she thought to herself, remembering the note pushed under her cabin door. 'Well,' she said, 'I'd better be off. Time to dress for dinner.'

'Keep your eyes peeled, Genevieve.'

'Oh, I will. For my own sake.'

'Why?' he asked, concerned. 'Is someone pestering you?'

'Not exactly.'

'Would you like me to have a quiet word with him?'

'That's very sweet of you, George,' she said, kissing him on the cheek, 'but I can cope. Besides, you can't have a quiet word with him when I don't know who he is.'

'A mystery stalker, is he?'

'Only time will tell.' She was about to leave when something else popped into her mind. 'Doesn't it strike you as odd?'

'What?'

'The fact that Hirsch had that briefcase with him.'

'Not really, Genevieve.'

'Nobody walks around a ship with a briefcase.'

'I suppose it lent him a businesslike air.'

'That's my point,' she said, puzzled. 'It's so odd. I mean,

what sort of thief steals people's property with a businesslike air?'

'They're called bank managers,' he explained.

Dressed for dinner, Ruth Constantine waited for her friends in the first-class lounge and whiled away the time by glancing through a newspaper. Her black evening gown was plain and unrelieved by jewellery, her one concession to style and colour being the red rose pinned into her hair. When a shadow fell across her, she looked up to see Orvill Delaney, at his most debonair in white tie and tails.

'Good evening, Miss Constantine,' he said, inclining his head.

'Hello, Mr. Delaney.'

'May I say how attractive you look this evening?'

'Then I obviously failed in my mission,' she said crisply. 'I don't believe in striving to look attractive with a new hairstyle and an expensive gown. Why betray nature's intentions? I let people take me as I am.'

'That's an attitude I find very attractive in itself.'

'Even though it's not one you share,' she observed, running an eye over his well-groomed appearance. 'You cut a fine figure, Mr. Delaney.'

'Thank you. But I didn't know that newspapers were delivered on board,' he said. 'I would have thought it beyond even Cunard's ingenuity.'

'This one is days old,' she explained, putting aside her copy of the *Westminster Gazette*. 'I brought it with me but haven't had time to read it until now. My friends don't allow me room to do anything as normal as reading a newspaper.'

'So I've noticed. You make a lively party.'

'It can get tiresome on occasion.'

'Not with someone like Miss Masefield around, surely?' he said. 'She seems a most interesting and charming young lady.'

'Genevieve is a delight.'

'How long have you known her?'

'Why do you ask?'

He gave a shrug. 'No reason. Ignore the question if it's offensive.'

'I find it rather unnecessary, that's all,' she said tensely. 'You've spoken to Genevieve on more than one occasion, so I'm sure you've figured out that she's a very recent addition to our circle. In point of fact, we met on the boat train.'

'Yet she fits into your group so well.'

'It's been one of the consolations of the voyage.'

'You sound like a reluctant passenger, Miss Constantine.'

'I never expect to enjoy myself.'

'What a pity! I always do.'

'I can see that, Mr. Delaney.'

He gave her a cordial smile and she returned it. 'Coming back to Miss Masefield,' he said casually. 'What exactly does she do?'

'Do?'

'What profession or line of work is she in?'

'Really!' she said with mock scorn. 'That's not the sort of thing you should ask about a lady. It's so vulgar. All I can tell you is what Genevieve is doing on this ship.'

'And what's that?'

'What every unattached young lady is doing, Mr. Delaney. Keeping clear of the elegant male predators who always come out panting at a time like this.'

'Is that what *you* do, Miss Constantine?' he asked with amusement. 'Keep clear of panting predators?'

Ruth was brusque. 'I don't need to,' she said. Her manner softened as she picked up the newspaper again. 'But there was something in here that might interest you.'

'Old news is dead news.'

'This was a report of the Carlsbad Tournament.'

'Why should that have any appeal for me?'

'Because it involves the finest chess players in the world. The grandmasters of the game. You told me that you play chess yourself.'

'From time to time.'

'Rubinstein was in the lead when this was published,'

she said, finding the appropriate page. 'He'd won eight games out of ten. Maroczy was hot on his heels, though. How would you rate your chances against men of that calibre?'

'I wouldn't, Miss Constantine.'

'Why not? Do they make you feel intimidated?'

'No,' he replied easily. 'They make me feel grateful that I don't approach the game in the spirit they do. I'm a practical man. While they play for pride, I only play for money. It's far more exciting.'

'Not if you lose, surely?'

'I do my best to ensure that I don't.'

'And how do you do that?'

'That's a trade secret.' He gave her a quiet smile and offered his hand. 'May I escort you into the dining saloon, Miss Constantine?'

'Thank you,' she said, putting the newspaper down once more and letting him help her up. 'You're a gentleman, Mr. Delaney.'

'That sounds better than being an elegant male predator.'

'The two are not mutually exclusive.'

He laughed, then conducted her toward the dining saloon. Ruth was pleased to be seen with him. It would raise eyebrows among her friends and provide a good talking point. She liked Orvill Delaney, and he seemed to appreciate her idiosyncrasies. It prompted her to give him some friendly advice.

'Don't become too curious about Genevieve Masefield,' she warned.

'Why not?'

'You can see how beautiful she is.'

'Are you telling me that I'd have lots of younger rivals?'

'Put it this way,' she said. 'If you went to tap on her cabin door tonight, you might find yourself at the back of a very long queue.'

He laughed again. 'They must've heard about that magazine with the story by O. Henry in it,' he said amiably. 'I've read it, so I don't need to join the queue.'

*

Until he sat down in the second-class dining saloon, Dillman did not realize just how hungry he was. It was suddenly borne in on him that he had eaten almost nothing since breakfast. Sharing a table with the Jarvis family and a few other friends they had acquired, he addressed his food with a zeal that was matched only by Lily Pomeroy, though he consumed his meal at a slower pace and without any of the weird gurgling noises the old woman managed to produce. Alexandra was very subdued and he deduced that Bobo still had not been found. What made the girl's suffering more acute was the fact that she could not confide in him during the meal because her father was listening and would be furious if he learned about the way she had coaxed her grandmother into taking her off in search of the ship's mascot. Dillman gave her a friendly wink, but even that did not revive her.

'What's the weather apt to be like in New York, Mr. Dillman?' asked Oliver Jarvis.

'Much the same as in London, I expect.'

'Cold, dull, and dreary.'

'But there'll be so much to *see*,' said Vanessa Jarvis. 'My sister was quite overwhelmed when she first went to America. She said the buildings were so tall that she felt like a tiny ant crawling along the street. Ernestine never thought she'd actually end up living in New York.'

'Then your sister shouldn't have made the mistake of marrying a handsome American,' said Dillman pleasantly. 'He must have swept her off her feet if she was willing to leave her own country.'

'He did,' recalled Mrs. Pomeroy. 'Ernestine was always the impetuous one, Mr. Dillman. She fell head over heels in love with him. I think she'd have followed him to the North Pole if he'd asked her. Ernestine is not like my other daughter.' She lowered her voice. 'Vanessa is the cautious one. That's why she chose a banker.'

'Mr. Dillman doesn't want to hear tittle-tattle,' said Jarvis, frowning.

'It's the truth, Oliver.'

'Be that as it may.'

'The strange thing is,' she continued, ignoring him, 'that Wesley is not handsome at all. To be honest, he's rather ugly in some ways, but Ernestine loves him and that's all that matters. Wesley has been very good to her, Mr. Dillman. According to my daughter, they live in a wonderful house. I've always wanted to see it.' She loaded her fork with another cargo of food. 'That's why we're making the effort to visit them for their silver wedding anniversary.'

Dillman had heard the details before, but he nevertheless showed interest. After the trials of his day, it was a relief to spend time with the Jarvis family and experience a return to normality. There were no daring thefts and missing passengers in their world. The most dramatic thing to touch one of them was the disappearance of a cat, and that, he felt, was only a temporary problem. Catching her eye again, he gave Alexandra another wink. She responded with a grin this time, then pretended to stroke a cat before hunching her shoulders to indicate bafflement. Dillman nodded to show that he understood.

'What are you doing, Alexandra?' asked the watchful Jarvis.

'Nothing, Daddy.'

'Don't bother Mr. Dillman. Let him eat his food.'

It was an order that the detective obeyed with alacrity.

Kept up beyond their usual bedtime, both Alexandra and her brother began to tire. Their parents finished their meal, made their excuses, and whisked the weary children off to their cabin, leaving Mrs. Pomeroy to attack her dessert and dispense more wheezing reminiscences about her American son-in-law. Other tables were beginning to shed their diners and Dillman watched them go, garnering smiles of gratitude from the people whose stolen property he had recovered. He waited until Mrs. Pomeroy and his other companions had finished their coffee, then he quit the table himself.

An elderly couple waylaid him as he left the dining saloon. 'We didn't want to interrupt you during your meal,

Mr. Dillman,' said Stanley Rosenwald, 'but we just had to thank you.'

'Yes,' said his wife earnestly. 'To be frank, I never thought we'd get our things back. Then Mr. Buxton handed them over to us. He was full of praise for you.'

'I did have some help, Mrs. Rosenwald,' admitted Dillman. He turned to her husband. 'I noticed you took a pill out of your snuffbox during the meal.'

'Just like old times,' said Rosenwald, patting his waistcoat pocket. 'It's back where it belongs and it's going to stay there. As a matter of interest,' he asked, moving in closer, 'who was the thief?'

'He's not in custody yet, Mr. Rosenwald.'

'But you know who he is?'

'We think so.'

'Good. You deserve our congratulations.'

'Thank you.'

Another elderly couple passed, and Miriam Rosenwald broke away to exchange a few words with them. Her husband took the opportunity to express a concern.

'We haven't seen Mr. Hirsch all day,' he said.

'No?'

'It's a great pity. He did enliven the table so much. We were supposed to have dinner with him last night, but he didn't turn up then either. Have you any idea of why not?'

'None at all,' said Dillman.

'Miriam has grown quite fond of him. And so, of course, has Mrs. Cameron.'

'Yes, I did notice a friendship developing there.'

'It may be more than a friendship,' said Rosenwald with a sly grin. 'Perhaps that's where he is – dining in private with Mrs. Cameron. She's a fine-looking woman. Mr. Hirsch was so kind to her when that bad weather was brewing yesterday. He escorted her to her cabin even though he felt queasy himself.' He scowled as he remembered something. 'Though he didn't look at all queasy when I saw him later on.'

'Oh?' said Dillman, his interest quickening. 'When was that?'

'Yesterday afternoon. During the bad weather.'

'Could you put a time on it, Mr. Rosenwald?'

'Three o'clock. Three-thirty at the latest.'

'And where exactly did you see him?'

'Walking along the corridor as jauntily as if he were strolling down Fifth Avenue on a sunny day. It was almost as if he enjoyed the rolling of the ship.'

'Did he see you, Mr. Rosenwald?' asked Dillman.

'Oh, no. I was on my way to the dispensary to get some tablets for Miriam, so I was going in the opposite direction. I would have called out,' he explained, 'but he vanished up those stairs and I was too law-abiding to follow.'

'Law-abiding?'

'I always obey printed warnings, Mr. Dillman.'

'What did this one say?'

' "Only First-Class Passengers Allowed Beyond This Point." '

'That didn't deter Mr. Hirsch?'

'I don't think anything could do that,' said the other with affection. 'He's his own man, Mr. Dillman. He goes wherever he likes. That was the other surprise.'

'What was, Mr. Rosenwald?'

'He was carrying a briefcase. With the ship heaving violently, he was walking along without a care in the world, holding this briefcase in his hand.' He bared a set of yellowing false teeth. 'It was almost as if he were going off to an important meeting.'

Dillman was glad he had restored the silver snuffbox to Stanley Rosenwald. In return, and without even knowing it, the man had just given him some valuable evidence.

Dinner in the first-class saloon that evening was a heady mixture of high fashion, sophistication, wealth, decorum, arrogance, and blatant glamour. The orchestra wrapped the whole occasion in a cocoon of light music. Rich men brought their gorgeous wives into the room like champion sportsmen displaying their trophies. New friendships took on more substance around noisy tables. Romances were blossoming between couples who had never met until they stepped aboard. Wit and repartee dominated. The tone was set by the captain and his entourage, occupying pride of place and acting as the hub around which the glittering wheel spun with dizzying speed. A veritable banquet was served, each course surpassing its predecessor, each glass of wine coinciding with the right food to produce a sense of consummate wholeness. It was difficult not to be caught up in the atmosphere of privileged joy, and Genevieve Masefield had to remind herself to hold out against its seductive effect.

Seated with her friends at a table for six in the lower half of the saloon, she noticed the glances that Patrick Skelton was sending her, a worrying blend of hostility and lust. He was situated at a large table some distance away, but his interest in her still managed to be oppressive. Genevieve wondered why he took so little part in the conversation of those around him. Orvill Delaney, by contrast, was completely at ease with his dinner companions. His table was much closer to Genevieve's and she could hear his laugh clearly and catch an occasional comment. Apart from the warm greeting he had exchanged with her, Delaney took no notice of her. Genevieve was nonplussed.

As the evening wore on, the shortcomings of tying herself to one table became increasingly apparent. Genevieve felt restricted. The badinage was as amusing as always, but she wanted to share in the hilarity at Delaney's table, or hear the captain's anecdotes, or try to cheer up the Goldblatts, or sit beside the ramrod figure of Edgar Fenby in a bid to make him relax, or compete with Katherine Wymark at the table of which she was the acknowledged queen, or even listen to sad Clifford Tavistock talking about his beloved eyeglass case. Genevieve was simultaneously urged to leave her table, and denied the opportunity. She was also beginning to miss Dillman more painfully than ever.

'Be serious, Ruth,' said Donald Belfrage. 'You can't really admire the man.'

'Yes I can,' said Ruth Constantine.

'Mr. Delaney is almost twice your age.'

'So? Don't be so conventional, Donald.'

'He's being realistic, darling,' said Theodora with a giggle. 'Do I need to spell it out? Some things just don't improve with the passage of time.'

'Do you speak from direct experience?' challenged Denning.

'Of course I don't.'

'No wild affairs with ancient suitors?'

'Harvey!'

'Then don't make disparaging remarks about virility and the older man,' he warned. 'Look at the king, for instance. Well over sixty and still in his prime. You can hardly call Edward the Seventh a martyr to impotence or half the women in England would shout you down.'

'That's a very tasteless remark, Harvey,' chided Belfrage.

'Why else do you think I made it?'

'I want to hear about this romance between Ruth and Mr. Delaney,' said Susan Faulconbridge, draining her glass. 'When I saw the two of them coming in here this evening, I couldn't believe my eyes. As a rule, Ruth has so little time for men.'

'One day you'll discover why, Susan,' said Ruth.

'What's different about Mr. Delaney?'

'He *knows* himself.'

'That's an absurd thing to say,' complained Belfrage. 'We all know ourselves.'

'Not in the sense that Ruth means,' commented Genevieve. 'Most of us have never really plumbed the full depths of our character. We've never had to battle against the odds, survive tragedies, and explore the extremities of life. Mr. Delaney gives the impression of having done all those things. He's been through the flames and come out a better man as a result.'

'We are into high-flown rhetoric!' mocked Denning.

'Genevieve is right,' said Ruth. 'Mr. Delaney has lived, while you merely exist.'

'I've lived,' asserted Belfrage.

'And I've survived tragedies,' said Theodora.

'Yes, darling,' prodded Denning. 'You met Donald and married him.'

'I was talking about the operation to remove my wisdom teeth,' she said over the laughter. 'It was touch and go. Then there was the time I had that strange disease.'

'He's sitting beside you,' murmured Ruth with a glance at Belfrage.

'I'm not letting you off the hook, Ruth,' said Susan, wagging a finger. 'I think there's something between you and Mr. Delaney. What is it?'

'Three thousand miles of ocean and a cultural chasm.'

'You came into dinner with him.'

'So? That doesn't mean the banns are being read, Susan. Look behind you,' she suggested, nodding toward Delaney. 'I can count five attractive women at his table and they're all salivating over him. He's completely forgotten me.'

'I haven't, Ruth,' said Denning, twitching his lips. 'Name the time and place.'

'You never give up, Harvey, do you?'

'Some things are worth the wait.'

'Come back in fifty years' time,' she said curtly. 'You might be civilized then.'

The chatter rolled on and Genevieve contributed her fair share. Because he had taken charge of the seating arrangements, Belfrage had put her at his side, but there was no contact with his foot this time. Genevieve was more disturbed by the ongoing surveillance by Patrick Skelton, a smart figure in his white tie and tails, yet uneasy in his surroundings. The more he stared, the more certain she became that he had slipped the message under her door. Harvey Denning was unlikely to resort to pen and ink; voice and appearance were his calling cards. He could be ruled out, along with Orvill Delaney. The American would be too gallant to resort to three words on a piece of paper. He would realize the distress they might cause her.

Having gone through a process of elimination, Genevieve was left with a man who had hardly exchanged a word with her on the one occasion when they met. Yet here he was now, looking up at regular intervals, watching her intently, conveying a desire of some sort, even rising to a cold smile at one point. Presentable as he was, the young accountant seemed faintly menacing to her. She wondered how she would cope with the situation if Patrick Skelton came to her cabin that night. He would have gone beyond the stage of pushing a note under her door; she had seen how much he had been drinking in the course of the evening. That might spur him on. Genevieve had never needed Dillman beside her as much before, but he was out of reach. She would have to deal with Skelton on her own and repulse the man she was now convinced had sent her the note. At that point, something happened to change her mind.

Donald Belfrage put his warm hand familiarly on her thigh.

FOURTEEN

Though the third-class dining saloon was crammed to
capacity, Glyn Bowen heard nothing of its cacophony and
smelled none of its pungent odours. As he sat at one of the
long tables, he hardly touched the food that was set in front
of him. Waiters moved swiftly up and down the rows of
hungry diners in a continual stream, but they were just a
blur before his eyes. Apprehension filled him. Thanks to
his friend, he was committed to an enterprise that was
foolish, dangerous, and potentially catastrophic. Bowen
had little faith in the plan. All that he could see were the
hazards. Instead of arriving in America to start the new life
they had promised themselves, he and Mansell Price might
find themselves held in custody before being handed over
to the New York Police Department. He began to wish he
had stayed in South Wales. There might be hardship, but
there were also basic certainties there.

Mansell Price had no fears about the task that lay
ahead. Far from robbing him of his appetite, the idea of
breaking into the security room only served to sharpen it.
Sitting opposite his friend, he chewed happily through his
food.

'Eat up, Glyn,' he urged. There was no response. 'Glyn!'

The kick against his shin brought Bowen out of his
morose introspection. 'What's wrong?' he said, blinking.

'You haven't touched your grub.'

'I'm not hungry.'

'It's good stuff, mun. Get it down you.'

Bowen picked up his fork and pronged a potato. He ate
without enthusiasm, then took a drink of water. Setting the
fork down, he pushed the plate away.

'Don't you want it?' asked Price.

'No, Mansell.'

'Well, it won't be wasted,' said the other, grabbing the plate and using a knife to scrape its contents onto his own. 'Cheer up!' he said, putting Bowen's plate aside. 'It's a big night for us. A nice meal would set you up.'

Bowen shook his head. With other passengers all around them, it was impossible to discuss the projected crime with his friend. He knew, in any case, that it would be futile to protest. Even when they were boys, Price had been the unchallenged leader of the local gang. He was big, strong, and decisive. Nobody dared argue with him. As they grew older and the other boys fell away, Bowen remained at his side like a faithful hound. Price's friendship had its advantages; it gave Bowen protection in a boisterous community, and a feeling of being needed. There was another bonus. Price had a knack of making girls like him. He not only found girlfriends for himself, he provided the more tongue-tied Bowen with an occasional girlfriend as well. It never troubled the latter that Mansell Price always had first choice.

'Remember that girl from Porth?' asked Price.

'What?' Bowen was jerked out of his reverie again.

'That girl, mun.'

'Which one?'

'From Porth. What was her name again?'

'Catrin.'

'That's it. Catrin.'

'Catrin Thomas,' said the other bleakly.

'She liked you.'

'Nice girl.'

'How nice?' asked his friend with a grin.

'Nice, Mansell. Easy to be with.'

'But you took her out for weeks.'

'Yes,' said Bowen sadly. 'Then I told her about going to America.'

It was one of the many things he had left behind him. The burgeoning friendship with the girl had been scotched instantly when she learned of his plan to emigrate. Bowen winced as he recalled their last meeting. He had grown very fond of Catrin Thomas and she had been drawn to him. The girl had been stunned by the news of his imminent departure. His mumbled promises to send for her once he was settled in America were met with scorn and disbelief. He could still see the pain on her face.

'I bet you wish she was here now,' said Price.

'Who?'

'Catrin. At least *she* wouldn't play the mouth organ in our cabin.'

'No.'

'Might even enjoy this voyage myself if I had Catrin Thomas on board. I know one thing. She'd be livelier company than you.' He kicked the other shin. 'Wake up, mun. You're still asleep. I need you with your eyes open.'

The reminder sent a mild shudder through Bowen. He felt ill. What he really wanted to do was to get up from the table and go back to the cabin to lie down, but he was afraid to move. Price would not accept sickness as an excuse. There was no way out of the predicament. Bowen would simply have to go through with the plan.

'What's *wrong* with you?' demanded Price.

'Nothing.'

'You sure?'

'I'm fine, Mansell,' he muttered.

While his friend ate heartily on, Bowen continued to suffer in silence.

When the festivities were over in the first-class dining saloon, most of the passengers began to gravitate toward the lounge or the smoking room. Genevieve Masefield's own party began to disintegrate. Harvey Denning and Susan Faulconbridge were partnering each other in a game of bridge and went off immediately to find their opponents. Donald and Theodora Belfrage adjourned to the lounge for drinks but soon peeled off to have an early night. Genevieve was left alone again with Ruth Constantine.

'Susan was in a peculiar mood this evening,' she observed.

'Peculiar?' said Ruth.

'She was as jolly as ever at the start of the meal but it didn't seem to last. I had the feeling that she was on edge.'

'In her shoes, you might be the same, Genevieve.'

'What do you mean?'

'Susan was sitting opposite Donald. How would you like to watch the man you love being pampered by his wife? And what a wife!' sighed Ruth. 'Theodora is like some little bird, twittering away and flying here, there, and everywhere. Susan must want to throttle the woman. Then, of course, there's the problem of Harvey.'

'Problem?'

'Will he or won't he?'

'I got the impression that he – and they – already had.'

'Not on this voyage, Genevieve. I can tell from the look in her eyes. What's the point of sitting up late in your cabin if your beau forgets to call? Or what's far worse, if you suspect he's paying a visit elsewhere.' Ruth lowered her voice. 'That's why Susan gave you those envious glances.'

'I didn't notice her doing that.'

'You wouldn't. She's very discreet about it.'

'Why should Susan be envious of me?'

'Since her bridge partner is not showing interest in her, she's bound to wonder if he's transferred his affections to you.'

'Not in the sense you mean,' said Genevieve firmly.

'We know that. Susan doesn't.'

'I'd hate for her to get the wrong idea.'

Ruth grinned. 'I'd do everything I could to encourage it.'

Genevieve had never met anyone so unashamedly candid as Ruth Constantine. In the woman's honest, fearless, sardonic way, she said things that others only dared to think. It was a little startling at times, but Genevieve found it refreshing also. She was sorry to hear that Susan was feeling vague pangs of jealousy because of her, and she hoped to find a way to disperse them. Harvey Denning was not the suitor who had courted her at the table. The hand on her thigh had belonged to someone else.

'You don't like Donald, do you?' she asked.

'Don't I?'

'I think you despise him for marrying someone like Theodora.'

'Not at all,' said Ruth. 'I'm more likely to despise her for having married him without realizing exactly what she was letting herself in for. Theodora's pillow will be soaked with tears before too long. As for Donald…well, it's impossible not to like someone who gives me so many opportunities to fire my arrows at him.'

'Why does he put up with it?'

'Because it keeps me around.'

'You mean it's a price he has to pay?'

'Something like that,' said Ruth, smiling to herself. 'The truth is that I fascinate Donald Belfrage. I'm unattainable. I'm the one woman he can't have at his feet. Susan worships him, Theodora dotes on him, and there are dozens of others who think he's a Greek god in the shape of an English aristocrat. But I'm not drawn by that combination of money, pomposity, imbecility, and good looks.'

'Don't you find Donald attractive?'

'Of course,' confessed Ruth. 'He has a wonderful body and great stamina, but I doubt that he'd bring any finesse to an intimate moment. Subtlety is not Donald's forte. He's more likely to grab a woman as if she's an oar in a rowing eight. Then,' she added with a roll of the eyes, 'there's his other fatal shortcoming.'

'What's that?'

'You've heard him talk.'

Genevieve laughed. 'I take your point.'

'Can you imagine what Donald would say to you afterward?'

'I'd rather not, Ruth!'

'Harvey has his drawbacks,' sighed the other, 'but at least he'd be relaxed and amusing in those circumstances. He'd know the right words to say to a woman. But not Donald Belfrage. Oh, heavens! You'd get his views on the British Empire or his memoirs of the Boat Race. He has no lightness of touch.'

'How did you meet him?'

'When he was playing polo down in Sussex. He looks quite splendid astride a polo pony. Let me be honest – I was struck by him. It was only later that I discovered I might have got more intelligent conversation from the pony.'

'Yet he has a degree from Oxford.'

'A fourth in Greats. He barely scraped through.'

'I got the idea that he'd had a dazzling university career.'

'Oh, yes,' said Ruth. 'Donald likes to dazzle.'

Genevieve felt much better about the incident at the dinner table. In cutting Donald Belfrage down to size, Ruth had made him seem less threatening. The hand on the thigh was no longer a menacing prelude; it should be dismissed as an improper gesture and quietly forgotten. She was grateful that Susan Faulconbridge had not been aware of what was going on beneath the table or her jealousy would have been fuelled even more. Theodora Belfrage, she suspected, would have been far more than jealous. The maiden voyage was like an extended honeymoon to her. It saddened Genevieve that the woman's husband was already taking a first look outside the marriage.

'Whom would you choose, Genevieve?'

'Choose?'

'Yes,' said Ruth with cool directness. 'You've been on the ship long enough to take stock of the possibilities. I'm sure you have the good sense to ignore both Donald and Harvey. So which man would you pick?'

'Do I have to pick any?'

'Not in reality. I'd just be interested in your taste.'

'Well, it's difficult to make a decision,' said Genevieve, gazing around. 'There's something about a man in uniform that always impresses me. In the dining saloon, I might even have selected Captain Pritchard.'

'What about Mr. Delaney?'

'He wasn't in uniform, Ruth.'

'Oh, yes he was. You didn't recognize it, that's all.'

'Tell me more.'

'In a moment,' said Ruth, nudging her. 'We have company.'

Genevieve tensed slightly when she saw Patrick Skelton walking toward them. He was on his way to the exit and had to first pass them. There was a quiet determination in his manner as he paused beside them to exchange pleasantries.

'Have you enjoyed the evening, ladies?' he inquired.

'Very much,' said Ruth.

'And you, Miss Masefield?'

'Yes, thank you.'

'What about you, Mr. Skelton?' asked Ruth. 'You're not a good sailor, I hear.'

'I prefer solid ground beneath my feet.'

'Don't we all?'

He switched his gaze to Genevieve. 'I like to know where I stand,' he said.

'You'll have to put up with it for a few more days,' she pointed out, 'I hope you can find some consolations on the ship.'

'So do I, Miss Masefield.'

'What do accountants do when they want to cheer themselves up?' asked Ruth with a mocking smile. 'Count money?'

'Something like that.' He gave a stiff bow. 'Good night, ladies.'

They bade him farewell and watched his compact figure move on toward the exit. Skelton had been very polite, yet he left Genevieve feeling uneasy. She recalled those three words on the note that was put under her door and she bit her lip involuntarily. Ruth Constantine sensed her friend's discomfort.

'I take it that Mr. Skelton is not your ideal man, Genevieve?'

'No,' said the other with feeling. 'Now, tell me about Mr. Delaney's uniform.'

Dillman kept on the move. The search for Max Hirsch had been abandoned for the day, but he was still involved in his own personal hunt, walking down passageways, opening storerooms, investigating the laundry area, peeping into larders, looking into cabins that were not being used on the voyage, wandering into the hairdressing salon, and racking his brains to think of anywhere else a missing man might be. When he made his way to the purser's office, he found Maurice Buxton lighting up his pipe.

'You don't smoke, Mr. Dillman, do you?' the purser asked.

'No, Mr. Buxton, and I never have.'

'I can recommend a pipe. Very soothing.'

'I'll bear that in mind.'

'The funny thing is that I smoke it only aboard ship. When I'm ashore, my garden is my consolation. An hour or two out there does wonders for my frayed nerves. Once we set sail again, however,' he said, raising his pipe, 'I reach for my tobacco.'

'Are your nerves feeling that frayed?' asked Dillman.

'Yes, it's been a long day. Not without its triumphs, mark you. But it's still left me feeling in need of a restorative pipe. What about you? Resting on your laurels?'

'There's no time for that, Mr. Buxton.'

'But you recovered that stolen property. You've earned a break.'

'I can't take one while Max Hirsch is still missing. I want to know what happened to him. In any case,' he added, 'Genevieve Masefield deserves as many plaudits as I do. Her interview with Mrs. Cameron was the turning point.'

'How is the lady?'

'Grief-stricken.'

'I can imagine.'

'Mrs. Cameron won't even leave her cabin.'

'Was she that involved with Hirsch?'

'No doubt about it.'

'What would have happened if he'd still been around?'

'I'm not sure, Mr. Buxton,' said Dillman. 'The chances are that Hirsch would have enjoyed his little romance until we reached New York, then dropped the poor woman like a stone. Either way, she was heading for disillusion.'

'Perhaps it's better that it came sooner rather than later.'

'Hardly.'

'Why do you say that?'

'In spite of everything, Mrs. Cameron still cares for him. Deep in her heart, she believes that Hirsch is being maligned and that he could explain everything if only he were here. Yet he's disappeared. That's causing her more distress than the thought that he might have misled her.'

'The cunning devil *used* her. Can't she see that?'

'It'll take time for her to get it all into perspective.'

'Meanwhile,' said the purser, brightening, 'the good news I have to report is that there's been no bad news to report.'

'No more thefts?'

'Lose a thief and you lose his crime dossier.'

'There are still two victims to be appeased, Mr. Buxton,' said Dillman. 'The items taken from first class were – if my guess is right – hidden in that briefcase, and that's gone missing as well. I know that he had it with him. Mr. Rosenwald actually saw Hirsch sneaking into the first-class section on Monday afternoon.'

'What about the third-class galley?'

'Not much chance of solid silver being down there.'

'Those tools were stolen, Mr. Dillman. Let's not forget them. What would Hirsch want with crowbars, a chisel, and a lump hammer?'

'We don't know that he took them.'

'Somebody did. Where are they?'

'If we search hard enough, they'll turn up.'

'I hope so,' said Buxton, exhaling smoke. 'We don't want another thief aboard. By the way, a word of warning. Somebody's on to us.'

'What do you mean?'

'That busy little American journalist, Mrs. Littlejohn, has been hounding me. She's spotted our men searching the vessel and wants to know what we're after. I made no comment, naturally, but that only made her more inquisitive.'

'Yes,' said Dillman. 'Mrs. Littlejohn is indefatigable.'

'Watch out for her. It was bad enough when she was trying to stir up the crew to mutiny, a real female Fletcher Christian. She seems to think that the Cunard Line is the twentieth-century equivalent of Captain Bligh. Mrs. Littlejohn has been scouring the ship for underpaid malcontents. She's looking for a nonexistent scandal to expose. Let her carry on,' he said wearily, 'as long as she doesn't discover what's really been happening aboard.'

'The lady is very well intentioned, Mr. Buxton.'

'They're always the worst kind.'

'She has the curiosity of a cat.'

'Don't mention cats!' wailed the other with mock horror. 'That's another name on the Missing Persons' list. Bobo, the ship's mascot. It's incredible. Since we set sail from Queenstown, we've somehow lost a passenger, an eyeglass case, a set of cutlery, a collection of tools, a trolley, since returned, several windows on the promenade deck, and a large black cat. What's next in line?'

'Wait and see.'

'I daren't look.'

'Then I'll leave you to enjoy your pipe. Oh,' he said, checking himself, 'I need to ask you a favour first. Where might I find an attractive young stewardess?'

Buxton was surprised. 'Are you that desperate, Mr. Dillman?'

'Of course not.'

'The duties of a stewardess extend only so far, you know.'

'I understand that, Mr. Buxton. It's not a personal request.'

'I'm relieved to hear it,' said the other, grinning.

'I need a stewardess to perform a very special service for a jaded passenger. Somehow, I feel that the lady would appreciate it.'

'What lady?'

'A hungry one.'

Agnes Cameron spent the whole day in her cabin, regretting her decision to book a passage on the *Mauretania*.

Setting out on a journey in memory of her husband, she had found herself embroiled in a situation that would have appalled him. She had been foolish, impulsive, and unguarded. What shocked her most was that she had not behaved like the respectable, middle-aged woman she took herself to be. Max Hirsch had unlocked something in her that she had not even known was there, and it was, in retrospect, quite frightening. Mrs. Cameron had been duped. She had to accept that, even though it was difficult to believe that a man who had been so tender could also be so devious. Yet she still had a vestigial fondness for him. Whatever he had done to her, she did not wish him to come to any harm. While agonizing about her own problems, she still found a moment to worry about Hirsch and to speculate anxiously about his whereabouts.

When the tap came on her door, she sat up with a cry of surprise, wondering at first if Hirsch had come back to her. How should she react? With pleasure or disgust? Was it conceivable that he might not, after all, be the villain that she imagined?

A second tap brought her to her feet, but she could move no farther.

'Mrs. Cameron?' said a female voice. 'Are you in there?'

'Who is it?' she asked.

'A stewardess, madam. I have something for you.'

'Wait a moment.'

Mrs. Cameron looked in the mirror while she tidied her hair, then straightened her dressing gown. Wondering what her visitor had brought, she crossed to the door and opened it a few inches. A pert young stewardess was standing there with a tray of food covered by a linen cloth. The visitor gave her a kind smile.

'With the compliments of Mr. Dillman,' she said.

'Mr. Dillman?'

'He thought you might be hungry.'

'Oh…well, yes.'

'Would you open the door a little wider, please?'

'Of course.'

Mrs. Cameron opened the door and stepped back so the

stewardess could bring the tray into the cabin and set it on the table. Mrs. Cameron was touched. As the stewardess was leaving, she called after her.

'Thank Mr. Dillman for me, will you?'

The pleasures of discovering his new kingdom were starting to wane after twenty-four hours. Bobo was both lonely and famished. Several circuits of the cargo hold had shown him that he would get neither company nor food down there. He yearned for release. Most of the time was spent sleeping near the door through which he first came, but one ear was always cocked for the approach of any rescuers. Eventually his patience was rewarded. He heard footsteps coming and dropped at once to the floor. Something was inserted into the keyhole. There was a scraping sound as the blade of a knife tried to coax the lock into obedience. After some delay, there was a click that made the cat tense himself in readiness. He did not linger for any introductions. When the door swung open, he sped through it as if his tail were on fire.

Glyn Bowen gave a yelp as the animal brushed past his leg again. 'There!' he said. 'I told you it was a cat.'

'A black cat,' noted Price, recovering from his own surprise. 'You know what that means, Glyn. It's a sign of good luck.'

'But it was running away from us.'

'So?'

'Doesn't that mean the opposite?'

'No,' said the other, bending down to grope behind the box. 'Of course not.'

'I don't like it, Mansell. That cat was a warning.'

Price gathered up the bundle of tools and handed them over to his friend. 'Carry these,' he ordered, 'and stop worrying.'

'I'm bound to worry. Look, I'm shivering.'

'Get a grip on yourself.'

'I'm scared of what might happen, Mansell.'

Price was grinning with sheer excitement. He gave

Bowen an encouraging push. 'Trust me,' he said. 'Nothing can possibly go wrong.'

The population of the first-class lounge was steadily thinning as people drifted off to bed or to private parties in their cabins. Genevieve had been so absorbed in her conversation with Ruth Constantine that she did not notice the passage of time. It was only when she glanced around that she saw how few people were still left.

'Heavens!' she said. 'We're almost the last ones here.'

'Not quite, Genevieve. The urbane Mr. Delaney is still over there in the corner with his friends, and I think there's another group behind those potted palms.'

Genevieve surveyed the room. Orvill Delaney was reclining in a chair, talking to two elderly men and their wives. He seemed almost youthful in their company. Though she could not see the people who were screened by the potted palms, she could hear Katherine Wymark's voice as she held court among an admiring circle. The one member of the group who was visible was Edgar Fenby, holding a pose in his chair and looking as relaxed as a dummy in a menswear department.

'I must let you get to bed, Genevieve,' said Ruth.

'But I'm not tired.'

'I am. Let's talk again tomorrow.'

'I'd like that. And thank you, Ruth.'

'For what?'

'Giving me a few insights.'

'Fair exchange,' said the other. 'You provided me with a few of your own.'

As they were rising from their chairs, they heard a succession of farewells from behind the potted palms. Katherine Wymark then swept into view on her husband's arm. They were a striking couple. She had chosen an evening gown of white satin with elaborate patterns sewn into it with gold thread. Her diamond necklace and earrings shimmered as she glided across the lounge. Walter Wymark was mocked rather than flattered by his apparel, but that did not concern him. He looked smug and happy

as he escorted his wife along. Genevieve waited to intro-
duce Ruth to them.

'I believe I saw you at the captain's table yesterday,' said
Ruth.

'That's right,' said Wymark easily. 'It was an honour.'

'Captain Pritchard is such a darling man,' added
Katherine. 'It's so reassuring to have someone of his vast
experience at the helm.'

'Especially during that terrible storm,' said Genevieve.
'Let's hope there's calmer weather ahead. We haven't been
out on deck all day.'

'Nor have we, Miss Masefield. But then, there's so much
to do indoors.'

'Yes,' agreed Wymark. 'It's a swell boat, honey.'

'Ship, Walter,' she corrected gently. 'Remember what
the captain told us. The *Mauretania* is a ship and we refer
to her as "she". I'm not quite sure why, though. Do you
know, Miss Constantine?' she asked, turning to Ruth. 'Why
should an enormous ship like this be designated a female?'

'Because she'll spend her entire life carrying men
around,' suggested Ruth.

Genevieve laughed at the rejoinder, but Wymark
merely scowled.

'I never thought of that,' said Katherine with a studied
smile. 'You're a perceptive woman, Miss Constantine. We
must stick together. There aren't many of us about.'

'Time to go, honey,' said Wymark.

'There's no hurry, Walter,' she replied before looking
across at Genevieve. 'My husband is always trying to move
me along. Like a tugboat pulling an ocean liner. Or are
tugboats female as well?'

'You'll have to ask the captain, Mrs. Wymark.'

'But I had the feeling that you were a veteran sailor.'

'No, I'm still a relative novice,' said Genevieve.

'Katherine,' murmured her husband.

'Yes, yes,' she said, squeezing his arm, 'I'll be there in a
moment. Have *you* ever been married, Miss Constantine?'

'I can't remember,' said Ruth lazily. 'If I have been, it
wasn't a success.'

'Perhaps you didn't work hard enough at it.'

'She's teasing you, honey,' warned Wymark.

'I can see that, Walter. I like a woman with a sense of humour.'

'I prefer mine plain and simple.'

'Then you shouldn't have chosen me.'

'But I had the feeling that you chose your husband,' said Ruth.

Wymark scowled again, but Katherine gave a serene smile. She raised a hand in farewell as they moved off to the door. Genevieve watched them go.

'I take back what I said about Donald,' commented Ruth. 'Compared to someone like Walter Wymark, our Mr. Belfrage looks like a perfect husband.'

'Not for a woman like that, I suspect,' said Genevieve.

'Oh, no!'

'He's not used to that degree of potency in a wife.'

'Mrs. Wymark would terrify him.'

'I fancy that her husband would terrify me,' admitted Genevieve, suppressing a yawn. 'Oh, dear. I'm more tired than I thought.'

'Being among so many inferior men is very taxing.'

They strolled to the door, chatted for a few minutes, then went their separate ways. Since Ruth's cabin was on the deck below, she descended the stairs, but Genevieve merely had to walk along a couple of passageways on the boat deck. Nevertheless, she hesitated, worried that she might return to her cabin to find another note waiting for her. What she really feared was being intercepted before she even got there. It was not fear of attack; she was certain that would not happen. It was fear of being the target for someone else's emotional needs, fear of somehow being taken for granted by a man. When she was with Ruth, she was safe, but she was on her own now. She realized how much she missed Dillman at that moment.

Gritting her teeth, she set off briskly along the passageway. She had gone only a dozen yards when she had the feeling that she was being followed. Not daring to look back, she maintained her pace, came to a junction and turned to the right. Then she darted into an alcove, pressing herself against the wall so she was out of sight. She heard heavy footsteps reach the junction and she braced herself, but they did not attempt to follow her. Instead, the man turned to the left and walked off. Genevieve emerged from her hiding place and looked to see who it was. Alarmed that Patrick Skelton might be in pursuit of her, she was astonished to see instead that the man was Edgar Fenby, moving furtively along the passageway as he checked the numbers on the cabin doors.

It was late when he made his way to the third-class kitchens, and most of the staff had already retired to their quarters. All that remained were a few people washing the last of the dinner plates and a lacklustre youth mopping the floor as if it were a punishment rather than a duty. Dillman introduced himself and took the youth aside.

'I understand that you had some tools taken,' he said.

'That's right, sir,' replied the youth, leaning on his mop. 'Crowbars and a few others.'

'Where were they kept?'

'In the cupboard with the brooms and mops.'

'And where's that?'

'Just outside, sir.'

'So someone could rummage in the cupboard without being seen from here?'

'Yes,' said the youth. 'Nobody in here would be looking, anyway. We're rushed off our feet. We got thousands of meals a day to prepare and serve. There's so much steam in here, it's like being in a thick fog.' He indicated his companions. 'Then there's all the washing up to do. They can build a ship that'll carry over three thousand people, but they can't invent a machine that washes dishes. Nor one that mops the floor.'

'They're not such high priorities, I'm afraid.'

'They are to me.'

'Is the broom cupboard locked?'

'No, sir.'

'Why not?'

'We're in and out of it all the time. Be a nuisance if we had to use a key. Anyway, who'd want to steal anything from there?'

'Someone did.'

'They might just have borrowed those tools, sir.'

'Were the other galleys checked?'

'I think so. Our stuff wasn't there.'

'Then where else could it be?'

'No idea, sir,' said the youth, biting a fingernail. 'But things do sort of come and go aboard ship. When I sailed on the *Lucania*, some frying pans went missing from the third-class galley. They turned up two days later. One of the laundry stewards told me that somebody walked off with six pillows during the night, but they came back as well. That kind of thing happens all the time. You get used to it.'

'A trolley disappeared from the first-class galley, but that showed up again.'

'There you are then.'

'On the other hand,' said Dillman reflectively, 'nobody would take a crowbar unless he meant to use it on something.'

The youth sniggered. 'Maybe he lost the key to his cabin, sir.'

The detective forced a smile. 'Thanks for your help,' he said, moving away. 'I'll leave you to your work. I can see that you enjoy it so much.'

'I love it!'

While the youth dipped his mop disconsolately in the bucket once more, Dillman let himself out and walked around the public rooms in steerage. They were virtually empty at that time of night, though a few stragglers were dotted around the lounge, playing cards or talking idly to keep themselves awake. He walked on past the long rows of cabins, noting that the passageways were much gloomier than elsewhere on the ship. It was not the kind of area that would have the slightest temptation for Max Hirsch. He was unlikely to find much expensive silverware among the meagre belongings of the immigrants or the luggage of the other third-class passengers. Hirsch enjoyed the luxuries of life, preferably at someone else's expense. If the man had been the victim of foul play, Dillman decided, then a passenger from first or second class was involved.

As he headed back to his own cabin, his feet took him past the security room, and something made him pause outside it for second. There was nobody in sight, and yet he sensed a presence of some kind. He gave the door a cursory inspection. It was thick, strong, and equipped with a battery of locks. Dillman relaxed. It was a relief to know that the gold bullion was beyond the reach of any thieves. Beside that cargo, Hirsch's little haul had been almost negligible.

Moving away, Dillman suddenly remembered Mrs. Dalkeith. The old lady's gold watch had vanished, then reappeared mysteriously in a brown envelope. Though he now had proof that Hirsch did venture into first class, Dillman did not believe he had stolen the watch, still less responded to an altruistic impulse to return it. The purser had been delighted when the object reappeared and he'd had the satisfaction of restoring it to its owner. Having been savagely berated by Mrs. Dalkeith, he felt entitled to bask in her praise. To the purser's mind, the incident was closed, but Dillman was less inclined to write it off. The problem of who returned the watch and why was a mystery that he hoped would eventually be solved.

Someone else aboard was committed to solving mysteries. When he walked up the grand staircase, he saw her coming down toward him. Hester Littlejohn's face lit up with a smile. Still in her evening gown, she held a purse in one hand and a pad and pencil in the other. Dillman recalled the warning about her from Maurice Buxton.

'What are you doing up at this hour, Mrs. Littlejohn?' he asked.

'I might ask you the same thing, Mr. Dillman.'

'I was just taking a stroll.'

'Counting the rivets in the hull, no doubt,' she teased. 'Or calculating how many square yards of carpet the *Mauretania* has.'

'Actually, I was trying to work out how much corticine was used.'

'What's that?'

'The material out of which the decks are made.'

'But that's wood, surely?'

'Look again, Mrs. Littlejohn,' he advised. 'There's a whole forest of timber used throughout the interior of the vessel, but the decks are constructed of corticine because it's lighter in weight. Corticine is made from ground cork mixed with India rubber.'

She narrowed an eye. 'Are you pulling my leg, Mr. Dillman?'

'Not about the corticine. That was in the specifications. But,' he confessed with a smile, 'perhaps I haven't been out there with a ruler to measure it.'

'So where have you been?'

'Getting the feel of the ship when there aren't so many people about.'

'I have another word for it.'

'Sleepwalking?'

'Snooping, Mr. Dillman.'

'I would have thought you'd be tucked up in bed by now.'

'Not when there's an exclusive story beckoning. In my experience, some of the most interesting things tend to happen at night.'

'Yes, but they usually involve two people and some privacy.'

She laughed. 'I'm no Peeping Tom. I'm just trying to get to the bottom of this mystery,' she explained. 'Something important has gone missing and the purser has organized a detailed search. I've seen the men at it. Unfortunately, Mr. Buxton won't tell me what they're looking for. Don't you think that's suspicious?'

'Not really, Mrs. Littlejohn.'

'I think he's hiding something.'

'Such as?'

'The disappearance of a passenger!' she exclaimed.

'Nothing evades you,' he said with admiration, seeing

the chance to shake her off the scent. 'As it happens, I'm in a position to tell you that you're perfectly right. I had it from one of the crew earlier. They *were* searching for a missing passenger. A very important passenger.'

'I knew it!' she said, grabbing his arm. 'What's the passenger's name?'

'Bobo.'

'Who?'

'Bobo,' he repeated. 'The ship's mascot.'

'All that fuss over a black cat?'

'As far as the crew is concerned, no passenger is more important than Bobo. Sailors are very superstitious, Mrs. Littlejohn. The cat has vanished and that worries them deeply. They see it as a portent of evil.'

The woman was deflated. 'Is that what all this is about?'

'I'm afraid so,' he said impassively. 'I'd like to be able to tell you that ten first-class passengers are missing, presumed drowned, but they were all hale and hearty at the last count. So will you be,' he counselled, 'if you have a good night's sleep.'

'There's still the other business,' she argued, rallying slightly.

'What business?'

'The theft from the galley.'

'That trolley was returned, Mrs. Littlejohn.'

'I know,' she said. 'Mr. Buxton told me. But those other items haven't come back yet, have they? There were those tools taken from the third-class kitchen. That's a crime that needs to be solved very quickly.'

'I'm sure there's an investigation in progress.'

'Well, I hope the villain is caught soon. It's rather frightening to think of someone wandering around with a crowbar in his hand. While he's at liberty, no woman is safe,' she said anxiously. 'He could break into any of our cabins.'

'That would give you a good story for your readers.'

'I'm serious, Mr. Dillman!'

'I know,' he said, soothing her with a kind smile. 'But I can guarantee that you're not in any danger. The chances of the thief having a grudge against *the Ladies' Weekly Journal* are very slight. You can sleep safe in your bed, Mrs. Littlejohn.'

'Why would anyone steal those tools?' she pressed.

'I've no idea. I'm not even certain they were stolen. After all, that trolley was returned in due course. Maybe the tools are already back where they should be by now,' he said easily. 'I wouldn't have thought it was worth missing your sleep over.'

'You're probably right, Mr. Dillman.'

'If you're still worried about being accosted by a homicidal maniac wielding a crowbar, I'd be happy to escort you to your cabin.'

'How kind!' she said, taking his arm. 'I accept your offer, sir. I knew that my nocturnal wanderings would bring some reward.' She beamed happily as they walked along. 'Tell me more about this missing cat, Mr. Dillman.'

With his food supply restored, Bobo was enjoying the freedom of the ship, padding along silently until he met anything that aroused his curiosity. Apart from an occasional steward on patrol, he encountered nobody in the floating maze that was the *Mauretania*. When he turned into the passageway that led to the security room, however, he saw something that made him stop, watch, and marvel. Shirt stained with sweat and face glistening, a muscular young man was inserting something under the door before using his foot to press down hard. Bobo began to groom himself. One eye on the man, he licked a paw and used it like a loofah on the back of his head.

It was at that point that Glyn Bowen saw him. He gave a grunt of surprise that caused Mansell Price to abandon his work and swing around with sudden fear. The two men spoke in hoarse whispers.

'It's that cat again,' said Bowen, pointing.

Price relaxed. 'Is that all? I thought someone was coming.'

'They will before long, Mansell. Stewards patrol past here on the hour.'

'But they're not always on time, as we found out last night when we kept watch down here. Anyway,' said Price, 'I'm almost there. I can feel it.'

Breaking into the security room was taking longer than he had anticipated. He was having to call on all the power and experience developed during his years down a coal mine. Leverage was the secret. He used the bolster chisel as a wedge, tapping it in position with the lump hammer and muffling the noise with strips of sacking. His aim was to weaken the hinges of the door so he could twist it slightly out of shape and burst the locks one by one. It required strength, patience, and experimentation. Bowen was there as a lookout, moving between the two ends of the passageway to check that nobody was coming in their direction. His friend might be doing the hard physical work, but Bowen himself was also dripping with sweat and troubled by prickly heat. Certain that somebody might come any minute, he was on tenterhooks.

When he walked toward Bobo, the animal fled around the corner. Bowen reached the turn, saw the cat disappear up a companionway, waited for half a minute, then went swiftly back past the security room to keep vigil at the other end of the passageway. The sound of a metallic click made him jump. In the confined space, it seemed much louder than it really was. He hurried back to his friend, who was now straining with all his might, one foot on the crowbar wedged under the door and both hands heaving on the second crowbar, worked into the side of the door close to another lock.

'Give us a hand here, Glyn,' ordered Price.

'Someone is bound to hear that noise.'

'One more heave is all it needs. Take this,' he said, giving Bowen the crowbar that was positioned by the lock. 'When I tell you, pull as if your life depended on it.'

'I will, Mansell,' agreed the other, trembling.

Price adjusted the crowbar under his foot; then he tapped the chisel into the narrow slit at the side of the door, directly below another lock.

'Two birds with one stone, Glyn.'

'What if it doesn't work?'

'Then we're not pulling hard enough. Ready? Now!'

Bowen obeyed the hissed command and heaved on his crowbar until his muscles went taut. Price was using his foot and hands to apply pressure elsewhere. Nothing seemed to happen at first, and Bowen felt the flames of panic starting to lick him all over. The defects of his friend's plan became apparent with a new immediacy. What if they could not spring the door open? How would they cope if there was a second door to negotiate behind the first, or some kind of security devices? Would they have any strength left to carry off some of the gold bullion? Where would they take it? Price had talked about rousing the purser with tales of having foiled the robbers, but how could he do that when he was running with sweat and panting stertorously? His appearance would arouse suspicion at once. Bowen was more terrified than ever. The plan could not possibly succeed.

'Harder, mun!' urged Price.

'I'm trying my best.'

'Harder!'

They both gave a final heave and the locks were jerked clear of their sockets simultaneously. The door swung back on its weakened hinges, and Bowen almost fell through it, grabbing at the wall to steady himself. Price let out a wheeze of triumph and dived into the security room. Sufficient light spilled in from the passageway to reveal the wooden boxes, stacked neatly in rows, each box containing gold bars for delivery to New York. Price did not hesitate. Still grinning wildly, he used a crowbar to pry the lock off one of the boxes, then lever it open. His joy suddenly turned to anguish.

'Bloody hell!' he exclaimed.

Instead of containing gold bars, the box was filled with house bricks.

FIFTEEN

George Porter Dillman had just drifted off to sleep when
he was awakened by a loud noise. Somebody was rapping
hard on his cabin door. Climbing out of his bunk, he pulled
on his dressing gown and opened the door. A steward
gabbled the message at him.

'Mr. Buxton's compliments, sir, and would you please
meet him outside the security room as soon as possible?'

Dillman was surprised. 'The security room?'

'Yes, sir.'

'Do you know what the problem is?'

'The purser will explain.'

Dillman closed the door, dressed quickly, then hurried
off to the security room. The light was on and the purser
was inside with four members of the crew. Dillman noticed
that the men had all been issued side arms. They were
sealing up the last of the boxes. Maurice Buxton turned to
give the newcomer a baleful smile.

'We've been robbed, Mr. Dillman,' he said.

'But how?'

'See for yourself.' He indicated the door. 'They used
crowbars to weaken the hinges and spring the locks.
There's the evidence,' he said, pointing to the tools that
had been abandoned on the floor. 'They took the gold bars
out of two boxes and filled them with bricks laid over a
lining of lead so they weighed exactly the same as all the
other boxes. My guess is that they were interrupted. If
they'd had time to reseal the lids and lock the door again,
we might never have known the stuff had been taken.'

Dillman examined the door. 'They'd have had a job

closing this from outside,' he surmised. 'Are you sure that's what they were going to do?'

'What other explanation is there?'

'I don't know, but I'm sure there is one. Have you checked all the boxes?'

'Yes,' sighed the other. 'Every one of them is accounted for.'

'And these two open boxes had gold bullion in them when we left Liverpool?'

'No question about that. We checked each box as it was handed over by the railway police.' He spread his arms. 'This is a disaster, Mr. Dillman. If we arrive in New York with a big chunk of the gold missing, there'll be an unholy rumpus. We can't solve a financial crisis with a set of house bricks. The press will crucify us. Cunard will probably make me walk the plank,' he said with a grimace, 'or set me adrift in an open boat. What are we going to do?'

'Keep the whole incident to ourselves,' said Dillman decisively. 'Have you impressed the need for secrecy on your men?'

'Oh, yes!'

'Captain Pritchard will have to be told.'

'He already has been, Mr. Dillman. After roasting my ears off, he ordered me to find the missing gold before we dock in New York. I assured him that we would. If worse comes to worst, we simply search every passenger before they disembark.'

'That won't be very popular, Mr. Buxton. The last thing the Cunard Line wants you to do is to upset the passengers. If you institute a search when we dock, you simply advertise the fact that the gold was taken.'

'What's the alternative?'

'Recover it before we get anywhere near New York.'

'But that will involve a cabin-by-cabin search, surely?'

'Not necessarily,' said Dillman. 'That would give the game away. Besides, it would take ages to go through the entire ship. The thieves would see us coming and simply move the loot ahead of us each time.'

'How, Mr. Dillman? Those gold bars are extremely heavy.'

The detective pondered. 'The trolley!' he said at length, snapping his fingers. 'That's why it was borrowed from the first-class galley. To wheel the bullion away.'

'But it was returned yesterday morning.'

'Check to see if it went missing tonight.'

'I will.'

'And find out the exact time when it went astray on Monday night.'

'One problem is solved, anyway,' observed the purser, pointing to the tools on the floor. 'We know why they were taken.'

'But why steal them from third class when the trolley was taken from first class? It doesn't make sense,' said Dillman. 'There's a supply of tools in the first-class galley. Why not take everything from there?'

'Your guess is as good as mine.'

'When was the theft discovered?'

'About half an hour ago,' said Buxton, running a hand across his brow. 'One of the stewards walked past here on patrol. He thought he heard the sound of running feet as he approached, but he saw nobody when he turned the corner. What he did see,' he went on, waving an arm to include the entire room, 'was this little bombshell.'

The men had completed their search. One of them collected the tools, then they all stepped outside. After switching off the light, the purser used his keys to shift back the levers in the locks before closing the door with care. It sank back down on its hinges with a squeal, allowing him to lock it properly again. He gave a grunt of satisfaction.

'I'll have a man on patrol outside here every fifteen minutes of the day and night.'

'Too late for that,' said Dillman. 'They've already got what they wanted.'

'But they didn't. The object of the exercise was to commit a crime that was not even discovered on board. The first we would have known about it was when some treasury official opened those boxes in New York.'

The man with the crowbars, chisel, and lump hammer

came forward. 'What shall I do with these, Mr. Buxton?' he asked.

'Take them back to the third-class galley,' said the purser. 'It's unlikely there'll be anybody there in the middle of the night. But if there is, don't say where we found them.' He looked at the other men. 'That goes for all of you.'

They nodded. The man with the tools walked off, and at a signal from Buxton, two of the others disappeared as well. The last man was left to patrol the passageway. The purser led Dillman off to his cabin. When they got there, Buxton went straight to a cabinet and took out a bottle of rum.

'This is what I need!' he sighed. 'Will you join me, Mr. Dillman?'

'No thanks.'

'I just never thought it was possible.'

'What?'

'Stealing that gold,' said the other, pouring a tot of rum into a glass. 'We took such precautions. They wouldn't have entrusted that amount of gold bullion to us if they hadn't been a hundred-percent certain we'd deliver the lot in one piece.' He drank some of the rum and licked his lips. 'That's better! You've got to hand it to them,' he said bitterly. 'It was a cunning scheme. Pinching those tools to force their way into the security room, then substituting those house bricks for the gold bars.'

'But that isn't what happened, Mr. Buxton.'

'Isn't it?'

'No,' said Dillman, thinking it through. 'There are too many contradictions. This robbery was planned before we even set sail. Someone clever enough to devise the scheme would never resort to such a crude means of getting into the security room. It would have taken a long time, and there was no guarantee of success. In any case,' he argued, 'if they managed to smuggle those house bricks aboard, surely they would have brought their own tools with them as well.'

'I never thought of that.'

'We may be dealing with two different crimes here, Mr. Buxton.'

'Two?'

'Yes. Suppose that somebody gained entry on Monday night, removed the gold, inserted the bricks, and left everything appearing exactly as it should? I'm sure they used the trolley that went astray. Then,' he speculated, 'another robbery is planned for tonight by the villains who stole those tools. Suppose they went to all the trouble of getting into that security room, opened the first box and saw that it was filled with house bricks.' He turned to the purser. 'What would you do under the circumstances?'

'Swear till my tongue turned blue!'

'I think most people would get out of there fast.'

'They had to make a run for it. They heard the steward coming.'

'And what did he find when he got there?'

'The door wide open and the lid of one box off.'

'Just one?'

'They didn't have time to seal it like the other.'

'But they weren't trying to close it,' insisted Dillman. 'Didn't you see the way it had been forced off with a crowbar? The wood was split. If they'd wanted to cover their tracks, they'd have been more careful when they opened that lid to take out the gold and put in the bricks. No, Mr. Buxton. I'm sorry, but I don't accept your theory. It simply doesn't hold water.'

'Hang on for a moment,' said the other, finishing the rum in one gulp. 'There's something you haven't explained, Mr. Dillman. Assuming that we *are* looking for two sets of thieves, how did the first ones gain access to the security room? We've seen how they forced the door open tonight, but how was it done last night?'

'With keys, Mr. Buxton.'

'But that's impossible.'

'Why?'

'I'm the only person who has a set.'

'And where are they kept?'

'In a locked cabinet in my office. When I'm not there,

the office is locked all the time. Besides,' he said, taking a bunch of keys from his pocket, 'they never went missing at any point. Here they are, safe and sound.'

'May I take a closer look at them, please?'

'Of course.'

Dillman took the keys to inspect them. 'When did you last use them, Mr. Buxton?'

'When I showed you around the security room.'

'And you haven't touched them since then?'

'Not until now.'

'Well, someone else did,' said Dillman, licking the tip of a finger to remove a speck from the end of one key. 'This is wax. Copies have been made of these keys.'

'Copies?'

'An imprint was taken in wax so that a duplicate could be fashioned.'

Buxton was horrified. 'They broke into my office?'

'They used a skeleton key probably. If they have the equipment to make keys, then one of them has had experience as a locksmith. No wonder the robbery went unnoticed,' he said, handing the keys back. 'They were able to let themselves into the security room in a matter of seconds. And because the crime was unreported, they'd have got away with the gold and nobody would have been any the wiser. We ought to be grateful to the thieves who made their bid tonight. They uncovered the truth for us.'

'There's wax on this one as well,' said the purser, scrutinizing another key. 'The clever devils! It never crossed my mind that anyone had invaded my office.'

'That's because they're professionals,' said Dillman. 'Just like Max Hirsch. He went in through locked doors at will. So did these people. I'm absolutely certain that we're investigating two separate crimes here. One was committed by professionals and the other by amateurs.'

'Amateurs?'

'They came unprepared. No tools, no careful planning. They took a huge risk, forcing their way in like that. Think of the noise they might have made. Somebody could easily have caught them in the act. I mean, it must have taken a fair amount of time for them to break in.'

'And a lot of strength,' noted the purser. 'Whoever got in through that door tonight must have muscles the size of coconuts. Do we have any prizefighters aboard?'

Dillman went silent as two faces suddenly popped into his mind.

— — —

Genevieve Masefield slept soundly, relieved that no anonymous note had welcomed her back to her cabin on the previous night. As she lay in bed, she reflected on the events of the day before and on the characters into whose lives she was getting so many new insights. Ruth Constantine remained the most engaging companion, but the one who occupied her thoughts most was Katherine Wymark. She was an enigma. The woman was astute enough to work out Genevieve's true role on board, and articulate enough to dominate the conversation at any table, yet she had married the unprepossessing Walter Wymark, linking herself for life to a man who so obviously lacked grace, dignity, and good looks. The difference in their ages did not worry Genevieve. Happy marriages could make light of a gap of twenty years or more. In the case of the Wymarks, however, there seemed to be a much bigger gap between husband and wife in terms of their outlook and social behaviour. It was perplexing. It was not happiness that Katherine Wymark exuded, but a kind of deep satisfaction over a favourable business deal.

When she got up, Genevieve slipped on her dressing gown and walked out of the bedroom. She came to an abrupt halt. Lying on the floor was a white envelope, pushed under the door at some time during the night. Her stomach tightened. Forcing herself to pick it up, she saw that the envelope bore no name on it. Inside was a message in the same hand as used in the earlier note. It was even more terse this time.

'Tonight?'

One word on a piece of paper was enough to set her mind on fire. She felt hurt, invaded, and obscurely threatened. It was almost as if the mystery correspondent had gained access to her cabin. Who had sent the note? It could hardly be Donald Belfrage; he would have been sharing a bedroom with his wife that night and would not have been able to contrive enough time away from her to woo Genevieve. Harvey Denning was a more likely person, but she still had reservations about that. Orvill Delaney was somehow more circumspect with her since their first meeting, and he had made no attempt to even speak with her after dinner. That left Patrick Skelton as the main contender, but why did she catch a whiff of enmity from a man who – if her guess was correct – might have designs on her?

Was her correspondent someone else entirely? Could it, for instance, conceivably be the strange Edgar Fenby, whom she had seen on the prowl nearby and who had a telling hint of quiet desperation beneath the formal manner? Or might it even be the egregious Walter Wymark, a man with an obvious inclination to possess an attractive woman? The very thought made her crush the piece of paper and hurl it into the wastepaper basket.

Genevieve was trying to compose her thoughts when there was a knock on the door. She was thrown on the defensive immediately, wondering if it might be her stalker, coming early to claim his prize. She took tentative steps back to the door.

'Who is it?' she called.

'A steward, Miss Masefield,' replied a man's voice.

'What do you want?'

'I have an important message for you. I was told to put it into your hands.'

'By whom?'

'Mr. Dillman.'

She relaxed at once and opened the door, taking the letter from the steward and giving him a smile of thanks. When she closed the door, she rested against it to open the envelope, confident that she would have at least one note that would neither distress nor mystify her. Anything that

Dillman wrote was always welcome. Simply to see his neat handwriting was a tonic in itself. Then she read the contents of the letter and gasped in astonishment. When she absorbed the impact of the news, she hurried back into the bedroom and began to get dressed.

The attempted robbery had been a fiasco. The plan had completely backfired. Bowen spent a sleepless night, blaming himself for having been drawn into committing the crime. He feared the consequences. All that effort had produced nothing more than a nasty shock. He and Price had been lucky to get away when they'd heard someone approaching. They were sweating even more by the time they let themselves into their cabin. Since it was shared with the two men from Huddersfield, they could not even discuss what had happened or console each other. Night was one long torment for Bowen, and he could hear his friend gnashing his teeth in the bunk below. When the old man and his companion woke up, Price could not wait for them to go on their way. He sat impatiently on the edge of his bunk and watched the pair of them dress.

'You two were back late,' remarked the old man.

'What's it to you?' asked Price aggressively.

'Nothing, nothing.'

'We didn't want to come back here and find you playing that mouth organ. It drives me mad. You play the same tunes over and over again.'

'They're all I know, friend.'

'Practise them somewhere else.'

The old man was about to reply, but his companion gave him a warning nudge, sensing that the truculent Welshman was in no mood for argument. Pulling on the last of their clothes, the two men mumbled a farewell and let themselves out of the cabin.

'Good riddance!' said Price. 'I thought they'd never go.'

'There's no point in upsetting them, Mansell,' said his friend, dropping down from his bunk. 'I mean, we have to share with them for two more nights yet.'

'Don't remind me!'

'What are we going to do now?' asked Bowen anxiously.

'Nothing.'

'But we broke into that security room, mun.'

'So?'

'They'll come looking for us.'

'Who will?' retorted Price. 'Nobody saw us, did they? Nobody knew that we nicked those tools. There's nothing that leads back to us, Glyn. We're in the clear.'

'Are you sure?'

'Trust me.'

'I made the mistake of doing that once before,' said the other despondently. 'The plan couldn't go wrong, you said. It was bound to work.'

'How was I to know those boxes would be filled with bricks?' snapped Price. 'We got in, didn't we? Exactly the way I told you we would.'

'But we came away with nothing.'

'That's because we were cheated. I bet those boxes of bricks are just a decoy. They must have the gold stashed away somewhere else.'

'Well, I don't want to know where,' said Bowen, asserting himself for once. 'That's it for me. I'm not getting involved in any more risks.'

'But it could so easily have come off, mun.'

'It didn't.'

'Only because they tricked us.'

'No, Mansell. We tricked ourselves.'

'What do you mean?'

'It was doomed from the start.'

'No it wasn't,' said the other, giving him a shove. 'We had bad luck, that's all.'

Bowen said nothing. He brooded in silence while he got dressed, trying to cope with a strong feeling of guilt. Price was untouched by remorse. He pulled on his clothes and sought to justify himself.

'It's always the same,' he said harshly. 'Whenever I set something up, you simply complain. It's not fair. The least I deserve is some thanks. I mean, if everything had gone the way I planned it, we might be heroes who foiled a robbery by now. They'd be all over us. Would that have happened if I'd left it to you? No. What ideas have you ever come up with, Glyn? I'm the brains around here. All you can do is to bleat and whimper like some old woman. Honestly, mun!' he said, confronting the other. 'Sometimes I don't know why I bother with you.'

There was a long pause before Bowen had enough courage to spit out his opinion. 'I think we should own up, Mansell.'

'What?' howled the other.

'They might go easy on us if we explain that we never meant to steal anything.'

'Have you taken leave of your senses?'

'We did wrong. It's preying on me.'

'That doesn't mean to say we rush off to the purser and confess everything. Do you want to spend the rest of the voyage locked up?'

'No,' said Bowen.

'Do you want to face a prison sentence in America and then be deported? Because that's what would probably happen to us. We broke into that security room. They wouldn't show us the slightest mercy.'

'They might if we cooperate.'

'Listen,' said Price, grabbing him by the shoulders to force him against the wall. 'The only person you cooperate with is me. Got it? All right, the plan blew up in our faces. I give you that. But we escaped scot-free. They can't touch us, Glyn. As long as you keep your big mouth shut, that is.' He slammed him even harder against the wall. 'Understand?'

With no strength or willpower to resist, Bowen nodded sadly.

Dillman had breakfast in his cabin with Genevieve so they could compare notes.

'I couldn't believe it when I read your letter,' she said, stirring her tea. 'I thought that gold was in the safest place on the vessel.'

'It is, Genevieve.'

'So how did someone manage to steal part of it?'

'By careful preparation.'

'But they couldn't hope to get ashore with that number of gold bars.'

'Why not?'

'Think of the weight.'

'Do you imagine they haven't already considered that?' he said. 'They weren't expecting the crime to be discovered, remember. It's one of the things that marks them as professionals. The longer you delay discovery, the more chance you have to get away with the loot.'

'But how, George?'

'By using accomplices to take it off the ship in small quantities.'

'We're dealing with a gang?'

'I think so. One of them might even be employed on the *Mauretania*. They had inside help from somewhere. They knew where the keys to the security room were kept and how often a steward went past the place on patrol. We might be looking for five or six people altogether.'

'In first or second class?'

'Both probably. So that they wouldn't be seen together on the voyage.'

'It won't be easy to root them out.'

'That's why I sent for you this morning – to devise our plan of campaign.'

He speared a piece of bacon into his mouth and munched it hungrily. Having been up for most of the night, he felt in need of sustenance. Genevieve drank her tea and tried to assimilate all he had told her about the situation.

'So where do we go from here, George?' she asked.

'The first thing we must do is to keep this to ourselves. Mr. Buxton is frightened that the press might get a hold of it. The cat will really be out of the bag then. Especially if a particular journalist stumbles on the truth.'

'Who's that?'

'Hester Littlejohn. A one-woman tornado.'

'You've told me about her. She writes for an American magazine. Isn't she the one who's trying to uncover the seamier side of the Cunard Line?'

'That's her,' said Dillman tolerantly. 'Mrs. Littlejohn believes that almost everyone in the crew is being exploited by ruthless employers. If it was left to her, she'd divide that gold bullion between the stokers and the stewards. I can see the headline in her magazine – "Cunard Makes Millions While Crew Suffers Misery". Whatever we do, we must keep Mrs. Littlejohn at bay.'

'I'll stay well clear of her.'

'You may have to keep well clear of your friends for a while too, Genevieve. This is going to take your full concentration. You'll have to scour first class for anyone who looks even faintly suspect. That trolley was stolen from your galley, so you have at least one of the gang operating there.'

'What about you?'

'I want to clear up the other crime,' he declared. 'We have more to go on there. The finger points to third class in that case.'

'But there are over a thousand passengers there, George.'

'How many of them are strong enough to pry open a reinforced door with a couple of crowbars and a bolster chisel?'

'Very few.'

'Exactly. I think it was a two-man job, Genevieve, and I might just have met the two men involved. It takes guts to do what they did. Stupidity as well, of course, but we can't deny them guts too. Leave them to me,' he said, slicing a corner off his fried egg. 'If we can solve the second crime, it may give us clues that help us solve the first one also.'

'I hope so, George. We don't have much to go on so far.'

'No,' he conceded. 'That's true.'

'And there's still the problem of the missing passenger.'

'I've got a hunch about that. I think that Hirsch's disappearance is linked in some way to the bullion robbery. Maybe he was an accomplice. Maybe they used him to get those keys from the purser's office. Hirsch was obviously a master at getting into places that were supposed to be safely locked up.'

'So what could have happened to him?'

'Perhaps he and the others fell out,' suggested Dillman. 'Or they simply decided to get rid of him once he'd done his part. Look at the time sequence, Genevieve. Hirsch vanishes on Monday afternoon. The gold – I'm quite certain – vanishes on Monday night. So does the trolley that was taken. It's too much of a coincidence.'

'I agree.'

'The other thing we must do, of course, is to carry out a discreet search of all the unoccupied cabins. There are quite a few. I've already made a list of the ones in first class, and I got the master keys from the purser.'

'Is that where we're likely to find the gold?'

'It's possible. The thieves certainly won't keep it in their own cabins. That would be an outright confession of guilt. No, they'll follow Max Hirsch's example and find a hiding place somewhere else. It may just be an unoccupied cabin.'

'I'll take the list and get started immediately.'

'Finish your breakfast first,' he said, touching her arm with affection. 'The one good thing about this crisis is that it's allowed me to spend a little time with you in private. Don't rush, Genevieve. The missing gold bars are not going to go anywhere.'

'Then neither am I,' she added, blowing him a kiss.

They ate their food and discussed the various possibilities that the crimes had presented. After the meal was over, Dillman went into his bedroom to get the list of first-class cabins. When he came back, he flipped through the pages.

'I came across something rather surprising,' he said, stopping at the last sheet. 'Do you remember that friend to whom you introduced me? That American woman who knows exactly how to make the most of her charms?'

'Mrs. Wymark?'

'That's the one. What do you make of her?'

'It's strange that you should ask,' said Genevieve. 'She baffles me. I'm afraid that she saw through my disguise. I couldn't fool her for a minute. Katherine Wymark likes to point that out. But there's something odd about her. I can't put my finger on what it is, but I sense it's to do with that husband of hers, Walter Wymark. Why pick him when she must have had a hundred other suitors?'

'Why pick me when you must have had a thousand?'

Genevieve laughed. 'That's another mystery I haven't yet solved.'

'Tell me more about Katherine Wymark.'

'There's nothing more to tell. Except that she has half the men in first class gaping at her whenever she walks into the room. Harvey Denning is intrigued by her, I can see. She even makes Donald Belfrage's eyes bulge, and he doesn't like Americans. Mrs. Wymark is a very special woman.'

'With a not very special husband.'

'I find him quite repulsive.'

'But excessively rich, no doubt.'

'Katherine Wymark would never marry a pauper. She's an expensive lady.'

'Obviously. What does her husband do?'

'She was evasive about that. All she would tell me was that he buys and sells.'

'That could mean anything.'

'Mrs. Wymark introduced me to a business associate of his, one Edgar Fenby. A real English gentleman of the old school. I'm surprised that he has anything to do with Walter Wymark. The two of them are like chalk and cheese'

'You clearly have a low opinion of Wymark.'

'He lets his wife down so badly, George. She must realize that.'

'She does. I have the evidence right here.'

'Evidence?'

'Look,' he said, handing the sheaf of papers over. 'Bottom of the last page.'

Genevieve ran a finger down the list of names until she reached the right ones. 'My goodness!' she said, mouth agape. 'Is this true, George?'

'According to the passenger list.'

'Mr. and Mrs. Wymark are in separate cabins.'

'Quite close to each other.'

'But she gave me the impression that they shared the same bed.'

'That was deliberate,' said Dillman. 'It might be instructive to find out why. I think that the Wymarks will bear further investigation, Genevieve, don't you? Find out what sort of a marriage they really have.'

Ruth Constantine was seated at a table with Harvey Denning in the first-class dining saloon, waiting for their breakfast to be served. Ruth was wearing another nondescript dress from her wardrobe, but Denning was impeccably smart and preening himself discreetly. Donald Belfrage came over to join them. Greetings were exchanged as he lowered himself into a chair. He surveyed the room with a freedom that he never enjoyed when his wife was at his side.

'This *is* an honour,' said Denning sarcastically. 'We thought you'd be having breakfast in the privacy of your regal suite.'

'Theo won't wake up for hours,' explained Belfrage, 'and I couldn't wait that long. She took one of her sleeping tablets last night. It's knocked her out completely.'

'That's not much of an advertisement for the joys of marriage.'

'Theo is very tired. She needs a good long sleep.'

'About forty years,' said Ruth with a wicked smile. 'By the time she wakes up, you might have rowed yourself off to the Great Boat Race in the sky.'

'I thought you'd appreciate my company at breakfast, Ruth.'

'We do, Donald. It spices things up no end.'

The waiter brought two meals, then took Belfrage's order before going back to the kitchen.

'Where's Susan?' asked Belfrage.

'She'll be here directly,' said Denning.

'She seemed a little off colour last night.'

'Only because she sat opposite you. Susan was in great form afterward when she and I had another night of triumph playing bridge.'

'What about Genevieve? Doesn't she usually join you?' asked Belfrage.

'No sign of her at all, unfortunately. Maybe I should go and tap on her door.'

'I could do that,' volunteered the other hastily. 'I know which cabin she's in.'

'Leave her be,' said Ruth, restraining him with a hand. 'Genevieve will come in her own sweet time. We mustn't crowd her too much. Or hold her back.'

'From what?'

'Her other admirers.'

'Admirers?' said Belfrage enviously. 'What admirers? They don't include that frightful American, do they?'

'Mr. Delaney is only one of a number. Genevieve turns heads,' Ruth told him.

'Well, that's understandable, I suppose. She's such a wonderful creature.'

Denning laughed. 'You make her sound like a thoroughbred mare.'

'She certainly is a thoroughbred.'

'Just like your wife,' Ruth reminded him.

'Theo is in a class by herself,' said Belfrage dutifully.

'Then why does she have to take sleeping pills?'

'I won't hear any criticism of her, Ruth. My wife is unique.'

'So is this lady,' remarked Denning, watching the couple about to enter the dining saloon. 'Most men would think she gave both Genevieve and Theodora a run for their money, though quite how thoroughbred a mare she is remains to be seen. Smile, Donald,' he warned, digging an amiable elbow into his friend's ribs. 'You're about to meet two of those Americans you love so much.'

'Oh, Lord! Must I?'

Belfrage summoned up a resemblance of a smile as Walter and Katherine Wymark came strolling toward them, arm in arm. Wymark had a proprietorial air about him as he sailed past, acknowledging them with a curt nod. His wife bestowed a gracious smile on the trio before joining her husband at a table nearby. Belfrage stared after her with mingled curiosity and distaste.

'Now if you were married to Mrs. Wymark,' said Denning with soft lechery, 'I don't think you'd allow *her* to forgo the delights of the marital couch by taking a sleeping pill.'

'That isn't why Theo took one,' retorted Belfrage. 'I must say, Harvey, some of your comments are exceedingly personal at times, and I resent that. As for the American lady, she has a certain flashy charm, I grant you, but could you honestly see someone with my background lowering myself to her level?'

'And what level is that?' asked Ruth.

'Well, look at her. There's a touch of vulgarity about the lady.'

'I like vulgar women,' said Denning. 'And any other kind, for that matter.'

'Donald is being unkind,' said Ruth. 'I think the lady has real style.'

'She doesn't compare with Theo,' argued Belfrage. 'Nor, for that matter, with Genevieve. They're two English roses, while Mrs. Wymark is an American cactus.'

Denning seized on the metaphor. 'I'm sure she has plenty of prickles, if that's what you mean. But she also has a natural splendour. Look at the way she holds herself, positively bristling with pride.'

The waiter returned with the other breakfast, and both men began to eat with relish. Conversation soon turned to politics, and Denning undertook to bait his friend in the usual way. Ruth picked at her food and studied Katherine Wymark. The latter was seated at a table with four men, including her husband, indulging in meaningless chatter, yet managing to hold her companions enthralled. Wymark was in an appreciative mood, patting his wife on the arm and laughing at her remarks as if he were hearing them for the first time. Ruth watched the faces of the other three men and noticed their expressions slowly change from interest to fascination.

Dillman borrowed a spare third-class cabin for the interview. Deciding to talk to them both at the same time, he led the two Welshmen in and closed the door behind them.

'You'll have to sit on the edge of a bunk,' he said. 'These cabins don't run to plush armchairs, I'm afraid.'

'We found that out, Mr. Dillman,' said Price warily. 'Now, what's all this about? Why have you brought us here?'

'To have a nice quiet chat. I've explained my position on this vessel.'

'I'd guessed it already. I know a copper when I see one.'

'I'm a private detective employed by the Cunard Line, Mr. Price.'

'Comes to the same thing.'

'Is that what you think, Mr. Bowen?' asked Dillman, turning to the other man.

'I don't know,' he grunted.

'Make yourselves comfortable, anyway.'

'We'll stand,' asserted Price, shooting a look at his friend.

'This may take some time.'

'We got things to do, Mr. Dillman.'

'Not until you've spoken to me.' He extracted pad and pencil from his inside pocket in order to take notes. 'I wonder if you'd care to tell me where the pair of you were just after midnight.'

'Fast asleep,' said Price firmly.

'Is that true, Mr. Bowen?'

'Yes, yes,' murmured the other. 'It's like Mansell says.'

'Did you leave the cabin at any time in the night?'

'Why should we?' asked Price.

'You don't have a bathroom. If you wanted to use one in the middle of the night, you'd have to go out. Did you?'

'No, Mr. Dillman. Neither did Glyn.'

Bowen nodded in agreement, glad to be spared the task of speaking again.

'Do either of you know a man named Arnold Higgs?' They looked blank. 'You ought to. Mr. Higgs has been sharing a cabin with you since Saturday night. He and his nephew, Benjamin Higgs.'

'We don't have anything to do with them,' said Price. 'The old man plays his mouth organ all the time and the other one sits there and grins. We never caught their names proper. The young one calls the old man "Uncle Arnie". That's all we know.'

'I've met them both. Nice people. From Yorkshire.'

'That's why they have those funny accents.'

'I didn't think there was anything funny about them, Mr. Price. They were very helpful. So was Eamonn Casey. Do you recognize that name?'

'Never heard of him.'

'He remembers you. He's one of the stewards in steerage.'

'What about him?'

'You quizzed him about the whereabouts of the gold bullion we're carrying.'

Bowen started, but Price looked unruffled. He put his hands on his hips. 'What if I did?' he said airily. 'Everyone was talking about it. I mean, it's not often you're sitting on a gold mine, is it? I just wanted to know where it was being kept. Not in steerage, that's for sure. We're at the bottom of the heap down here.'

'Let's go back to Mr. Higgs. Uncle Arnie, that is. The older of the two men whose names you couldn't be bothered to find out. Do you know what he used to do for a living, Mr. Price?'

'It certainly wasn't playing the mouth organ!'

'He was a timekeeper in a textile factory for the best part of forty years. Can you hear what I'm saying?' asked Dillman, looking from one to the other. 'The man you share a cabin with was tied to the clock all his working life. You might say he has an ingrained sense of time.'

'So what?'

'According to him – and his nephew says the same – you and Mr. Bowen were out of the cabin last night from about eleven o'clock until well past one this morning.' He saw the shifty look in Bowen's eye and picked on him. 'Is that correct?'

'No,' said Price with vehemence. 'They're bloody liars!'

'I was asking Mr. Bowen.'

'He'll tell you the same as me.'

'Then let him have a chance to do so,' said Dillman, giving him a hard stare. 'I've never liked ventriloquism, Mr. Price. Especially when the pair of you haven't rehearsed your act very well.' He looked back at Bowen. 'Two witnesses tell me that you were out of the cabin for over two hours last night, yet Mr. Price insists that you were both fast asleep in your bunks. Who's telling the truth?'

'Mansell,' said Bowen, glancing nervously at his friend.

'There!' said Price. 'Told you.'

'I'm inclined to believe Mr. Higgs and his nephew.'

'It's their word against ours.'

'No,' said Dillman levelly. 'Their word is backed up by Eamonn Casey's evidence and by the fact that I caught you wandering around the other night in a restricted area of the ship.'

'We got lost.'

'Is that what happened last night? Did you get lost again, then find yourselves – quite by accident of course – outside the security room?' He saw Price's eyes blaze. 'Is that what you were doing when you weren't in your cabin?'

'We never left it, Mr. Dillman.'

'I think you're lying,' said the detective, pocketing his pad.

'Watch what you're saying!' warned Price, squaring up to him.

'Go easy, Mansell,' said Bowen.

'Keep out of this.'

'Calm down, mun.'

'Listen to your friend,' advised Dillman. 'You'll get nowhere by threatening me or by continuing to lie your head off. I put it to you, Mr. Price, that you and Mr. Bowen were not asleep in your cabin at midnight because you were too busy trying to force open the door of the security room to get at the gold.'

Price's anger flared. He clenched a fist to throw a punch, but he was far too slow. Seeing the danger, Dillman took swift action. The first punch sank into Price's midriff to take all the breath out of him, and the uppercut caught him flush on the chin. Gasping with pain and surprise, the Welshman staggered back. Dillman opened the door and beckoned in the two men standing outside.

'Mr. Price objects to being questioned,' he said calmly. 'Please take him away and ask the master-at-arms to lock him up for the time being.'

Price howled with rage and lunged at Dillman, but the two men overpowered him and dragged him out. His yells echoed along the passageway. Bowen had gone white. He shifted his feet uneasily. Dillman had deliberately provoked Price, but his friend required a very different approach. The detective sat down on the edge of a bunk and indicated the one opposite. Bowen slowly lowered himself, sitting with his elbows on his knees and his hands knotted together. His face was a contour map of desperation.

'Now,' said Dillman gently, 'suppose you tell me what *really* happened.'

After an exhaustive search of the cabin, Genevieve Masefield crossed another number off the list that Dillman had given her. Working her way through the unoccupied first-class cabins had taken her all morning, but it was a necessary exercise even though nothing had come to light. The theft of the gold bullion preoccupied her. If it was not recovered before they reached New York, it was not only the captain and the purser who would be held responsible. The unsolved crime would reflect badly on Dillman and herself. They had already traced one cache of stolen property; it was vital to locate another. Genevieve checked her list. There was one more empty cabin to search on the promenade deck.

Letting herself out, she pulled the door shut behind her and turned to walk along the passageway, only to see a familiar figure coming toward her. She froze. It was not the first time she had encountered Edgar Fenby unexpectedly. Was his arrival a coincidence, or had he been following her? She forced a smile. Fenby stopped to give a polite nod.

'Good morning, Miss Masefield,' he said.

'Good morning.'

'I thought your cabin was on the boat deck.'

'Yes,' she said. 'I was just...visiting a friend.'

'I see. You didn't appear for breakfast this morning. It was difficult not to notice,' he said with gallantry. 'Someone as attractive as yourself is conspicuous by her absence.'

'There are plenty of other attractive ladies in the dining saloon.'

'That's true, Miss Masefield.'

'I don't believe I stand out that much.'

'These things are a matter of personal opinion.'

Fenby gave nothing away. The black beard concealed the expression on his face. Words came out smoothly, but they seemed at odds with the cold look in his eyes. He was dressed in business attire and might have been off to a day at the office. Genevieve could almost see the invisible bowler hat on his head. Fenby was appraising her quietly, but she fought off the sensation of unease. Recalling what Dillman had said earlier, she took the opportunity to probe for information.

'Mrs. Wymark told me that you're a business associate of her husband's.'

'That's right,' he said.

'Have you known the Wymarks for long?'

'I've met him a couple of times before, but this is the first time I've had the pleasure of being introduced to his wife.'

'She's very striking.'

'I'd certainly have to agree with that.'

'And highly intelligent into the bargain.'

'That's also true. No disrespect to English ladies,' he said briskly, 'but they're a little less forthcoming than their American counterparts.'

'Blame that on the way we're brought up, Mr. Fenby.'

'I don't believe it's a case for any blame, Miss Masefield. I merely indicated one of the differences between English and American ladies.'

'What are the others?'

'I'm hardly qualified to judge.'

'They seem a strange couple, don't they?' she said artlessly.

'Mr. and Mrs. Wymark?'

'Yes. When I first met her, I had a very clear impression of the sort of man she would marry, but Mr. Wymark is not at all as I would have imagined.'

'They're a well-matched couple,' he said defensively.

'I'm sure they are. They seem quite happy together.'

'Very happy.'

'What line of business is Mr. Wymark in?'

'I don't see that that's any concern of yours.'

'No, of course not.'

'Then why do you ask?'

She gave a shrug. 'Simple curiosity.'

'Why not direct it to Mr. Wymark himself,' he suggested, 'instead of trying to wheedle the information out of me? Be prepared for a vague answer, however. Walter Wymark is a successful businessman who likes to shed his professional burdens when he's on board a ship. Voyages are occasions for pleasure. Like me, Mr. Wymark has put all his business affairs aside for a week.'

It was an odd remark from a man who seemed unable to relax and enjoy himself. Genevieve watched him as he walked away. His manner had been uniformly polite, but she sensed that she had offended him. Edgar Fenby let himself into a cabin farther down the passageway. Since his accommodation was on the promenade deck, she wondered why he had been wandering around the boat deck the previous night. A glance at the list in her hand gave her a clue. The passageway in which she had seen him contained the cabins of Walter and Katherine Wymark. Had he been going to play chess with his business associate? Or did he have another reason to pay a nocturnal visit?

SIXTEEN

Maurice Buxton swung like a pendulum between elation and despair. One crime had been solved with admirable speed, but a far more serious one remained. There was also the continuing problem of a passenger who was missing, along with property he might have stolen from two first-class cabins. The purser did not know whether to celebrate the arrest of the two Welshmen or bemoan the lack of progress on other fronts. Feeling the need for another tot of rum, he instead settled for a comforting pipe of tobacco. Smoke curled up lazily in his office and the familiar aroma began to spread.

'Let's begin with the good news, Mr. Dillman,' he said. 'Bobo is back.'

'I'm glad to hear that.'

'Mr. Reynolds heard him crying outside his cabin and gave him a feed. The cat was starving. He must've been locked in somewhere.'

'I'll pass that information on to a young friend of mine,' said Dillman, thinking of Alexandra Jarvis. 'She'll be very relieved.'

'Nice to know that someone on board this ship is happy.'

'I take it that you aren't, Mr. Buxton?'

'How can I be with this business hanging over us like the sword of Damocles?'

'We've cleared up one crime. Doesn't that reassure you?'

'Only up to a point, Mr. Dillman,' said the purser. 'You caught that pair of jokers who forced their way into the security room last night, and you're to be congratulated.

But they were rank amateurs. How on earth did they expect to get away with it? They could hardly stroll down the gangplank with all those bars of gold in their pockets.'

'That wasn't the plan.'

'Then what was?'

'According to Bowen, they were going to break in, then come to you with a tale of having stumbled on the thieves and fought them off. It was Price's idea,' explained Dillman, 'but how he thought they'd ever get away with it, I don't know. They expected to be praised for their bravery and, more to the point, given some kind of cash reward.'

'That's lunacy.'

'Price thought it was sound common sense.'

'How would they account for the fact that they were near the security room at midnight in the first place? It's completely outside the reach of steerage passengers.'

'Price would have told you they'd got lost.'

'They must think I was born yesterday.'

'They didn't think at all, Mr. Buxton.'

'That's obvious.'

'The crime owes more to impulse than to careful planning. In some ways, I feel sorry for them. They're two ex-miners, down on their luck and looking to make some money.' He heaved a sigh. 'Mind you, I can think of easier ways to do that than by struggling with a steel door for the best part of an hour.'

'You arrested them, Mr. Dillman. That's the main thing.'

'Bowen is not such a bad man. He was more or less bullied into it by his friend.'

'Some friend!'

'There are more details to come out yet,' said Dillman, 'but I thought I'd let the two cool their heels for a while. The master-at-arms has them both under lock and key.'

'They'll need more than a crowbar to get out of those cells.'

'Yes, Mr. Buxton. Price and Bowen won't be getting into any more mischief.'

'It was rather more than mischief.'

'Agreed.'

'Still, we can now put them aside for a moment.'

'Yes,' said Dillman, 'and turn our attention to the real criminals.'

'They won't be quite so easy to unearth.'

'I'm very afraid not.'

'What steps are you taking?'

Dillman told him about his discussion with Genevieve Masefield and detailed the lines of inquiry he now intended to follow himself. Buxton was only partially satisfied.

'Can't we work any faster, Mr. Dillman?'

'We're slow but methodical. That way, we don't attract attention to ourselves. The last thing you want is someone like Hester Littlejohn hammering on your door.'

'I wish the master-of-arms could lock *her* up for me!'

Dillman grinned. 'She's only doing her job. Just like we are.'

'Yes, but her job impedes ours.'

'All that Mrs. Littlejohn wants is a good story.'

'Let her go to the library. The shelves are full of them.'

'Coming back to the matter in hand,' said Dillman seriously, 'I've had some time to reflect on it. The two Welshmen might have been bungling amateurs, but the men who staged the earlier theft were cool professionals. Just think of the planning involved. They not only worked out how to get into that security room with the minimum of fuss, they knew the exact weight of the gold in those boxes. That was why they used the lead lining in addition to those house bricks.'

'How did they get the bricks aboard?' asked the purser, exhaling smoke. 'They're not exactly the kind of things you pack in your bag.'

'We need to go farther back than that.'

'What do you mean?'

'This crime was planned before the gold bullion even left London. The thieves knew everything that was necessary beforehand.'

'All they had to do was to read the newspapers, surely?'

'No, Mr. Buxton,' said the other. 'There were lots of articles about our cargo, I know. I read some of them. But they didn't give precise details about the size and weight of those boxes. Only a privileged few would have that information.'

'A privileged few?'

'At the source.'

'The Bank of England?'

'Where else? The robbers must have had a contact there. There's no other way they could be so well prepared. The average man would have no idea of how gold is refined into bars. Only a banker could know that.' A smile touched his lips. 'Yes, that's right. Why didn't I think of that before? Excuse me, Mr. Buxton,' he said, opening the door. 'I have to go.'

'Where?'

'To see a friend about banking procedures.'

'But we haven't finished our chat, Mr. Dillman.'

'I'll be in touch,' said the detective.

And he was gone.

Eager not to get ensnared at a table with her friends, Genevieve had decided to miss luncheon and complete her tour of the unoccupied cabins. By the time she finished, most of the diners were leaving their seats. After rehearsing her excuse, Genevieve went into the lounge in search of her circle. Pausing at the door, she saw that Ruth Constantine was sitting in a corner with Susan Faulconbridge. Before she could join them, however, a pleasant voice sounded in her ear.

'Ah!' said Orvill Delaney. 'The return of the prodigal!'

'Hello, Mr. Delaney,' she replied.

'I'll tell them to kill the fatted calf immediately.'

'Why?'

'We thought we'd lost you. There was no trace of you at breakfast. According to Miss Constantine, nobody has seen you all morning. When you didn't show up for luncheon, we began to think of sending out search parties.'

'I don't think I'm *that* important a feature of the dining saloon.'

'You are to me,' he said with an affectionate smile.

'Thank you, Mr. Delaney.'

'Welcome back. I won't hold you up from joining your friends.'

'Before you go,' she said, stopping him with a raised hand, 'I wanted to ask you something. You seem to know the Wymarks quite well, and you played chess with Mr. Wymark the other night.'

'So?'

'Don't they strike you as an unlikely couple?'

'No more unlikely than you and I, Miss Masefield.'

'But we're not married.'

'Perhaps not,' he said with a grin, 'though if we stand here together long enough, I'm sure we'll provoke a lot of curiosity. Rumours will soon spread. "Isn't he too old for her? Too ugly? Too American?" Exactly the things they say about Walter Wymark.'

'I'm more interested in his wife, actually.'

'Then you must talk to someone else.'

'Why?'

'Because I never discuss one beautiful lady with another,' he said evasively. 'It would be very ungentlemanly. A beautiful lady is like a concert pianist, Miss Masefield. Nobody needs two at the same time.'

He gave her another smile and went off. Genevieve made her way across to her friends, apologized for her absence at lunch and sat down. Both of them had watched her exchange with Orvill Delaney.

'It's just as well that Donald didn't see you,' observed Susan. 'He doesn't approve of fraternizing with American passengers.'

'More fool he!' said Ruth. 'Mr. Delaney is a charmer.'

'It looked as if Genevieve was doing the charming.'

'We only exchanged a few words,' said Genevieve. 'But I'll be the first to admit that I like Mr. Delaney – and I don't feel obliged to ask Donald's permission to do so.'

'Hear, hear!' said Ruth.

Susan was serious for once. 'Donald is not as stupid as he looks.'

'Nobody could be *that* stupid.'

'Ruth!'

'Donald is a lovable fool. Quite harmless, really. As long as you feed him four times a day and cosset him all night, he can even pass for a civilized Englishman.'

'You don't know him as well as I do.'

'That causes me profound gratitude, Susan.'

'Why bicker about it?' intervened Genevieve, noting the colour rise to Susan's cheeks. 'Donald is a kind, generous man and we all like to have him around. I don't see why you two should fall out over him.'

'Excuse me,' announced Susan, leaping to her feet.

She hastened across the lounge to the door and went out without a backward glance. Genevieve was puzzled and concerned. She looked for elucidation.

'You came at a sensitive moment,' explained Ruth.

'What do you mean?'

'Susan is in rather a bad mood. She and Harvey had a successful night at the card table and reeled off happily together. But he wouldn't go beyond her cabin door.'

'I see.'

'Over luncheon,' continued Ruth, 'it was Donald's turn to upset her, albeit unwittingly. But then, almost everything about Donald Belfrage is unwitting.'

'What did he do?'

'Talked obsessively about you, Genevieve.'

'Oh dear!'

'He touched another raw nerve in Susan. He also irritated Theodora so much that she dragged him off to their cabin after luncheon to have a row with him. That's why they're not here with us.' She gave a slight chuckle. 'He may have to give her another of those pills just to shut her up.'

'Pills?'

'Sleeping pills.'

'Is that what Theodora takes?'

'Occasionally. She took one last night and didn't wake up until ten o'clock this morning.'

The information rang an alarm bell in Genevieve's

head. She might not be as safe from Donald Belfrage as she thought. If his wife resorted to a sleeping pill, she might have no idea of whether or not her husband was still in the cabin with her. Belfrage would be at liberty to pay a visit to the boat deck and knock on Genevieve's door.

'That's why Donald joined us for breakfast,' said Ruth. 'Theodora was lost to the world and he got bored with waiting for her to wake up. He was hypnotized by Mrs. Wymark during the entire meal. Donald pretends to despise the woman, yet he couldn't stop looking at her.'

'Was her husband with her?' asked Genevieve.

'Oh, yes. He was in attendance. But it was the other three men at the table who interested me. I don't know what she was saying to them, but they were completely enraptured by her. Mrs. Wymark was *playing* with them, Genevieve.'

'How did her husband react to that?'

'He was helping her as much as he could. That's what intrigued me. I watched the pair of them carefully throughout the meal, and I had this bizarre feeling.'

'About the Wymarks?'

'That might be his name, but I'm not at all sure that it's hers.'

'What do you mean, Ruth?'

'I don't think they're married at all.'

Pressure of work obliged Dillman to forgo his luncheon as well. He was glad that he had taken the precaution of eating a large breakfast, and even more glad that it had been shared with Genevieve. Hoping to find the Jarvis family, he made his way to the second-class lounge, but someone emerged as he reached the door. Agnes Cameron's face lit up.

'There you are, Mr. Dillman. Is there any news of Max?'

'I'm afraid not, Mrs. Cameron.'

'Wherever can he be?'

'If he's still on the ship, we'll find him sooner or later.'

'And if he isn't?'

'Be patient,' he advised. 'And don't fear the worst.'

'But that's already happened,' she sighed. 'One way or another, I've lost him forever, haven't I?' She made an effort to compose herself. 'I must thank you for arranging to send me that meal yesterday. It was so kind of you.'

'I hope you enjoyed it.'

'I did, Mr. Dillman. I hadn't realized how hungry I was.'

'Good,' he said. 'And I'm pleased to see you out and about again.'

'I can't stay locked away in my cabin for the rest of the voyage. That would be silly. I mean, it's not as if I committed those thefts myself, is it? I told myself that I had to get over my disappointment. Max may have gone,' she said bravely, 'but I've made other friends on the voyage. I had luncheon with the Rosenwalds.'

'Mix with the other passengers as much as you can. It may help.'

'That was my feeling. But I'm so glad that I bumped into you.'

'Are you?'

'Yes, Mr. Dillman. The thing is that I remembered something Max said to me and I thought it just might be useful to you.'

'Go on.'

'When he brought that briefcase into my cabin on Sunday, he said it only contained his overnight things. Obviously, that wasn't the whole truth.'

'Mr. Hirsch was very skilled at concealing the truth, Mrs. Cameron. He told you only what he wanted you to hear. That's the way such people operate.'

'I believed him when he told me about his friends.'

'What friends?'

'Well, you see,' she explained, 'Max was so fond of talking about the number of times he'd crossed the Atlantic in both directions. Since he was such a gregarious man, I said that he must have made lots of friends among the regular travellers. I asked him if any of them were on the *Mauretania*.'

'What did he say?'

'That he did know one couple, but they were in first class.'

'Did he give their names?'

'Mr. and Mrs. Wymark.'

'Can you recall what he said about them?'

'Only that he knew them well and had done business with Mr. Wymark.'

Dillman was so grateful that he wanted to embrace her. A tenuous link had been established between Max Hirsch and two passengers in first class who had aroused Genevieve's suspicion. The information might prove critical.

'Is that helpful?' asked Mrs. Cameron.

'Extremely helpful. Thank you.'

'I was too flustered to remember it when you and Miss Masefield questioned me.'

Dillman chatted with her for a few minutes, then eased her on her way. As soon as he went into the lounge, he saw the Jarvis family ensconced in their chairs. Oliver Jarvis was talking to his wife, Alexandra was nestled against her grandmother, and Noel was gazing through the window at the rise and fall of the waves. Dillman's appearance was welcomed. The parents smiled, the girl giggled with pleasure, and the old woman released one of her celebrated cackles. Even the boy managed to show interest. Dillman apologized for not having seen as much of them as he would have liked and explained that he had been tied up in his cabin with work.

'But I heard one piece of good news, Ally,' he announced.

'Did you?'

'Bobo has been found.'

'Wonderful!' she cried, clapping her hands. 'Where had he been?'

'He hasn't told us yet.'

She giggled again. 'Thank you, Mr. Dillman. Thank you for telling me.'

'I'm sure he'd love to see you,' said Dillman, trying to compound the girl's joy. 'I know that your parents don't want you running off on your own, but I daresay they wouldn't mind if someone else went with you. Mrs.

Pomeroy perhaps?' he suggested, looking hopefully at the old woman. 'The two of you might want to go and see Bobo being fed in a little while.'

'Yes, please!' said Alexandra. 'Can we go, Granny?'

'It's not up to me, Ally,' said the other.

'You'd have no objection, Mr. Jarvis, would you?' asked Dillman persuasively, making a request that he knew would be denied if put forward by the girl herself. 'That cat is very fond of Ally. It seems unfair to keep the two of them apart. Perhaps Noel would like to go along as well?'

'I don't like cats,' said the boy.

'Then your sister can go with Mrs. Pomeroy.' He turned back to the father. 'With your permission, that is, Mr. Jarvis.'

Vanessa Jarvis endorsed the request by squeezing her husband's arm. Unable to refuse, Jarvis gave a nod of approval and collected an impromptu hug from his daughter. Alexandra was far too impatient to wait and insisted that they go off in search of the cat immediately. Dillman offered his hand to help Lily Pomeroy up from her chair. When the two of them left, he settled down opposite Oliver Jarvis.

'I hope you didn't mind my breaking that piece of news,' he said.

'Not at all,' replied Jarvis. 'Alexandra has been moping ever since the animal disappeared. You've cheered her up again, Mr. Dillman.'

'I have a feeling that she'll cheer up Bobo as well.'

'Mother will enjoy a little break from us,' said Vanessa.

Jarvis almost smiled. 'We all need a little break from each other at times.'

'It's so nice to see you again, Mr. Dillman.'

'Thank you, Mrs. Jarvis,' he replied. 'I'm sorry that we haven't been able to see more of each other. At least there's been an improvement in the weather,' he went on. 'It's still too cold and miserable to tempt anyone out on deck, but we don't have Monday's gale that battered the *Mauretania*.'

'I'm so glad about that. We were frightened.'

'I thought we were going to sink,' said Noel mournfully.

'No chance of that,' Jarvis reassured him.

'But you were scared as well.'

'Of course I wasn't,' said his father, flicking him a stern glance. 'My only concern was to comfort you and your mother. There was no real danger of foundering, was there, Mr. Dillman?'

'None at all,' said Dillman, moving the conversation in the direction he wanted. 'If there had been, they'd never have entrusted the best part of three million pounds in gold bullion to the vessel. It must impose a huge responsibility on the captain. Carrying such a cargo, I mean. But I expect that you're used to that kind of thing, Mr. Jarvis,' he reasoned. 'As a bank manager, you must have the responsibility for large amounts of money on a daily basis.'

'We don't keep anything of that value in our vaults.'

'But the bank must have a sizable amount of cash.'

'It does, Mr. Dillman.'

'What sort of security arrangements do you have?'

'Very stringent ones.'

'The same goes for that gold bullion, I'm sure.'

'Yes,' said Jarvis knowledgeably. 'It would have been guarded every step of the way. I've been inside the Bank of England, so I know the kind of security it has in place. Even with an army, you couldn't break in there.'

'Where is the gold refined?'

'There's a special department for that, Mr. Dillman.'

'But who actually does the refining, and what sort of process is it?'

'I'm not really the best person to tell you that, I'm afraid.'

'Why not?'

'Because I've had no direct experience with it,' said Jarvis. 'We have no gold bullion at my branch in Camden. We deal almost exclusively in paper transactions. If you really want to know about refining, you ought to talk to someone from the Bank of England.'

'How can I do that?'

'You can't, unfortunately. Unless you could somehow get into first class.'

'First class?'

'Yes,' explained Jarvis. 'There's a passenger I recognized when he was boarding the boat train. An old colleague of mine, actually. He moved to the Bank of England some years ago and has done very well there, by all accounts. Well,' he added with a rare laugh, 'the fellow is travelling in first class, while we lesser mortals are down here.'

'What's the man's name?' asked Dillman.

'Fenby,' said the other. 'Edgar Fenby.'

Harvey Denning was at his most trenchant. When he joined them in the lounge, he kept them amused with a series of cutting remarks about the other passengers, singling out Walter Wymark for particular scorn. Ruth sometimes added her own caustic observations, but it was Denning who was in full flow.

Genevieve let them bicker on. She was far more interested in keeping Walter Wymark under surveillance than in participating. In view of Ruth's earlier comments about the Wymarks she would have preferred to see husband and wife together, but Katherine Wymark had not come into the lounge at all. Walter Wymark talked briefly to Orvill Delaney, then to another man, and finally to Edgar Fenby. Taking a seat beside him, Fenby was soon locked in an intense discussion with Wymark. Genevieve was mesmerized. The two men were less like business associates than conspirators plotting a coup d'état. Incongruous as they might at first look, they were somehow harmonized by a mutual interest in something of vital interest to both.

When a suggestion was made by Wymark, the other man nodded and looked at his watch. Wymark then handed him something, and Fenby slipped it into one of the pockets of his waistcoat. Genevieve could not see what the tiny object was. Wymark soon rose, shook hands with Fenby, then went quickly out. Fenby immediately checked his watch again and sat back with controlled impatience. Harvey Denning was lampooning all and sundry, but only Ruth heard him; Genevieve was too busy watching Edgar Fenby. Ten minutes after Wymark's departure, he consulted his watch for the third time, got up and strode slowly out of the room.

Genevieve felt impelled to follow him. She sensed that it might pay dividends. 'You'll have to excuse me,' she said, standing up.

Denning was peeved to lose half his audience. 'Deserting us already?'

'I'm afraid I have to, Harvey.'

'Shall we see you for dinner?' asked Ruth.

'Probably. Goodbye.'

She turned away as they waved her off. Heading for the grand staircase, she was just in time to see Fenby's distinctive figure ascending the steps. Wherever he was going, it was not to his own cabin on the promenade deck. Instead, he went up to the deck above and followed the route he had taken on the previous night. Guessing his destination, Genevieve was able to stay well back in order to avoid discovery. When he reached the junction at the end of the passageway, he turned to the left. She scurried forward. Keeping close to the wall, she peered cautiously around the corner. Edgar Fenby did not need to search for a number this time. He reached the cabin he wanted, took a key from his waistcoat pocket and let himself in.

Genevieve was mystified. A hazy idea began to form at the back of her mind, but it had no time to take on shape or substance. She heard footsteps coming and turned around to see Patrick Skelton walking in her direction. Her mouth went dry.

'Good afternoon, Miss Masefield,' he said calmly.

'Good afternoon.'

'We haven't seen much of you today.'

'Is that a complaint?' she asked.

'Take it as you wish.'

'To be honest, I'm surprised that you even noticed I wasn't there.'

'Oh, I noticed, believe me.'

'I didn't know that you had a cabin on the boat deck, Mr. Skelton.'

He gave her a cold smile. 'I don't.'

He walked past her and turned to the right. Halfway along the passageway, he paused outside her own cabin just to let her see that he knew where it was. Throwing a glance over his shoulder, he continued on and turned the next corner. Genevieve shuddered.

Dillman stayed long enough in the second-class lounge to learn as much as he could about Edgar Fenby and his role at the Bank of England. Oliver Jarvis was glad to have such an attentive listener. He waxed lyrical about the joys of working in a bank and talked about his relationship over the years with Fenby. It was clear that the latter's career had accelerated with far more speed than Jarvis's own, a fact that drew a frown of disapproval from his loyal wife. When he had heard enough, Dillman thanked the bank manager for his help, proffered his excuses, and withdrew. He was making his way up the grand staircase when he met Genevieve descending it.

'Thank heavens!' she said. 'I was coming to look for you.'

'Why? What's happened?'

Genevieve was concise, abbreviating her suspicions into a few telling sentences. Dillman needed no time to absorb the information. Matching it with his own discovery, he decided it was time for action. They went back up the stairs together.

'There's a clear connection between them,' he explained. 'Hirsch knew the Wymarks. Mrs. Cameron told me that. And this Edgar Fenby turns out to work at the Bank of England. Mr. Jarvis thinks the man is travelling in an unofficial capacity to hand over that gold bullion in New York. I think he may have had other designs on our cargo. Three links in the same chain – a known thief, an employee at the bank who could furnish vital details about the bullion, and Walter Wymark.'

'What's his role?'

'We'll soon find out.'

They retraced Genevieve's footsteps and came to the passageway on the boat deck to which she had trailed Fenby. She pointed out the cabin he had entered.

'Leave this to me,' Dillman insisted.

'Are you sure, George?'

'Go back to your own cabin. If you leave the door slightly ajar, you'll be able to observe this end of the passageway.' He checked his watch. 'Give me five minutes. If I'm not out by then, go to the purser and raise the alarm.'

'Why not get more support first?'

'There's no point in charging in there with a small army until we have more proof, and I think I have a better chance of getting that on my own.' He kissed her softly on the lips. 'By stealth.'

'Suppose they're armed.'

'Suppose you stop worrying and do as you're told.'

She nodded, brushed his cheek with a kiss, then hurried off to her cabin. When she was safely inside, Dillman went to the cabin into which Edgar Fenby had let himself with the key. He knocked hard on the door. There was no response. He rapped again with his knuckles. A door opened this time, but it belonged to the cabin directly behind him. The burly figure of Walter Wymark confronted him.

'What do you want?'

'To talk to the people inside.'

'There's nobody in there.' Wymark squinted. 'Say, don't I know you?'

'Yes, Mr. Wymark. I'm George Dillman. I was told someone was in there.'

'Then you were told wrong.'

'Let's see, shall we?'

Dillman raised his fist to knock again, but Wymark grabbed his wrist.

'Excuse me,' said Dillman coolly, 'but you seem to have hold of my wrist. Perhaps I should tell you that I'm a private detective employed by the Cunard Line. Unless you wish me to arrest you for impeding an investigation, I suggest that you release me right now. Otherwise, I might start to get annoyed.'

Wymark saw the determined look in his eye. Dillman was younger, taller, and fitter than he was. He could not be frightened away. Letting him go, Wymark forced an apologetic smile and took a step back.

'Sorry, Mr. Dillman,' he said. 'I didn't mean to get in your way. Truth is, I get a lot of guys trying to pester my wife. I thought you were one more of them.'

'I need to talk to her and Mr. Fenby.'

'Who?'

'Edgar Fenby. He's your business associate, I understand.'

'Yeah, he's a banker. Helped to arrange a couple of loans for me.'

'To be honest, I expected to find you in there with them.'

'Hell, no,' said Wymark, thinking fast. 'You've got it all mixed up. Mr. Fenby did call by to pick up my wife, but only to take her off to that concert in the music room. That's where you'll probably find them, Mr. Dillman.' He raised his voice slightly. 'If you want a word with me, step inside. We have two cabins so that I can use one as my office. Come and see for yourself.'

Dillman knew that a signal was being given, but he also knew that Genevieve was still watching the proceedings. He accepted the invitation and stepped into Wymark's cabin. A full minute elapsed before Katherine Wymark opened the door of her own cabin and peered out. She was wearing a silk dressing gown. Believing that the coast was clear, she disappeared again. When the door opened once more, a flustered Edgar Fenby came out and walked away hurriedly. Genevieve Masefield watched it all. The idea that had earlier danced at the back of her mind now pirouetted to the forefront.

— — —

Alexandra Jarvis was thrilled to be reunited with Bobo, and the cat expressed his own pleasure freely. When he finished his meal, he leaped up into her arms and let her stroke him again. Lily Pomeroy gave a sentimental sigh and turned to the officer.

'Oh, isn't that nice!' she cooed.

'Bobo is very fond of your granddaughter.'

'Ally is something of a cat herself. One minute she'll purr quietly in your lap and the next minute she's tearing off somewhere as if you never existed.'

Reynolds could not resist the pun. 'She's a real alley cat, you mean?'

The old woman went off into such peals of laughter that Bobo jumped from the girl's arms in fear and fled along the passageway. Alexandra went after him pleading with him not to run away again. Reynolds stepped out of the cabin with Mrs. Pomeroy to watch the two of them. Bobo relented. Stopping at the end of the passageway, he began to groom himself as if waiting for Alexandra to join him. She walked slowly up to him and reached out, but he was in a playful mood and darted between her feet. When the girl giggled and went after him, he eluded her with ease. The spectators gave indulgent smiles.

'He wants to play games,' said Alexandra excitedly.

'Well, he'll have to play on his own,' said her grandmother, 'because we have to be getting back soon.'

'Oh, not just yet. *Please*, Granny. Five minutes more, that's all.'

'I'm not sure.' She winked at the officer. 'What do you think, Mr. Reynolds?'

'I think we can allow them five minutes together,' he decided, producing a whoop of joy from the girl. 'Bobo's missed her.'

'He has,' confirmed Alexandra, kneeling down so the cat could rub himself against her thigh. 'And I've missed him. Haven't I, Bobo?'

'Can I offer you anything while we wait, Mrs. Pomeroy?' asked Reynolds.

'Don't bother on my account,' she said, almost simpering.

'It's no trouble. I can rustle up a cup of tea in no time. Unless, of course,' he added, raising an eyebrow, 'you'd prefer something a little stronger?'

'Mr. Reynolds!'

'I'll get you a tot straightaway,' he said, going into the cabin. 'I'd love to join you, but my watch starts soon and I can't be tipsy on the bridge. Come on in for a moment, Mrs. Pomeroy.'

'Thank you,' she said, tickled at the notion of being offered a drink of rum by an attractive officer. 'Perhaps we should make that *ten* minutes.'

Bobo wanted more fun. As soon as the adults disappeared, he turned tail and fled in the opposite direction, pausing at the corner to give his friend a teasing look before he vanished. Alexandra sprinted after him at top speed, ready for any game he chose.

'Bobo!' she shouted happily. 'Come back here! Bobo!'

The chat with Walter Wymark was brief, but revealing. Dillman quickly realized that the man was not involved in the gold-bullion theft and that the verbal charade he was putting up was meant to mask a different crime altogether. Giving Wymark the impression that he believed what he was being told, he took his leave and walked down to Genevieve's cabin. When she told him what she had seen from her vantage point, it confirmed his suspicion.

'I think you should take over now, Genevieve,' he suggested.

'It will have to be handled with care.'

'That's why I'm bowing out.'

She grinned. 'What you mean is that under the circumstances, you're frightened to be left alone with Mrs. Wymark.'

'Let's just say that this is a job for a woman, Genevieve.'

He gave her a kiss, let himself out and headed for the grand staircase. Dillman was disappointed that his assumptions about Wymark and the others had been proved wrong. At the same time, he was grateful that he had chosen to make the call alone instead of forcing his way into Katherine Wymark's cabin with armed men in support. That, he now saw, would have been highly embarrassing for all concerned. Intending to report to the purser and apologize for his earlier abrupt departure, Dillman was disconcerted to approach the man's cabin and see Hester Littlejohn coming out of it. Her expression changed from irritation to pleasure in a flash.

'Hello, Mr. Dillman,' she said. 'You're just the man I want.'

'That sounds ominous, Mrs. Littlejohn.'

'I've had the most frustrating interview with Mr. Buxton. I thought the function of the purser was to help passengers, not to keep them at arm's length.'

'What happened?'

'He refused to give me the information I need.'

'And what's that?' asked Dillman warily.

'Well,' she said, moving him away from the door, 'one of the British journalists – I think it was the correspondent from *The Times*, actually – overheard a lady in first class saying that her gold watch went astray but a woman detective found it for her within a day. I didn't know there were such things as female detectives.'

'But *you* are one, Mrs. Littlejohn,' he pointed out.

'Not that kind. Who is she, Mr. Dillman?'

'I can't help you there, I'm afraid.'

'Neither could the purser. He was quite infuriating.'

'Mr. Buxton was only protecting the lady's identity.'

'But I want to do an interview with her.'

'That would be very unwise.'

'Unwise?'

'And unfair, Miss Littlejohn,' he argued. 'You'd break the lady's cover and that would make her far less effective in her work. In fact, she'd probably lose her job as a result and you, of all people, wouldn't want to be responsible for that.'

'No, no, Mr. Dillman.'

'If the lady exists – and it's only hearsay that she does – I'm quite sure she'd prefer to remain anonymous.'

'Like that man who helped secure the anchor in a gale?'

'Exactly like him.'

'That means I have to miss out on *two* exclusive stories,' she complained. 'No female Sherlock Holmes and no courageous passenger. On top of that, the purser tells me that not only has the missing cat been found, but that those tools that were taken from the third-class galley turned up out of the blue.'

'I had a feeling they might.'

'What am I to do, Mr. Dillman? I need a theme for my articles.'

'I would have thought that you already have one.'

'Do I?'

' "Unsung Heroines." This lady you mention might be one of them, except that you'd jeopardize her position by saying so. But there are other women on board whose work should be celebrated. The stewardesses, for instance.'

'I've spoken to all ten of them,' she said, warming to his suggestion. 'And to the two matrons. They get the most pitiful wages.'

'Tell that to your readers.'

'Oh, I will. And I won't pull any punches.'

'Don't forget to say that none of those women are forced to work on the Cunard Line,' he warned. 'They do it by choice, so there must be rewards of the heart that are not reflected in their wage packet.'

'Exploited, Mr. Dillman,' she insisted.

'Then sing their praises from the rooftops.'

'They do a remarkable job. Each and every one of them.'

'That includes the most important lady of all, Mrs. Littlejohn.'

'Who's that?'

'The *Mauretania* herself, of course,' he explained. 'She's done wonders under trying conditions. Put her at the top of your list of "Unsung Heroines".'

'I'd never have thought of that. Thank you, Mr. Dillman.'

'My pleasure – but I'll let you go now.'

'Oh, yes. I'll have to speak to all twelve women again.'

'Why?'

'To check my facts,' she said earnestly. 'I always try to fit in a second interview, if at all possible. No matter how meticulous you are, there's usually something you miss, some tiny but crucial detail that only comes out the second time.'

'Yes,' he said thoughtfully. 'That's a good point.'

'And at least, they'll cooperate. Unlike the purser. He wouldn't tell me a thing. I still don't know if that silver cutlery has been recovered yet.'

'Don't worry about that, Mrs. Littlejohn. You already have your story.'

She nodded and bustled off. Dillman acted on her advice; a second interview was a wise precaution. Instead of going to see Buxton, he headed straight for the master-at-arms' cabin. A few minutes later, a penitent Glyn Bowen was being unlocked from his cell. The prisoner was haggard with fear and anxiety. There was no Mansell Price to tell him what to do and say now. He was completely on his own.

'How are you getting on?' asked Dillman.

'It's miserable in here.'

'You can hardly expect a first-class cabin after what you did.'

'That's what Mansell reckoned we'd get. A big reward from the purser and a cabin among the toffs. Never thought we'd end up in a cell.'

'Are you sorry for what you did, Mr. Bowen?'

'We were so *twp*,' he admitted. 'That means stupid.'

'What drove you to it?'

'Mansell.'

'But what put the idea in his head in the first place?'

'I told you, Mr. Dillman. He's always been a bit wild.'

'Tell me again,' invited Dillman softly. 'Step by step. Give me the details you left out last time. How you stole those tools, for example.'

'That was Mansell's doing.'

'When did he take them?'

'On Monday,' said Bowen, keeping his voice down for fear his friend would overhear him from the adjoining cell. 'The problem was that we couldn't keep them in the cabin, see? There was nowhere to hide them. If those blokes from Huddersfield didn't spot them, the steward would when he changed the bed.'

'So where did you hide them?'

'In the cargo hold.'

Dillman was astonished. 'The cargo hold?'

'Seemed like the safest place. Mansell opened the lock with his penknife. He's good at things like that. We stuffed the tools inside.' He shivered: 'It was so creepy.'

'Why was that, Mr. Bowen?'

'This cat ran past me in the dark. Made me jump.' He grimaced at the memory. 'Then he did it again when we opened the door to get our tools. He shot out like he was in some race. Even Mansell was surprised by that.'

Dillman's mind was alight. The team of men who had worked their way through each deck of the vessel had finished up in the cargo hold, but they had been looking for a missing passenger. Since the theft from the security room was undiscovered at that point, they would have had no reason to look for hidden gold bullion, yet where better to conceal it than among the luggage, which would not be moved until they disembarked? Hester Littlejohn's advice was sound; the second conversation with Glyn Bowen had supplied a new and important detail.

At a signal from Dillman, the master-at-arms eased Bowen back into his cell in order to lock the door again. The Welshman reached out a pleading hand.

'Mr. Dillman!' he called.

'Yes?'

'What will happen to us, sir?'

'I don't know, Mr. Bowen. It's not up to me.'

'But you'll have to give evidence against us, won't you?'

'Yes,' said Dillman, hearing what he was being asked, 'and I'll point out that you were very cooperative. Unlike Mr. Price. That may well be taken as a mitigating factor.'

'What does that mean?'

'It should help you.'

When she was admitted to the cabin, Genevieve saw that Walter Wymark was also there. He gave her a hostile glare but she held her ground. Katherine Wymark took control of the situation and ushered him out. Unperturbed, she offered her visitor a chair, then sat down opposite her with a bland smile.

'I had a feeling you'd call on me sooner or later, Miss Masefield.'

'Did you?'

'Yes,' said Katherine. 'You had to take off your mask eventually.'

Genevieve was brisk. 'I won't beat about the bush. You've met Mr. Dillman, a colleague of mine. Not long ago, he came to visit you.'

'I wasn't here when he called.'

'But you were, Mrs. Wymark. He took the precaution of stationing me where I could watch your cabin in case there was a problem. Mr. Dillman was diverted by your husband, who took him into the cabin opposite. I saw you peer out, and I couldn't help *but* notice that you weren't wearing what you have on now,' she said, glancing at the other's fashionable green dress. 'I also couldn't help observing the furtive way in which Mr. Fenby had to break off negotiations with you.'

Katherine laughed. 'Negotiations!'

'I was trying to use a polite word.'

'Use the one that fits the situation, Miss Masefield. Or do you think it will stain that pure English tongue of yours? Go on – say it.'

'Is it necessary?'

'I want to see if you have the nerve to speak it.'

'It's not a question of nerve,' said Genevieve sharply, 'and you know it. The Cunard Line does not condone the use of its vessels for prostitution.'

'Well done!' said Katherine, clapping her hands. 'You made it at last.'

'Mr. Fenby came here for an assignation.'

'How do you know, when you weren't in the cabin at the time?'

'Why deny it, Mrs. Wymark? I saw your husband give Mr. Fenby a key in the lounge. When I followed Mr. Fenby, I also watched him let himself into this cabin. So please don't insult my intelligence by telling me that you put on a dressing gown simply in order to make Mr. Fenby feel at home.'

'But he's *not* at home, Miss Masefield. That's the whole point.'

'Is it?'

'Of course.' A long sigh. 'You're not as worldly as I thought you were.'

Genevieve was blunt. 'I think we've each disappointed the other.'

'What was that word again?' teased Katherine.

'Mrs. Wymark…'

'Please. Just once more. I like the prim way you say it.'

'Prostitution,' said Genevieve firmly. 'Engaging in sexual intercourse with a man for monetary reward. In your husband's case, there is the associated charge of procuring and living off immoral earnings.' Katherine laughed again. 'I'm glad you find it so amusing, Mrs. Wymark.'

'I just wish you'd hear what you actually said. Engaging in sexual intercourse with a man for monetary reward? That sounds like a pretty good definition of marriage to my ear. The man gets the pleasure, the woman gets the financial security. And as for Walter living off my immoral earnings,' she continued, 'why should he do that? He already has a very lucrative business.'

'Buying and selling. I think we both know what you sell, Mrs. Wymark.'

'Did you see any money change hands?' challenged the other.

'No, I didn't.'

'How do you know that a sale of any kind was involved? I trade, Miss Masefield. I barter. I give some of this for some of that. Who are you to say that I didn't invite Mr. Fenby in here out of the kindness of my heart?'

Genevieve looked her in the eye. 'I've met him, remember.'

'A fair point,' conceded the other, amused.

'Also remember that I saw your husband give him the key to this cabin. Mr. Wymark not only condoned what took place, he actively promoted it.'

Katherine was scathing. 'Nothing took place, believe

me! Mr. Fenby is an English gentleman. He needs fifteen minutes just to undo a shoelace, and that colleague of yours, the dashing Mr. Dillman, didn't give him enough time for anything else.'

'I gathered that.'

'When he banged on the door like that, he put the fear of death into my visitor.'

'You're getting away from the point, Mrs. Wymark.'

'And what's that?'

'The Cunard Line has a strict policy.'

'No whores in first class,' said Katherine sourly. 'Well, that's what you're calling me, isn't it? I'm the whore and Walter is my pimp. So what do you propose to do, Miss Masefield? Tar and feather us? Feed us to the sharks?'

'I'll report the matter to the purser and he'll take the necessary steps. My job is simply to confront you with the evidence. I'm sorry you've been so obstructive.'

'Obstructive? What am I supposed to do when you're about to ruin my reputation? Lie back and let you do it? I'm obstructive, okay,' she warned. 'I'll obstruct you, the purser, and the interfering Mr. Dillman as much as I damn well can.'

'None of this is helping you, Mrs. Wymark.'

'Who says I want to be helped?'

'You've done wrong. You've been caught.'

'No,' snapped the other. 'I live my life the way I choose. I resent you coming in here with your moral certainties and calling me a scarlet woman. I'm not a prostitute, Miss Masefield!' she said emphatically. 'I'm not a common hooker. If I were, why did Captain Pritchard have me at his table in the dining saloon? Why have the most respectable people on this ship been glad to spend time with me?' She pointed a finger. 'The only name I may just answer to is "courtesan". That's a woman with real class who consorts only with selected courtiers. Highly selected at that. They don't choose me, Miss Masefield. I choose them.'

'I'm glad we agree on the basic point.'

'Have *you* never taken a man for the sheer pleasure of it?'

The directness of the question made Genevieve pause. She did her best to conceal her discomfort. The conversation was not taking the course she had hoped for. When she was put on the defensive, she could hear the self-righteous tone in her voice, and the last thing she wanted to do was to appear a prig. She made an effort to relax.

'Look, Mrs. Wymark,' she said reasonably, 'I'm not enjoying this any more than you are. I'm sorry if I offended you or if I appear to be handing down moral judgments from up on high. That's not the case at all. What I want to say is this: We have certain rules on board. In our view, you've broken those rules. How, when, and to what degree is, frankly, your business.' Her voice hardened slightly. 'But we can't ignore them, I'm afraid.'

'You didn't answer my question, Miss Masefield.'

'We're not talking about me.'

'But we are, don't you see? We're talking about *every* woman.'

'My private life is my own,' said Genevieve quietly, 'but you're perceptive enough to deduce certain things about me, so you can make your own judgment. After all, you saw through my disguise as if it were a thin veil. I should've realized then that you were seasoned in the art of spotting detectives in order that you could steer clear of them.'

'In your case, that's not what I did,' said the other. 'I rather enjoyed taunting you with the fact that I knew your little secret.' She gave a shrug. 'Now you know mine. A part of it, anyway.'

'I won't press for details.'

'You wouldn't get any, Miss Masefield.'

'There is just one thing I'd like to ask.'

'Let me save you the trouble. No,' she said, eyes smoldering. 'Walter is not my husband. Do you think I'd let a man like that anywhere near me? I do have standards. He's a useful bodyguard, that's all. We trade. Both of us profit.'

'I won't pretend that I understand.'

'Yours is one world, mine is another.'

'I accept that,' said Genevieve, 'but the purser will still have to know.'

'Tell him,' replied Katherine airily. 'I'm not ashamed of anything I've done, and I fancy that Mr. Buxton might be more amenable to reason than you are. You surprise me, Miss Masefield. I need hardly tell you that I don't like detectives or policemen of any kind, but you were the exception. Until now, that is.'

'I'm sorry it had to end this way. I enjoyed our earlier conversations.'

Genevieve got up from her chair and moved to the door. Katherine followed her.

'By the way,' she said casually, 'I'm pleased that Mrs. Dalkeith got her gold watch back. It was very foolish of her to walk out of the ladies' room and leave it lying there on the basin. In a sense, she almost deserved to lose it, didn't she? I wonder how it made its way back to you, Miss Masefield.'

'I wonder.'

'It's just as well we have detectives working on the ship, isn't it?'

'Yes, Mrs. Wymark.' Grateful that the mystery of the watch had been solved, Genevieve gave her an appreciative smile.

'Goodbye, Miss Masefield. I hope that we won't have to speak again.'

'No,' said Genevieve, 'I'm afraid that we won't.'

Bobo was relishing the game, staying close enough to Alexandra to remain in sight but too far ahead of her to be caught. The girl was in her element, giggling merrily as she chased him and oblivious to the passage of time. As she followed his twists and turns and plunges down companionways, she was quite unaware of the fact that she was now completely lost. Eventually he paused outside an open door to lick at a paw. Alexandra stopped to catch her breath, then crept forward very slowly. He let her get within a foot of him before taking off through the door. She went after him and found herself in the cargo hold. The girl was not alone.

'Ally!' said Dillman in amazement. 'What are you doing here?'

'I was chasing Bobo.'

'Is the cat here as well? Bobo got locked in here once before. We don't want that happening again. Let's find him quick.'

Dillman was leading a search party of four men who were working their way through everything in the hold. The girl stared at them in bafflement.

'What's going on, Mr. Dillman?'

'Oh, I found I needed some of my luggage and these gentlemen are very kindly helping me find it. But let's get Bobo out of here first. We can't lose the ship's mascot again. He is definitely "Wanted On Voyage." '

Eager to get rid of the girl, Dillman joined her in the hunt for the cat. Bobo was not going to be caught easily. He jumped on crates, hopped down between trunks, dodged between boxes, and crawled into places where they could not reach him without shifting several items. Dillman tried to remain patient. Searching for a cache of gold bullion, the last thing he wanted to do was to waste time chasing a black cat, but it had to be done. Bobo was eventually cornered, but he had one more hiding place. As Dillman and the girl closed in on him, he spun around and dived underneath the impressive new Lanchester automobile that was gleaming in the light.

'Get out of there, Bobo,' ordered the girl with a laugh.

'Come on,' coaxed Dillman. 'Come on, Bobo.'

But the animal was deaf to any blandishments. Instead of leaving his refuge, he simply curled up in a ball as if about to go to sleep. Dillman moved with caution. Lowering himself to the floor, he crawled under the vehicle until he could reach out a long arm. His hand fell on Bobo.

'Give him to me, Mr. Dillman,' pleaded the girl.

'If I do, hold him tight.'

'I will, I promise.'

'When I pass him back,' said Dillman, 'take him from me.'

Still full-length under the vehicle, he handed the cat to her. Alexandra cradled the animal in her arms, alternately stroking and scolding it. Bobo was content. He'd had his fun and wanted to be cosseted now. Dillman, meanwhile, was trying to wriggle back out from under the car. When he made the mistake of lifting his head too high, it collided with something solid. He rubbed his scalp and looked up ruefully. Then he saw what he had struck and the pain vanished miraculously.

'Quick!' he shouted. 'Someone bring a light over here!'

Orvill Delaney pored over the chessboard for several minutes before he moved a white bishop. He then turned the board around so that he was now in charge of the black pieces. Playing chess against himself was, he found, a stimulating way to pass an hour or two. It tested his mettle and kept him in readiness for any opponent he might take on. Delaney was about to use the black queen to swoop on another pawn when there was a sharp tap on the door. He opened it to be confronted by Dillman. When he had introduced himself, the detective was invited into the cabin. His host was relaxed and hospitable.

'Do take a seat, Mr. Dillman,' he said, indicating a chair. 'I suppose I can't tempt you to a game of chess?'

'I'm afraid not, sir. And I'd rather stay on my feet, if you don't mind.'

'That means it's a short visit.'

'Not necessarily.'

'In that case, you won't mind if I sit down, will you?'

Delaney lowered himself into the chair beside the table. He was impeccably dressed and seemed both unsurprised and unworried by the visit from the detective. Dillman appraised him carefully before speaking.

'I understand that you own an automobile, sir,' he began.

'I own three actually, Mr. Dillman. The Cadillac and the Great Chadwick Six are back home in the States. The Lanchester 12 H.P. is down in the cargo hold.'

'I know, sir. I've just been examining it.'

'Wonderful vehicle! Four-litre engine with fully automatic lubrication and a three-speed epicyclic gearbox. I hope you were impressed.'

'I didn't have time to admire it, Mr. Delaney.'

'A pity,' said the other. 'You'd have seen some real craftsmanship.'

'The only feature that interested me was the one that was out of sight,' said Dillman, watching him shrewdly. 'A steel box has been welded onto the vehicle just in front of the rear axle.'

Delaney chuckled. 'What on earth were you doing under my Lanchester?'

'That doesn't matter, sir. The point is that I found the steel box and when we unscrewed the front panel, I saw what it contained.'

'And what was that?'

'I think you already know, Mr. Delaney.'

'But I don't. Surprise me.'

'Gold bullion.'

'You're joking!' said the other, getting up. 'That's a design feature that wasn't mentioned in the specifications. Gold bullion? Do I get to keep it?'

'No, Mr. Delaney. It's already been put back into the boxes from which it was stolen. There's a twenty-four-hour guard on the security room now so that nobody will be able to break in there again. It was a very clever plan,' he said, looking over at the chessboard. 'Worthy of someone with a sharp mind that he keeps in trim.'

Delaney spread his hands. 'Do I hear you properly, Mr. Dillman?'

'I think so, sir.'

'You're suggesting that I actually *knew* about that gold bullion?'

'Don't play games with me, Mr. Delaney,' warned the detective.

'I could say the same to you,' returned the other. 'I don't find it at all amusing to be accused of something I didn't do. Is this some new game that Cunard has devised? What do you call it, Mr. Dillman – "Insult the Passengers"?'

'I call it making an arrest, sir.'

'On what evidence?'

'On that of my own eyes,' said Dillman smoothly. 'So it's

no use wearing that expression of injured innocence, sir. If you want me to tell you exactly how the gold bullion was taken, I will.'

'Please do. I'd love to hear.'

'You planned the whole thing well in advance. Knowing that the difficult part of the operation was to get the gold bars safely off the vessel, you bought the car and had the metal box welded underneath it. Then you stole the security-room keys from the purser's office and took an imprint to make duplicates. That enabled you to let yourself into the security room on Monday night. Am I right so far, sir?'

'No, but I'm fascinated nevertheless.'

'The crux of the plan,' said Dillman, 'was to make sure the theft was not discovered until you were off the vessel and driving away fast. When you took out the bars, therefore, you put house bricks into the boxes instead, and added a lead lining to bring them up to the exact weight required.'

Delaney grinned. 'House bricks? Lead lining? Really, Mr. Dillman. Do I look like the sort of man who carries things like that around in his pocket?'

'The materials were brought on board in the box beneath your automobile so that they could be retrieved when needed. A trolley was stolen from the first-class galley to facilitate the movement of the bricks and then of the bullion.'

'You have a remarkable imagination for a detective.'

'It doesn't quite match yours, Mr. Delaney.'

'I still haven't heard any evidence that *I* am the man who committed the crime. All you've offered me so far is this incredible story of how you think it was done.'

'How I *know* it was done, sir.'

'By whom?'

'You and your accomplices.'

'Oh, I see,' mocked the other. 'I have a gang of desperadoes, do I?'

'You had a contact at the Bank of England who provided you with details about the size and weight of those boxes in the security room. And you had someone on board who could steal keys and make duplicates.'

'And who might that be?'

'A possible name is that of Max Hirsch.'

'Who?'

'A passenger from second class who inexplicably went missing during the storm on Monday afternoon. My guess is that Hirsch was mixed up in this business somehow.'

'But I've never even heard of the man.'

'So you say.'

'Nor have I any idea of how that gold bullion came to be found under my vehicle. Somebody must have known I was shipping my new automobile to the States and decided to use it for his own purposes. That's the only conclusion I can reach.'

Dillman was brusque. 'The only one that I can reach, Mr. Delaney, is that you're a barefaced liar. I'd better warn you now that no judge will be taken in by your denials either. It's my duty to place you under arrest,' he said, taking a firm hold of the man's arm, 'before I start to round up your accomplices.'

'And who are they?' asked the other coolly.

'I propose to begin with Mr. Patrick Skelton.'

Genevieve Masefield was in a state of exhilaration. After being told by Dillman of the discovery in the cargo hold, she was able to link Delaney's name with that of Skelton's and to provide other information that sealed the culprits' fate. Everything was now clear. Orvill Delaney was a criminal with well-developed cultural interests. Genevieve was also certain that he had preceded Edgar Fenby into the arms of Katherine Wymark, using the mention of a game of chess with her putative husband as a euphemism. The woman had warned him that Genevieve was no mere fellow passenger, and Delaney had passed on that intelligence to Patrick Skelton. It explained the subtle alteration in Delaney's manner toward her, and it also relieved her of one anxiety. Skelton was not the man who had pushed the notes under her door.

When he had paused outside her cabin, he was not issuing a covert warning; he was taunting her. Skelton was supremely confident that he had helped to commit the perfect crime. He believed it would not come to light until long after he and Delaney had disembarked, and even then there would be nothing to incriminate them. During their brush on the boat deck, Skelton was simply indicating that he knew all he needed to know about Genevieve Masefield. He knew where she slept and what her official position was on the *Mauretania*. Delaney's cabin was also on the boat deck, so Skelton had a legitimate reason to be there. That is where he must have been heading when he encountered her.

Skelton was not there now. He was chatting to a steward in the first-class lounge. When she saw him, Genevieve was even more exhilarated. Dillman had gone to confront Delaney, but she did not wish to be left out of the action. Since she still had the list of first-class passengers, she could easily identify Skelton's cabin. One of the master keys that Dillman had given her was bound to let her into it. Reassured that the man himself was occupied in the lounge, she checked her list, then hurried off to the cabins on the promenade deck. She had to try three keys before she found one that fit. Once inside, she felt a surge of fear and excitement, worried that he might catch her there, yet fired by the thought that she might find some damning evidence against him.

Her search was swift but thorough. This time she did not have the disapproving presence of Agnes Cameron to hamper her. She went through every drawer and examined all the garments in the wardrobe. She also searched the bedroom and the bathroom, but none of them yielded what she hoped to find. It was only when she looked under the bunk that she saw the briefcase. Pulling it out, she took it through into the main area to place it on the table and open it. A briefcase was a normal accessory for an accountant, and she expected to see it filled with documents and business papers. Instead, Genevieve saw something wrapped in a scarf. When she unwound the scarf, she was looking in wonderment at solid silver cutlery. Amid the knives was a silver-and-ivory eyeglass case with tissue paper around it.

'What are *you* doing in here, Miss Masefield?' said a menacing voice.

The key had been inserted so silently in the lock that Genevieve had not even heard it. Patrick Skelton stepped into the cabin, closed the door and kept his back to it. He looked down at the briefcase on the table. Shocked at his sudden arrival, Genevieve stood there with her heart pounding.

'That was very silly of you,' he warned. 'I had a feeling that you were up to something when I caught a glimpse of you in the lounge. You were checking to see where I was.'

'With good reason, Mr. Skelton.'

'Oh?'

'You've got stolen property here.'

'From where I stand, you look more like the thief than I.'

Genevieve faced him boldly. 'The game is up, Mr. Skelton. The gold bullion that you stole has been found in its hiding place in the cargo hold. My colleague is arresting Mr. Delaney at this very moment.'

'But that's impossible,' said the other, stunned by the news.

'We may also wish to ask you about the disappearance of Max Hirsch.'

'Who?'

'Another passenger,' she explained, pointing to the briefcase. 'The man who in all probability stole these things from their rightful owners.'

'Hirsch, eh?' said the other, taking a step toward her. 'So that was his name.'

'You did meet him, then?'

'Oh, yes. He made the mistake of stumbling on us when we were testing the keys to the security room. It was in the middle of that gale, when the ship was rolling heavily. We thought that nobody would be about at that time.'

'Mr. Hirsch was.'

He smirked. 'Not anymore.'

Genevieve hid her apprehension. Skelton was too strong for her to overpower, and there was a vengeful glint in his eye as he moved even closer. All she could do was to keep him talking until Dillman arrived.

'Who made the duplicate keys?' she asked.

'I did.'

'But I thought you were an accountant.'

'I am, Miss Masefield,' he explained. 'But my father was a locksmith and I learned the rudiments of the trade at his knee. Making a duplicate is not too difficult. All you need is a blank key, the right tools, and lots of patience. The tools fell over the side of the ship on Monday night. That's why you didn't find them in your search.'

'But I found this briefcase, Mr. Skelton.'

'You're going to regret that, I'm afraid.'

'Am I?'

'I can't have you telling people what happened to Mr. Hirsch, can I?'

'You killed him, didn't you?'

'Why not ask him when you meet him?' he said, grabbing her quickly and clapping a hand over her mouth to stop her from calling out. 'Because you're going to make the same journey he did – over the side of the ship!'

Genevieve struggled hard, but his grip was too powerful. She was finding it difficult to breathe with his hand over her face. When she tried to bite it, he rammed her against the wall by way of punishment. Slightly dazed, heart thumping and body sagging, she began to fear the worst. She was trapped by a man who had already committed one murder and would not hesitate to commit a second. Genevieve made one last effort to squirm free, but Skelton tightened his hold.

It was then that Dillman knocked on the cabin door. 'Mr. Skelton?' he called. 'Are you there, sir?'

Standing behind her, Skelton put an arm around Genevieve's neck. 'Quiet!' he whispered. 'Make a noise and I'll break your neck.'

Another knock. 'Mr. Skelton? Are you in there?'

It was Genevieve's only chance. If Dillman believed that the cabin was unoccupied, he would go away and leave her to Skelton's mercy. The briefcase still lay open on the table, projecting over the edge. She kicked at it with all her might. There was a clatter as sixty-four pieces of cutlery and an eyeglass case were tipped out of the falling briefcase. Skelton went berserk, hurling her against a wall, then using both hands to try to strangle her. The attempt was short-lived. Dillman's impetus was much too strong for the cabin door. The force of his shoulder broke the lock and he came hurtling in. He was on Genevieve's attacker in a flash, tearing him clear of her and hitting him with a relay of punches that sent Skelton to the floor. Dillman sat astride him, raining blows to his face and body until the man's spirited resistance eventually stopped. Gasping for breath, Skelton was now covered with blood.

Orvill Delaney, held by two of the crew, watched through the open doorway.

'I *told* you to get rid of that stuff,' he said with disgust. 'What's wrong with you, Patrick? Wasn't your share of the gold enough for you?'

Dillman was on his feet, comforting Genevieve. She rubbed her neck gingerly. 'They threw Mr. Hirsch over the side of the ship, George. He admitted it.'

'What do you say to that, Mr. Delaney?' asked Dillman.

'You'll have to return my magazine, Miss Masefield,' he said politely. 'It looks as if I may have plenty of time to read O. Henry's stories now.'

The ordeal in the cabin had shaken Genevieve badly, but Dillman's consoling arms made her feel much better. He pointed out the grave danger of having acted on her own in such a situation, though he admitted that she had obtained a confession of murder that could not have otherwise been had. The whole episode was now over. The gold bullion was back in its boxes, the cutlery and the eyeglass case returned to their owners, and the mystery of Max Hirsch's disappearance solved. Held in custody, Orvill

Delaney and Patrick Skelton would face charges of murder and robbery when they reached New York.

Genevieve's recovery was further helped by the praise showered on her by the purser, followed by an invitation to dine at the captain's table that evening. Lying in her bath, she mused on the crucial role played by a black cat and a little girl. Dillman had explained how the pursuit of the ship's mascot had led to the discovery of the gold. In her own way, Alexandra Jarvis deserved her share of the thanks, but that was impossible without telling her the whole story, and at the purser's insistence, a blanket of silence had to be thrown around the various crimes. The ship had been through enough turbulence already, and Maurice Buxton did not want to undergo another interrogation at the hands of Hester Littlejohn. As far as the other passengers were concerned, everything was going smoothly. Genevieve felt happy, relaxed, and fulfilled. On her first outing as a detective, she had helped to solve serious crimes. She could now start to enjoy the voyage properly.

Choosing a white-satin gown for the occasion, she dressed with care and raided her jewellery box for a diamond brooch and matching earrings. When she saw the effect in the mirror, she was satisfied. Genevieve Masefield would be the centre of attention that evening, and deservedly so. Katherine Wymark would have withdrawn discreetly from the field. Delaney and Skelton would also be unavailable, as no doubt would the embarrassed Edgar Fenby, but there would be male admirers enough for Genevieve. That thought was a timely reminder. She was forgetting her mystery correspondent. While most of the men merely looked at her with pleasure, one had clear designs on her. He would make his move that very night.

Genevieve's pleasure slowly ebbed, replaced by a nagging fear. Would the man be Donald Belfrage or Harvey Denning? Or would it turn out to be someone else? Though Delaney and Skelton could be firmly discounted, that still left plenty of possible contenders. Genevieve was vexed. She could always turn to Dillman for protection, but she felt that this was a problem she should face and resolve on her own. It was not as if she was unused to dealing with unwanted suitors. The knock on the door made her gasp with surprise. It sounded threatening. She sensed that it might be the author of the two unsettling notes and needed a moment before she could speak.

'Who is it?' she called.

'Me,' replied Harvey Denning. 'Your faithful escort.'

'I'm not ready yet.'

'Then I'll wait.'

'No, you go on ahead, Harvey,' she said, trying to get rid of him. 'I'm dining at the captain's table tonight.'

'We *are* going up in the world!' he teased. 'But I need to speak to you before you go, Genevieve. It's important. It's about that unsolicited mail you've been receiving.'

Genevieve winced. It was Harvey Denning, after all. From the tone of his voice, she could not determine whether he had come to apologize or to pay his attentions. At least the truth would finally come out. She steeled herself to open the door. After letting him in, she stood waiting with her arms folded.

'You look absolutely gorgeous!' he said without irony.

'Thank you, Harvey.'

'That, of course, is part of the problem. Look, Genevieve,' he said seriously. 'I have an apology to make. Two notes were put under your door. They probably upset you. I know they were meant to do that.'

'Then why did you leave them there?' she demanded.

'But I didn't. I'm here on behalf of the person who did.'

'Donald Belfrage?'

'No,' he said. 'Susan Faulconbridge. "Hell hath no fury like a woman who thinks she's being scorned." Susan and I had a long chat this afternoon and she admitted what she'd done. She seemed to think that you and I were…' He flicked a hand in the air. 'I gave her my word that nothing of that sort had or, unfortunately, would occur, and out it all came. Susan is terrified that you won't ever speak to her again.'

'Nonsense!' said Genevieve with relief. 'Tell her that I hold no grudge.'

'I knew you wouldn't.'

'To be honest, I thought that you might have sent the notes, Harvey.'

'Me?'

'Or Donald.'

'No, Genevieve. I'm too circumspect to even commit myself to paper where a lady is concerned, and Donald would never dream of such a thing. He's a hand-on-the-knee merchant.' He grinned broadly. 'You should be quite safe from his wandering digits at the captain's table.'

'Thank you,' she said. 'Thank you for coming to tell me all this.'

'Does that mean I can carry you off to the dining saloon?'

Genevieve smiled sweetly. 'I already have an escort.'

George Porter Dillman was delighted with the opportunity to dine with the first-class passengers for a change. Five of them were missing that evening, but nobody seemed to notice or to mind. Dillman was pleased. He felt that he had cleansed the room of its seamier elements. Genuine passengers could now breathe a purer air. The room was awash with beautiful dresses and expensive jewellery. Soft violins lent a romantic air to the scene. Delicious fare was served on silver trays. Happy conversation bubbled on all sides.

Dillman had no doubt that he was sitting beside the most attractive woman in the whole room, and Genevieve had already told him how dashing he looked in his white tie and tails. Both of them collected admiring glances from Captain Pritchard that had nothing to do with their appearance. The captain was the most contented man in the room, and he was signalling his congratulations to them. Dillman and Genevieve felt able to bask in their success for once.

Over the dessert course, he leaned across to whisper to her. 'That woman is still staring at me, Genevieve.'

'They *all* are, George,' she replied.

'This lady is at the table in the corner,' he said, nudging

her to look in the right direction. 'The one in the plain dress.'

'Where?'

'Next to that large young man with the curly hair.'

'Oh, that's Ruth Constantine,' she said, seeing her friend. 'Next to the famous Donald Belfrage. I'm not surprised that Ruth is so interested in you, George. She's just picked you out of the identity parade.'

'What identity parade?'

'The one she's held since we set sail.'

'Ah,' he recalled. 'You told me about Ruth. She's very intuitive, you said. Ruth is convinced that you have someone special tucked away in the corner of your life.'

'That's why she's been lining up the suspects.'

Mock indignation. 'Is that all I am – a suspect?'

'A prime suspect.'

'That's something, I suppose.'

'You're now under arrest.'

'Does that mean a sentence will be imposed on me?'

'Oh, yes.'

'By whom?'

'I think I might take over the judicial role myself, actually.'

'And where will the verdict be given?'

Genevieve made him wait for a long minute before she made her decision. 'In my cabin.'

He grinned. 'I thought we agreed to stay well apart during the voyage.'

'Yes, we did.'

'So?'

'I'm only inviting you back to play chess with me.'

'But you don't have a chess set, Genevieve.'

'No, I don't,' she said fondly. 'In that case, we may have to improvise.'

⚓ ⚓ ⚓

By noon on Thursday of her maiden voyage, the *Mauretania* had spanned 624 miles in twenty-four hours, creating a new record for the distance covered in a single day. The captain was toasted, and a grateful American passenger, Mr. W.J. White, gave the stokers $1,000 in appreciation of their sterling work. But the Blue Riband eluded them. Slowed by bad weather throughout and hampered by thick fog off Sandy Hook, the *Mauretania* did not dock until 6.15 p.m. on Friday, November 22, 1907. In spite of the adverse conditions, her average speed was a respectable 21.22 knots.

After a refit the following year, the *Mauretania* went on to capture both the eastbound and westbound records in April 1909, holding the Blue Riband for the next twenty years.

Also available

In 1907, the world applauds as the Cunard Line launches a history-making ship. The magnificent *Lusitania*, hoping to capture the Blue Riband for the fastest crossing from Liverpool to New York, attracts both the beautiful and the damned for its maiden voyage. Among its privileged passengers strolls the debonair American George Porter Dillman, a shipbuilder's son - and a detective secretly hired to find the con artists, gigolos and thieves who prey on the rich and unwary. But the robbery of the ship's blueprints and a shocking murder take Dillman by surprise. Now, attracted to a woman who may not be what she seems, Dillman plunges into a drama of love and intrigue set in the glittering salons of this floating palace. And perhaps plays right into a killer's hands...

'Delightful escapism'
Chicago Sun-Times

'Well-drawn characters and precise
historical details'
Booklist

Temporarily forsaking the Cunard Line to work as private
detectives aboard the *Minnesota*, a combination freighter and
passenger ship owned by the Great Northern Steamship
Company, George Porter Dillman and Genevieve Masefield
are eagerly anticipating the prospect of a cruise bound for the
Far East. Once aboard, the two begin to establish separate
social circles in order to keep an eye on as many of the passengers and crew as possible. As the ship gets underway it's
smooth sailing, and George and Genevieve are hoping that
perhaps this will be their first uneventful cruise.
Unfortunately, their luck turns quickly as a fiery Catholic
missionary is murdered in what proves to be the first in a
series of crimes that will stretch them to their limit. Dillman
and Masefield have to use all their skills to combat danger on
more than one front and to prevent an otherwise idyllic (and
romantic) trip from becoming a terrifying nightmare.